Snapshot

Also by Garry Disher

Snapshot

Garry Disher

First published in Australia in 2005 by
Text Publishing Company, Pty Ltd.

First published in the United States in 2006 by
Soho Press, Inc.
853 Broadway
New York, NY 10003
Library of Congress Cataloging-in-Publication Data
Disher, Garry
Snapshot/Garry Disher
p. cm.
ISBN 978-1-56947-460-0
eISBN 978-1-56947-743-4
I. Police—Australia—Melbourne Region (Fic.)—Fiction.
2. Melbourne Region (Fic.)—Fiction.
3. Australia—Fiction. I. Title.
PR9619.3.D56S72 2006
813'.54—dc22 2005055459

Printed in the United States of America

10 9 8 7 6 5 4 3

For Chris

1

On Saturday she watched Robert have sex with four women. She had sex with two men. And now it was Tuesday and she was driving along the highway with her seven-year-old daughter. Sex with strangers on a Saturday evening, driving around with her daughter in the family station wagon on a Tuesday morning: were these the twin poles of her existence? Not any more. Janine McQuarrie had done something about that.

'Are we there yet?' asked Georgia in her piping voice.

Another cliché in a life of them. 'Not yet, sweetie. Bit further.'

She needed to concentrate. The weak, wintry sun was casting confusing shadows but, more than anything, she'd be obliged to make right-hand turns pretty soon. A right turn off the highway, another off the Peninsula Freeway, and another off Penzance Beach Road, which wound in a dizzying climb high above sea level. She slowed for an intersection, the light green. She should make a right turn here, but that meant giving way to the oncoming traffic, which was streaming indifferently towards her, and what if some maniac failed to stop before she completed the turn? She tried to swallow. Her mouth was very dry. Someone sounded their horn at her. She continued through the intersection without turning.

All those people there last Saturday, as close as bodies can get to one another, yet Janine hadn't expected, sought or found any kind of togetherness. She knew from past experience that the other couples would look out for each other, the wives watching out for their husbands, always with a smile, a kiss, a comforting or loving caress, 'Just checking that you're happy' kind of thing, and the husbands checking on how their wives were doing, 'Are you okay? Love you' kind of thing, even stopping to have sex with them before moving on to another play area. But that wasn't Robert's style. He would never so much as say 'Enjoy yourself' but go after the single women and younger wives, a glint of grasping need in his eyes, and last Saturday hadn't been any different. He'd kept her there until three in the morning, long after most of the others had gone home.

'Mum?'

'What?'

'Can I have a Happy Meal for lunch?'

'We'll see.'

Beside her, Georgia began to sing.

It had taken her husband about three months to wear her down. When he'd first proposed attending one of the parties, late last year, Janine had thought he was joking, but it soon became clear that he wasn't. She'd felt vaguely discomfited, more from the tawdriness and risk of exposure than realising he probably didn't want her sexually any more. 'Why do you want to have sex with other women besides me?' she'd asked, putting on a bit of a quiver.

'But you can have sex with other men,' he'd said reasonably, 'as many as you want.'

'You're pimping for me, Robert?'

'No, of course not, it will spice things up for us.'

Things had been low-key to non-existent, she had to admit. They still were—with Robert at least.

For three months she'd let him think his wheedling and cajoling were seducing her into it. 'You'll meet lovely people,' he said one day. 'Very open-minded.'

That confirmed it: he'd had experience already. She waited a beat and said in a little voice, 'You mean you've already been to one of these parties?'

Yes, he told her, trying not to sound ashamed or evasive but open, honest and a little defiant and courageous. She'd felt a surge of anger, but kept it bottled. He was so plausible, so *small*. Playing shy and a little threatened she'd asked, 'So they let single men in?'

'Some parties do,' he said. 'It costs more, and you're soon barred if you're a sleazebag.'

Robert wasn't a sleazebag, or not to look at. Nondescript, if anything. His morals were sleazebag, though.

'There's no need to feel threatened or jealous,' he'd said gently, stroking her arm, her neck, her breasts, and she'd actually tingled, her body betraying her. 'It forges a deep trust between couples,' he went on. 'It's not just physical, it's also spiritual. A mutual trust. It's a fundamental thing.'

On and on, for three months.

'I don't want to have sex with a boilermaker,' she'd told him finally, knowing just what to say.

He shook his head, the picture of top-drawer gentlemanliness. 'Potentially, you have people from all walks of life,' he said, 'but I'll make sure we attend only the better parties.'

Yeah, those that admit right-wing, think-tank sons of police superintendents, she thought now, at the next intersection, her insides clenching. Finally she found the nerve to turn right across oncoming traffic. Soon the car was climbing steeply inland from the coast and heading across the Peninsula along narrow roads lined with pines and gums, sunless, dank and dripping on this early winter morning.

Eventually she'd let Robert see that he'd worn her down, and in February had let him start taking her along with him to his banal little suburban orgies. She went partly out of curiosity and partly to get something on him. On the first three occasions she'd insisted they attend as observers—Robert itching to get into it, of course.

At her fourth party she drank a lot first, to convey the impression that she needed Dutch courage—but then discovering to her irritation that she *did* need it. 'Good on you, sweetheart,' Robert said.

To her surprise, it all turned out to be quite erotic. A house in Mornington, lots of plane trees along the street, tall hedges to screen the house from passersby or nosy neighbours. Robert pointed it out to her, and then parked in the next street. 'What we're doing isn't illegal,' he said, 'but we don't want to attract unnecessary attention.' They walked to the house, dressed as if for an ordinary party, and were greeted at the door. Ten o'clock, and most people were already there, about twenty couples and a dozen single women. Janine recognised several of them from observing on earlier occasions. They stood around, drinks in their hands, talking about football, the stock market, who was minding the kids tonight—in Janine's and Robert's case, Janine's sister, Meg.

By 10.30 everyone had loosened up. Jackets came off, lights were dimmed, there was kissing, a porn film flickered on a widescreen TV in a corner of the sitting room.

Soon men and women were in the 'change' rooms, hanging up trousers, jeans, dresses, shirts, and emerging, the men in G-strings, the women in sheer black slips, camisoles, knickers. Janine was accustomed to this by now, after those three preparatory visits. You had to 'dress down' in order to watch.

She drank another vodka, then stripped to her knickers and walked topless to one of the bedrooms, a large room where two double beds had been pushed together. Black satin sheets, candles placed where they cast a suggestive light but couldn't be knocked over, a bowl of condoms and a pump dispenser of lubricant on a side table. Two couples were having sex; others watched in the shadows, fondling themselves, sometimes darting forward to peer at all that moist

4

coupling. Cruising nicely now after the vodkas, Janine felt desire hit her, a little hot and nasty in the pit of her stomach. She perched on the end of a bed and touched a woman's breast, a man's penis, saying, 'Do you mind?'

It was important to ask and not simply barge in. They smiled. No, they didn't mind. Join in, why don't you?

She still wasn't sure. Most of her wanted to, part of her didn't. Perhaps if she just stretched out on the bed...Time passed. People stopped to watch, moved on to another play area, or joined in. 'Like this?' they asked, 'or like that?' 'Here, or there?' 'What would you like me to do?' 'Do you mind if I do that?' 'What turns you on?' By midnight, that first time, Janine had had sex with three men.

It had been her awakening—though not in the way Robert intended—when, a few weeks ago, she'd found love and excitement in the arms of a man who *wasn't* part of that scene.

She shook off the memory and concentrated on her driving, feeling safer now that she was on Penzance Beach Road. She was heading through a region of sealed roads and dirt side roads, amid wineries, berry farms, craft galleries and more cars than she cared to encounter. And a heavy fog had rolled in from the Westernport side of the Peninsula. She tried mentally to map her way, but she'd never driven this route before. Robert was the driver in the family.

Robert and his bullshit about a higher form of sexual freedom. Right from the start Janine had known that Robert and the others were trying to put a spin on things to make themselves feel better about what they were really doing. 'The suspension of jealousy' they called it. 'True sharing' and 'The highest form of sexual freedom'. Janine, checking out a couple of the websites, had found more of the same: 'All-in-together fun and erotica,' one site said, and featured personal ads aimed at getting like-minded couples together.

The same tone came through in the rules. Of course, they didn't call them rules, but 'etiquette': shower before you arrive; practise safe sex; no anal sex; respect the wishes of others; no means no; ask first and choose the right moment; feel free to watch, but erotic dress in the play areas, please; by all means have a drink to loosen up, but no one wants to partner a drunk.

Despite the claptrap it had been exciting, that first time, and for a while continued to be. Sometimes all of the elements—the smells, the sounds, the images—conspired to make her really horny. But she'd never felt liberated, alive or sweetly wicked, to quote some of the garbage the others spouted from time to time. None of it had translated into a better relationship with Robert—not that she'd wanted that at the time, and certainly not now, with a genuine man, genuine love, in the wings. It all seemed like hard work to Janine, and she felt contempt, everyone so nice, so conscientious about making sure everyone got an opportunity to enter this, touch that, suck this, stroke that, do this, please, do that again, please. By profession she was a psychologist but you didn't need a university degree to see that the whole sex party scene suited the needs of men, not women, and was symptomatic of fundamental anxieties, like desperately clinging to youth, seeking self-esteem, and wanting to be desired.

It was all about needing to be loved, and that was pathetic and illusory. Robert and his mates needed a good dose of reality, and the means to that had fallen into Janine's lap. Exactly a week ago, the Waterloo *Progress*, a small weekly newspaper, had published a long article on the swingers scene. The editor had apparently attended a party somewhere on the Peninsula and written it up with the blessings of the organisers and the participants. Caused quite a stir amongst the good and the decent who secretly hankered for a bit of spice in their lives. No photographs, no real names used—and that had given Janine her idea. Yesterday Robert and three of his mates would have opened their mail and found photographs of themselves in all of their glory, having sex with women not their wives in front of a bunch of other naked people.

There was no way she could have used an ordinary camera, not even a little spy camera. But a mobile phone with camera and video facility, that was a different story. You needed to have a mobile handy at these parties, wrapped up in your towel, G-string or camisole, in case there was an emergency call from the babysitter.

A few quick snaps, a few seconds of video, family doctors, businessmen, headmistresses, lawyers and accountants bonking strangers in some ghastly suburban bedroom. Even a few snaps of Robert. Janine shivered with glee. What if she showed them to his father, the superintendent of police, the custodian of good order?

Nah, maybe some other time.

She'd posted one photograph to each of the four men whose faces were clear enough for ID purposes. No demands for money, no note of any kind. She wanted to infect the swinging scene with a bad case of nerves, that's all. She grinned now, like a shark. The fear of finding themselves posted on the internet can't be too far from the surfaces of their tiny little minds, she thought.

Clearly Robert had opened his envelope at work yesterday. She'd had a little fun when he got home, rubbed up against him, felt for his cock, and said, 'Can we go to another party next weekend? I can't stop thinking about it. You were right, it's been liberating.'

He'd squirmed away from her, mouth wrenched in panic and distaste. 'I don't think that would be a good idea,' he'd said in a choked voice, before turning nasty and almost striking her. She'd always suspected that he had a propensity for violence. Robert was the kind of man to kill his wife and plead a provocation defence, and Janine knew there were plenty of other men—judges and defence lawyers—who'd allow him to get away with it. In the end, he'd shut himself in his study all evening. At 6 a.m. tautology, he'd flown to Sydney.

Just then her daughter's voice cut in on her reverie. 'Can I put the heater on?'

'Sure.'

It was chilly for early July—meaning a long, dreary winter, Janine supposed. She watched Georgia expertly adjust the Volvo's heater and fan controls, the concentration fierce on her sweet face with its halo of fine blonde curls. How did Robert and I produce her? she wondered. They drove on through the misty landscape, and eventually Georgia was perched alertly on the edge of her seat, asking, 'Mum, is it far now?'

'Don't think so,' Janine said, sounding more confident than she felt.

They were on a ridge road, with milk-can letterboxes every couple of hundred metres, signs for 'horse poo', and dense trees and bracken concealing driveways that led down to houses and cottage gardens tucked into the hillside. 'I think it's this one,' Janine continued, indicating squat brick pillars and an open wooden gate. She braked cautiously, not wanting to alarm the driver of the car behind her. She signalled, steered off the road, and drove in a gentle curve down a gravelled track to a parking circle beside a weatherboard house.

'Look, sweetie,' she said, pointing ahead, the fog parting briefly to offer gorgeous views across a dramatic valley, the sea and Phillip Island beyond. But Georgia wasn't buying it. 'It's creepy,' she said, meaning the grimy old weatherboard house. 'Do I have to wait in the car?'

'I'm sure you'll be allowed to watch TV or something,' Janine said.

She was double-checking their location with the street directory, completely rattled, and welcomed the sound of the car that came in behind them with a growl of its tyres.

2

There were two of them, wheelman and hard man, and they rolled down the driveway in a Holden Commodore, a model dating from 1983 but still plentiful on the roads, though maybe not in dirty white with one light yellow door.

A woman, that's all Gent knew. He didn't know what she'd done, only that Vyner had to sort her out, a warning, maybe a slap around the chops. That was Vyner's expertise, not his. He was the wheelman, along to provide the car and knowledge of the twisting roads in and out of this part of the Peninsula, an area of small towns, orchards and vineyards. And a sea mist had rolled in, choking the roads and waterways, providing good cover for the job.

The driveway was a steep plunge from the main road above, the Commodore's brakes dicey. 'Shitheap car,' said Vyner in the passenger seat.

Gent shifted uncomfortably behind the wheel. Vyner had told him to steal a decent car, plenty of power but nothing fancy. 'Best I could do,' Gent muttered, guiltily pumping the brakes of his cousin's Commodore.

The guy's a whinger, thought Vyner in the passenger seat, drawing out a pistol with one gloved hand and screwing on the silencer with the other. He waited with barely concealed patience for Gent to stop the car, then got out and advanced on the woman's car, a silver Volvo station wagon. The woman got out; big, apologetic smile. Vyner despised that. Where he came from, you acted first and asked questions later. Children's Court at thirteen, ward of the state at fourteen, sentenced to a youth training facility at fifteen. Then the Navy, where for a few years he channelled all of that energy into useful skills like long-range, technologically enhanced killing techniques. He was discharged in 2003, an incident in the Persian Gulf, the shrink who assessed him concluding: *Leading Seaman Vyner possesses a keen intelligence but is manipulative, lies compulsively and has demonstrated a capacity for cruelty.*

Well, as Vyner had noted in his journal this morning, *No comet has showered sparks of joy and light over me.* Life snapped at his heels even as he sought higher rungs of knowledge.

Like now, what it meant to gun a woman down in front of her kid—for there was a kid in the passenger seat, should have been at school, given that it was a Tuesday. The kid not scared yet, merely curious, but the woman was, the woman had seen the gun.

She held both hands out, pleading, 'No, please, it was just a joke, I wasn't going to show them to anyone, I wasn't going to ask for money.' Then she slammed the door on her kid and began to back away from Vyner. Said a few other things, too, like 'You've got the wrong person' and 'What did I ever do to you?' and 'Don't hurt my daughter', but Vyner was here to do a job.

He strode on, and when the woman turned and scuttled around to the front of the Volvo, Vyner didn't alter pace, merely raised the pistol and closed in on her. She rounded the front of the car, ducked back along the other side, towards the tailgate, so Vyner turned patiently, retracing his steps to meet her. It was cat and mouse, the woman whimpering, Vyner registering the measured rate of his own heart and lungs. Lines for his journal: *Today I was served by angels.*

Nathan Gent, behind the wheel of the Commodore, came to a shocking realisation. Sitting there with his mouth open, the Commodore shaking arrhythmically on about four out of the six cylinders, he finally twigged that this was a killing he'd been hired for. He closed his mouth with a click of rotting teeth and goosed the accelerator a little, hearing the motor idle more evenly. 'A bit of business,' Vyner had said. 'Won't take long.' Vyner—as hard, thin and snapping as a whip—had always been tough, but Gent had never known him to kill anyone except maybe a few Iraqi ragheads. Gent felt himself go loose inside. He watched, squeezing the old sphincter, and saw Vyner and the woman reach the rear bumper of the Volvo simultaneously, from opposite sides of the car. The woman jerked, ran back the way she'd come, half bent over. Vyner, all the time in the world, went after her.

Then she broke cover. She knew the end had come and intended to draw Vyner away from the kid trapped there in the back seat—or so Gent hoped, an old bitterness rising in him as he flashed back to his own mother, who'd never sacrificed a thing for him. He watched the woman dart away from the carport towards a little garden shed, a tangle of rakes, shovels, fence pickets, whipper-snipper and mower—looked like a Victa to Nathan Gent, he could come back with a mate's ute, load up, flog the mower for fifty bucks in the side bar of the Fiddlers Creek pub.

Maybe not. Crime-scene, police tape around it, the cops wanting to know what business he had on the property.

But a murder. Jesus, accomplice to a murder. For comfort, Gent rubbed the stump where his right ring finger had been, the finger torn off by a ship's chain somewhere in the Persian Gulf.

Again he remembered what Vyner had said about stealing a car, and silently thanked God for the concealing fog. And for the location: the house was below road level, the road winding along the top of a ridge, the ground sloping steeply away on either side. Passing drivers would have to get out of their cars and stand at the head of the driveway and look down on the turning circle and carport in order to witness anything. No neighbours to speak of. But Jesus, why hadn't he *stolen* a car like Vyner said?

While Gent watched, Vyner aimed at the woman, now cowering beside the garden shed, and shot her twice, a couple of pops, softened by dense fog and silencer. Then Vyner returned to the woman's car, hurrying a little now.

The kid knew. A little girl, maybe six or seven, she came bounding out of the Volvo in her red parka, running, curls bouncing, Vyner tracking her with his pistol. Gent saw him fire, miss. Now she was heading towards the Commodore, Gent thinking, no, piss off, I can't help you. He put his hand out of the window, waved her away. She gaped at him for a long moment, then darted towards a belt of poplars at the edge of the garden. Gent saw Vyner take aim, pull the trigger. Nothing. Vyner looked at the gun in disgust, then strode back to the garden shed, searching for ejected shells. A moment later he was piling into the Commodore, shouting, 'Let's go.'

Keep the prick moving, Vyner thought. Gent had been sitting too long—though it was what, less than two minutes, tops? He hoped the guy wouldn't turn out to be a liability. Gent was only in his early twenties but going to seed rapidly through beer and dope; a pouchy, slope-shouldered guy who claimed to know every back road—and probably every backyard and back door, Vyner thought—of the Peninsula.

Well, Gent was getting $5000 for his part in the hit, and knew what would happen if he didn't keep his mouth shut.

They neared the top of the driveway, Vyner removing the clip from his Browning and cursing it. You'd think the Navy would stock reliable handguns, border protection and all that. Not that he'd ever intended to hang on to this gun, keep incriminating evidence around. He'd do what he'd done before, seal it in a block of concrete, and toss it into a rubbish skip on some building site. There were two more Navy Browning pistols in the wall safe of his Melbourne pad, and he'd better examine and clean them tonight. Didn't want them jamming on him, especially when firing in self-defence. Shit gun. Unfortunately it was too late to get back his $500 per weapon because the Navy armourer who'd sold them to him was dead. Shot himself in the head.

He unscrewed the silencer—at least *that* worked—and slid it into the inside pocket of his jacket, then shoved the Browning into another pocket, the hammer catching, tearing the fabric. Useless fucking thing. Vyner had wanted something more cutting edge from the armoury, a Glock automatic or a Steyr short-barrelled carbine and a high-end night-aiming device, but all the Navy guy would sell him was three old Brownings from the stock used for cadet training and which were gradually being phased out. 'I can lose these in the paperwork, no dramas,' his mate had said, 'but the new stuff, no way.'

Vyner removed his gloves and folded down the sun visor to check himself out in the vanity mirror. Nothing caught in his teeth. His old familiar face looking back at him. He pocketed his cap, smoothed back his hair.

'Shit!' shouted Gent, braking hard as the Commodore levelled out at the top of the driveway. It rocked to a halt just as a taxi came out of the fog and disappeared into the fog, gone in an eyeblink.

3

Normally Hal Challis started the day with a walk near his home, but he wanted to catch Raymond Lowry unprepared, to ask about the stolen guns, so at 6.30 that morning he shrugged into his coat, collected his wallet and laptop, and got behind the wheel of his Triumph. Five minutes later, he was still trying to start it. When finally the engine caught it fired sluggishly, with a great deal of smoke, and he made a mental note to book it in for a service and tune.

He set out for Waterloo, heading east through farmland, a sea fret licking at him, shrouding the gums and pines along the side of the road, reducing the universe. 'Sea fret'—as if Westernport Bay, vanished now but normally a smudge of silvery water in the distance, was chafing. Challis supposed that it was chafing, in fact: there'd been a sudden and bitter chill in the air last night, which had come into contact with sea water still warm from a mild autumn, and the result was this dense, transfiguring fog. He knew from experience that it would sit over the Peninsula for hours, a hazard to shipping, school buses, taxis and commuters. And a hazard to the police. Challis's job was homicide but he pitied the traffic cops today. Maniacs passed him at over 100 kmh, before being swallowed up by the fog; irritated with him, the sedate driver in his old Triumph. Old, lacking in compression and the heater didn't work.

Soon he reached a stretch of open land beside a mangrove belt, and finally the tyre distributors, petrol stations and used-car yards that marked the outskirts of Waterloo. New, cheap houses, packed tightly together, crouched miserably in the fog. There was high unemployment on the new estates; empty shops in High Street; problems for the social workers. Yet on a low hill overlooking the town was a gated estate of million-dollar houses with views over Westernport Bay.

Waterloo was the largest town on this side of the Peninsula, hemmed in between farmland along one flank and mangrove swamps and the Bay on the other. Three supermarkets, four banks, a secondary college and a couple of state and Catholic primary schools, some light industry, a fuel refinery across from the yacht club, a library, a public swimming pool, a handful of pubs, four $2 shops, several empty shopfronts. A struggling town to be sure, but growing, and less than an hour and a quarter from Melbourne.

Challis slowed for a roundabout, and then headed down High Street to the shore, where he passed the swimming centre and the yacht club on his way to the boardwalk, which wound through the mangrove flats. Here he parked, got out and walked for an hour, his footsteps muted and hollow on the treated pine boards. Beneath him the tidal waters ran, and once or twice there was a rush of air and a hurried warning bell as a cyclist flashed past him, too fast for such a narrow pathway in such struggling grey light.

Seven-thirty. He stopped to watch a black swan and thought about his dead wife. She'd never understood his need to wake early and walk, or his need to walk alone. Maybe the rot had set in because of that essential difference between them. His solitary walks focused him: he solved problems then, plotted strategies, drafted reports, did his best loving and hating. Other people—like his wife—wanted to chat or drink in their surroundings when they walked, but Challis walked to think, get his blood moving and look inwards for answers.

Strange the way he kept referring to her in his mind. Strange the way she continued to be the person to whom he presented arguments and information, as if she still mattered more than anyone else, as if he still hoped to shine in her eyes, as if she hadn't tried to kill him and her own death hadn't interrupted everything.

Seven forty-five. He swung away from the swan, returned to his car and drove back to High Street. Here the early birds in the bakery, the café and the newsagency were opening their doors, sweeping the footpath, seeding their cash registers. He entered Café Laconic, bought takeaway coffee and a croissant, and consumed them in his car, watching and waiting.

At five minutes to eight, Lowry appeared, walking from the carpark behind the strip of shops. The man wore jeans, a parka and a woollen cap, a tall, thick-bodied guy who liked to show a lot of teeth when he talked. Challis watched him fish for keys and open the door to his shop. Both the windows and the door were plastered with advertisements for mobile phones and phone plans. Waterloo Mobile World the shop was called.

Challis gave Lowry a couple of minutes and then entered, setting off a buzzer. 'We don't open until...' Lowry began, then something stopped him, some stillness and focus in Challis. 'What do you want?'

'Another talk, Mr Lowry,' Challis said.

Raymond Lowry showed indignation and bafflement with his mouth and shoulders. 'What about?'

'The inquest's on Thursday,' Challis said. 'I'm finalising my report to the coroner.'

'Let me get the door,' Lowry said resignedly. He locked it, then gestured for Challis to follow him into a cramped back room, where he immediately sat at a desk and began to make notes in a ledger. It was airless in the little room. A fan heater blew scorching air at Challis's ankles. Eventually Lowry looked up. 'Sorry about that. There's a lot of paperwork in this job.'

Challis glanced around at the grey steel shelves loaded with boxes of mobile phones and phone accessories. 'Business doing all right?'

'Can't complain.'

'Better than life in the Navy?'

Lowry shrugged.

The Navy base was a few kilometres away. Lowry had served there for a while, met a local girl and eventually quit. 'You can't raise kids in that kind of environment,' he said, 'getting posted all over the place. And I make a decent living at this.'

Lowry, the solid businessman and decent family man. Challis didn't reply but waited, an old trick. 'Look,' said Lowry with a disarming grin, baring his large, glorious teeth, 'what more can I tell you? I barely knew the guy.'

On a Saturday night in May, an armourer from the Navy base, high on a cocktail of alcohol and drugs, had been ejected from the Fiddlers Creek pub. Two hours later he'd returned unnoticed with a pistol from the armoury and shot dead a bouncer, then returned to the base. Later still, he'd killed himself with the same pistol. The fallout was far-reaching: eighteen cadets had been dismissed after testing positive to drugs, and the operation of the armoury was under investigation. According to a preliminary check, some of the pistols were missing, older stock that was being phased out. Challis badly wanted to know where those guns were.

'Barely knew him? That's not what I heard,' he lied. 'I heard you were pretty pally with him. Were you his contact on the outside? He falsified the paperwork to cover the theft of several guns, and you fenced them for him?'

'No way. Not guns.'

Meaning that yeah, he'd been caught handling stolen property last year, but no way would he handle stolen handguns. 'Then who did handle the guns for him?'

Lowry opened his arms wide. 'How the hell would I know?'

'How's the wife?' said Challis.

Lowry faltered at the direction change. He had close-cropped hair and now he floated a hand above the spikes as if to gather his thoughts. 'We're separated.'

Challis knew that from Lowry's file. Mrs Lowry had taken out an intervention order on her husband last year, and later left him and been given custody of their children. Lowry had joined an outfit called Fathers First and made a nuisance of himself. 'Sorry to hear that.'

Lowry flushed. 'Look, am I under arrest? Are you going to charge me or what?'

Challis smiled without much humour. 'We'll see,' he said, and returned to his car, hoping it would start and not let him down with Lowry watching from his shop window.

The police station was on two levels; offices, cells, canteen and interview rooms on the ground floor, and conference rooms, the Crime Investigation Unit and a small gym on the first floor. Challis entered by the back door and headed for his pigeonhole in the corridor behind the front desk. He reached in, took out a sheaf of memos and leafed through them.

Most he shoved into the overflowing bin nearby, but paused in futile wrath over one from Superintendent McQuarrie, addressed to all senior officers: *The Assistant Commissioner will be asking some tough questions this year, and you will be expected to deliver balanced budgets. The budget situation is taking over as the main management challenge for the region, and so every order, every item of expenditure, will be reviewed with a critical eye.*

Challis had lived through budget constraints before. The usual result was that paper expenditure skyrocketed, to deliver the ever-increasing flood of memos, while the money for torch batteries, interpreters, pens, cleaning materials or calls on mobile phones dried up. More seriously, any squad could be charged for using the services of another squad, access to telephone records of victims and suspects had been reduced, and there was only minimal funding for phone taps. Crime fighting by committee, that was Challis's view.

He turned and made for the stairs that led to the first floor. 'Hal,' said a voice before he reached them.

He swung around. Senior Sergeant Kellock—a bull of a man, befitting his surname, and the uniformed officer in charge of the station—was beckoning him. Challis nodded a greeting and entered Kellock's office. 'This came for you,' Kellock said.

It was a parcel the size of a wine carton wrapped in heavy brown paper. Complicated feelings ran through Challis when he saw the senders' names: his dead wife's parents. He was fond of them, and they of him, but he'd been trying to draw away from them. 'Thanks,' he muttered.

'Mate, we're not a postal service,' said Kellock.

Challis knew that the parcel would have been delivered to the front desk. There was no reason, other than nosiness, for Kellock to take charge of it. Profoundly irritated, Challis carried the box upstairs to the first floor.

The Crime Investigation Unit was a vast room of desks, filing cabinets, phones, wall maps and computers. Ellen Destry, the CIU sergeant, was having a half-day off work; Scobie Sutton, one of the DCs, was spending the morning in court. A third DC was taking a week-long intensive course in the city, and the fourth was on holiday. It was going to be quiet in CIU today.

Challis's own office was a partitioned cubicle in one corner, offering a dismal view of the parking lot behind the building. Here he dumped the box on the floor, switched on his office computer and checked his e-mail. There was only one message, from Superintendent McQuarrie, who wanted him to write a paper on regional policing. Challis printed it out and tried to make sense of the guidelines, a low-level fury burning in his head. Was there a clear distinction between a 'mission statement', an 'aim' and an 'objective'? Words, meaningless words, that's what policing had become.

Fed up, he brewed coffee and reached behind him to the dusty radio on his shelf of law books, police regulations and tattered manilla folders. With the 9 a.m. news murmuring in the background, Challis fired up his laptop, got out his notes, and brooded over his report for the coroner on the Navy shooting.

But really, he was putting off the inevitable. Retrieving the parcel from the floor, he tore open the paper and found a sealed cardboard box with a note taped to the lid.

> *Dearest Hal,*
> *These things of Angie's arrived here a few days ago. Apparently they'd been in storage at the jail and overlooked. We thought you should have them to do with as you wish. Take care, dear Hal. We often think of you.*
>
> *Love,*
> *Bob and Marg*

Challis opened the lid and looked at the sad remnants of his wife's life: paperback novels, a brush and comb, makeup, a pocket-size album of photographs, a wristwatch, the clothes she'd been wearing when arrested. He swallowed and wanted to cry. And then, as the habits and imperatives of his days asserted themselves, he dumped the box and all of its contents in the bin.

Too soon to know if it was a gesture that meant anything.

He returned to his report. The phone rang. It was Superintendent McQuarrie, but a broken McQuarrie, not the dapper golfer and Chamber of Commerce toady.

4

According to the DC who greeted Challis at the murder scene, the 000 switchboard had given the job to Rosebud police. Suspecting a prank, a kid playing around with her mother's mobile phone, they had eventually sent two uniforms in a divisional van. The uniforms had taken one look at the scene, secured it and called in Rosebud detectives. Then the child, remarkably calm but smeared in her mother's blood, had revealed that her grandfather was a policeman, an important policeman, Superintendent McQuarrie.

'I mean,' the Rosebud DC said, 'we had to contact him.'

Challis nodded. He gave his name to the uniformed constable who was keeping the attendance log at the head of the driveway, and paused for a moment to take in the wider scene. Sealed road, with various police vehicles, including his own, parked on the grassy verges. There was also a hearse from the firm of undertakers on contract to the government to deliver suspicious-death cases to the lab. Gum trees, suffering from dieback, pittosporums, pine trees and bracken. A couple of distant letterboxes. And, closer to, a steep gravelled driveway leading down to a small weatherboard house, where a silver Volvo station wagon was parked with all of its doors open.

Various men and women were there, too, dressed in white or blue disposable body suits and overshoes and standing beside and under an inflatable forensic tent, which would protect the body and the immediate surroundings from wind or rain. A photographer was taking stills and video of the body, and of the body in relation to the car, the garden beds, the house and a small aluminium shed. The pathologist on duty, Freya Berg, knelt beside the body. Challis couldn't see McQuarrie anywhere.

He started down the driveway, accompanied by the Rosebud detective, a man with an off-centre nose and a crumpled grey suit. 'Where's the super?'

'Took the kid home with him.'

'Damn,' Challis said. A part of him knew that the child would need comforting; another part wanted to get her side of the story before she'd told it to too many others. McQuarrie was an experienced police officer, but he was also the kid's grandfather, and bound to be protective, bound to want to question her, maybe even put notions in her head about what she remembered.

'Sir?' the Rosebud detective said.

Challis smiled at the man. He didn't want him to think he rode roughshod over the sensibilities of grieving children. 'I'd hoped to catch up with him, that's all.'

'He wants you to meet him at his place, late morning.'

Christ, Challis thought, looking at his watch. He needed to talk to McQuarrie's granddaughter immediately, not later. He greeted some of the crime-scene technicians, then shouted a sharp '*Oy*' at a uniformed constable who'd popped a stick of chewing gum into his mouth and tossed the balled foil wrapper under a shrub. The Rosebud man hurried over, saying 'You prick, what if we'd taken that into evidence? Pick it up.'

When he came back, Challis said, 'Did the kid say anything?'

'Her name's Georgia,' the Rosebud man said, a mild rebuke. 'She said there were two men in an old white car with a yellow door. One of them shot her mother, the other one waited in the car.'

'What were they doing here? Why wasn't Georgia in school?'

The air was clammy, the sea fret that morning reaching well inland of the coast. The Rosebud detective tried to shrug deeper into his suit coat, his face pink and white with the cold, his balding scalp leaching body heat into the air. 'It was curriculum day, meaning no classes, so she was spending the day with her mother. I couldn't get much else out of her. Didn't want to push it. In fact, she refused to talk to me until the uniform guys confirmed that I was a copper. Then McQuarrie showed up.'

I'd better take Ellen Destry with me to question her, Challis thought. 'So she called 000 using her mother's mobile?'

'Yep. We found it in the car,' the Rosebud man said.

'Why didn't her father pick her up?'

The Rosebud man checked his notes. 'Name of Robert McQuarrie...lives with the victim and their daughter in Mount Eliza...in Sydney today on business. He's flying home.'

'So he wasn't the shooter.'

'He could have hired someone.'

'Very true.'

The statistics say that nine in ten homicides—murder, manslaughter—are committed by someone known to the victim, and about five in ten are direct family members. That's where Challis always started. He'd say to a man grieving for his murdered wife, 'I'm sorry for your loss,' but also look long and hard at him, for whatever his face and eyes revealed there and then, and for what his hidden life—bank statements, letters, credit card receipts—might reveal in the longer term. On occasion he'd even said gently, to husbands, wives, lovers, friends, 'Forgive me, but you are my first suspect. Until I can eliminate you from this inquiry, I cannot move forward.'

Challis looked at the little house. 'Anyone home?'

'No.'

'Do we know who lives here?'

The other man checked his notes. 'The uniforms came up with one name, Joy Humphreys.'

'Did Georgia say why they'd driven here?'

'No, only that she had no school today, and the childcare arrangements had fallen through, so she was spending the day with her mother.'

'Do we know what the mother does?'

'I found this in her wallet.'

A small embossed business card, with the name Janine McQuarrie in bold, followed by Bayside Counselling Services in cursive script, and the words 'Mediation, reconciliation, parenting issues, stress management, self-esteem and assertiveness training, specialist counselling'.

'Psychologist? She was visiting a client?'

'No idea.'

'Any other witnesses?'

'We've sent uniforms door to door. So far no reports of witnesses.'

Challis examined the little house. It looked at once run down and old fashioned, as though an elderly person lived there and had relinquished hope and energy.

'They could have been followed,' he said, 'or it's a case of wrong person, wrong place. Maybe you can make a start on tracking down this Joy Humphreys.'

The Rosebud detective shook his head with an air of satisfaction. 'No can do. The super said he's handing it all over to you, and Waterloo. Told me to hang around until you got here.' He paused. 'Read that article in the *Progress* last week,' he said, with a faint air of blokey interrogation.

Challis scowled. His involvement with the editor, Tessa Kane, was past history. They were back to being uneasy acquaintances, but ever since her article about sex parties in last week's issue of the *Progress*, he'd had to endure smirks and nudges. It was as if people assumed he'd always attended orgies with her, and still did. He gazed levelly at the Rosebud DC and saw the guy swallow.

'Well, good luck.'

Challis nodded a sour farewell. Just then Freya Berg announced that she was releasing the body, so he joined her. 'What have we got?'

It was a joke between them. The dialogue on one of the American crime-scene programs they professed to hold with scorn seemed to consist solely of the lead investigator saying 'What have we got?' and 'Keep me posted.'

Freya's mouth was serene, her eyes permanently amused. 'Well-nourished female, blah, blah, blah, shot once in the back, once in the back of the head, been dead less than two hours.'

The dead woman had been found sprawled face down on the ground, but Freya had turned the body over during the examination and now the woman lay slackly dead, her face stretched in anguish. Her trousered thighs and knees were damp, her cream-coloured top twisted at the waist, her unbuttoned jacket streaked with mud.

Challis glanced across to the crime-scene techs. 'Any shells?'

'Nothing, Hal.'

He turned to Freya again. 'Exit wounds?'

She shook her head. 'Still inside her.'

'When can you do the autopsy?'

'Later today.'

'Keep me posted,' Challis said.

Returning to his car Challis checked his mobile. As expected, he'd had several calls from reporters, including Tessa Kane. He sighed, feeling beset. There was going to be intense media interest in this case. Meanwhile, Tessa would want an inside story. Challis felt he owed her that at least, but at the same time, she'd often been critical of the police. The Waterloo *Progress* was quite unlike other small-town weeklies—with their ninety per cent classified advertisements and ten per cent feel-good stories about local sporting heroes, the barking dog that saved a widow from a house fire, the mayor planting a tree—in that it regularly spoke out on local social justice issues, including the detention centre near Waterloo and poverty and distress on the newer estates. Not surprisingly, Tessa Kane was loathed by many, including Superintendent McQuarrie.

Challis tossed the matter around. He didn't feel ready to speak to her yet. Maybe he lurked in her mind, never far from her consciousness, just as she often lurked in his, but the days when he'd immediately and automatically phoned her with details of a story were long past.

In the end he made two calls, one requesting updates on stolen, abandoned and burnt-out cars on the Peninsula, and the other to McQuarrie.

'My granddaughter's still very upset, Inspector,' the super told him firmly. 'I know you need to speak to her while things are fresh in her mind, but she needs a little time, okay? We'll see how she feels at lunchtime.'

'Sir,' Challis said.

Now to establish if there was a link between the victim and the woman who lived at number 283. He was reluctant to break into the house, so coaxed the Triumph into life and drove two hundred metres to the nearest neighbouring property, a long mudbrick house with a clerestory roof. Here a woman in overalls was pushing a wheelbarrow load of mulch around a garden at the rear. She had a smooth, youthful face and gave her name as Lisa Welch.

'You're the second policeman to come knocking this morning,' she said warily, knuckling a strand of hair away from her face. 'I know it's something to do with next door, but he wouldn't say what. Not that I saw or heard anything.'

'I know it seems like a waste of manpower,' Challis said, 'but we need to contact the woman who lives there.'

'Mrs Humphreys. Joy. But she's in hospital at the moment.'

He stared at her intently. 'Do you know why?'

'Hip replacement. She's in her late seventies.'

Challis tried to process this. Could an elderly woman be the intended target? Could a young woman be mistaken for an elderly one? 'Which hospital?'

'Waterloo.'

Well, that was convenient. 'Does she live alone?'

'I think her husband died a few years ago.'

Challis said patiently, 'But since then—any long-term visitors, tenants, anyone like that?'

The woman shook her head. 'I wouldn't know, really. I'm new to the area and I don't know all the comings and goings.'

Challis pocketed his pad and pen. 'Thanks, you've been very helpful.'

He saw her swallow. She was holding herself tensely. 'Can you tell me what happened? Was her house broken into?'

Challis hesitated. It was always possible that *this* woman was the intended target. If so, would she run when she learnt what had happened next door? Rather than make another trip out to question her, he said, 'Ms Welch, there was a shooting. A woman is dead. Not Mrs Humphreys,' he said, holding up his hand, 'but a younger woman.'

'Oh, God.'

'Do you have any enemies?'

She shrank away from him. 'Everyone has enemies. You really think they went to the wrong house?'

'We have to check everything.'

'What if they come back? I live alone here.'

'Is there anyone you can stay with tonight or the next few nights?'

'My parents live up in the city.' She gave him an address and phone number in Highett.

He said gently, 'I don't think you're in any danger. Whoever did this is long gone. But it would be wise for you to stay with your parents for the next couple of days until we sort this out.'

He agreed to wait while she packed a suitcase, locked up and drove away in her car. He noted the make, model and number, and then headed for Waterloo.

Unfortunately, his route took him past the local airfield. Inside one of the hangars was a Dragon Rapide, a 1930s biplane that he was supposed to be restoring, but some things had gone wrong for him and the old plane was still only seventy per cent complete. He'd lost all enthusiasm for carrying out the remaining tasks, such as hunting down the correct tyres. Besides, the hangar spooked him. He could feel Kitty there sometimes, at work on restoring her World War II Kittyhawk fighter. Of course, both plane and woman were long gone, but she'd been a companionable presence—almost a friend—until her husband had sneaked in one evening a year earlier and shot her dead while she worked. Challis had arrested the man but that had been the start of a shift in him, a loss of faith. His visits to the hangar had tailed off; meanwhile he'd recently received an invoice to renew his lease of the hangar space. Deciding that this was a good time to cut his losses and sell the Dragon, he'd fired off an e-mail to a Californian collector who'd expressed interest in buying it at the air show last March.

He reached Waterloo's little hospital and parked beside a line of golden cypresses. The interior colours were pastelly pinks and greys, the air scented with lemon, the rooms and corridors flooded with natural light. Even so it was a cheerless place.

'Mrs Humphreys?' the receptionist said. 'She's being operated on this morning. No visitors until much later today.'

Challis returned to his car and called Ellen Destry. It was her morning off, but he needed officers to work the Bayside Counselling angle as soon as possible.

5

Detective Sergeant Ellen Destry had begun her half-day off with a walk on Penzance Beach with Pam Murphy, a senior constable who lived nearby and was also based at Waterloo. The fog had been dense and clammy around them, the foghorns distant and muffled as Pam had told Ellen about a local conservation group called the Bushrats that she'd recently joined. 'We spend one Sunday morning a month clearing cape weed and pittosporum from roadsides and nature reserves,' she said. 'It's fun, educational, the Shire helps out with tools and sprays, there's even a newsletter. And we finish with a slap-up lunch.'

'Sounds good,' said Ellen neutrally.

On the surface, there were more differences than similarities between the two women. Where Ellen was forty, married and content to limit her exercise to a daily walk, Pam was twelve years younger, single and outdoorsy, an athlete. But Pam was tired of wearing a uniform and working as a patrol cop. She had shown investigative skills and initiative on a couple of important cases, so Ellen had taken the younger woman under her wing with a view to grooming her for plainclothes work. They were not exactly friends—the differences got in the way—but enjoyed walking and talking together when their schedules allowed it.

'The next working bee's in four weeks' time,' Pam said. 'We're clearing pittosporum in the north-west corner of Myers Reserve, if you'd like to come.'

'Not my cup of tea,' Ellen said. 'Sorry.'

She was not as bad as Hal Challis, who'd once advised her, 'Never join anything,' but couldn't comprehend people like Scobie Sutton and his wife, who joined everything from the school council to the pool of Meals on Wheels volunteers, or Pam, who belonged to four sporting clubs and was involving herself in the community. If pressed to join a club, Ellen would have said she was too busy, but in truth she'd never been asked and it had never occurred to her to join anything. As for the community, she kept it at a healthy remove.

They walked on, Ellen changing the subject. 'How's your new job?'

Pam shook her head ruefully. 'It's a bullshit gig, Sarge.'

It was an initiative of Senior Sergeant Kellock, and involved the Road Traffic Authority, Victoria Police and a few businesses with vague automotive connections. Pam and her partner were to tool around in a dinky little sports car for several weeks, rewarding courteous drivers with showbags that contained goods worth $150: a Melways street directory, a book of touring maps covering the entire continent, a BP fuel voucher, five McDonald's coupons, a free wheel balance and alignment from Tyrepower, and a bumper sticker that read 'Drive Safely and Live'.

'Tell yourself it's character building.'

'Yeah, right,' said Pam.

At the end of their walk, Ellen said, 'Coffee?'

Pam looked briefly stricken, then rallied. 'No thanks, Sarge,' she said gracefully. 'Stuff to do before my shift starts, you know.'

Ellen nodded, thinking: She doesn't want to encounter Alan. Ellen's husband liked to refer to Pam as 'That pushy little uniform from down the road' his contempt for her thinly veiled on the few occasions they'd met. He didn't like his wife mentoring the younger woman.

They parted at the store and Ellen walked home. Home was a fibro-cement beach house on stilts. On the plus side it was two minutes' walk from the beach and ten minutes' drive from her CIU office in Waterloo, but it was also uninsulated and difficult to heat and keep warm. The mornings were the worst, and the late afternoons. She hated waking up in, or coming home to a cold house. And Ellen felt the cold, always had. Finally, she had no one to talk to, except her husband, Alan, and he was no comfort. Things had been better when their daughter had lived at home, but Larrayne was studying up in the city now.

Ellen entered the kitchen and found her husband at the kitchen table, in uniform, eating breakfast, wound hard with frustration and grievances. 'Have you seen the power bill?'

She hadn't. She'd dumped it unopened and forgotten in the little cane bowl beside the phone at the end of the kitchen bench, where all the bills and junk mail ended up. She poured muesli and soymilk into a bowl. 'How much is it for?'

'Only almost double what it was for the same period last year,' Alan said.

He actually grabbed a fistful of bills and credit card statements and shook them at her. 'With just the two of us living here I thought our costs would *de*crease,' he said.

He was a solid man, close to being fleshy from all those hours spent sitting in a patrol car. He'd been transferred to the Accident Investigation Squad recently, but for many years before that had worked Traffic. He always tanned up a little over summer, looked healthier, but in winter his gingery fairness went a shade too pale, an unhealthy paleness. Not for the first time, Ellen wondered why she stayed with him, for theirs had long been a loveless marriage. And what did he get out of it? The sex was perfunctory, they didn't nourish one another and they always bickered. It would be easy for them to separate, now that Larrayne no longer lived at home or depended on them.

But it would destroy him if she left. He'd be helpless and hopeless. That was no reason for staying with him, but it made the first step towards leaving him difficult.

He narrowed his pouchy eyes as she sat opposite him with her muesli and a mug of coffee. 'Have you ever left the heater switched on during the day?'

She had, two or three or maybe a dozen times this winter. 'No,' she said emphatically.

'Liar.' Then he was doubtful. 'Maybe it's the meter, giving a false reading.'

'It has been a cold winter so far,' she said, and, as if to reinforce the observation, the foghorns boomed from Westernport Bay.

'So?'

'I think we should install central heating.'

'We've been through this.'

We? There's no 'we', Ellen thought. And if I'm serious about leaving him, why am I thinking about installing central heating? Is it because I'm assuming I'll get the house? Whoa, she thought, you're getting ahead of yourself.

'Another thing,' Alan said, 'sometimes you sit there with the heater on and a window open. How stupid is that? It's like trying to heat not only the room but also the rest of Australia.'

'Central heating.'

'No.'

A stupid, futile, demeaning squabble, symptomatic of her husband's simple but dangerous failings and grievances, which boiled down to two things: he'd failed his sergeant's exam, and his wife had been fast-tracked because she was a woman.

The phone rang and Alan sprang for it, listened, said curtly, 'She's got a morning off, sorry,' and banged the handset down.

'Who was it?'

'Challis.'

'Jesus, Alan.'

Ellen picked up the phone and dialled Challis's mobile. 'Hal, I'm sorry—'

He cut her off, telling her that the super's daughter-in-law had been murdered and outlining the circumstances. 'I'll set up an incident room and brief everyone at lunchtime. Meanwhile I need you to sniff around Bayside Counselling: get a feel for Janine McQuarrie and the people she worked with, see if her diary or calendar tell you anything about her movements today.'

'I'll take Scobie with me.'

'If he's finished in court.'

6

Scobie Sutton stifled a yawn; he was sitting in the Frankston Magistrates' Court, a thin man with the look of a mournful preacher. Heather Cobb was appearing this morning on drugs charges and Scobie, who'd arrested her, was there to ensure that she wouldn't go to jail.

It had started two weeks ago, when he'd been called to a Waterloo primary school. At show-and-tell that morning Sherry Cobb, barely nine years old, had presented the class with a marijuana plant in a plastic pot. Scobie's interview with the child, and subsequent visit to her home, had uncovered a typical story of poverty, addiction and neglect. There were five children in the Cobb family, ranging in age from three to eighteen; father in jail; mother an alcoholic. They lived in a two-bedroom weatherboard shack between the railway line and a timber yard.

Now, in the Frankston Magistrates' Court, Scobie glanced at Natalie Cobb. She was the eighteen-year-old, in Year 12, wagging school today to provide moral support for her mother. When he'd first gone to question Heather Cobb, Natalie had been there, dressed in a tracksuit and slumped in front of the TV. She was a fine looking young woman, but it was two o'clock in the afternoon and she should have been at school. Today she looked not eighteen but twenty-eight, and as poised—in her best clothes, not her school uniform—as any of the young female lawyers you saw around the Magistrates' Court. Natalie smiled at her mother, then gave Scobie a complicated look.

Complicated girl, Scobie thought.

The cases droned by, and then it was Heather's turn. As expected, the magistrate let her off with a caution. 'While I accept that you didn't grow the plant, Mrs Cobb, you nevertheless allowed your premises to be used for the cultivation of marijuana.'

Heather, dressed in a thin summer dress and ragged parka, glanced worriedly at Scobie through pouchy eyes. He smiled at her, nodded, and mouthed the word *sorry* to her across the courtroom.

Heather brightened, brushed a greasy comma of hair away from her eyes, and looked confidently at the magistrate. She told him how sorry she was, it would never happen again, the man who'd grown the plants was a bully and she'd been scared of him, but he was in prison in Brisbane now, and no way was she going to let him back into her life.

She means it, too, Scobie thought.

Outside afterwards, Heather Cobb trembled as her tensions eased. 'Mr Sutton, I don't know how to thank you.'

'That's okay,' Scobie said. 'It was a good result.'

'The magistrate listened to your recommendations,' Natalie said. 'You swung it for us. Thanks,' she said, and pecked him on the cheek.

He blushed. 'My wife knows you. The youth club on the estate?'

Natalie looked guarded. 'Mrs Sutton, the social worker? She's your wife?'

Damn, Scobie thought. I should have kept my big trap shut. If Natalie refuses to work with Beth as a result, I'll have set back community relations and all of my wife's good work.

A small van pulled into the kerb, the driver tooting. 'Got to go,' Natalie said. 'See ya, Mr Sutton. See ya, Mum.'

'Boyfriend,' Heather Cobb said, watching the van peel away.

Somehow Scobie didn't think the boyfriend was taking Natalie back to school. His mobile rang. It was Ellen Destry. 'You finished?'

'Yes.'

'I need you back here,' she said, but didn't explain.

'Come on,' he said to Heather, 'I'll give you a lift home.'

7

Tessa Kane had heard about the murder at 9.45 a.m., a call from an ambulance officer, one of her many contacts. She'd immediately rung Hal Challis, but he was apparently out of the station and not answering his mobile phone—or not to her, at any rate. Ellen Destry and Scobie Sutton weren't available. And nobody else at the Waterloo police station would talk to her. She felt frantic for thirty minutes, then asked herself what the point was. She published a weekly paper: the dailies would have all the scoops on this story, and she'd have to be content with an overview in next Tuesday's edition, when no doubt the case would be long closed.

And then, at 11 a.m., Challis returned her call, suggesting they meet for coffee. Five minutes later she was walking down High Street to Café Laconic, where she sat at a window table, looking out at the canopied, unoccupied footpath tables, a public phone booth and a plane tree. There had been a dense fog all morning, but it had lifted here on High Street, as if burnt off by human endeavour. Tessa drew her coat tighter around her shoulders and glanced at the corkboard on the adjacent wall: this week's program at the drive-in cinema in Dromana, a couple of garage sales—she loved garage sales—a scattering of business cards and a federal election poster eighteen months out of date.

Then a waiter was standing there, looking appreciatively at her legs, stockinged today, slim and dark under a skirt. She normally wore jeans or trousers, but liked to dress up on Tuesdays, publication day.

'What can I get you?'

She smiled. 'Nothing just yet, thanks. I'm waiting for a friend.'

'Fair enough,' the waiter said, and went behind the counter again, a slab of jarrah fronted by corrugated iron. There was wood and iron everywhere, she noticed, her eyes alighting on the election poster again. Her vote had made no difference back then. She came from a family of Labor voters, but Labor had long ago sold out on the things that mattered to her: social justice issues and an independent foreign policy. Back when Labor first showed signs of decline, she'd voted Communist a few times, to register her protest, but Communism was a spent force. Now she voted Green, for the Greens actually held values and beliefs, unlike Labor. She'd probably call herself Red-Green, like the political movement in Germany, favouring both social justice reforms and green reforms. Unfortunately the Greens were widely seen as tree-huggers—and indeed there were plenty for whom that was as far as their beliefs extended. She'd never vote Liberal or Democrat, and would never again vote Labor, the party whose ex-prime ministers were now millionaires, its ex-senators and ministers into tax evasion and cozying up to the richest men in Australia.

She was sitting there getting quietly steamed up when the lean frame of Hal Challis passed by the window. Theirs was a complicated relationship. They'd been lovers for a while, things fading away rather than ending convincingly. Now she saw him at press conferences and at times like this, when they exchanged information.

Not that it mattered any more, but she wondered if he felt free of his wife yet. Angela Challis was dead, but that didn't mean she was dead in Challis's heart. It had been a huge story at the time, for

Challis's wife had started an affair with another policeman, the pair of them luring Challis to a lonely rendezvous on a back road one night, intending to kill him. The attempt had failed and Challis's wife had been jailed for conspiracy to murder. But instead of divorcing her, washing his hands of her, Challis had felt obscurely responsible, as if he'd failed Angela, driven her to taking drastic action. He'd gradually stopped loving her—so he said—but for years had let her call and write to him from prison, let her talk out her guilt and regret. 'Move on, Hal,' people had said, and God knows Tessa herself had said it often enough, but he'd not moved on, and whenever she was with him he'd seemed disengaged, sad.

And then last year Angela Challis had killed herself in the prison infirmary. Tessa had taken heart. She'd not rushed Challis, not jumped for joy, but been patient, kind and commiserative. Where had that got her? Exactly nowhere. Challis had grown more disconnected, as though the guilt he felt had not disappeared but compounded itself. Eventually she'd stopped seeing him, stopped waiting, but for a long while the whole business had been a permanent ache inside her, composed of loss and emptiness.

She'd known that he was struggling. Back when they'd slept together Challis had too often scurried off home afterwards, or the next morning, as if he had to clear his head. He seemed to want her, then feel crowded, compounded by a desire not to hurt her or lead her on.

Anyway, that was Tessa's two-dollar analysis. She thought all of these things in the time it took for him to spot her, smile, cross the room and kiss her cheek. He pulled out a chair and sat. Their knees banged together; they moved apart politely, almost automatically.

'This is a privilege,' she said, 'morning coffee with you in a trendy café.'

'As trendy as Waterloo gets, anyway.'

She studied his face. 'You look tired.'

'It's a nasty one,' he said, and told her all he knew. She made notes, trying not to be distracted when his sleeve rode up, revealing a bony wrist and a centimetre of crisp white shirt. Normally she hated white shirts, but Challis was suited to them, with his leanness, and the olive cast of his skin.

'What happens next?'

'We speak to the child.'

'Could I speak to her?'

Challis said tiredly, 'McQuarrie would never allow it. She's too young, and he doesn't like you.'

She smiled ruefully. McQuarrie had friends in Rotary, local businessmen who didn't want a local newspaper that was left-wing and edited by a woman.

'But you won't keep me out of the loop, Hal?'

He shook his head.

'Of course, you might solve it this afternoon,' she muttered, 'and this time next week it will be stale news and no good to me.'

He gave her a twisted grin. 'So write another story like the one on well-mannered and well-run suburban orgies, where there's no time imperative.'

'Yeah, yeah, rub it in.'

'People look at me oddly, kind of smirkingly,' Challis said, 'as if I'm still involved with you and we're always having kinky sex.'

'Poor you.' She stared at him challengingly. 'Aren't you going to ask me what it was like?'

He shook his head. 'Your article pretty much covered it. Apart from a mild titillation, it left me unmoved. And it's hardly a police matter, not unless any of the players are underage.'

She sighed. 'I've had so much crank mail, my head's spinning. Distribution's up, but advertising is down.'

'Crank mail in addition to the other stuff?'

By 'other stuff' he meant a string of hate mail she'd been receiving for the past few months, along with anonymous phone calls and hang-ups, messages in soap smeared across her windscreen, and on one occasion a rock heaved through the glass panel of her front door. It all seemed to be the work of one man, who called her a bitch and said she'd get what was coming to her, one day soon. There hadn't been much that the police could do about it.

'It will all blow over eventually,' she said.

'What else are you working on?'

'The detention centre.'

'But isn't it being phased out?'

Tessa shrugged. Very few asylum seekers were left in the Waterloo centre. Most of the detainees now incarcerated there had breached or overstayed their visas, and were quickly processed and repatriated. But Tessa, in her role as editor of the *Progress*, had been critical of the centre from the outset, in the face of massive local apathy, and wanted one last shot at Charlie Mead, the manager. 'There are still abuses there, Hal.'

She paused. 'It looks like I'll be moving on.'

He looked at her quizzically. 'Moving on?'

'They're pulling the plug on me. The sex-party story was the last straw.'

She explained. Challis knew some of the details. The *Progress* was owned by a wealthy man who had a social conscience and tolerated Tessa's stance on most issues. What Challis didn't know was the man also leaned towards the Christian right and was furious with her for attending the sex party and writing about it. 'I've got three months of my contract left.'

Challis squeezed her hand and let it go. 'You'll be missed,' he said.

'I'll be missed, or you'll miss me? Which is it, Hal?'

'Both.'

She sighed. 'I thought about you the other day. I was out at the airfield doing a story and had a peek at your Dragon, hoping to find you working on the engine or something.'

Neither the plane nor its restoration had meant much to her, when she was seeing Challis, but they'd clearly meant something to him, and his obsession with such an arcane interest had been oddly appealing at the time.

'I'm thinking of selling it.'

'No! Why?'

'I haven't worked on it since Kitty was shot. It feels like bad luck.'

'Hal, I've never heard you talk like that before.'

'I'll take up golf with McQuarrie instead,' he said.

He grinned, but didn't mean the grin and she didn't return it.

Then he was on his feet and planting a kiss beside her ear. 'I'd better get back,' he said.

When he was gone, she stayed in Café Laconic for a while, checking messages on her mobile phone. Then, on a whim, she tried the detention centre again, and twenty seconds later, against all odds, was put through to Charlie Mead, who for months had been 'unavailable'. 'How did you get this number?' he demanded.

She frowned. 'Your secretary switched me through.'

'She's a temp, stupid cow. What can I do for you?'

'Now that the centre is winding back its operations, I thought it would be a good time to run a survey article.'

'The usual crap? Riots, self-mutilation, bullying guards?'

'Well, you were never available to give me the other point of view, Mr Mead,' Tessa said carefully.

'Sure, why not, one-thirty this afternoon.'

Unbelievable. Tessa returned to her office, forgetting all about Challis.

Ellen and Scobie were in Mount Eliza, where Bayside Counselling Services occupied a new but nondescript two-storey building in the main street. The bistro and the delicatessen on either side of it might have been lifted from one of the lifestyle magazines, and were inhabited, so far as Ellen could tell, by people who'd stepped from the pages of a lifestyle magazine. She wondered if they ever made independent decisions, and said so.

'Sorry?' said Scobie.

'Never mind,' Ellen said. Scobie Sutton liked to think the best of people. There wasn't a sour bone in his body.

They went in, finding an unoccupied reception desk. Ellen picked up a glossy brochure and showed it to Scobie: Janine McQuarrie was a good-looking woman, if surfaces counted for anything. The face in the brochure was contained and humourless.

Just then a man approached the reception desk, looking furious. He was about fifty, balding and as neat as a pin. Ellen disliked him immediately. 'Excuse me, sir,' she began.

'Yes?' he snapped. He didn't meet her gaze but addressed a point several centimetres above her head.

'We need to see—'

'Make an appointment—*when* our esteemed receptionist returns from wherever she is.'

'It's important,' Ellen said. 'We need to see someone in authority.'

'And you are?'

They showed their warrant cards. 'Well, I'm Dominic O'Brien, one of the senior partners,' the man said, still refusing—or unable—to make eye contact.

'Mr O'Brien, I'm afraid I have some bad news. Your colleague, Janine McQuarrie, was found murdered in Penzance North earlier this morning.'

There was a moment of silence, a throat-clearing cough, and O'Brien said, 'Sorry? Who did you say you were? What are you saying?'

Ellen repeated herself. O'Brien's voice gained in strength and passion. 'And you thought you'd just bowl up and drop this little bombshell on me?'

Oh God. Ellen said gently, 'I'm terribly sorry, Mr O'Brien, of course you're right, but there's no easy way to break this kind of news, and we need to act swiftly. Do you know why Mrs McQuarrie was in Penzance North this morning?'

'No idea.'

'Was she seeing a client? I understand that she was a psychologist, a counsellor.'

'She was. Are you suggesting one of her clients murdered her?'

'I don't know. Do *you* think that might have happened?'

'You'd better come into my office,' O'Brien said.

He took them upstairs to a vast, oppressive corner room. God help the poor soul who seeks solace here, thought Ellen. 'We need to see Mrs McQuarrie's files,' she said.

O'Brien was on firm ground now; resistant ground. 'Janine appointed me to look after her records in the event of anything happening to her. It's standard practice,' he said, to forestall any objections that the police might like to make.

'May we see those records? We need to identify anyone who has a volatile background and rule out everyone else.'

'A fishing expedition? Request denied. You'll need a warrant, and even then you'll need a good reason, *and* we'll challenge it.'

Ellen sighed. She knew that a magistrate would grant a subpoena without hassle, for this was a murder inquiry, but only if the police could present a compelling case for the murderer being one of the dead woman's clients rather than anyone else. 'All right, then perhaps you can tell me the *sorts* of people Mrs McQuarrie counselled.'

O'Brien breathed out heavily. 'Children—bedwetting kids and troubled teenagers. People grieving the death of a loved one. Women finding the strength to leave unhappy marriages. All kinds of ordinary afflictions, and none that might give rise to the impulse to murder, I wouldn't have thought.'

Ellen agreed privately. According to Challis's descriptions of the circumstances, Janine McQuarrie's murder had been a carefully arranged contract killing, not the product of impulsive or skewed reasoning. Her mind drifted. *Women finding the strength to leave unhappy marriages*, she thought. Is that what I need?

Scobie Sutton broke in. 'We'll need to see her desk calendar, and talk to everyone in the clinic, before the press do.'

O'Brien rolled his eyes. 'I'll see what I can do.'

He showed them to the conference room and for the next hour they interviewed the staff: O'Brien, three other therapists, the office manager and the receptionist, all of whom had solid alibis for earlier than morning. The office manager, a vigorous, no-nonsense woman named Iris, was the most helpful, but her information merely bore out in clearer terms what everyone was saying: that Janine McQuarrie had been a real piece of work, not only considered a poor therapist but also reviled. A woman whose bitter personality had permeated the building, she had minions, not friends. She was manipulative, a gossip, and would spread rumours against those whom she believed had wronged her. At staff meetings she liked to chuckle over her clients' sad secrets and off-the-wall phobias. She wasn't motivated to help, Iris said, but to bring down people and institutions, and she was obsessed with money: accumulating it, not spending it.

Scobie Sutton stirred, as if money, or all of this dirt being spread about Janine McQuarrie, was distasteful to him. 'Was she a gambler?'

'Not her,' Iris said. 'Gambling is a sign of weakness, quote unquote.'

'Any irregularities in the firm's bookkeeping?'

Iris bristled. 'I keep the books.'

Scobie back-pedalled. 'I mean, did she have access to the books? Was she keeping income back from the firm? Anything like that?'

'Not that I'm aware of.'

'Her clients,' said Ellen. 'Were any of them unstable enough to murder her? Did she offend any of them?'

'She whisked them in and out, or met them elsewhere, so I wouldn't know,' Iris said.

'What about her private life? Anyone in the background? Friends? Enemies?'

'Look,' said Iris. 'We pitied her more than anything. We avoided her. She was most probably lonely, but everything about her said "back off". I wonder how on earth she found herself a husband and mothered a child, frankly.'

'Do you know who she was seeing this morning?' Ellen had examined Janine McQuarrie's desk calendar, and the day's entry was typically cryptic: *Penzance North 9.30.*

'No.'

That was all they could get. Ellen called Challis's mobile number. 'We're on our way back to Waterloo.'

'Good. I want a quick briefing before we talk to the super's granddaughter.'

'Be there in twenty minutes,' said Ellen.

9

Scobie drove, with Ellen sitting tensely in the passenger seat, her hands braced on the dash, her foot on a phantom brake pedal. Sutton's driving style was full of fits and starts, swivel necking, and hand gestures as he talked, punctuated with occasional swigs from a bottle of mineral water.

'You know the Cobb family?' Scobie said. 'From one of the estates?'

'One of the kids took a marijuana plant to school for show-and-tell,' gasped Ellen.

'Correct.'

'What about them?'

'My wife's had dealings with them.'

Ellen knew that Scobie would get to the point eventually. She'd met Beth Sutton a few times, at police picnics and Christmas parties. A plain, good, churchgoing woman who worked for Community Health and was given to helping the unfortunates of the Peninsula. Nothing wrong with that, except that people involved in good works often seemed to wear an air of piety and satisfaction, which often grated on

Ellen. She waited, said 'Really?' to prompt Scobie.

'When I was in court this morning I let slip that I was married to Beth. Now Natalie's going to be suspicious of her.'

'Scobie, suspicion of the police is inbred on those housing estates.'

'I know, but it needn't be. Beth keeps her work and mine completely separate.'

They lapsed into silence. The road was wide and flat now and Ellen relaxed fractionally. Her mind drifted. There was a possibility that one of Janine McQuarrie's clients was the killer, but getting access to her records was going to be a headache. At the same time, all of the circumstances of the murder indicated a degree of planning and professionalism, as if the killers had been hired.

The woman's finances would have to be examined minutely. Did everything come back to money? Ellen wondered, thinking about her husband's own futile rants centred on money. They *were* struggling, despite their combined salaries—one of their cars was for the scrap heap, and their daughter's rent and university tuition fees were crippling—but Alan's resentment sometimes took strange turnings. Only last night he'd said, with a sidelong glance, 'Don't you think it's interesting that it's always plainclothed police who go up on theft or corruption charges?'

Plainclothed police like her, he meant. 'Your point being?'

'They bring decent police into disrepute.'

Guys like him, he meant. Rarely was the Ethical Standards department of the police force obliged to investigate the guys who worked in the Traffic and Accident Investigation squads.

Alan was full of undercurrents. It was very possible that he was depressed. But, more than anything, Ellen was scared that he'd found her out. Now and then over the years she'd pocketed money at crime-scenes, $50 here, $500 there. Probably no more than $2000 in all, over a ten-year period, and she'd even put one haul, of $500, into a church poor box. But the pathology was there in her and she was afraid. It had started with chewing gum at the corner shop when she was eight years old and although she'd more or less stopped, the impulse hadn't. Maybe she needed a psychologist. Maybe she needed to make an appointment with Dominic O'Brien.

God, what would Challis think of her if he ever found out? She felt sick at heart at the thought. Her palms were damp. She dried them on her thighs, letting Scobie Sutton wander all over the road and talk and talk.

They arrived to find that Challis had brought in two DCs from Mornington and, with their help, set up the first-floor conference room as an incident room: extra computers, phones, fax machines, whiteboards, photocopiers and scanners, and a TV set. But, more than anything as far as Ellen was concerned, he'd brewed coffee and placed a box of pastries in the centre of the conference table. She sipped and nibbled as he introduced the Mornington detectives and outlined the case, reading from his laptop.

Finally he turned to her. 'Ellen?'

She brushed flakes of pastry from her lapels and summarised the results of the Bayside Counselling interviews. 'We need to look at those files,' Challis said. 'Meanwhile, I carried out a Google search on the husband. He's a well-known hard case in the finance world, good at firing and downsizing, so no doubt he's got some enemies. When Ellen and I have finished talking to his daughter we'll head up to the city and check him out.'

Scobie Sutton had eschewed the pastries and was fastidiously peeling and slicing an apple. 'Will the daughter make a good witness, boss?'

Challis shrugged. 'We won't know until we talk to her, but she did tell the first officers at the scene that the killers came in an old car, white with a yellow door. That will be your job,' he said to one of the Mornington DCs. 'I've put in a request for lists of cars stolen, abandoned and burnt, so keep updating it and check with Traffic for cars caught speeding, the usual thing.'

'Sir.'

'The car could have come in from outside,' Scobie said, 'or they were dumb enough to use their own car.'

'Or Georgia was quite wrong about the car. Either way, we'll release details to the media,' Challis said. 'Someone might recognise the description.'

They looked doubtful. Cars with mismatched doors, boot lids, bonnets and panels were common in a country where the poor were getting poorer.

Challis glanced at the other Mornington detective. 'Go back to Lofty Ridge Road and talk to any of the neighbours who weren't at home this morning. Find out who delivers the mail and the newspapers, supermarket orders, the usual.'

'Boss.'

'Scobie, I want you to check Robert McQuarrie's flight movements and find out what you can about Mrs Humphreys and whoever else might have lived at that address. When she's recovered from her hip operation, interview her. We need to establish if she knows Janine McQuarrie or if she herself has any enemies.'

'Boss.'

'Ellen, the superintendent awaits.'

'Whoopee-do,' said Ellen, immediately regretting it, for surely the super was grieving.

10

They signed out an unmarked Falcon from the motor pool and drove to Mornington in intermittent sunshine that was hard and bright on the wetness all around. Above them a high, scudding wind blew scraps of cloud across the sky. Normally they chatted when they were together, settling quickly into comfortable patterns with each other, but Ellen was withdrawn, a heavy presence in the passenger seat. 'Anything wrong?' said Challis.

'Nup.'

He wondered if it was her husband again, remembering the man's brusqueness on the phone that morning. Ellen was loyal and private by nature, but had revealed enough over the years to indicate that the marriage was under strain. Challis had never liked Alan Destry. The man was chronically surly, and so tightly wound that he might one day do something violent. We're a fine pair, he thought, me morose about my wife this morning, Ellen about her husband now.

'Everything okay at home?'

'Peachy,' said Ellen, her eyes fixed on the road.

Time to change the subject. 'So this Dominic O'Brien character is going to be obstructive?'

Ellen seemed to bristle at the wheel. 'What happens when an immovable object meets an irresistible force?'

He grinned. He'd always liked looking at her, a woman full of coiled energy and every muscle expressive, her beautiful eyes now taking on their familiar tuck of suspicion and anticipation. She was ready for business.

'Uh oh,' she said presently. 'We've got company.'

They'd reached a hilly street behind the Esplanade in Mornington. No fog on this side of the Peninsula, but a rainsquall had come in across Port Phillip Bay, causing movement in a huddle of reporters and camera crews camped on a nearby nature strip. 'Be friendly,' Challis said.

Shouted questions reached them through the windows of the car, but Ellen didn't stop, easing the CIU Falcon off the street, onto a gravelled driveway and past dense shrubbery and slender gum trees, to park nose-up to a railway sleeper barrier. They got out, locked the car and Challis followed Ellen down the steps to the front door, careful on the slicks of moss.

McQuarrie greeted them, holding his granddaughter's hand. She'd been crying, but glanced up at them solemnly, as if shy but also aware that she was at the centre of something momentous. She wore jeans, a pink long-sleeved top, pink socks, pink clips holding back unruly blonde hair. Her grandfather looked faintly lost, a slightly built senior policeman who'd seen the underside only from behind a desk. He didn't make introductions but stood back, saying, 'Come in, come in,' before glancing at their feet. 'Would you mind…'

There were shoes and gumboots heaped on both sides of the door. Challis and Ellen slipped off their shoes, curling their toes on the cold concrete of the verandah, waiting for McQuarrie to stop dithering on the doorstep.

Finally they were in a hallway, pale green carpet expensively thick beneath their feet, a phone off the hook on an antique hallstand.

McQuarrie led them to a sitting room: a red leather sofa and armchairs, massive antique sideboards, two small Turkish rugs. A huge window looked out onto a barbecue pit, a brick courtyard, a rose arbour and shrubs in bulky terracotta pots. McQuarrie's wife Barbara—often called Mrs Super—stood beside an open fire, as neatly put together as her husband but snootier, more readily offended. Challis tried a commiserative nod and smile and got a scowl in return. He introduced Ellen, who earned only a flickering glance.

'Have you found out who did this?'

McQuarrie said hastily, 'It's too soon, dear. Hal is here for information.'

Barbara McQuarrie came forward a few centimetres, the strain apparent in her face. 'I don't want you upsetting Georgia.'

'Some tea, love, we could all do with a cup of tea.'

'I'll help you,' Ellen said, expertly shepherding McQuarrie's wife out of the room, piling on admiring comments about the décor, the house, the landscaping. Challis and McQuarrie watched them go, Challis appreciating her tact and her instincts.

McQuarrie said, 'Hal, this is Georgia. Georgia, this is Inspector Challis.'

Challis put out his hand and the child shook with him gravely, her palm moist, her bones like a tiny bird's inside his grip. 'Pleased to meet you.'

'Pleased to meet you.'

Challis didn't know what McQuarrie had said to his granddaughter. He'd hoped to be briefed before meeting and questioning her. Did Georgia know that her mother was dead? If so, what did she, a six-year-old, understand that to mean? 'Perhaps we should all sit down,' he said.

'Grampa, can I have a hot chocolate?'

'Of course you can. Run and ask Nana.'

Relieved, Challis watched her leave the room, and then turned to McQuarrie. 'Sir, are you okay with this, my questioning her?'

'I am. My wife's not.'

'Does Georgia know her mother's dead?'

Some of McQuarrie's brisk superintendent's manner had come back. 'Yes. Died and gone to heaven.'

'She's remarkably poised.'

'She's incredible. She's finished her crying for now. Even so, we'll see that she gets proper counselling.' He paused. 'If your questioning upsets her I'm putting a halt to it, Hal.'

'Sir.'

McQuarrie was the only super in Challis's experience who expected to be called 'sir' by the more senior of his officers. Most preferred 'boss' or even first names and affectionate nicknames. McQuarrie insisted on 'sir' and Challis believed that it was a measure of the man's insecurity—compounded today by the fact that he was grieving.

There was the distant ping of a microwave oven, and moments later Georgia appeared with a mug of hot chocolate, a frothy moustache on her upper lip. Ellen Destry came in behind her with a teapot and sugar bowl on a tray, Barbara McQuarrie with plain Ikea mugs and shortbread biscuits in a bowl, her disapproval obvious. She wanted Challis and his sergeant out of her house.

When they were settled—Georgia perched on her grandfather's knees—Challis glanced at Ellen, who leaned forward and said, 'Georgia, we want to catch the bad men who hurt your mother.'

Georgia, small and tawny, shrank into McQuarrie's lap, hot chocolate splashing on his tie. 'I want my dad. Where's Daddy?'

'He's on his way, sweetheart,' McQuarrie said, rocking her. 'His plane's already landed.'

'What if they shoot him, too?'

'Hush, hush,' McQuarrie said, out of his depth.

'We're stopping this right now,' his wife said.

Challis signalled to Ellen and they got to their feet, but Georgia seemed panicked by this. 'Where are you going?'

'To catch the bad men,' Ellen said.

'Where?'

'We'll look for them everywhere.'

Challis was wondering if Ellen's answer would add to Georgia's fears, make her housebound, when Georgia said, 'But you don't know what they look like.'

Barbara McQuarrie said, 'It's all right, Georgia. Let the man and the lady go off and do their job.'

'I know what they look like,' Georgia insisted, recovered now. She climbed out of her grandfather's lap and left the room, returning moments later with several drawings. She aligned the edges awkwardly, shoving them at Challis. 'Here.'

Challis glanced inquiringly at McQuarrie, who said, 'The crime-scene people arrived before I did, and Georgia watched them sketching the scene. She came home and wanted to do her own sketches.'

Challis swallowed. 'Thank you, Georgia. These will be very helpful.'

He examined the top drawing: a bird's eye view of the area, showing both cars and her mother's body. There was a border of trees and a curious smudge amongst them. 'Is this...?' he asked, indicating it to her.

'That's me hiding from the man who wanted to shoot me.'

'Uh-huh.'

Ellen came to stand beside him. There were three other drawings, and Georgia identified them one by one. 'That's the man who shot Mummy, that's the other man in the car, that's Mummy.'

Mummy from before the murder, a woman with long hair and a big smile.

'These are terrific,' Ellen said. 'Have you remembered anything else about the car? Maybe you remember some of the letters and numbers on the numberplate.'

'It was just an old car.'

'Well, that's helpful. Now, shall we sit and talk some more about what happened this morning?'

'Okay.'

Ellen guided Georgia to the sofa and sat with her. Challis sat in a nearby armchair and watched and listened.

'You didn't have to go to school today,' Ellen said, 'is that right? No lessons?'

'Mummy had to take me to work with her.'

'Was she meeting someone before going to the clinic?'

'I think so.'

'Do you know who?'

Georgia shrugged, a child's quick, jerking shrug.

'Did your mum notice a car behind you at any stage?'

Shrug.

'Did she say anything to you about being lost?'

Head shake.

'You came to a house and your mum stopped the car,' Ellen said, briefly stroking Georgia's forearm. 'Then what happened?'

Afterwards Challis was to remark on how fiercely Georgia had concentrated. There were two men, she said. One stayed in the car and she hadn't seen him clearly, except that he wore dark glasses and had a kind of round face. The man who'd shot her mother wore a beanie and a jacket with the collar up, so she couldn't give a clear description, except that she thought his face was thin. The jacket was blue, no, black, no, blue. The car was kind of white.

The gun was a little one, not a rifle, but it had something stuck on the end of it, and the man carrying it had chased her mother around and around the car. She'd undone her seatbelt to fetch something from her Hi-5 backpack by that stage, and so she was able to move about inside the car and follow the action. Then her mother had made a break for it and she saw the man point the gun and her mother fell to the ground.

'Did you hear the gun?'

'It made a kind of *phht* sound.'

Challis exchanged a glance with Ellen: probably an automatic and fitted with a suppressor.

'I wanted to go to her but I was scared and he turned around and looked at me.'

That was when she darted out of the car and ran towards the other car. 'I thought he would help me, but he didn't.'

'You mean the man driving?'

'Yes. He just waved me away, so I ran into the trees. I tried to hide but it wasn't a very good hiding place and the man with the gun could see me, but when he tried to shoot me nothing happened and he said something bad and looked at his gun and went back to the car.'

McQuarrie murmured, 'Any ballistics, Hal?'

'Not yet.'

'Automatic pistol, do you think? It jammed on him?'

'Possibly. What did you do then, Georgia?'

When she heard the white car start up she raised her head and watched it leave. It made a lot of smoke. Yes, a white car. A kind of old car, she thought, with a funny door.

'Funny door?'

'Not the same colour. Kind of a yellow. Look,' she said, pointing to one of the drawings. An off-white car with a pale yellow door and the driver inside, his arm out of the window, presumably waving her away.

'If the original door was rusted or damaged,' Ellen murmured to Challis, 'it may have been replaced by one from a wrecking yard.'

Challis nodded. It was a job for Scobie.

'Do you think you could look at some photographs for us, Georgia?'

That quick shrug again. 'Don't know.'

'Pictures of men's faces, sweetheart,' her grandfather said. 'You might recognise the men who hurt Mummy.'

'Okay.'

'If you do,' he said, 'we'll catch them and have an identity parade. Do you know what that is?'

Challis let the super prattle on. Identity parades were only useful to back up solid evidence. A failed lineup was like manna from heaven to a defence lawyer. And the idea of putting Georgia McQuarrie through an identity parade was galling to him. He'd tried, and failed, to observe a distance with regard to the child. The job swamped you if you didn't learn to see the blood and the damaged flesh and lives as outcomes or problems to solve. But you couldn't go on thinking like that without giving the pressure some kind of outlet. Humour—of the blackest kind—was a common outlet; booze; a hobby; the exclusive company of other cops. Without an outlet, your heart would fracture. That little girl with her wintry face...Challis didn't have children but Ellen and Scobie did. What went through their minds every day? Did they ever stop worrying about their kids? Abused kids, bloodied kids, orphaned kids.

'Is there anything else you remember about the two men, Georgia?'

'What colour was their skin?' Barbara McQuarrie wanted to know.

'Dear, please,' McQuarrie said.

'Same as mine,' Georgia said.

Challis rested his forearms on his knees. 'You couldn't see their faces very clearly.'

'No. The man with the gun had a beanie on. It was all pulled down and his collar was turned up.'

'Was he fat? Thin?'

'Medium.'

'Tall? Short?'

'Medium.'

'What about the way they spoke?' Barbara McQuarrie asked. 'Did they speak English?'

'Love, please,' McQuarrie said.

'It's a fair enough question.'

Ellen broke in. 'What about the other man, Georgia, the driver of the car. Was he wearing a beanie, too?'

'No.'

'What colour was his hair?'

'He was kind of bald.'

'Bald, or had he shaved his hair off?'

'I think shaved.'

'Did he say anything?'

'He just waved at me to go away.'

'Anything else about his face that you can remember?'

'He was kind of a bit younger than the other one.'

'As old as your dad?'

Georgia screwed up her face assessingly. 'Younger.'

'Anything else?'

'Sort of a round face, a bit fat,' Georgia said.

Then she went alert in McQuarrie's arms as a door opened in the hallway and a voice called, 'Mum? Dad? Georgia?'

She hurled herself out of the room.

11

Robert McQuarrie came in looking pale but composed, frowning a little as the clamouring hands of his daughter pulled his suit askew. Then his mother rushed to him with a small, incoherent cry, which seemed to break his resolve. He blinked his eyes. Finally the superintendent was clapping an arm around him in a clumsy embrace.

Challis watched, unmoved. Robert McQuarrie seemed to notice him then over the shoulders of his parents. He had an open face, smooth and well tended, like his hands. A little button nose, inherited from his mother, gave him the appearance of a plain, over-sized schoolboy dressed in a costly suit.

He broke the embrace and approached with his hand out. 'Robert McQuarrie,' he said. 'And you are?'

Challis made the introductions, McQuarrie scarcely glancing at Ellen.

'I'll be available later, but right now I need to comfort my daughter.'

'I understand,' Challis said. He glanced at Ellen, and by unspoken agreement they edged towards the door. The superintendent followed them into the hallway. 'You're going?'

Challis nodded. 'I'm not sure that Georgia can help us any further at the moment. We may need to show her photographs of cars later, and mugshots.'

McQuarrie waved a hand as if to say, 'Of course, of course.'

'And we'll need to speak to your son.'

McQuarrie looked at the floor, then up at Challis. 'My son is devastated by this.'

'I can imagine.'

'I know you're just doing your job. I'm a policeman myself, remember? I know you have to eliminate him from your inquiries. But go gently, all right? He's exhausted, in shock, he's just lost his wife. His daughter has just lost her mother.'

Challis nodded, waiting for McQuarrie to wind down.

'And he couldn't have shot Janine. He was in Sydney.'

Sooner or later, Challis thought, he'll make the necessary leap: *Did my son hire someone to shoot Janine?*

'I understand.'

'Should be plenty of witnesses, too. He was guest speaker at a seminar.' McQuarrie gave a ragged sigh. 'Look, Hal, whatever resources you need, they're yours. Extra manpower, overtime, anything at all. But for God's sake keep the media out of this.'

'We'll have to tell them something.'

'It's an unholy alliance, sometimes, police and press. But this is my son and his wife and daughter we're talking about, so no quiet words in the ear of that girlfriend of yours.'

Challis flushed angrily. Ellen saved him. 'Sir, before we go, could you tell us a bit about your daughter-in-law?'

McQuarrie glanced at his watch, looked back over his shoulder to the sitting room and sounds of grief and bewilderment. 'Can't it wait?'

'Just some basic background, sir, to get us started.'

'Oh very well, come with me.'

He led them to a study, a cluttered, cheerless room at the rear of the house. There were framed diplomas and graduation photographs on the walls, golfclubs in one corner, a shelf of trophies, a ship in a bottle, very few books, golfing clothes tossed over a sombre leather armchair, computer, printer and fax machine on a leather-inlaid wooden desk. It seemed to Challis that McQuarrie had staked out this space as his own and his wife could go to hell.

'Another cup of tea?' McQuarrie said, not meaning it.

'We're fine, thank you, sir,' Ellen said, glancing at Challis to see if he'd regained equilibrium.

'Well, what do you need to know?'

Challis saw Ellen take out her notebook and move unobtrusively to one side. He'd ask, she'd record. 'We'll start with her personality, sir. What was she like?'

'Lovely girl. Good family.'

'She's a psychologist?'

'Has—had—her own clinic, in Mount Eliza,' McQuarrie said. 'A very bright girl.'

'We've begun interviewing her staff and colleagues.'

'Of course.'

'Did she see clients at the clinic, or travel to see them?'

'Both, I suppose. I don't really know.'

'And today?'

McQuarrie was impatient. 'It was a curriculum day at Georgia's school, which is another way of saying that her teachers gave themselves a day off, and when Janine couldn't arrange childcare she had no option but to take Georgia with her.'

'Was Janine going to the clinic afterwards, or visiting other clients?'

'Hal, for God's sake, this is basic police work. Talk to her secretary, check her calendar.'

'Sir.' Challis thought for a moment about his next question. There was no easy way to ask it. 'Would you say that Robert and Janine were happily married?'

The super said, through compressed, bloodless lips, 'See? That's the kind of innuendo the media love. That Janine had a lover and so Robert shot her. Or that Robert had a lover and wanted Janine out of the way.'

'We need to examine all scenarios,' Challis said, hating the word but it was a useful one and by now deeply ingrained in the police lexicon.

'To hell with that. I hope you're not going to ask my son that same question.'

Challis tilted his chin a little. 'I'm afraid I'll have to, sir.'

And you know it, too, was the unspoken part of his reply.

McQuarrie flushed. 'Just remember who I am and who my son is and who you are, mister.'

'Getting back to Janine,' Ellen said hastily.

'Lovely girl.'

Challis reflected that he wouldn't get more than that from McQuarrie, who seemed incapable of discerning individual quirks in people. Janine came from a good family, was successful in business and had been chosen by his son, so no further scrutiny was required. She'd passed the only tests that mattered.

Poor woman. Had she struggled to be seen and heard by the family?

'Did Janine ever mention particular clients who were threatening or abusive?'

Challis watched the superintendent absorb the implications. 'No, but that's a promising avenue, Hal, very promising. Follow it up.'

Challis nodded, despite his reservations. 'Would Mrs McQuarrie have anything to add, do you think? Not now, perhaps tomorrow?'

'You keep my wife out of this.'

'Sir, I have no desire to upset anybody, but isn't it possible that she knows things you don't? You're very busy, after all. Were they close?'

'Janine was like a daughter to both of us.'

'Yes, sir. How about her parents? Have they been told?'

'They're both dead, I'm afraid—killed in an accident some years ago. But there is a sister, Meg. Now, will that be all?'

'Thank you sir,' Ellen said.

They were halfway to the car when McQuarrie caught up with them, taking Challis by the arm and saying, 'It's time I spoke to the media.'

Challis exchanged glances with Ellen and they followed the superintendent up the driveway to the street and the reporters, who were standing with hunched shoulders against the driving wind. McQuarrie lifted a hand and said, 'I wish to make a brief statement,' and confirmed that his daughter-in-law had been shot dead at approximately 9.30 that morning. Challis and Ellen endured; cameras flashed at them. Meanwhile McQuarrie had apparently cast off his grief and strain; this was the McQuarrie who wore a costly suit and carried himself with a military man's brisk snap and fearless gaze, like a British Army officer in a stiff-upper-lip film from the 1950s. He impressed the cameras, but it seemed to Challis that the man knew more about golf than crime, more about wealthy Rotarians than criminals or the police officers under his command. Tessa Kane arrived halfway through, earning a frown from McQuarrie, but he didn't falter, talking at length, answering questions, and finally clapping a hand on Challis's back, saying, 'This is the man who will find my daughter-in-law's murderer.'

The cameras and microphones turned questingly to Challis but he declined politely and returned to the car with Ellen. While she drove, heading across to the Nepean Highway, Challis sat slumped against the passenger door full of thoughts and with Georgia's drawings clasped in his lap.

Ellen broke the silence. 'I notice you didn't tell the super we're going to his son's place of work.'

He stirred and grinned. 'I didn't, did I?'

'First impressions of the son?'

'Smooth, a charmer, in a private school kind of way.'

'Professionally charming, not personally charming. Did you notice that he didn't once look at or talk to me?'

'I did.'

'And it had nothing to do with rank. I'm a woman, ergo I don't have a brain.' She paused. 'Be interesting to know what his relationship with Janine was like.'

'Yes.'

After a pause she said, as if testing the waters, 'Hal, what did you make of the super and his wife?'

Challis cocked his eyebrow at her. 'Not exactly heartbroken.'

'No.'

'They praise Janine, but secretly didn't like her, or thought her unworthy of their son.'

Ellen nodded. 'That's the impression I got.'

'And if you're asking should we consider the super, or even Mrs Super, a suspect, the answer's yes.'

There, it was out in the open. With anyone other than Ellen, he'd have kept his suspicions to himself. He saw her nod. 'And your reasons are…?' she said.

'Little things: lack of grief, being protective of his son and granddaughter, being faintly obstructive and wanting to guide the investigation. All explicable, but we can't rule him out, or not entirely, and we can't rule out the possibility that he suspects his son and is protecting him.'

'Yes,' said Ellen simply, confirming that she'd come to the same conclusions. 'He can't take over the investigation, can he?'

Challis shook his head. 'Regulations won't allow it.'

'But he'll meddle?'

'Yes.'

Then a little Mazda sports car was beside them, tooting. Ellen tooted back and the Mazda shot away along the rain-slicked highway. Challis stirred. 'Who was that?'

'Pam Murphy and John Tankard.'

Challis frowned, then twigged. 'Kellock's safe driving campaign.'

12

Constables Pam Murphy and John Tankard, dressed as if they belonged to the Special Operations Group or the FBI, with peaked caps, waisted jackets and pants tucked into their boots, promptly began discussing Challis and Destry. Tankard thought they had a thing going.

'No way.'

'They're always together.'

'Tank, *we*'re always together.'

He subsided, muttering, but it was short-lived. 'What about the newspaper chick?'

'What about her?'

'Is he still giving her one?'

'I don't know and I don't care. It's none of my business.'

Then, with his old nudge nudge, wink wink: 'Has he given you one yet?'

'Tank, grow up, okay?'

It was no joke, cooped up with John Tankard in the little sports car. It was bad enough that he was a big, fleshy man, but ever since coming back from six months' stress leave for shooting dead a deranged and armed farmer, he'd been a little unstable. His mood today was pretty typical of the Tankard she remembered, the racist and bully who'd been called a storm trooper by the locals, the partner who was more interested in her tits than police work, but he was also given to moments of moody daydreaming and insecurity—which she attributed to counselling that hadn't taken very well.

She could sense him looking at her, and confirmed it with a quick, sideways glance, disturbed to see and feel a queer, sulky heat coming from him as he asked, 'Could you do it?'

'Do what?'

'What that newspaper chick did, have sex with a lot of guys, everyone watching.' He cocked his head at her assessingly. 'Nah, can't see you doing that.'

As if throwing her a crude challenge, hoping she'd rise to it and come across for him. 'She didn't have sex with anyone. She was there as a reporter.'

'Yeah, yeah, whatever. Bet Challis was pissed off. But if you can't keep your chick in line, what do you expect?'

She ignored him.

'I mean,' he went on, 'he couldn't even control his wife. She sleeps around on him and tries to have him killed.'

'Tank,' Pam snarled, 'only Neanderthals feel the need to keep their women in line.'

He sniggered to see her riled. She drove on, cross with herself. Early afternoon, and still the fog persisted. As they approached a roundabout, she said, 'Mornington, Tyabb or straight ahead?'

But Tankard was in a reverie beside her and failed to answer. Maybe he was looking inwards again, at his sorrows. Pam was suspicious of Tank's new-found introspection, wondering if it would slow his response times, blunt his survival instincts. Well, she wasn't put on earth to cure him. Still, she'd always known where she stood with the old Tankard. He'd been reliably suspicious of everyone, confrontational but not unsteady, with the instincts of a cop driven by self-preservation rather than ambition. In fact, he'd been entirely lacking in ambition, relying on the police force for a sense of brotherhood and security, even as he distrusted or despised his fellow cops.

She chose to drive straight ahead, which would take them to Penzance Beach and Waterloo.

He stirred. 'Did you say something?'

'Forget it.'

Tankard struggled like a dim schoolboy caught staring out of the window. Finally he said, in the faintly lost manner of the new John Tankard, 'Do you see the point of this? Spending four hours a day on the roads thanking people for the one time in a thousand they happen to show courtesy to another motorist or signal before turning a corner? This is bullshit.'

'True,' Pam said.

They were passing the detention centre near Waterloo when she was forced onto the gravel verge by an oncoming Subaru, which veered across in front of her and onto the centre's main driveway, narrowly missing a silver Passat that had emerged to wait for a gap in traffic. Tessa Kane, who clearly didn't deserve a showbag. Pam tooted, and so did the Passat.

13

Whoops, she'd cut off those cops in their sports car and nearly collected a Passat. Tessa Kane grinned ruefully, shrugging an apology at Pam Murphy and John Tankard. Pam returned the grin, her cap at a rakish angle. A tough little broad, Tessa thought, heading towards the main gate.

The detention centre was a cheerless expanse of chilly cement-block huts behind razor wire. Originally intended for 350 inmates, it had held almost 500 asylum seekers at one stage, in a concentrated knot of misery. Now the 'flood' of asylum seekers had dried up and most of the detainees had been shipped back and a few granted residence visas. Eighty were left: a handful of asylum seekers from the Middle East, and people who had breached or overstayed their tourist visas. Soon all would be deported.

The centre had delivered no benefits to Waterloo that Tessa had seen. Most of the locals had been apathetic, a handful angry and ashamed, and the remainder rubbed their hands together at this God-given opportunity to relish their prejudices. They seemed to applaud the perimeter guard who'd shouted at a detainee: 'You are one ugly fucking Arab.' There had been plenty of letters to the editor after Tessa had published that quote, objecting to the word 'fucking'; none objecting to the matter of detention itself, of course, or the centre, or the mindset of the guard. It had been—still was—an unhappy place. Last week there had been a riot—termed a 'disturbance' by corrections staff—and today Tessa could see men and children on the flat roof of the gymnasium, displaying banners: *We Are Human Not Animal.* In the first six weeks of operation, two men had been trapped on the razor wire; over a ten-month period in the second year, seven inmates had sewn their lips together; and most had gone on a hunger strike at one time or another. Fires had been lit, rocks thrown, tear gas used.

That had been the public face of almost all of Australia's detention centres, the one you saw on commercial television's current affairs programs. Tessa had been interested in the hidden stories: mental illness; treatment refused for sexually abused children; the dubious backgrounds and qualifications of the guards; the attitudes of the Refugee Review Tribunal and Department of Immigration staff. There had also been whispers of corruption. Apparently Charlie Mead and his section heads had routinely defrauded the federal, state and local governments by artificially inflating the cost of repairs, provisions, services and wages, the benefit flowing to their employer, ANZCOR, an American company that managed prisons and detention centres under contract to the governments of Australia and New Zealand. They operated out of Utah and had branches in Canada and the UK.

And soon the detention centre would close its doors. Tessa wanted one last opportunity to nail the detention system itself, and Charlie Mead's role in it, to the wall.

Why had Mead agreed to see her? For the past three years he'd been typically contemptuous of the media seeking interviews, and do-gooders befriending the inmates. Perhaps he'd got sick of the way she always concluded her articles with the words 'Centre management declined to comment', or he simply didn't care, now that he'd be moving on.

Tessa ran through her mental notes on him. Born in Durban, South Africa, fifty-five years ago; served in the army for ten years before completing a law degree in Johannesburg and an MBA in London. Worked in prison management in the UK, then successfully applied for the position of deputy manager—and later manager—of a maximum-security prison in Brisbane. There his tough line had alienated guards and inmates alike, but that had been no handicap to his being hired to manage the Waterloo Detention Centre. Arrived Waterloo, January 2002. Married to Lottie, about whom Tessa's research had found no information. No children.

She was obliged to wait outside the main gate while the guard confirmed with the administration building by telephone, then was directed to an adjacent carpark. She got out, locked her car, and was turning towards the gate, tucking her keys in her briefcase, when a guard materialised in front of her. She'd not heard his approach. He jerked his head and she followed him, a solid, swaggering figure, through the outer and inner razor-wire perimeter fences and across a paved area to the administration block. It was separated from the other buildings by high, tubular steel railings. A child smiled at her through the bars; two women appeared to be painting the doors to a dormitory; several men stared at her, cigarettes in their hands, while others booted a soccer ball from one side of a stretch of cracked asphalt to the other.

Tessa closed her coat more thoroughly at her throat, as if to dispel the dense fog and the air of hopelessness. No one glanced at her in curiosity or hope: she no doubt represented another branch of an unfeeling government. She'd been to plenty of prisons over the years as a reporter and newspaper editor. This was worse than a prison because, for many of these inmates, further abuse—even death—awaited them on their repatriation to home countries.

Her briefcase was scanned electronically, then searched manually, and her mobile phone and microcassette recorder confiscated. 'You'll get these back when you leave,' said the man who'd searched her. She was obliged to step through a metal detector and even then her coat was removed and the seams, cuffs and collar searched minutely by hand. Tessa stared at the walls, which were bare and painted a comfortless white.

Finally she was shown to a straightbacked chair in a corridor and told to wait. White walls, photographs of the US president and the Australian prime minister. After fifteen minutes a young woman stuck her head out of a nearby doorway and beckoned to Tessa. 'Mr Mead will see you now.' Her look of appalled fascination was a sure sign that she'd read last week's *Progress* and half expected Tessa to take her clothes off and have group sex with the guards.

Tessa entered an office dominated by a desk and the man behind it. As expected, the room was furnished with filing cabinets, shelves of books and spiral-bound reports, and a barred window that looked out onto an exercise yard, but the desk was set up as a security and communications centre, with several telephones, an intercom system, security monitors, two computers, a laptop and a fax machine. The walls were bare but for a couple of framed certificates and a photograph taken during the centre's opening ceremony, the mayor and councillors grinning as they clapped Charlie Mead and other ANZCOR dignitaries on the back. Pricks. If you looked closely enough, you could even see the $100 bills changing hands. Even more would change hands once approval was given to refit the detention centre as some other kind of facility.

Camp for disadvantaged children? thought Tessa sourly. Community centre for the people of the housing estates?

She caught Mead looking at her. He was a rangy man, all bone and sinew, with a knobbly hard skull and quick, sharp, coldly humorous eyes. He rose—he was very tall—from behind his desk, reached across it and squashed her hand in his. He pointed to the chair opposite. 'Sit.'

A growling voice. He watched while she took out her notebook and tested the ink flow of her pen. Then she gave him a brief, automatic smile, and was halfway through thanking him for his time when he said, 'Kane: is that a Jewish name?'

Well, hello, she thought. Was she going to get the full treatment? Ironical amusement, raised eyebrow, frank appraisal of her legs, overt anti-feminism, overt anti-Semitism, and a whole arsenal of other shock tactics, gestures and attitudes intended to rattle her?

So she said at once, 'It could be argued that your guards have been dehumanised by their work here, an attitude encouraged by management. Would you care to comment?'

It was as if he'd become bored. He swung back in his chair, crossed his long legs and stared up at the ceiling. He splayed the fingers of his left hand, examined his nails. '"Dehumanised"? Another meaningless word among many.'

'According to an ex-employee of—'

'Who?' he demanded.

'I can't divulge that. According to an ex-employee, your guards wake detention centre detainees at random times throughout the night, demanding they quote their detention numbers. Is that meaningless?'

Mead shrugged. 'Security,' he said.

She stared at him, and went on. 'Inmates have attested that the Refugee Review Tribunal is often only one individual rather than a panel, and some of these individuals make it a point to refuse all applications.'

'Take it up with the RRT,' Mead said, jerking forward, his fingers flying over a keyboard. Then, with a soft, impatient grunt, he leaned back again. 'Next question.'

Mead was tapping his pen against his teeth now, staring out of his window. She could see the back of his neck, his tough, tanned skin. There was a photograph on the windowsill and Mead picked it up, put it down again. A watchful, dark-haired woman offering a reluctant smile to the camera. Lottie Mead, presumably—and, Tessa realised, the driver of the Passat.

'Care for a tour of the place?' said Mead.

14

'Let *me* drive,' said John Tankard after the near miss with the Subaru.

He didn't expect Murph to accede, and she didn't. The incident hadn't rattled her, and hadn't been her fault in the first place, but he felt in a take-charge mood suddenly, in reaction to her superior attitude, the particularly girlie quality of the wave she'd exchanged with the Kane woman, his cramped seat and the job itself. He felt rage building, fine and liberating. Sometimes he worried that his six months of stress counselling hadn't worked; sometimes he was glad that it hadn't.

And now some prick was tailgating them, flashing and tooting. He turned around in his seat and saw the Passat that had been waiting to merge with the traffic passing the detention centre. A woman was driving, and he felt obscurely satisfied by that. 'What's *her* problem?' he snarled.

'Keep your shirt on, Tank,' said Murph, pulling over to the side of the road.

'Stay here,' he said, getting out.

He adjusted his gun belt, jacket and cap, and advanced grimly on the Passat. The driver, spotting his uniform, blanched, then looked sulky, and began to open her door.

'Lady, get back in the car,' he said.

She complied. He stood beside her door, gestured for her to wind down her window, then stood there, crowding her space. It felt great. They were near the Fiddlers Creek pub and patrons were streaming in for the all-you-can-gorge buffet lunch, which finished at two. 'Got a problem?' he said.

'I didn't know you were the police.'

'Well, now you do.'

She recovered some of her composure, a woman in her forties with dark hair and a narrow face. 'I would like to get out of the car,' she said.

'No.'

'Do you know who I am?'

'Don't know and don't care,' said Tankard.

'You'll need to know my name if you intend to warn or fine me,' the woman pointed out.

That wasn't what her question had meant and they both knew it. Tankard decided to call her bluff and got out his citation book. 'Fire away,' he said.

'My name is Lottie Mead.'

'So?'

'My husband is director of the detention centre,' she said.

Tankard was filled with emotions: a natural obedience towards authority figures, fear and resentment of stroppy women, and respect for those, like Charlie Mead, who did their bit in the war against terror. He wanted to charge Lottie Mead with something, but feared a whole heap of trouble if he did.

To make it worse, Pam Murphy joined them. 'Is there a problem, madam?'

Lottie Mead took that as permission to get out of her Passat and cross to the front of the car. She was a lean, springy figure in tailored pants and a black woollen jacket. 'There,' she said, pointing.

A cracked headlight. 'Your car did that,' she said. 'I saw and heard it.'

'How?' demanded Tank, wishing Murph would get back in the Mazda and leave him to deal with it. To make it worse, she seemed to know what the Mead woman was on about. 'A stone,' she said apologetically.

'Exactly.'

'You can't prove it was us,' Tank said, trying to wrestle something back. 'That could have happened yesterday, last year.'

He felt Murph's hand on his arm. 'Leave it, Tank, all right? Madam, if you'd care to make a formal report I'm sure we can—'

The woman back-pedalled and Tank was glad to see it. 'That won't be necessary,' she said. 'It's my husband's car, and his company will take care of costs.'

'Then why,' sneered Tank, 'did you cause such a fuss?'

'I couldn't allow you to just drive off without acknowledging that something had happened,' Lottie Mead said, as though there were lots of things she didn't allow.

'Duly acknowledged,' said John Tankard through gritted teeth.

'Tank,' warned Murph, and he got back in the Mazda feeling that he wanted to sort her out as well.

15

Challis and Ellen stopped for petrol and lunch in Frankston, Challis glancing at his watch as they left. It would take them an hour to get to the city, then fifteen minutes for parking, and later they'd have the longer trip back to the other side of the Peninsula: almost two and a half hours of the afternoon would be spent in travelling. He turned on the radio. Someone had tuned to a station that broadcast music of the 1980s. He hurriedly found Radio National.

'Hal, come on, eighties music.'

He snorted. 'There was no music in the eighties.'

She thought. 'Duran Duran.'

'I rest my case.'

She grinned, amusement transforming her, and he felt a sudden urge to touch her cheek. Why? Because her bullying husband was making her miserable? Because he was her friend, and he wanted to show simple comfort and affection? And how simple was the affection? Challis believed that an element of physical attraction existed in most friendships. If he wasn't drawn to her, could he have been her friend? He was relieved when she said, 'Tell me more about the super's son.'

He quickly paraphrased the results of his Google search. Robert McQuarrie ran an investment and brokerage firm, but also belonged to the Australian Enterprise Institute, a neo-conservative think tank that advised the federal government on policy matters and carried out smear campaigns against charities and welfare and aid agencies, which it accused of taking a public advocacy stance on issues of human rights, corporate social responsibility and environmental protection. In fact, Robert McQuarrie had headed an inquiry into the role of non-government organisations, and had been quoted in the press as saying that NGOs were shifting away from direct work in the community to political lobbying and activism. He recommended that certain NGOs earn lower grants, lose their tax-exempt status and meet strict compliance conditions. The tone of his speeches was mean and self satisfied, the voice of a humourless bully.

Ellen sighed. 'So plenty of potential enemies.'

'You think someone killed Janine to get back at her husband?'

Ellen shrugged. 'It's as good an answer as any at the moment.'

By 2.30 p.m. they were fronting up to McQuarrie Financial Services' coldly gleaming marble reception desk, thick carpet under their feet, hemmed in by walls hung with posters discreetly designed and framed. The receptionist, a young woman with a pert nose, poised in a business suit, said, 'May I help you?'

Challis explained the circumstances of their visit, and saw her swallow and go white. 'Mrs McQuarrie?' she whispered.

Challis asked for a room gently. 'We'll need to interview everyone, I'm afraid.'

'I'll need Mr McQuarrie's permission for that,' the receptionist said, recovering her colour.

'Let's not bother him now,' Challis replied. 'He's comforting his daughter. In any case, this is a murder inquiry and I don't really need his permission.'

'But he's just come in to work. Just one moment.'

Stunned, Challis and Ellen watched her make the call. Then Robert McQuarrie was striding towards them, looking more spruce than grieving. 'This really isn't a good time.'

Various thoughts raced through Challis's mind. Robert McQuarrie had spent scant time with his daughter. He apparently valued his work over her, or the memory of his dead wife. And he hadn't yet informed his staff or colleagues. The murder had been reported on the midday news, but Janine hadn't been named. Challis felt a twist of acute displeasure, but concealed it, saying softly, 'This won't take long. Perhaps we could go to your office?'

McQuarrie seemed to come to his senses. 'If you insist.'

Challis gave a mental shake of his head. The super and his wife hadn't seemed particularly grief-stricken about their daughter-in-law, and now the woman's husband rushes into the office rather than stay with his daughter. Challis knew something about grief—he'd felt it, he'd observed it, and knew it took many forms—but he'd never seen grief expressed as an inconvenience before. Who are these people? he wondered.

Ellen was clearly thinking the same thing. When they were settled in a huge corner office with views across the city to the bay, she said, 'I must say I didn't expect to see you here, Robert.'

The use of the man's first name was a deliberate slight, an indication that she was in a dangerous mood. But it failed to chasten the superintendent's son. 'What are you implying? That I'm not observing a decent period of grieving? That I should be at home with my daughter?'

Challis stepped in. 'Some people might think that, Mr McQuarrie.'

'Listen,' Robert McQuarrie was saying, 'I have responsibilities. Two hours here, then I'm driving straight back to be with her. How dare you presume to question how I feel or deal with things? Georgia's in the loving care of my parents today, and tomorrow will go to stay with my wife's sister. I don't want to take her home yet.' His eyes filled with tears. 'We'd only rattle around there and be surrounded by memories. Georgia needs mothering and plenty of distractions, okay? Meanwhile I am the chief executive officer of a company that employs a hundred people Australia-wide.'

With a warning glance at Ellen, Challis said, 'Then we'll be as efficient as possible, but we do need to question everyone.'

'Very well then,' Robert McQuarrie said.

And so Challis and Ellen asked their questions. McQuarrie answered with barely restrained fierceness. No, he could not think of anyone who hated him sufficiently to kill his wife. He vouched for everyone employed by his firm, and as for the Australian Enterprise Institute, it was comprised of men handpicked from law, business, politics, sport, agriculture and the universities, men who were above reproach and met irregularly in various locations, hosted by sympathetic companies around the country. Nothing sinister, nothing underhand. The Institute did not rent premises anywhere or employ staff. It was not that kind of organisation.

'Do you receive hate mail?'

Something, a flicker, in the man's face. 'Naturally,' he replied, reverting to his old manner. 'We at the Institute make the kinds of hard observations that offend sad and mad individuals from the loony left.'

'Loony left,' muttered Ellen.

'Have you kept any of these letters?' said Challis hastily.

'Generic hate,' Robert McQuarrie said. 'Not worth preserving. Will that be all?'

'We need to speak to your staff and colleagues.'

A weary sigh. 'If you must.'

They were given a small conference room. A dozen men and women came to them one by one, and it was soon apparent that none could think of a reason why anyone would want to harm Mr McQuarrie—Mack, Robert, old Rob—by killing his wife. He was an exacting boss and partner, but fair. He wasn't sleeping around. As for his wife, she seemed nice enough. Sad about Georgia, a sweet kid.

They were so crisp and clean, those employees and fellow executives. Buffed and shined and expensively dressed. Yet Challis sensed an awful fear gnawing at them, and could almost hear their thoughts: Am I a winner? Am I being noticed? Is this suit the right cut, this tie the right colour? Will I get a bonus this year? Will I be promoted? Will my ideas be adopted?

Is anyone listening to me?

On the way back they called at a house in Sandringham, which had views over the choppy waters of the bay. Janine's sister, Meg, answered their knock on the door and her resemblance to Janine McQuarrie was startling. She'd been weeping; her face was raw with grief. 'You're lucky to catch me: I'm just on my way to Robert and Janine's house—Georgia needs me.'

Challis exchanged a glance with Ellen. Was 'Georgia needs me' code for 'Robert needs me'? Had he murdered his wife to have the sister?

She showed them through to a cloyingly warm sitting room. Ellen took over, encouraging Meg to talk about herself. Married, but childless; Janine's youngest sister ('There are three of us'); a high-school teacher currently on stress leave.

Challis studied her as she talked. A kindly woman, he decided. Motherly. Unsophisticated. Perhaps a woman who'd wanted to have children but couldn't. Hardly someone to murder or inspire murder. She wore all of her emotions on her face: pity for Georgia and Robert; dismay and apprehension that her sister could be murdered. 'I'm glad our parents aren't alive—it would have killed them.'

'Did Janine have any enemies? Any altercations with anyone recently? Anything like that?'

'No. Nothing. I have no idea who would have wanted to kill her.

I'm sure it was a mistake.'

Challis gazed at her for a couple of beats, then decided to bypass those polite conversational gambits that are intended to comfort the bereaved but waste police time. 'Your sister was a forceful woman,' he said.

Meg blinked. 'Janine had a demanding job,' she said stoutly, 'full of responsibilities.'

Ellen saw where Challis was going, and also pushed. 'Would you say she was happily married?'

Meg smoothed her thighs as though to dry her palms. 'Of course!'

'We heard that she was seeing someone,' Challis lied.

A barely concealed flicker, the eyes shifting sideways. 'She wouldn't do that.'

Perhaps Meg meant that *she* wouldn't do that, but couldn't vouch for her sister, thought Challis. Meg clammed up then, visibly distressed, and they left, feeling small.

16

Scobie Sutton had received word that Mrs Humphreys was ready to see him, but when he reached the hospital, the first thing he saw was his wife's car parked in one of the reserved slots. He went inside, showed his ID at the reception desk and explained the purpose of his visit. 'But first,' he said, blushing a little, 'could you page my wife? Beth Sutton?'

A call went out on the public address system, and then Beth was there, beaming, and they gave each other a chaste kiss. 'I wanted to warn you,' Scobie said, leading her to a vinyl bench seat beside a rubber plant in a huge brass pot.

His wife was round, pink, and easily flustered. Her hand went to her throat. 'What about?'

He told her what had happened in court that morning. 'Now that Natalie knows you're married to a policeman she'll be suspicious.'

Beth blinked away sudden tears, shook her head, and clenched her fists in frustration and pain. 'I'm fighting a losing battle, Scobe,' she said, and it was an old story between them, the social problems on the blighted estates of Waterloo, Rosebud and Mornington. She knew the Cobb family, and dozens more like them, and sometimes it was all too much, there was too much misery, ignorance and indifference for her to bear.

'There, there,' said Scobie, rocking her gently, listening as she told him about Seaview Estate, where the Cobbs lived, which offered views of the refinery stacks and wore an air of defeat.

'There's this little community hall,' she said, 'but no one on the estate ever uses it. Don't get me wrong, it's booked solid every day, but by outsiders, like the Gilbert and Sullivan players, the Penzance Beach Cubs and Scouts, the Yoga Club. I'm trying to get the local kids to make it their clubhouse, but we need funds to employ a youth worker, and whenever I approach the Shire for money, the manager of finance and the manager of marketing say no. Their bottom line is always cost. I try to get them to *feel* something, but they have no feelings. Oh, it makes me so cross.'

That was as close to an oath as his wife could get.

'The only ray of hope among the kids on that estate is Natalie Cobb,' she said.

'Sorry if I've stuffed it up for you.'

'Oh Scobe, you haven't.' She brightened. 'What brings you here?'

He told her about Janine McQuarrie and the connection with Mrs Humphreys. She was appalled. 'Janine McQuarrie?'

'Do you know her?'

'All the welfare agencies know her,' Beth said. She paused. 'I don't want to speak ill of the dead.'

'That's all right,' he said resolutely. 'We need to know everything we can, the good and the bad. Then we can sort the relevant from the irrelevant.'

Beth's hands were washing against each other dryly, restlessly. 'This could be relevant,' she said.

'You'd better tell me,' he said.

He watched her stare into the distance, gathering her thoughts. 'It was as if she deliberately set out to antagonise people, turn them against each other,' she said slowly. 'She was autocratic, had to get her own way all the time.'

To encourage his wife, Scobie said, 'We heard much the same thing this morning, from the people she worked with.'

Beth nodded. 'In one case I know of, a fifteen-year-old girl from one of the estates was referred to her because of problems at home. She told the girl to leave home immediately, but failed to do a follow-up, and the girl joined a shoplifting gang so she could buy drugs. It turned out there weren't problems at home, not really: the girl didn't like being thwarted by her mother, that's all. If she'd carried out a proper mediation involving the girl and her family, she would have saved everyone a lot of heartache.'

Scobie nodded encouragingly.

'Her job was to listen and advise, and if necessary refer people on to other specialists, or place them in shelters or whatever, but often she'd be openly antagonistic, act like judge and jury.'

'Such as?'

'Well, let's say a wife came to her for counselling because her marriage was unhappy or acrimonious: Janine would go after the husband, challenge him directly.'

'Ah,' said Scobie musingly.

'In another case I heard about, a man came to her because his wife was beating him. Janine thought he was lying in order to cover up his own acts of violence, and reported him to the police. She doesn't double check, Scobie. She doesn't follow up.'

He sighed. 'Well, someone sure followed up on her.'

'Who would do such a thing?'

It's what good people, innocent people, said at such times. Scobie himself still said it, even after years on the job. He suspected that Challis and Ellen didn't say it: they knew, or were past being baffled.

But Scobie was patient. He waited, and his wife went on: 'No one deserves to die like that, but she was awful sometimes, just awful. She was a relief psychologist for the prison service, but rarely got invited back. Children's Services stopped referring kids to her. She'd insult them—you know, blame the victim—and us.'

'Can you give me any names? Social workers? Kids?'

'Oh, Scobie, I don't think any of the social workers would shoot her. And where would a kid get a gun?'

You'd be surprised, Scobie thought. 'Even so, she clearly made enemies, Beth.'

'It was all hearsay, I shouldn't even be telling you this,' his wife said, and gathered her things to go.

'What about lovers?'

'Oh, Scobie, how would I know a thing like that?'

'Ask around, could you, love? Discreetly? Who she kept company with. Anyone heard making threats, anyone harmed by one of her decisions…We need their names, even if only to cross them off the list.'

Beth's face twisted in anguish but she gave him a hurried peck goodbye. 'I'd better call on the Cobbs,' she said, and a moment later was hurrying out to her car.

Scobie sighed and returned to the reception desk. A minute later he was shown to a corner room where the afternoon light struggled to reach a high, narrow bed and the woman in it, who was observing him with sly good humour, as if she'd never had an operation in her life. 'Police, eh?'

She was a down-to-earth, big-boned woman aged in her seventies, and Scobie hated to think of those bones failing her. He sat, mustering a knockabout look on his face to suit her canny, expectant expression. 'Mrs Humphreys, I understand you live at 283 Lofty Ridge Road in Penzance North?'

'Call me Joy. And out with it, no beating about the bush.'

So he told her.

'Good lord. You think those jokers were after me?'

'Were they?'

'Blameless, son, a blameless life,' she said, twinkling. 'All of my enemies are too old and tired to do me in, or I've outlasted them. Who's the dead woman?'

'Her name's Janine McQuarrie.'

'Never heard of her.'

'You weren't expecting any visitors to the house today?'

'No.'

Scobie showed her the photograph of Janine McQuarrie from the Bayside Counselling brochure. 'Have you seen this woman before?'

'No.'

He sighed. 'It's possible she was lost and went to your house by mistake.'

'Followed,' Mrs Humphreys said, 'or ambushed? If ambushed, why at my place?'

Scobie grinned. 'You're trying to do my job for me.' He paused. 'Reporters will want to talk to you.'

'Let them,' Mrs Humphreys said.

She was tiring now, winced once in pain, and struggled to muster a return grin. 'I don't have a soul in the world but my goddaughter.'

Scobie stiffened. 'God-daughter?'

'She was staying with me a couple of months ago but she's in London now.'

Scobie uncapped his pen. 'I think you'd better tell me all about her.'

17

Mead showed Tessa around the detention centre, a tour that avoided any contact with the detainees, and took her back along an exposed path to the administration wing. 'Coffee before you go? Tea?'

'We haven't finished, Mr Mead.'

'Call me Charlie,' he said automatically. 'What else do you need?'

A chilly wind was blowing from the southwest, right off the bay. Tess shivered, as much from Mead's indifference as the wind. 'Some grave allegations have been made.'

'There are always allegations. There always will be. But spit it out: what allegations?'

'According to a nurse, a guard and a section manager who once worked for you, ANZCOR systematically defrauded the Department of Immigration to the tune of millions of dollars.'

'Prove it.'

'For example, you and your staff created artificial riot situations in which equipment and buildings were damaged, in order to submit inflated repair bills.'

'Is that a question or an opinion?'

'If any of your section managers raised concerns, they were threatened with the sack and their reports were censored or conveniently lost.'

'Lady,' Mead said, leaning towards her menacingly, 'put up or shut up.'

'Do you care to comment on these allegations, Mr Mead?'

'Call me Charlie,' Mead said, swinging around to face her again. 'Will that be all? Good,' he said, opening a side door. 'Someone will show you out.'

As Tessa left the main building, a guard, bored and scowling, ran his metal detector over a steel door idly, listening to it squawk. He did it over and over again. No one else seemed to notice. In fact, a vicious kind of indifference was the pervasive atmosphere of the place, and Tessa wondered if that was all down to Charlie Mead: who he was and who he had been.

She stopped dead in her tracks. Why continue to look at who he was now? He'd be leaving soon, and she continued to run into brick walls. Why not look at who he had been and where he'd come from?

Andy Asche was driving Natalie Cobb back from the city. He marvelled at how great she looked, despite being stuck in court all morning holding the hand of her fucked-up mother, followed by an afternoon ripping off gear in South Yarra. He told her so.

'Thank you, kind sir.'

'Straight,' Andy continued, 'but sexy.'

Eighteen years old, still at school, but she could pass for a yuppie chick out shopping for her yuppie pad in Southgate, where all the yuppies lived, and that's what mattered to Andy and Natalie.

It went like this: the people they worked for owned pawnshops in the city and a discounted homewares outlet on the Peninsula, which made for a two-way flow of stolen gear. Andy liked the neatness of it: goods from the city ended up on the Peninsula, goods from the

Peninsula ended up in the city. The Chasseur frying pan that he and Natalie might shoplift in South Yarra went straight to Savoury Seconds (frying pan, savouries, get it?) in Somerville. The cops weren't likely to venture outside of the city to look for a stolen frying pan, even if it did cost $300. Meanwhile the pawnbroking stores in the city sold gear burgled from homes on the Peninsula. A retiree down in Penzance Beach isn't going to stumble by chance on her VCR in a barred shop window in Footscray. The people that Andy and Natalie worked for weren't too worried by tax audits or CIU inquiries either. They had 'paperwork' to prove that the new Chasseur frying pan in Savoury Seconds had come from a bankrupted shop in Cairns, the VCR in Footscray pawned by a waitress in Abbotsford.

Andy's and Natalie's first hit today had been Perfecto Coffee, in Chapel Street, the shelves stocked with coffee pots and machines, filters, ring seals, milk frothers, you name it; Bialetti, Gaggia and other big names. Coffee beans, too, but the order was for espresso machines, percolators and plungers. Natalie, in her long, loose woollen overcoat over tailored pants, leather shoulderbag and artfully tousled hair, browsed the shelves while Andy chatted up the shop assistant. No security cameras that he could see. Then Nat was at his elbow, doing her sulky look—'Can we go now?'—as if shopping, and Andy, and this shop, made her dangerously bored, not something you wanted to see in a beautiful woman. Andy slipped the shop assistant a wink—she sympathised—and followed Natalie out of the shop, Natalie's overcoat barely registering the spacious hidden pockets that were now full of top-end coffee making machines.

They hit a couple more places, had lunch in a bistro, and now, mid afternoon, were nearly home, Waterloo free of fog at last. Andy dropped Natalie outside the tattoo parlour next to the railway line. She had a fistful of money in her pocket: most would go to her mother, but she wanted a new tatt, a butterfly, high on the inside of her right thigh. Then she was going to score some dope. Andy didn't do dope, or booze, or anything else. He'd saved twelve grand so far, down payment on a BMW sports car.

'Tomorrow, yeah? You up for it?'

'Yeah,' she said.

He drove to the McDonald's on the roundabout for a Quarter Pounder, and read the local newspaper while he waited. Turned to 'Police Beat' on page 10. He liked the irony: here he was, a thorough crook, reading about the work of other crooks while sitting just across the road from the cop shop. Unimaginative crimes, too. A ride-on mower stolen in Penzance Beach. A woman robbed at syringe point outside an ATM in Mornington. A purse snatched here in Waterloo.

Andy Asche glanced up from his paper. The noon-to-four shift cops coming off duty, heading across the road for their Big Macs. And fuck me, there was John Tankard, his footy coach, getting out of a Mazda sports car with some female cop.

John Tankard and Pam Murphy logged off, deeply fatigued with one another, the only distraction during the long afternoon having been their encounter with Lottie Mead. They separated, showered, changed, then happened to meet in the staff carpark afterwards, Tankard noticing the gear that Pam was wearing: black lycra shorts, sweater and trainers. Great legs, notwithstanding the goosebumps from the cold air. Great body.

Suddenly the elements of his personality, fractured after he'd shot dead that farmer, were clashing inside him. He'd had counselling, and told himself he was a better person for it, but before he could stop himself he felt a carnal tug deep inside and was touching her smooth behind and pulling her towards him, and then he was crying wretchedly.

'I'm sorry, I'm sorry,' he gasped.

She pulled away angrily. 'What's got into you?'

'I'm sorry. Don't report me.'

'You deserve to be reported.'

'I know, I'm sorry, I feel all...all...'

She folded her arms and said, with vicious reasonableness, 'Yeah, I can see how that would work. Give me a quick grope, and if I object, you can blame it on stress.' She unfolded her arms. 'You're pathetic, John.'

'Pam, I'm sorry, I don't know what got into me.' His hands pressed against his cheeks. 'I've stuffed up big time, haven't I?'

The look she gave him then was weary and disgusted, but not angry or vengeful. 'You came back to work too soon,' she said.

'Mate, I was going stir crazy at home.'

'If you touch me again, I'll flatten you, and then I'll report you.'

'I know, I know. I'm really sorry.' He made an effort and said, without looking at her thighs, smooth in their lycra sheaths: 'Where're you going?'

'Training.'

'For what?'

'Triathlon.'

'When?'

'January.'

'That's six months away.'

'Exactly.'

The new Tankard struggled, finally remembering that she'd been in a bad car smash at her last station, so maybe she was trying to get fit again.

'What about you?' she said, more out of politeness than actual interest.

Tankard said shyly, 'I'm coaching footy this season.'

Pam went slackjawed. 'You're joking.'

'Nope.'

'Good for you.'

Good for me, good for the kids, Tankard thought. He was a copper, so that gave him some clout to begin with, but he was trying to be more than copper and footy coach. Like he'd intervened in this dispute between the club and the Fiddlers Creek pub. Some of the guys would get legless after training or a game on a Saturday and walk across the road from the clubrooms to the pub, where they'd get even more loaded, and brawl, swear, trash the bar or the men's room, reverse into patrons' cars on the way home. It had got so bad, the pub withdrew sponsorship from the team and banned club members from drinking there. John Tankard had a quiet word with the pub management, and then with the players, and now everything was sweet again.

'Well, gotta run,' he said. 'See ya.'

She shrugged and walked to her car. He got into his old station wagon—chosen because he could cart a lot of kids and gear around in it—and drove to the clubhouse, where he got kitted out before running a few gasping laps of the oval to warm up. Soon the kids were arriving, some straight from school, others driven by their parents, a few dropped by their girlfriends. And Andy Asche; that was a change. Half the time the guy failed to turn up. Tankard waited until they were all kitted out then called them to run a few laps of the oval.

Nathan Gent had spent all day smoking joints and sinking cans of Melbourne Bitter, but his anxiety wouldn't go away. Yeah, there'd been a heavy fog this morning, and no cars about, only that fucking taxi, but had the driver seen anything? Would he come forward when the shooting hit the TV news and tomorrow's newspapers?

Nathan had been paid, and he intended to stay clear of Vyner, but he'd crossed a divide this morning. Accomplice to a murder. Plus the kid had seen him. That little face, maybe six years old, sees her mum shot down in cold blood.

Nathan wanted to go, 'Whoa! Stop the world, I want to get off.'

But he'd crossed the divide. He was no longer his old self, a simple sort of bloke, likes to sink a few beers at the pub, watch the footy, see if he can use his missing finger to pull a chick at the Krypton Klub in Frankston. Choof on a bit of weed occasionally.

Three things gnawing at him: murder, the look on the kid's face, the car. Particularly the car. 'No worries,' he'd assured Vyner, 'it's stolen, can't be traced to us.' In fact, stealing a car had been harder than Nathan had expected, and he'd left it too late, and so he'd used his cousin's Commodore. Except it wasn't really Nora's; when she got the job in New Zealand she'd sold him the car for $975, leaving the paperwork up to him, the roadworthy certificate and the registration and insurance and stuff—which he hadn't got around to yet.

Fine, except when he'd dropped Vyner off after the shooting this morning, Vyner had thumped the Commodore and said, 'Burn the fucker.'

Nathan had driven away, saying 'No worries,' his mind racing.

Even if he burnt the Commodore, didn't the cops have ways of tracing ownership? Even if he removed and destroyed the numberplates, wasn't there some number on the engine block or something? What if someone came along while he was trying to set fire to it? He'd have to get rid of it some other way. Besides, he was kind of sentimental about the Commodore. He'd borrowed it off Nora stacks of times, and Nora was a good sort, and he hated to think of her car—his car—as a blackened ruin on some back road. Obviously he couldn't keep driving around in it—Vyner might see him, the vicious cunt—so he'd cleaned everything out of the car, wiped it down, and driven it to a wrecking yard in Baxter, still wearing his gloves (which hadn't raised any eyebrows because the weather was shithouse). What he did was, he drove past the yard for a few hundred metres, removed the oil filter and tossed it into a culvert at the side of the road, then drove back to the yard, by which time the engine had seized. He pushed the car into the yard, removed both plates, and walked out with $120 in his pocket, saying of the yellow door: 'That's a good door, no rust.'

But the kid, her little face.

Murder.

Nathan Gent went to the pub with his last ten dollars, downed a couple of pints, and fired up the jukebox beside the men's toilet, trying to decide what his next move should be.

18

The incident room, 5 p.m.

McQuarrie was there, making it clear that he'd be running the briefing. Challis acquiesced, vowing to hold another briefing as soon as McQuarrie left, to undo any damage or interference the man caused, intended or otherwise. Again he pondered the super's motives. Was he instinctively protecting his son? His daughter-in-law? His own reputation? Or was it obstruction of a more calculated kind? Challis waited for McQuarrie to sit at the head of the table, then stepped across to the wall and propped it up morosely. Ellen flashed him a grin.

The setting sun angled across the chipped table and McQuarrie's twitchy knuckles. 'Inspector? We'll hear from you first.'

Challis outlined his day. Then, true to form, McQuarrie double-checked every step of his account.

'You talked to my son.'

Said almost accusingly. 'I hadn't expected to see him,' Challis replied.

'He's got important commitments,' McQuarrie said. 'He made a racing visit up to the city, then came straight back to be with Georgia.'

You don't have to apologise for him, Challis thought.

'And you got nowhere,' McQuarrie said. 'He's well respected, well loved. No enemies.'

'Sir.'

'And no witnesses.'

'No.'

'This Lisa Welch woman didn't hear or see anything?'

'No.'

'But you think it's possible she was the intended target?'

Challis gave his head a brief, impatient shake. 'No, sir, not really. It's just a precaution. I thought it best to advise her of the danger, but on the face of it she's not involved.'

'Still, I want you to dig a little deeper. You never know.'

'Sir.'

'Good,' McQuarrie said briskly. 'Now, my daughter-in-law. Sergeant Destry?'

Ellen flashed McQuarrie an alert, humourless smile. 'Sir?'

'You spoke to Janine's work colleagues this morning, I believe?'

'Sir.'

'And?'

Challis, unseen by McQuarrie, made a fleeting axe-murderer face at Ellen, who composed herself and reported that the office staff and other therapists at Bayside Counselling Services had alibis and were clearly baffled by Janine's murder. 'Meanwhile, we still don't know who she was meeting this morning or why she was on Lofty Ridge Road. A note scribbled on her desk calendar simply says "Penzance North, 9.30".'

'Keep looking. What about disgruntled clients? Weird clients?'

'We're still looking into that, sir, but client confidentiality comes into it.'

'How closely did you look at her work colleagues? For all you know there could be simmering resentments, jealousies, that type of thing.'

'Not that we could see on a preliminary visit.'

'Keep looking. She was at the top of her profession, you know. Bright girl.'

'Sir,' Ellen said, wanting to tell the super what she'd told Challis in the car that afternoon, that husband and wife had been made for each other.

'Constable Sutton, anything to add?'

Scobie nodded. 'I spoke to Mrs Humphreys, and—'

'Who?'

'She owns the house where Janine was murdered.'

'And?'

'She's elderly, currently in hospital recovering from a hip operation.'

McQuarrie semaphored with his arms. 'What about her?'

'She has a goddaughter, Christina Traynor, who stayed with her for three weeks in April.'

The room went very still. McQuarrie cocked his head. 'Do we know anything about her?'

'Not yet.'

'Get onto it.'

'Sir.'

Challis uncoiled from the wall and sat at the table next to Ellen. He knew that McQuarrie would be leaving soon. 'Sir, thirty minutes ago I had a call from Janine's sister, Meg. She said something that might have a bearing on all this.'

McQuarrie looked put out. 'Such as?'

'Were you aware that Janine hated driving?'

McQuarrie looked puzzled. 'I fail to see—'

'In particular, she had a pathological fear of making right turns, of turning against oncoming traffic, and so whenever she had to drive anywhere she'd map out routes that involved mainly left turns, meaning that she often drove far out of her way to travel short distances. You weren't aware of that? Robert didn't tell you?'

'I think he mentioned something about it,' McQuarrie said evasively. Then he brightened. 'But don't you see? Everything points to one thing: Janine was the wrong person in the wrong place at the wrong time.'

'But there's no indication that Mrs Humphreys was the right person or that her house was the right house,' Challis said.

'And Janine might have been followed,' Ellen said.

McQuarrie said, 'Keep an open mind, that's all I ask. Any joy on the weapon?'

'No ejected shells were found,' Challis said, 'but ballistics confirm that the shooter used a 9mm automatic.'

The report had just come in. The usual kind of detail, two 9mm slugs, the lands and degrees of twist possibly indicating a Browning. 'If our shooter was a pro,' he went on, 'and it seems he was, he'd have used gloves and got rid of gun, gloves and outer clothing as soon as possible.'

'Not necessarily,' McQuarrie said briskly. 'We're probably not dealing with rocket scientists here.'

Challis gazed at his boss for a couple of beats. 'Quite right, sir.'

'Have you spoken to everybody yet?'

You never reach everybody, Challis thought. 'We will eventually.'

'No time to lose,' McQuarrie said, getting to his feet and making for the door in a faint eddy of aftershave. 'I want to be informed of everything of importance the moment it happens. Meanwhile I think our most promising course of action is to look closely at the woman next door and the goddaughter.'

When McQuarrie was gone, Challis stood by the window to watch and wait. After a couple of minutes, McQuarrie strode across the carpark to his personal car, a Mercedes, finding time to reprimand two constables on their way to a divisional van. One, Challis noted, gave McQuarrie the finger afterwards.

The world restored a little, he returned to the conference table, saying, 'That man's been like a father to me.'

Then he waited. Would they think his remark in bad taste? But they grinned. 'This job's expanding before our eyes, boss,' Scobie said.

Challis nodded. 'And we're going to be stepping on sensitive and powerful toes, so we do everything by the book. The super is going to stick his oar in at all stages, he's going to want to steer the investigation, and he'll try to protect his family. At one level, we're going to let him do that. We'll listen to him, we'll follow up the lines of inquiry he suggests, for they'll probably be those we've already thought of, and generally let him think he's the driving force. At the moment he's not calling for a full-scale task force. If things get too unmanageable, I'll do something about it. Just don't let him waste your time, okay?'

Ellen gathered her notes into a folder. 'Are we ruling out Janine McQuarrie as the intended victim?'

'No,' Challis said bluntly, 'no matter what the super thinks.'

He saw Ellen sneaking a look at her watch. 'Go home,' he said. 'I'll run Christina Traynor through the data bases; Scobie, I want you to keep checking for stolen cars, particularly older ones, pale in colour, but cast a state-wide net.'

'Boss.'

Ellen continued to pack up her notes. 'Did Janine's sister say anything else?'

Challis could read Ellen by now, and shot her a look. 'You think she's trying to divert our attention away from Janine's love life,' he said.

Ellen shrugged. 'I don't think she gave us the full picture this afternoon.'

Challis nodded his agreement, just as one of the phones rang. It was the switchboard, looking for him. They had a man on the line who claimed to have information about the shooting of Janine McQuarrie. Challis told them to record and trace the call and put the caller through to him. He switched to speaker mode and said, 'Inspector Challis.'

The voice emerged like a mouse from a hole. 'Are you the guy in charge of the murder of Janine McQuarrie? The one on the news?'

Challis leaned forward, listening hard to the voice, the background noise and everything in between. It was hard to pinpoint the age. Slurred, which meant he'd been drinking or was stoned. Suspicious and wary: owing to the situation, or because he'd had dealings with the police before? No extraneous traffic or other sounds.

He said carefully, 'Do you have something to tell the police?'

It was important to stay low-key: no hectoring, pushing or leading. It was also necessary to establish if the caller was a hoaxer or a sad character after a bit of attention.

In a rush the man said, 'What if something happened you didn't think was going to happen?'

Challis said gently, 'We're not in the business of blaming people for things they didn't do.'

'I didn't think he'd go this far.'

'Is this person a friend of yours? Are you afraid of him? We can offer protection.'

There was silence and the seconds ticked away and then the caller said, as if betrayed, 'I bet you're tracing this,' and hung up.

'Well?' Challis said, glancing around at the others.

'He wasn't on long enough for a trace,' Scobie said.

'What was your impression of him?'

'Genuine, boss.'

'Ellen?'

'Genuine.'

Challis said, 'Right, we need it to go out on the evening news and in the papers tomorrow. Reporters are already swarming over this, so we won't need to persuade them. The usual thing: Police are anxious to speak again to the anonymous caller who phoned with information regarding the murder of Janine McQuarrie. Who knows, it might shake something loose.'

19

In Challis's experience, very few criminals returned to the scene of the crime—not unless they were stupid, retrieving incriminating evidence, or actively seeking capture and punishment. But police officers often did, and on his way home that Tuesday evening, Challis called in at 283 Lofty Ridge Road, and stood for a while in the waning light.

The lowering sky was dripping and close around him. The crime-scene tape thrummed in the wind and the sounds of engines and tyres on the road above him were disembodied and distorted. His old Triumph ticked as the motor cooled. It had been a bugger to start, drawing amused glances in the carpark at Waterloo, but he'd booked it in for a service and tune tomorrow.

He shook that off and began to think himself into the minds and bodies of this morning's victims and killers. This was a natural condition: Challis did it automatically at every murder scene. In that way he was able to understood the impulse and the circumstances. Very little surprised him—which is not to say that he condoned or forgave, necessarily.

But this time his skin crept. All of his senses were resonating with another shooting, in another place, with other culprits and victims.

He'd been younger then, a detective sergeant based in a large town on the endless wheat plains in the west of the state. He was married, and had thought that he was happily married, but what he didn't know was that his wife was deeply unhappy. She started sleeping with one of his colleagues, a married senior constable. Their affair grew in hothouse circumstances and turned obsessive. In their minds, the only way out was to shoot Challis dead, so they lured him to a lonely place and ambushed him under a moonless evening sky. But Challis's senses had begun to tell him that something was wrong, and he half turned to fish out his service .38, an action that saved his life. The bullet plucked at his sleeve, putting a hole through his jacket and ploughing through the flesh of his upper arm. Alerted now, he'd circled around, shot his wife's lover in the shoulder and disarmed the man. He was currently serving twelve years. Angela Challis got ten years, but imprisonment had thrown her off course, and she'd killed herself in the prison infirmary last year.

Challis knew that he'd not have liked Janine McQuarrie if he'd met her, but had she been set up, too? Had *her* spouse wanted her out of the way? Ellen and Scobie had uncovered evidence that she'd been a poor therapist and a pain to work with: perhaps her bad judgment calls, contempt and secrecy were symptoms of a deep unhappiness, brought on by marriage to Robert McQuarrie and scrutiny by his awful family.

He stood there, knowing that he was missing something and hoping the scene would tell him what it was. He saw, in his mind's eye, the driver and the shooter. Why had the shooter needed a driver? Had they worked together before? From Georgia McQuarrie's account of the killing, the two men had not brought equal degrees of professionalism to the job. He could see her dialling 000, and made a mental note to check the records for Janine's car phone. Speaking of which, how had the killer got his instructions?—assuming that he'd been hired and didn't have a personal stake in the outcome.

This led Challis by degrees to the anonymous caller. Was he the driver? An acquaintance who'd supplied the gun or the car? Someone who'd hired others to throw a scare into Janine, only to see it all go wrong?

His bones were aching, the chilly dampness creeping into his core. He stamped his feet and began to move, pacing across the driveway to a muddy path along one side of the house. He peered up and saw smears of khaki-coloured mould, for the sun never penetrated here, and he envisioned Joy Humphreys's life of solitude, poverty and neglect.

He circled the house, wondering if love or desire, and their perverted forms, had had any role in the murder of Janine McQuarrie. Had she been an obstacle to love or desire, or inspired them? Challis thought of the women in loveless marriages: many endured, some walked out and a handful looked for drastic solutions.

As did husbands.

He tried to think of Janine McQuarrie's husband then, but Ellen Destry's took form in his mind's eye. The guy was paranoid, obsessive, authoritarian. He was wound so tight, and harboured so many grievances, that he'd snap one day, and maybe harm her.

It caught Challis like a blow then, an unbidden image of Ellen at the wheel of the CIU Falcon this afternoon, her fine jaw uptilted determinedly, and his wanting to touch her. He examined that desire, in his orderly way. It was more than friendship and less than knight-in-shining-armour. It was desire, plain and simple—and it probably wouldn't do.

He rounded the final corner and came again to the parking circle where Janine had tried to dodge her killer. Visualising that was enough to make an ordinary person's skin crawl and pulse race, but the McQuarrie men, son and father, had been strangely unmoved. Challis didn't think they were numbed, but if they were not involved in the killing, what were they hiding?

The light had faded to a mess of shadows in the little hollow. He returned to his car. He was still sitting there, cold and depressed, five futile minutes later. And because he'd flattened the battery, he couldn't even listen to the news.

Vyner, on the other hand, had been listening to the news all day. He liked being the lead item; an added bonus to learn that he'd topped the daughter-in-law of a senior cop. 'No leads,' the updates said, 'no leads.'

He'd hotfooted it back to his flat in the city after the shooting, glad to be free of dirt roads, cows and Nathan Gent, and now, reassured that the cops were running around in circles, he was working at his other job.

'Sammy was a hero,' he said, perched on the edge of a sofa in a Templestowe sitting room. He paused. 'You don't mind if I call him that? We all knew him as Sammy.'

Mrs Plowman, Sammy's mother, smiled damply. 'Everyone called him Sammy. I was the only one who ever called him Sam—or Samuel when I was cross with him about something.'

The tears flowed again, to think she'd ever been cross with her son, his life cut short guarding an oil pipeline in the Iraqi desert.

Vyner reached out, gently took her grieving hands and kneaded life and hope into them. 'Sammy always looked on the bright side of life. In a way, he held the unit together. If any of the younger blokes looked like chucking it in, Sammy was there for them. The Army lost a hero, Mrs Plowman.'

Mrs Plowman wiped her eyes. 'I try to picture his face sometimes and I can't, and that scares me. But you bring him to life for me.'

Vyner went very still. He didn't want to go too far. He wanted her to walk down memory lane but not so far that she'd be deflected from *him*, *his* needs.

The house was an architectural nightmare, amid other architectural nightmares. Architectural nightmares worth three-quarters of a million dollars, mind you, and no doubt full of vulgar, newly rich and idle women, but Mrs Plowman herself was a homely sort, grieving for the death of her only child, Lance Corporal Samuel Plowman. The husband grieved by working longer and longer hours in an office building, or attending interstate conferences, leaving Mrs Plowman alone with her memories—which Vyner had teased out with a few tears of his own, a bit of hand-holding on the four-thousand-dollar sofa in front of the bay window, and his trawl through the internet and various newspaper records last month.

'He was incredibly brave, Mrs Plowman. Not a risk taker, just a guy who kept his head. He got me out of a scrape once. I was pinned down by a sniper, and Sammy crawled across open ground and got me out. I'd lost my nerve. Paralysed. Your son saved my life.'

She looked up at him, hungry for word pictures. 'They didn't mention that in his record.'

Vyner waved dismissively. 'Typical Sammy. As far as he was concerned, he was just doing his job, that's all. I wanted to put his name forward for a commendation, maybe even a medal, but he wouldn't hear of it. "Mate, I didn't think twice," he told me. "You and the other guys, you're my family when I'm away."'

Mrs Plowman's hand was warm, damp and sad in Vyner's grasp. 'What hurts me is last time he was home on leave he had words with his father. They ended up not speaking, and now my husband is just quietly falling apart about that.'

Careful, Vyner told himself. The last thing he wanted was for the silly cow to bring her husband into this. It was harder selling consolatory stories to husbands and fathers than to wives and mothers. He patted her plump wrist. 'Sammy thought the world of his dad—of both of you, in fact. He spoke about you all the time. He looked up to you. I never heard him say a negative thing about either of you.'

Mrs Plowman's face was suffused with a dampish joy. 'You've brought me a great deal of happiness these past few days.'

'I'm glad.'

'I can't believe the Army,' she said. 'It's disgraceful.'

'They can't afford any negative publicity,' Vyner said. 'Sure, Sammy died a hero, but they didn't want to make too big a thing of it. Seventy per cent of the population thinks Australia should never have sent peacekeeping troops to Iraq.'

As quoted in yesterday's *Herald Sun*. But Mrs Plowman said sternly, 'I don't mean that. I mean it's disgraceful the way the Army treated *you*, Richard.'

For a millisecond then, Trevor Vyner wondered who Richard was. He reached for a biscuit—not some generic supermarket crap but Italian biscotti. Earl Grey tea, too, which he loathed, but it went with the lifestyle in this moneyed corner of the north-eastern suburbs.

'That's the way it goes,' he said.

He'd been dishonourably discharged from the Army for striking an officer—or so Mrs Plowman believed. Not only that, but the officer was a bully, and had been having a go at Sammy, Sammy who'd been sticking up for one of the younger guys, whom the officer had been picking on. Sammy, the selfless hero; Sammy, a protective older brother to the new recruit; Sammy, alive there in that Templestowe sitting room.

'Not everyone can take the pressure,' Vyner said. 'The heat was indescribable, dust storms, Arab fanatics taking pot shots at you all the time, no wonder some guys lost the plot. But Sammy was always there for us. Until one day this total—' he almost said 'arsehole', then did say it '—arsehole of a lieutenant tears strips off him for comforting a guy who'd crawled into a foxhole in tears. Well, it was totally unfair, so I punched him out.'

Mrs Plowman shook her head. 'And they discharged you? It's disgraceful, it really is.'

Vyner sighed. 'I feel good about myself in the sense that I know I did the right thing, even if it was an act of violence, but now I've got a black mark against my name and something like that follows you around, makes it hard to get a job, hard to get references…'

Mrs Plowman said firmly, 'Stay there,' and left the room. Vyner allowed himself a small grin, then strained to hear the start of the seven o'clock news on the old bag's TV set, which was quietly murmuring in a little nook on the other side of an archway in the open-plan room. He caught the words 'anonymous caller' and 'police are anxious to speak to' and his skin went cold. At the same time, his mobile phone rang. He had a text message, but before he could read it, Mrs Plowman returned with her purse, flushing, determined to do the right thing by a friend of her son, a friend who'd been tossed onto the scrap heap by an uncaring system to the tune—Vyner tried to count the notes in her little fist—of around $500.

Well, a guy had to eat. He was still due the remaining $10,000 for this morning's hit, but it wasn't like he got paid to top someone every week—or even every year—so meanwhile you took what you could get. Five minutes later, he was in his car, reading his SMS. It said simply: *elimin8 anon callr.*

It had to be Gent, the fuckup.

Vyner reached into the glove box for his notebook. A latex glove spilled out, a box of matches, a spare brakelight bulb, and finally his chewed Bic pen.

'I am the jagged tooth of a lone crag,' he wrote.

He thought some more.

'I am the doom maker.'

Too bad that he had to return to the Peninsula. Too bad that he wouldn't be paid for this hit.

Challis received two calls while he waited for a breakdown truck to cart his car away from Lofty Ridge Road and a taxi to take him home.

Tessa Kane got in first. 'How come I have to hear it on the seven o'clock news, Hal?'

'Honestly, it slipped my mind,' he said truthfully.

He was pleased to hear a friendly voice in the darkness, but the conversation went wrong in subtle and obscure ways. 'Exactly what did this person tell you?' Tessa demanded.

'Very little.'

'A man or a woman?'

'Is this off the record?'

'In the last few months you haven't thought highly enough of me to tell me anything *on* the record. It seems that I call you, you never call me.'

Challis felt a twist of futility and anger. A part of him wanted to appease her, a part of him wanted to help her, and a smaller part of him wanted to see her again. He tried to get comfortable in the cramped space of the Triumph. 'He said, quote, "I didn't think he'd go that far."'

Tessa absorbed that. 'What else?'

'Nothing.'

He waited. But Tessa could outwait him any day of the week. 'He asked if I was in charge of the case. I said yes. Then he got spooked and cut the call.'

Tessa said nothing.

'He got agitated and asked if I'd put a trace on the call. I had, and I'd taped it. But the trace failed.'

'Caller ID?'

'I rang the number, finally someone answered. It was a coin phone in a supermarket.'

'Which one?'

'Look, Tess, I can't say any more.'

He heard—and in his mind's eye, saw—her bristle, but the explosion didn't come. 'All right,' she said, and cut the call.

Challis sighed, and at once the phone rang again. 'Challis,' he said.

'McQuarrie here.'

'Yes, sir.'

The superintendent was clipped. 'Why wasn't I told?'

'Sir?'

'This anonymous tipoff.'

'Sir, I—'

'I have to hear about it on the evening news.'

'It wasn't a tipoff as such. A man called. He seemed rattled, as though a shooting hadn't been part of the plan this morning, but hung up before I could question him.'

'Didn't it occur to you that by plastering it all over the news you've scared the shooter off, not to mention that he might start killing his accomplices to shut them up?'

Challis said evenly, 'It's a calculated risk.'

'Be it on your head, Inspector, be it on your head. Anything else?'

'Not at present.'

'Well, keep digging.'

'Sir,' Challis said, but the line was dead.

Then he made a call of his own.

20

Ellen cooked lasagne for dinner, knowing that it would please her husband. She recognised the impulse, one familiar to social workers, counsellors and the police from endless domestic violence situations, in which women—and sometimes men—strove futilely to please their spouses, patch up squabbles, mend cracks, keep the peace—until it all blew up again.

She hated herself for it.

But did you just throw away twenty years of marriage without trying? She knew the pressure that Alan was under. The man she'd married—big, bluff, competent and cheerful—had gradually been ground down by disappointments. He felt left behind by his colleagues *and* his wife, and hadn't the strategies to adjust to or rise above the situation.

He'd been an only child, that was part of the problem. Because his parents had indulged him, and he'd never disappointed their modest expectations, or encountered significant setbacks or challenges early in life, he'd coasted uncomplicatedly through school and later the police academy. Life to him was easy, predictable and not all that serious.

But then had come the regular, mundane but testing responsibilities of full-time work, marriage, fatherhood and a mortgage. The world wasn't small any more, but big, and full of ambitious, talented and hard-working men and women. He was ill-prepared and only moderately talented. He didn't take to drink, drugs or sleeping around to make himself better; instead, he developed biting suspicions and grievances, which he kept barely contained. He fumed, his brow permanently dark. He hated the world and, Ellen suspected, hated himself.

There was a yellowing photo of him on the fridge, and she glanced at it while she cooked. Taken when he was twenty-two, he was a fine-looking man, grinning widely as he passed out of the police academy. It hurt her to think that so cheerful and invincible a man could be reduced to sourness and futility.

And so she was cooking him a lasagne, to make him feel better, to atone for the morning, to put the world right again.

She hated herself for it. Once upon a time, she'd cooked lasagne out of love. Now she cooked it because love had gone. Did lasagne ever bring love back? She thought of Janine McQuarrie then, and wondered about her strategies for enduring a loveless marriage. Ellen and Alan ate early, a habit set years earlier, when they'd had a child in the house.

'Like it?'

'It's delicious,' he said, chomping away. It occurred to her then that he did eat more than he used to, and exercised less. Maybe he's depressed, she thought, but she had no idea how she'd ever broach that subject with him.

Meanwhile he was comforted by the food he was eating, so she told him about her day: the circumstances of the murder, the unappealing personalities of the main players, the anonymous caller. 'Hal thinks—' she said.

He cut across her. 'Hal thinks, Hal thinks. You're always going on about what lover boy thinks.'

Alan's head was full of sour imaginings, and he half believed that she was attracted to or had even slept with Challis. Fed up suddenly, Ellen said, 'Keep it up, Alan, and you might get what you wished for.'

He flushed, scowled and looked away impotently, then swung his head back to her. 'Do you want to know how *my* day has been?'

'Why don't you tell me,' she said in an uninflected voice.

'While you and lover boy have been swanning around the Peninsula, mixing with the rich and powerful, *I* have been measuring skid marks and collecting chips of glass and paint at accident sites. I've been sloshing around in blood and motor oil, getting my hands dirty. Welcome to the real world, Ellen.'

This was another old refrain, life as a competition. She didn't buy into it but packed the dishwasher and settled herself in front of the TV, feeling small and alone. Alan joined her. At once she returned to the kitchen and phoned Larrayne, who was distracted and uncommunicative. The conversation faltered and then Alan was there, tapping his watch face to tell her this was becoming a costly phone call. 'Have to go, sweetie,' she said. 'Want to speak to Dad?'

It was a small victory and she relished it. Alan took the phone from her and talked for a few strangled minutes, clearly counting the mounting dollars and cents. Eventually he hung up and said ferociously, 'Why do women say in thirty minutes what can be said in five?'

'She's our *daughter*, for God's sake,' Ellen said.

She dodged around him and returned to the sitting room, where 'The 7.30 Report' was discussing legal definitions of the provocation defence in cases of domestic assault and homicide. 'Poor bastard,' said Alan feelingly of one of the studio guests, a league footballer and notorious wife-basher.

'What would you know,' muttered Ellen, aware that she sounded about fifteen.

Alan shrugged, strange, conflicting expressions passing across his face, as though he wanted to strike her and felt he had the right, as though he was scared to think he couldn't control himself, and as though he had access to secret knowledge and courses of action. Fed up, and not trusting herself, Ellen walked to the kitchen pantry and dug out the jar of chocolate biscuits, eating one standing up at the sink and staring out at the night.

'Don't I get one?' her husband said.

Wordlessly she nudged the jar towards him.

'Cat got your tongue?'

Ellen was saved by the wall phone above the bench. 'Hal!' she said, her eyes hard on her husband now.

Challis explained, in his mild, pleasant rasp, that his car was stuffed and asked if she could give him a lift to work in the morning.

'A lift? Sure, Hal, pick you up at eight,' she said, her voice animated for her husband's sake and her own.

21

At six-thirty the next morning, Challis walked along the dirt roads near his home, lubricating his stiff joints. He passed an orchard, a berry farm and a plaything vineyard owned by a Melbourne stockbroker. Challis was the odd one out. He had a salary and did nothing with his two hectares but watch the grass grow and turn the fruit from his old plum trees into jam every summer.

Another sea fret this morning, and apparently nothing and no one about, only the blasts of the foghorns, carried mournfully to him from the Bay, reminding him that he was not alone in the world. He increased his pace, his body responding, until he came to a bend in the road and face to face with a kangaroo, as surprised to see it as it was to see him. They faced one another for a taut moment; it was a big roo, at least two metres high, and probably from the small mob rumoured to live in uncleared land near the old reservoir. Then the animal turned powerfully, leapt a fence and was swallowed by the fog.

Challis went on, his heart hammering, to the top of the hill, passing the farm where, as always, four outraged dogs followed him along the fence line. There was no relief from the fog. He turned around and went back down the hill again, while the foghorns called and condensation splashed fatly on the fallen leaves around him. He thought about the child, Georgia, running from the killers, hiding, then emerging again to call for help on her dead mother's mobile phone, pressing 000, her tongue tip showing in the corner of her mouth. He'd listened to the tape yesterday: a precise little voice, very clear about her name and the name of the street, Lofty Ridge Road, and the street number, and assuring the operator that yes, her mother had been shot dead.

He wondered about the gun. Were the killers local? Had the shooter obtained the gun locally?

And who was their anonymous caller? Someone associated with Christina Traynor? Janine?

Finally, someone would have to interview Mrs Super some time today.

He stopped at his mailbox, retrieved the *Age* and a litre of milk, and walked up his driveway, avoiding the boggy lawn. At the back door he removed his boots and went inside to shower, dress and make coffee and toast.

He breakfasted where a patch of sunlight slanted across his kitchen table, flicking through the *Age*, which carried the news of Janine McQuarrie's murder on the front page, together with a couple of sidebars, one on himself and the other on the anonymous caller. He'd finished and was rinsing his cup and plate when he heard a vehicle and peered out of his kitchen window, which looked onto the gravelled turnaround where visiting cars parked. Ellen Destry. She was early.

She knocked on his back door and he stood aside to let her in. 'You've got pittosporum outside your front gate,' she announced. 'And blackberries.'

'Have I?'

'You need Pam Murphy. She belongs to a crowd called the Bushrats, who go around clearing weeds on public land.'

Ellen was cheerful but bore the chilly air with her, leaving behind cool, damp eddies as she passed him.

'Coffee?'

'Thanks. I love your coffee. Sorry I'm early.'

'You're early because you hope I'll offer coffee.'

'Nothing wrong with your deductive instincts.'

She strolled ahead of him to the kitchen, unbuttoning her jacket, and that single action, and her easy familiarity with him in his house, rattled Challis. Again he wanted to touch her. What was wrong with him?

It was scarcely easier in the kitchen. She hung her jacket on the back of his usual chair and sat, relaxed and confident, asking, with a kind of bright-eyed gaze, 'Can you froth the milk?'

'Sure.'

Challis busied himself with cleaning out the espresso pot and filling it with water and fresh coffee grounds. 'Something to eat?'

Out of the corner of his eye he saw her pat her trim stomach. She looked sharp and fresh: tailored pants, a long-sleeved top, wings of fair, staticky hair swinging about her shoulders. 'Better not.'

'I have croissants in the freezer.'

'Oh, God.'

He laughed, microwaved a frozen croissant, and placed it before her on a plate, together with a pot of his own plum jam. She reached out a hand challengingly.

'Go ahead,' he said. 'Give yourself a sugar hit.'

'I think I will.'

She tore the croissant into pieces, spread jam and began to eat, her tongue darting after crumbs. Then she froze: a car had pulled up in his driveway. She glanced tensely at the window. 'Expecting visitors?'

At that moment, he guessed exactly what was uppermost in her mind: she was fearful that her husband had followed her. It didn't matter that her presence here was warranted. Alan Destry was the type of man to harbour suspicions and act on them. Challis touched her wrist briefly, got up and went to the window. He didn't know the car.

Meanwhile, whoever had been driving it knocked on his front door. 'Probably Bible bashers,' he murmured. As he left the room he heard her get to her feet and move across to the kitchen window.

He opened the front door to two men, who were interchangeable in their plain grey suits and cropped hair, but one man was thin, the other bulky. Both looked as if they'd been up for hours. They flashed Federal Police ID and one of them said 'Christina Traynor' while the other watched him.

Federal? thought Challis. Have I got myself into a jurisdictional tussle? More and more did he feel that he was living through the clichés of TV cop shows. 'We could have done this in my office,' he said mildly.

'No we couldn't,' said the thin man.

Challis shrugged. 'What's your interest in Christina Traynor?'

'Wrong question,' said the thin one. 'What's *yours*?'

'Let's do this inside,' Challis said, and he took them through to his kitchen. Ellen sprang to her feet and watched guardedly.

The men stopped, glanced inquiringly at Challis, who thought that he might as well make everything clear. 'This is Sergeant Ellen Destry, from Waterloo. My car has broken down and she's giving me a lift to work. In fact, we should probably leave now.'

'No chance,' said the thin man.

Challis gave him an empty smile. 'Then may I offer coffee? Proper coffee, not instant.'

'We didn't know you'd have company.'

'If this is about Christina Traynor,' Challis said emphatically, 'then Sergeant Destry stays. She's part of the investigation and knows as much as I do. So, coffee?'

They shrugged, waited stonily while he brewed the coffee. 'Grab a seat,' he said, keeping it light.

The bulky man sat; the thin man didn't but started the pissing competition immediately. He crossed the room and pointed to a photograph that Challis had tacked to the corkboard on his kitchen wall. 'Dragon Rapide,' he said. 'You've been restoring one just like it in a hangar at the local airfield for the past five years.'

So you've done your homework, Challis thought. You've read my file and talked to people and know me inside and out. I, on the other hand, don't know a thing about you, which puts me at a disadvantage. He sat at the table and waited.

Eventually the thin man sat and said, 'You accessed the national computer yesterday afternoon at five thirty-five.'

'Yes, about then.'

'I'll ask again: what's your interest in Christina Traynor?'

Challis gazed at the man. Clearly by keying in Christina Traynor's name he'd raised a red flag in the federal system. He wondered idly why they hadn't expunged Traynor's name completely but let mugs like him get as far as the screen that read 'Access Denied', and then thought it was precisely so that they could catch people like him. Christina Traynor was apparently need-to-know, and he didn't need to know.

He sipped his coffee. They sipped theirs, and the bulky man nodded approvingly and said, 'Good brew.'

'Inspector,' prompted the other man.

Ellen acted then, pushing Challis's copy of the *Age* across the table towards them. 'Did you know we had a murder here yesterday?'

There was no response. 'A rural address,' Challis said, 'the houses a few hundred metres apart. The owner, an elderly woman called Joy Humphreys, was in hospital at the time. The victim is much younger, and apparently has no connection to the house or Mrs Humphreys. We don't know what she was doing there. But several weeks ago, Mrs Humphreys had a houseguest for three weeks, her goddaughter, Christina Traynor.'

'We're wondering if she was the intended victim,' Ellen said, cutting in seamlessly.

'It seemed like a long shot,' Challis said, 'but obviously now we're not so sure.'

They often did this when interrogating suspects, set up a smooth rhythm, a double act, but the two men waited expressionlessly, so he went on. 'Mrs Humphreys was tired and in a lot of pain yesterday. We've yet to interview her properly. But she did say that Christina stayed for three weeks in April and then flew to London. That's all we know at this stage. Naturally I had to run her name through the system. Access denied. Who is she? Has she done a runner?'

They ignored both questions. The thin man said, 'What do the neighbours say? Any strangers or strange cars lurking about?'

'Nothing, so far,' Ellen said. 'We've put in a request for Mrs Humphreys's phone records.'

'We'll also need to see those,' the bulky man said.

The thin one said, 'Do you trust your officers, Inspector?'

Ellen bristled. Challis gestured irritably. 'Why don't you tell us what's going on.'

They seemed to be gauging how much to reveal, or how far he and Ellen could be trusted, or how bent they might be. He was sick of the bullshit, and reached for his phone. 'I'm going to call my superintendent. The woman shot dead in Mrs Humphreys's driveway is his daughter-in-law.'

He saw the surprise in their faces. Maybe they weren't locals but had flown in from Sydney or Canberra last night. He dialled. McQuarrie was abrupt. 'Yes?'

'Sir, I've got two federal police officers with me. I trod on some toes when I ran Christina Traynor's name through the system last night. They've yet to tell me what it's about.'

McQuarrie was jubilant. 'Don't you see?' he demanded. 'Janine was lost. Wrong person in the wrong place at the wrong time.'

All along, the prick's been afraid something grubby might emerge in the life of his son or daughter-in-law, that he'll be tainted by association, Challis thought sourly. In the super's system of values, Janine murdered by mistake was better than Janine murdered by a secret lover or rival.

'Sir, could you have a word with them?'

Challis handed the receiver to the thin man and heard the tinny scratching of McQuarrie's raised voice. The thin man was scrupulously polite, unbowed by McQuarrie's bluster, but by the time he'd hung up it was clear that something had clarified for him.

'Let me explain,' he said.

22

An hour later, Ellen took her place at the incident room table and watched as Challis stood and announced, 'Before coming to work this morning I was visited by two officers from Witsec.'

Witsec was the federal witness protection program, and she saw Scobie Sutton and the others grow alert and intrigued. She tried to match their expressions, amused that Challis hadn't said she was with him, but also able to see his point: tongues would wag.

'Last year,' he went on, 'they gave protection and later a new identity to this woman, Christina Traynor.'

He tapped a photograph pinned to the display board behind him. 'Christina Traynor also happens to be the god-daughter of Mrs Joy Humphreys, who lives at 283 Lofty Ridge Road, where Janine McQuarrie was murdered. In fact, she stayed with Mrs Humphreys for three weeks in April.'

A groan went around the room. 'So back to square one,' said one of the detectives on loan from Mornington.

'Where's Traynor now?' asked Scobie.

'London, Mrs Humphreys says. She left in a hurry, apparently.'

Everyone glanced at the photo display again. The image of Christina Traynor supplied by the Witsec agents revealed only an approximate resemblance to Janine McQuarrie. Both women had fair, shoulder-length hair, but Christina's was stiff and thick, Janine's straight, fine and glossy. Christina's build was solid, Janine's slight. Christina's face was lively and ready for a laugh, Janine's shut down, almost suspicious.

'Not a close resemblance,' Challis said, as if reading their thoughts, 'but close enough if you're working from a description. What probably clinched it for the killer is that he *expected* to see Traynor, and so anyone resembling her was assumed to be her.'

'But he turned up there two months late,' Scobie said. 'A bit of a stretch, boss.'

Challis shrugged. 'Remember that this is the federal witness protection program we're talking about, so our man did well to track Traynor down that far. As to why someone would want to kill her,' he went on, 'it seems she got mixed up with the wrong people, informed on them, and needed protection and a new identity.'

'She must be important if Witsec agents turn up unannounced.'

'She is—or was.' Challis glanced at his notes, and then paraphrased. 'Christina Traynor grew up in Melbourne, and moved to Sydney with her parents when she was sixteen. She did law at Sydney Uni. Her parents now live up on the Gold Coast. Meanwhile Christina was doing well—junior in a law firm that took on a lot of criminal cases, owned a flat and a car, didn't booze or take drugs, no debts, only a couple of speeding fines. But then she got involved with Avery Blight.'

Blight by name and nature. Ellen had heard all of this before, in Challis's kitchen, so amused herself by glancing around at the others. She saw the recognition in their faces. Avery Blight was based in Sydney, but the police forces in each state—and New Zealand—knew who he was. Blight specialised in armed robberies with violence on banks and payroll vans and had been implicated in two murders, including that of a traffic policeman on the motorway between Sydney and Newcastle.

'Blight's married,' Challis said, 'but he spent a lot of time at Christina's flat, which he used as a kind of base whenever he pulled a job: planning, meeting other hard men, storing firearms, even stashing stolen getaway cars in the two parking spaces allocated to Christina. He's normally hyper-vigilant, but got cocky, assuming that Christina was hooked on him and would never turn him in.'

Ellen knew that it wasn't unusual for young female lawyers to fall for good-looking crims. She glanced around the room, saw the sour expressions: lawyers were often the enemy, and Christina Traynor's actions confirmed old prejudices.

'Then Blight went too far,' Challis said. 'A security guard was shot dead when they robbed a payroll van. According to Christina, Blight did it, laughed and boasted about it, so she contacted police and he was arrested.'

'But too late for the poor guy working security,' the Mornington detective muttered.

'Christina was placed in witness protection immediately,' Challis went on, 'and moved to a house in Melbourne, where she had armed minders twenty-four hours a day. Blight was tried and convicted largely on her evidence, and after he was jailed she was given a new identity and moved to a secret location. Then in April she came to stay with her godmother, and later flew to London.'

He gazed at them. 'Not even her parents knew where she was. She would call them from time to time, and sound forlorn, to use her mother's words, but they didn't think anything was amiss until recently, when she sounded extra jumpy.'

Ellen thought that she'd better say something. 'So Christina got wind that Blight was after her?'

'It seems so. She's running scared.'

'How come Witsec weren't keeping a better eye on her?'

'Once Blight was convicted and Christina had been set up with a new identity, that was it. They contacted her regularly, and gave her emergency numbers to call, but there was no watch over her as such.'

There was a general shaking of heads in the room. Christina Traynor had been foolish to get involved with a crim like Blight, but she'd done the right thing eventually and now had to spend the rest of her life looking back over her shoulder.

'If Witsec have finished with her,' Scobie said, 'why are they sniffing around here?'

Challis shrugged. 'I don't suppose they want to lose a witness, even an ex-witness. And maybe they think Blight has coppers on his payroll, prepared to do his dirty work for him on the outside. And they admitted there'd been stuffups they wanted to atone for. The date of birth on Christina's new passport doesn't match that on her driver's licence, for example, meaning she's had hassles when presenting documentation to organisations like banks for ID purposes. She'd complained several times, but nothing was done.'

Ellen stirred. 'She doesn't need the driver's licence to fly out of the country.'

'There's an alert out for her.'

'Any point in talking to Blight?' Scobie asked.

Challis looked weary and sardonic. 'Assuming the super gives permission and allocates expenses to cover the cost of a trip to Sydney, it's obvious that Blight will deny everything.' He shook his head. 'We keep this local for now, *and* we keep an open mind. For a start, if Janine was the intended target, we need to know who she'd arranged to meet yesterday.'

Scobie Sutton was dubious. 'If I were a betting man,' he announced, 'I'd put my money on Christina Traynor, and that means we need to know everything we can about Blight: who he might have contacted on the outside, who visited him in prison, who he shared a cell with, anything at all.'

'Yeah, right,' Ellen said, realising too late that she was echoing her daughter's favourite expression, 'the police and prison service of New South Wales are going to drop everything in order to help us.'

Challis grinned. 'In an ideal world,' he said.

She returned the grin.

'What's next?' asked Scobie.

'Ellen and I will visit Mrs Humphreys. The rest of you, keep digging into Janine McQuarrie. Scobie, I want you to speak to the super's wife if you can.'

23

'*Isolation brings purity and strength,*' Vyner wrote. '*I am the custodian of the codes.*'

He closed his notebook and settled deeper into the driver's seat of the Falcon he'd stolen from the carpark at Moorabbin airport. Mid morning now, a chill in the air, the weak wintry sun barely reaching him through the windscreen. He could run the heater, but didn't want to draw attention to himself. You don't necessarily notice a parked car, but you do if there's someone seated inside it, starting the engine every five or ten minutes.

He'd raced down to the Peninsula from the airport, but there was no one at home in the miserable weatherboard ruin that Nathan Gent had been renting for the past few months. Bayview Grove, Dromana, a defeated-looking collection of houses crammed close to each other and the sea nowhere in sight. Vyner, taking care of business, had been waiting for an hour. Had Gent followed up his anonymous call with a visit to the cop shop? Bayview Grove was dead; four vehicles in the past hour: the postman on a 100cc Suzuki, bouncing at low speed over kerbs and driveways, a couple of women strapping toddlers into shiny cheap Korean imports, a guy distributing leaflets and not giving a shit about the No Junk Mail notices.

Vyner gazed again at Gent's house. A few untidy plants on the front porch, weeds in the overgrown lawn, and no vehicle in the driveway but indications of one: muddy tyre impressions, flattened grass, oil leaks. He'd knocked when he first arrived, checked the meter box, and listened at doors and windows, but clearly Gent wasn't in. And he hadn't wanted to spend too much time poking around, for the house was too exposed. The street seemed dead, but it was probably chock-a-block with young mothers behind closed doors. Maybe with all of that post-natal depression they'd not be capable of identifying him, but he didn't want to chance it.

What was in it for Gent, contacting the police? Money? Get rid of the guilt? Treacherous little prick. Time passed; Vyner dozed.

Gent came home on a pushbike, of all fucking things, shopping bags swinging from the handlebars. Vyner ducked low in his seat, confident that the tinted glass would obscure him. He saw Gent swing into the driveway with a natty flourish, dismount, and prop the bike against the peeling front wall. Then Gent disappeared down the side of the house. Vyner checked the wing mirrors, checked the street ahead and behind, and swung the Falcon into the driveway at low speed and revs. He piled out, ran to the rear of the house, and charged through the door on the back porch just as Gent was about to elbow it closed. The shopping spilled all over the worn linoleum and Gent stumbled backwards and Vyner shot him in the heart with his second silenced Browning automatic.

24

Ellen sat in the CIU Falcon in the carpark behind the station, waiting for Challis to leave the building. She still felt buoyed by the events of the morning. She could have sworn that Challis was going to kiss her at one stage, before those Witsec goons arrived.

She saw the back door swing open and Challis appeared. He wore an overcoat at a time and in a place where men didn't wear overcoats but brightly coloured jackets of padded down or polar fleece. He was very slightly daggy and she liked that about him. He glanced about the yard for her, and in the second or two it took for him to find the CIU car, and her, his face was in repose, showing the true man underneath: fatigued, a little sad and careworn, his narrow face and hooded eyes faintly prohibitive. Then he smiled and it transformed him.

'All set?' she asked, as he got into the passenger seat.

'Waterloo Motors called as I was leaving,' he said, buckling his seatbelt.

'And?'

'It will take a few days to get the parts they need.'

'Buy yourself a new car, Hal.'

'Nothing wrong with my car. The motor's tired, that's all,' Challis said. 'Like the owner.'

She checked him for a ribald meaning, but as usual Challis was unreadable. Without trying to make it sound too significant, she said, 'I'm happy to take you to and from work until you get it back.'

He shook his head. 'They'll have a courtesy car for me later today.'

His lightness of mood was evaporating. To distract him, Ellen said, 'Alan wanted to know why you didn't get a cab to work,' and watched for his reaction. For reasons that she hadn't finished thinking through, she wanted Challis to know that her husband was jealous of him.

'Huh,' said Challis.

She gave up and they drove in silence to the hospital, Ellen feeling obscurely disappointed. At the hospital they walked into a close, dry heat: guaranteed to make you feel sicker, Ellen thought. A nurse directed them along a pastelly corridor, and they found the owner of 283 Lofty Ridge Road watching morning TV, her face registering a kind of fury. 'Nothing on but rubbish,' she said. 'Who are you?' she demanded, glaring at them both.

Challis told her. 'Mrs Humphreys, I need to ask you some questions about your god-daughter.'

Mrs Humphreys aimed the remote at the TV set and the screen gulped and went blank. 'I wasn't much help to your man yesterday, and I don't suppose I'll be much help now.'

Challis smiled. 'How are you feeling today?'

'Sore, but brighter in the head.'

'You told DC Sutton that Christina stayed with you for a while last April.'

'That's right. For about three weeks.'

'Was it unusual for her to stay with you?'

'Yes and no. I saw her often when she was little, before the family moved to Sydney, but haven't seen much of her in recent years. Look, is she in trouble?'

Challis wondered how much to tell her. 'Not with the police. She hasn't done anything wrong.'

Mrs Humphreys glanced at him shrewdly, her veiny hands kneading her pale blue hospital blanket. 'That woman who was shot at my house—do you think they were after Chris instead?'

'We don't know for sure. We have to look at all possibilities. Are you certain that Christina went to London?'

'I got a postcard from her. I recognised the handwriting. Do you think she'll be safe there?'

'Yes.'

Mrs Humphreys didn't seem convinced.

'How would you describe Christina's mood?'

'When she stayed with me? I've been going over that in my head all night. At the time, I thought she was nursing a broken heart—you know, some man had dumped her and she wanted to get away for a while. She was moody and sad. Wouldn't leave the house. But now I'm thinking she might have been more scared than sad.'

'Did she receive any unusual phone calls? Make any? Have any visitors?'

'No, nothing like that.'

'And she left suddenly?'

'Yes.'

'How did she seem when she said goodbye?'

'Elated. Like a weight was off her mind. Bought me a brand-new TV set to say thank you, silly girl.'

'So she must have left the house at some stage, in order to buy you the TV set and make travel arrangements.'

Mrs Humphreys shook her head. 'Did it all by phone.'

'You said she didn't make any calls.'

'No *funny* calls,' Mrs Humphreys said.

They got no more from the old woman, and Challis asked for her house keys. 'I'm afraid we need to search it for anything that Christina left behind, or anything that might involve you,' he said.

'You're mad.'

Ellen perched on the bed and reached for a veiny wrist. 'We won't pry unnecessarily, or disturb anything. We can get a warrant, but if you gave us your permission...'

Mrs Humphreys gestured impatiently. She seemed tired now. 'Suit yourselves, but you won't find anything.'

They were in the hospital carpark, strapping on their seatbelts, when Tessa Kane appeared, tapping on Challis's window. 'Hal, Ellen,' she said.

Ellen replied with a short nod, feeling a quickening of suspicion and resentment. She began to fiddle with her mobile phone, needing to occupy her hands while the other two talked.

'What brings you here?' Challis asked.

'Work.'

'Mrs Humphreys?'

'Yes.'

'She's just had an operation.'

'I'll go gently, Hal.' A pause. 'Well, mustn't keep you. Stay in touch.'

That was Ellen's cue to turn the ignition key abruptly and wheel them out of the carpark. Telling herself to grow up, she breathed in and out and said offhandedly, 'Hal, do you ever find it hard, knowing what cap to wear?'

'What do you mean?'

'You know, the cop who's a source, and the cop who's involved personally.'

She couldn't look at him but sensed that he was looking fully at her. Presently he said, 'I was involved with Tessa Kane. I'm not any more.'

Said coolly, so she gestured with one hand, saying, 'Sorry, don't mean to pry.'

She thought he'd leave it, but he treated her question seriously. 'It was complicated sometimes. There were issues of confidentiality, and I know half the station disapproved—but that's not why we broke up.'

Broke up. He'd actually said it. 'Hal, it's okay, I had no right...'

'Forget it,' Challis said, making an effort. 'Let's turn the old girl's place over.'

They reached the house on Lofty Ridge to find crime-scene technicians still at work, widening their search of the grounds, taking new photographs, making further sketches. 'Oh hell,' Challis said, darting out of the car and approaching one of the technicians. A moment later he was back, grinning at her ruefully. 'See that oil stain? That's where I parked the Triumph last night.'

Ellen gazed at him, experiencing a sudden insight into his solitariness. She found herself squeezing his hand. He laughed, and a kind of current sprang between them, opening them to possibilities. Ellen followed him into the house giddily.

He almost spoilt it then, saying, 'If there's anything here, you'll find it.'

She was alarmed. What did he mean? Did he mean that he knew she had light fingers, or that he valued her ability to find hiding places? She tried to read him. After a while she told herself there were no undercurrents in his observation.

They began the search. A preliminary run through the house yielded nothing but a postcard under a fridge magnet. Postmarked London, it depicted Big Ben, the Houses of Parliament and a barge on the River Thames. It was signed 'Chris' at the bottom of a couple of short sentences that said nothing about Christina Traynor's state of mind, whereabouts or intentions.

Ellen was thorough, but also intensely aware of Challis. They seemed to perform a kind of dance, almost touching, colliding and glancing away from each other, only to be drawn together again. They were both aware of it but said nothing. It wouldn't do. She tried to shake off the feelings even as she welcomed them. 'Anything?' he said at one point, his voice rasping. She didn't trust her own voice. 'Nothing,' she said.

They parted again and she made a more thorough search, looking under framed pictures for wall safes, kicking skirting boards for tell-tale hiding places, checking cupboards, drawers, photo albums, wardrobes and the laundry basket. It was fruitless: there were no indications of where the old woman's goddaughter was now, or that she'd been the intended victim, or even that she'd ever been in residence.

They met in the kitchen. By now Ellen was depressed by the house with its musty air and the faint grime of an old woman whose eyesight was failing. She turned to Challis. 'Hal—'

'Oh, Christ,' he muttered, glancing past her through the window.

She followed his gaze. Superintendent McQuarrie's Mercedes had pulled up at the yellow tape. The super got out with Georgia McQuarrie, who held a small bouquet of flowers, and together they approached the tape, ducked under it and made for the chalked area where Janine had died. Ellen watched curiously. The officer in charge of the crime-scene technicians seemed to argue with McQuarrie, before shrugging and stepping back to allow Georgia to place the flowers on the ground. Then McQuarrie and his granddaughter ducked back under the tape again and stood watching for a while, Georgia absorbed by the technician who was sketching.

Suddenly Challis was leaving the kitchen. Ellen watched, hearing him call, 'Sir, a moment?'

'Not now, Inspector,' McQuarrie said, bundling Georgia into the big Mercedes and driving away.

Ellen locked the house and joined Challis at the CIU car. The mood gone, the magic irretrievable, they travelled in silence. Then Challis's mobile phone rang. He listened attentively, switched off and glanced at Ellen. 'That was Scobie. A woman called Connie Rinehart from Upper Penzance just called the station. She had an appointment with Janine McQuarrie yesterday morning, nine-thirty, about the time that Janine was shot.'

25

On the other side of the Peninsula, John Tankard was saying, 'Look, about yesterday, I'm really sorry I made a grab at you.'

Pam Murphy, deeply bored, said, 'Forget it.'

They were in the little Mazda, patrolling the area between Mount Martha and Rosebud. Week Two of the Drive Safe campaign and that was two weeks too long. Pam had long exhausted topics of conversation with Tankard, the modern sports car doesn't necessarily offer much in the way of driving thrills, and safe and courteous drivers were few and far between. She'd much rather be out catching bad guys. Meanwhile, after what happened yesterday, she had to put herself on full alert in case Tank groped her again, or, worse, wanted a cuddle and forgiveness. Was he losing it? Could she rely on him if they did meet a bad guy? She watched from the corner of her eye as he twisted his large trunk and meaty legs to get comfortable in the passenger seat. He was too big for the tiny car, exacerbated this morning by soreness and stiffness brought on by football training.

He wouldn't let it go. 'It was out of line. I'm really sorry.'

'Tank? Can it,' she snarled.

'I was only saying...'

'Well don't.'

Fortunately they passed a building site shortly after that, a new housing development that faced the sea, a handful of men outside it picketing against scab labour. Tankard seemed to shake off his moroseness, some of his old intolerance showing as he shifted in the tight passenger seat and said, 'Look at those wankers.'

Pam had to laugh. In occupation, status and background he was thoroughly working-class, yet he always voted for the conservative coalition, approving of their hard line on law and order, immigration, terrorism and anything else that threatened white-bread, middle-class Australia. Maybe the prime minister, attorney general and immigration minister represented the strict father he'd never had.

Her own position was more complicated. Her father and brothers were university academics, intellectuals, which meant that Christmas Day table conversations in Pam Murphy's family were rapid-fire, elliptical, knowing and wide-ranging, leaving her far behind. She was the youngest child, good at sport, barely adequate in tests and exams, and had joined the police force, so...

'Do the maths,' she muttered now, heading from the freeway down into Rosebud.

'Sorry?'

'Nothing.' She had no intention of describing, to John Tankard, the remote, condescending love that her father and brothers bestowed upon her.

Two tedious hours passed. They decided to head across to the Waterloo side of the Peninsula, but on Dunn's Creek Road they encountered a white Falcon, sitting solidly on 80 in a 100 zone. The undulating road afforded Pam few opportunities to pass, and she cursed. 'There should be demerit points for driving too slowly,' she said.

Tankard, apparently still smarting, said, 'Don't get your knickers in a knot.'

She let it pass. The word 'knickers' had always inflamed the old John Tankard, and she wasn't taking any chances. 'Take down his number.'

'Why? He's not breaking any road rules.'

'Forget it,' Pam said, and she followed the Falcon all the way to Waterloo, by which time she'd decided the driver deserved a showbag.

Tankard, concurring, placed the portable pursuit light on the dash and sounded the siren. 'You moron,' said Pam, scrambling to turn them off.

Vyner, spotting uniformed police in the little Mazda sports car behind him, cast his mind back over the past couple of hours and wondered where and when he'd gone wrong.

He hadn't registered anything on his personal radar when he'd left his flat for his appointment with Mrs Plowman. He lived in a yuppie singles pad in Southbank, and even though he was surrounded by Asian students and young women with jeans so low in front you saw the fur line, the place was anonymous and close to everything. He felt out of his element whenever he left the city. That's why he'd hired Gent yesterday. Well, he wasn't making that mistake again.

No one had tailed him from Mrs Plowman's, or to and from the airport, or down the Peninsula to fucking Gent's fucking house in Dromana. No one saw him go in through the back door and shoot the bastard, then bundle him into the boot of the Falcon. So why were the cops following him? And why the fuck were they driving a sports car? Why the fuck were they wearing uniforms if they didn't want to be noticed?

It had been a toss-up between getting rid of the body first, or setting up a false trail. The latter, and maybe that's where he'd gone wrong. He'd spent a crucial thirty minutes in Gent's house, shoving the moron's computer into the boot with the body, emptying the fridge and propping the door open; filling a garbage bag with perishables, which he'd disposed of in a public rubbish bin; packing a suitcase as if Gent were going away for a month; closing the blinds and curtains and turning out the pilot lights for the oven and space heater; and finally leaving Gent's shithole and filling out a hold-mail application at the local post office.

Then he'd got rid of the pistol. Two good Browning automatics in two days. He'd sealed the one he'd used on the woman yesterday in a block of wet cement, dumping the block at the tip when it was dry, but dismantled the one he'd used on Gent—his Navy training coming in useful—and then he'd hacksawed the parts and tossed the scraps, along with Gent's computer and suitcase, into builders' skips in an area stretching from Rosebud to Mount Martha.

And now it was time to get rid of the body, and he was heading northeast across the Peninsula, towards Waterloo, observing all of the road and speed signs, and suddenly there were cops behind him. Dunn's Creek Road was snaking around one side of a pretty gully before flattening out along a high ridge lined with horse studs and plant nurseries set behind massive old pine tree avenues. There was more traffic than he'd expected, and on Penzance Beach Road and again on Waterloo Road he'd been obliged to give way to intersecting traffic, stop for a befuddled koala and not try overtaking a community bus full of old-age pensioners.

The little MX5 behind him all the way.

And when he got to Myers Reserve, dense with pittosporum, bracken and dying gum trees, the Mazda was still there, so he headed on down to Waterloo. He stopped for the give-way sign on Coolart Road, slowed to 70 kmh and then 60 kmh through the next township, signalled left at the T-intersection, did all the right things, and the Mazda stuck with him, never varying speed or relative position, and that, and the peaked caps worn by the driver and the passenger, really got Vyner's mind working.

And so he pulled the stolen Falcon into the carpark of the Mitre

10 hardware on the main street of Waterloo and got out, letting his body language spell *innocent do-it-yourself guy shopping for a packet of nails and a tin of paint*. But then a siren whooped and the Mazda purred in beside him, the cops getting out, a guy and a woman, dressed like SWAT commandos in boots, waisted leather jackets and peaked caps.

'Excuse me, sir.'

Vyner froze, his eyes darting. Hell of a place. Tattoo parlour across the road, McDonald's on one side of the carpark, railway line on the other. And further up the road, a roundabout and the Waterloo police station. He said innocently, 'Was I going too fast?'

The woman shook her head. 'The opposite, in fact. I'm Senior Constable Murphy, and this is Constable Tankard.'

Tankard, thought Vyner. The guy was built like a tankard, round and squat.

'We couldn't help noticing, sir.'

Noticing what? That I've got a body and a shovel in the boot of a stolen car?

Murphy flipped open her notebook. 'You were faced with constantly varying speed limits for the past few kilometres, and you observed all of them. You observed stop and give-way signs, you were courteous to other drivers, and you made commonsense decisions when faced by unexpected hazards, like that koala trying to cross the road.'

Vyner shook his head. He was waiting for the 'However…'

'On behalf of Victoria Police and the RTA, we'd like to reward you,' the woman said.

Vyner wanted to laugh. He gave them a frank and open grin. 'Well, thank you.'

The female cop leaned into the Mazda, emerging with a bulky plastic bag. 'To show our appreciation, sir.'

Vyner peeked inside. 'Great. Thank you.'

For a moment, he really meant it. He'd always driven safely. He'd never been ticketed, and now it was paying off.

'You're welcome sir. Have a good day, now,' the guy, Tankard, muttered.

Gloomy guy. Whoever said fat was cheerful?

Vyner went into Mitre 10 and bought saw blades to replace those he'd broken and blunted while cutting up the Browning.

Out in the carpark again, he saw that the Mazda was gone. He observed all of the speed limits and road rules from Waterloo to Myers Reserve, where he committed several misdemeanours, beginning with the lock on the gate that said Parks Victoria Vehicles Only.

26

Using her office phone in the *Progress* building, Tessa Kane posed as an insurance agent selling life cover. Having established that Charlie Mead was at work, she drove across the Peninsula to Rosebud and knocked on the front door of his house. 'Mrs Mead? Lottie Mead?'

A wary 'Yes.'

'My name is Tessa Kane, from the *Progress.*'

Tessa waited, wondering if she'd be recognised. Lottie Mead was slender and unsmiling, her gaze passing expressionlessly across Tessa's face and examining the street. 'What do you want?'

'I won't lie to you, Mrs Mead. My paper has been running a series of critical articles about asylum seekers and your husband's management of the Waterloo detention centre. I think it's time for a personal perspective, and would like to interview you. Perhaps we could start with your lives together in South Africa, and move on from there. Would that be possible, do you think?'

She waited. The house was a grim grey fortress on a slope overlooking the bay. Finally Lottie Mead said, 'I have nothing to say to you,' and began to close the door.

'Wait! Did your husband tell you not to speak to reporters? Does he have something to hide, do you think?'

'Perhaps you didn't hear me,' said the woman distinctly, shutting the door with a brisk click.

Ellen was in Upper Penzance, half relieved and half chagrined to be working with Scobie Sutton instead of Challis. Their interview with Connie Rinehart completed, she got behind the wheel of the CIU Falcon, flipped open her mobile phone and reported in. 'Hal? Rinehart never met Janine—it was all arranged by her doctor.'

'What can you tell me about her?'

'Thirty-four, suffers from agoraphobia, has scarcely left her house for the past five years. When Janine didn't arrive, she supposed she'd made a mistake with the date or the time, but hadn't got around to checking with the clinic or her doctor. She's very timid and withdrawn.'

'Does she live anywhere near Mrs Humphreys?'

'Several kilometres away.'

'Does she know her?'

'No.'

'Does she know Christina Traynor?'

'No.'

There was a pause, and Challis said, 'That leaves us with Janine's phobia about making right-hand turns. Yesterday she was obliged to visit Rinehart at home, so she mapped out a route that would avoid turning right, and found herself in an unfamiliar area and stopped to check her street directory. I've been looking at the map: someone driving from Mount Eliza to Upper Penzance without making right turns would probably pass through Penzance North. She was the wrong person in the wrong place at the wrong time, and got herself shot.'

'It's a theory,' Ellen said. 'See you back at the ranch.'

She started the car. Scobie promptly settled into yarning mode. 'Remember I was talking about Natalie Cobb yesterday?'

Ellen had been cooped up with him for hours, and forced herself to mutter, 'Yes.'

'Well, Beth went to see the Cobbs after work yesterday. She told me something interesting. She arrived just as Natalie was slipping her mother some money. She said it was clear Natalie hadn't been to school all day. I myself saw her being picked up outside the courthouse by her boyfriend, and I guess she spent the day with him.'

'Uh-huh,' Ellen said, and then thought she should make an effort. 'Doing what with the boyfriend?'

'Well, that's the question.'

'Is the boyfriend known to us?'

'Don't know. Don't know who he is.'

'Be worth finding out.'

'True.'

There was a blessed silence and then he said, 'Today was mad hair day.'

Ellen's mind raced, but not for long. He's talking about his bloody daughter again.

'If it's mad hair day, or wear-what-you-like day, we have to get Ros up at least half an hour earlier than usual. She gets in a real knot about it, poor little thing. "Do I look stupid in this?" "Are you sure it's mad hair day?" "You're doing it all wrong." And so on and so forth.'

The Suttons' only child was a pale, wispy eight-year-old. 'Uh-huh,' said Ellen.

'Maths, that's another thing that makes her anxious.'

I should be so lucky, Ellen thought. To break up the litany, she said, 'You spoke to the super's wife?'

Scobie groaned. 'Oh god.'

'Bad, huh?'

'She had plenty to say, but nothing to say, if you know what I mean.'

Ellen nodded. 'Janine was married to her son, and was therefore a paragon of virtue.'

'That about covers it,' Scobie said.

Meanwhile Andy Asche was driving past the secondary college in Waterloo. Lunchtime, and Natalie, hanging around the front gate, gave him a nod, their signal that she was still intending to slip away from school during an afternoon lesson break and meet him around the corner.

This afternoon they were hitting a house in Penzance Beach. Andy had a head full of potential targets. He worked part-time for the shire, in a job that took him all over the Peninsula. Last month, for example, he'd spent two days delivering the new-style recycling bins to every house in Penzance Beach. At other times he might accompany the property valuation surveyor, going around to every property noting improvements and taking measurements for the next hike in shire rates. Or he drove around back roads, marking for attention ditches and culverts that were clogged with sand, twigs and pine needles.

Whatever, he had a lot of facts at his fingertips. Such and such a house is always empty during the day. Another is only occupied on weekends, a third only in summer. This street's no good: there's always some busybody in her garden or staring out of her window. That street is full of barking dogs. There's a top-of-the-range security system in this house; there's no security system in that house, despite the sticker in the window.

Penzance Beach was always a good earner. A few locals lived there permanently, but mostly it consisted of beach shacks, which looked humble but were owned by wealthy city people who liked to come down on weekends or school holidays and maintain the level of comfort they'd grown accustomed to in the city: top quality TVs, VCRs, DVDs, microwaves, sports equipment, clothes, even mobile phones, cash and Walkmans left lying around in kids' bedrooms. Wealth made teenagers indifferent to wealth. Andy Asche's mother would have tanned his hide if he'd been as careless with his possessions.

27

Challis had put in requests for assistance from the police and prison services in New South Wales after the morning's briefing, but when nothing had transpired by lunchtime, he grabbed a sandwich from the canteen and checked his pigeonhole. The top circular read, *Where circumstances and protocol allow, Victoria Police and civilian staff members will use both sides of a sheet of paper rather than two sheets.* He almost crumpled it up and tossed it into the bin, but the circular's reverse side was blank, so he did the right thing and took it upstairs with him, to be used for making rough notes.

Then Waterloo Motors called to say that his loan car was ready. He shrugged on his coat and left the station through the rear door to avoid the reporters camped outside the front door. Waterloo Motors was choked with cars awaiting service or repairs or to be collected by their owners. He picked out his loan car quickly, a rusted-out Toyota, with mag wheels, a fluffy steering wheel and the words 'Waterloo Motors' pasted all over it. He collected the keys and drove it back to the station, enduring the blokey jibes of a few car-mad constables.

By mid afternoon some preliminary information had come in from

New South Wales. Blight's prison visitors consisted of his parents, wife, brothers and two men who'd once driven cabs for him. He'd shared a cell only once, with a man who was still incarcerated. Since then he'd been in a single cell in a segregated block.

What next? Fly to Sydney and interview every one of Blight's visitors, every inmate in the prison? A sheer waste of time, and Challis couldn't see McQuarrie giving budget approval.

Meanwhile he wasn't ruling out Janine McQuarrie as the intended victim—or not entirely—but was prompted to close certain avenues related to her case by a bleating phone call from Robert McQuarrie: 'When are the police going to release my wife's body?'

'Should be in the next day or two,' Challis said, making a note to check with the pathologist.

'There's also the car and her mobile phones. Surely you've finished checking them for evidence?'

A little chill crept over Challis's skin. Why the hurry? What was so important about these possessions ahead of the welfare of his daughter? 'These things take time in a murder investigation, sir,' he said.

McQuarrie said nothing but Challis could feel the man's irritation and impatience. 'You said "phones"? I understood that there was only one phone,' he said, searching through the files on his desk for the crime-scene inventory.

'*Two* phones: one that she uses—used—hands free in the car, and another that she carried around with her.'

Challis found the inventory. There was only one mobile phone listed, clip-mounted to the dash of the car. He'd assumed that was the phone Georgia had used to call 000. Had she used the second one instead? If so, where was it?

'It will still be in the property room,' he said confidently. 'I'll see that it's returned to you first thing tomorrow. My apologies.'

'I hope that light fingers haven't been at work, Mr Challis.'

Fuck you, thought Challis savagely. He immediately made two

phone calls. From the first he learned that Janine's car had been tested for prints but none were found to match those stored on the national computer. Then he called a number at the regional headquarters in Frankston, Superintendent McQuarrie answering on the first ring, saying peevishly, 'I was just on my way to a meeting.'

'Sorry, sir, a quick question: when you took Georgia home from the murder scene yesterday, did she have a mobile phone with her?'

'Not that I recall.'

'According to your son, Janine had two phones. We only recovered one.'

'Not to worry,' McQuarrie said, 'I've seen her office, home and mobile phone records, and there's nothing on any of them to arouse concern. Nothing dodgy, only business calls and calls to my son's mobile and work numbers. I'll fax them through to you, if you don't have them—though I'd be disappointed if you don't by now, Hal, I must say. Obtaining phone records is surely basic groundwork in a murder investigation.'

In fact, Challis had requisitioned Janine's phone records—except those for the second mobile phone, which he hadn't known existed. He wanted to drive to Frankston immediately and slap his boss about the face, demanding to know whether or not the man considered himself a proper policeman, or even a policeman, or even a man of ordinary decency and common sense.

He forced himself to calm down, but his mind raced. McQuarrie must have gone swiftly to work in getting those phone records, and as a superintendent he had considerably more juice than a humble inspector. But what was he playing at? Was he trying to bury evidence that might damage his son's good name, his own good name? What if he'd discovered that Janine had been phoning organised crime figures or toy-boys twenty times a day? Would he have revealed *that* to the investigating officers?

Is he, thought Challis, our killer?

'Sir, we need the second phone.'

'Why? I've got a record of the calls she made. All innocent.'

'I need to see the message bank,' Challis said patiently, 'the numbers listed in the memory, and the call list for the most recent incoming, outgoing and missed calls.'

'Well, *I* haven't got the damn thing,' McQuarrie said peevishly. 'Georgia didn't have it, I'm sure of that. Perhaps she gave it to Robert.'

'It was Robert who alerted me to the fact of its existence,' Challis said, trying to convey that he thought McQuarrie should have done so, too.

'Well there you are. It was collected at the crime-scene and has either been misplaced or stolen since then. Rosebud officers were the first to attend; have you tried them?'

Fuck off, Challis thought. He double-checked the record of calls made on Janine McQuarrie's car phone—there were no calls to the police on the morning of her murder, and so Georgia must have used a different phone. Then he spent a fruitless hour tracking down and calling the Rosebud CIU and uniformed officers. They knew nothing of a mobile phone being found with or near the body.

Finally he talked to Georgia.

'I used Mum's mobile,' she told him.

'Not the one she uses in her car?'

Georgia's voice went small, almost scared. 'No, the one in her bag. I'm not supposed to, but I grabbed it when the man started chasing her. Sorry.'

'Nothing to be sorry for,' said Challis gently. 'Can you remember what you did with it afterwards?'

There was a gasp and he pictured her hand flying to her mouth. 'I left it on the ground!'

'Where?'

'In the trees where I hid!'

'Don't worry, we'll find it.'

Challis thought about all of the things that might have damaged the phone since the murder: rain, dew, the chilly air, hungry rats, inquisitive magpies. Just then the fax machine sounded: as promised, McQuarrie was sending through Janine's phone records. Challis snatched up the sheets, and there was Georgia's call to 000. He noted the number of the missing mobile phone, then drove to Mrs Humphreys's house in the late afternoon gloom. The crime-scene crew had packed up and gone, and he walked unimpeded down her driveway. After checking the signal strength of his own phone, he dialled the number for Janine's. A moment later, very faintly, he heard it ring. A voice inviting him to leave a message cut in before he could isolate the location.

He approached the stand of poplars, which were leafless and choked by pittosporums. The latter would have promised a reasonable degree of shelter to Georgia, he supposed. He pressed redial, and this time found the phone, secure inside a small vinyl case deep in a tangle of grass and fallen leaves. He opened the Velcro flap and let the phone slide into his palm. It was a fancy, costly-looking thing; he couldn't figure out how to work it.

He encountered Ellen Destry in the station carpark, retrieving files from the back seat of the CIU Falcon. 'Our esteemed leader returns,' she said. She cocked her head at his loan car. 'Cool wheels.'

'It's a heap of shit.'

She laughed, then said with a slight catch in her voice, 'So I guess you won't be needing a lift home tonight.'

Challis gazed critically at the rattletrap Toyota. 'Too soon to tell.'

They went upstairs to CIU. 'You busy, Ells?'

'You know I'm busy. I think you mean, drop everything at once and help me with something tedious.'

'No one likes a smart-arse. See if you can figure out how to retrieve the numbers and messages stored in this mobile.'

'Whose is it?'

'Janine McQuarrie's.'

'What makes you think I'd be better at it than you?'

She was in a light, attractive mood. 'You have a teenage daughter,' he said, flourishing the mobile at her. 'I rest my case.'

'No one likes a smart-arse,' Ellen said, taking the phone from him. She turned it over, pressed buttons, and gave him a running commentary. 'Cutting edge. You can use this for calls, SMS, e-mail, video, photography...'

Challis watched her press more buttons, watched her face change as she said, 'The secret life of Robert and Janine McQuarrie.'

Instead of showing him the tiny screen, she attached the phone to the USB port of her computer, downloaded the contents to her hard drive and made CD copies. 'Here,' she said, handing him one of the CDs.

'What do you want me to do with it?'

'You're such a dinosaur. Copy the contents to your hard drive, then print it out.'

She showed him how. What he saw put Janine's murder in an entirely new light: ten photographs, low-resolution shots of men and women copulating, the women obscured, four of the men in sharp enough detail to be identifiable. Two had flushed, straining, heavy-lidded faces, one man was apparently emotionless, and the fourth was Robert McQuarrie, showing his teeth in a kind of ecstatic snarl.

'Oh boy,' said Challis, shifting in his seat. It was a powerful distraction, the snapshots, Ellen's joshing expertise and physical proximity.

'We have to assume that Janine downloaded these to her home or office computer,' Ellen said, 'or e-mailed them to herself.'

Challis shrugged. The technology was beside the point just now. He told her he was more interested in what had driven Janine McQuarrie to take the photographs, what she'd done with them, and whether or not they'd contributed to her being murdered.

Ellen was with him every step of the way. 'Blackmail?'

'Could be.' He tapped the photographs. 'But what are we looking at here?'

Ellen snorted, naming and describing a few body parts.

'Very funny,' he said, feigning severity. In fact, the mood was electric and precarious.

She sobered and made an effort. 'Dim lighting,' she said.

'Yes.'

'A suburban house.'

'So it's not a photographic studio or the set of a porn film?'

She shook her head. 'It's someone's house, and they're not making a film or posing for the camera.'

'Good. But is it a suburban house that doubles as a brothel?'

'We've both worked Vice in the past, Hal. This is no brothel.'

'Why not?' Challis demanded, wanting Ellen to pin it down for him.

'The body language,' she said. 'These people don't look like pros and their clients. They all seem a little self-conscious. Look here in the background: people standing around watching, and that looks like a bowl of condoms and that looks like a lubricant dispenser. The pictures on the walls, the knick-knacks, the furniture, all point to this being an ordinary house.'

'I agree.'

'Do you think the super knew Robert and Janine were attending sex parties?'

Challis shrugged. 'Could explain why he's been obstructive and interventionist.'

There was a pause. 'Hal,' Ellen said eventually, 'could you imagine being watched by a roomful of people while having sex?'

Challis couldn't imagine engaging in *any* kind of herd behaviour. 'No.'

'It doesn't turn you on?'

'No.'

'How about watching?'

'Unobserved?'

'No, watching in a roomful of others.'

'No. I'd still feel watched.'

She seemed to sway towards him a little. 'That's pretty much how I feel about it,' she said.

Then she destroyed the mood. 'You know what we have to do, don't you?'

He turned and looked at her. 'Talk to Robert.'

She shook her head determinedly. 'Talk to Tessa Kane. And I'm coming with you.'

'That's not a good idea.'

'You don't trust her?'

Challis didn't, not entirely. 'Robert can tell us where this took place.'

'And Tessa Kane can tell us if it's the same party that she attended. Of course we don't show her anyone's faces, only photos that identify the location. If she does recognise the place, then we start digging, making it clear to her that she'll face obstruction charges if she writes about the photos or tries to contact anyone.'

'You don't like her, do you?' Challis said.

'Not much.'

They stared at each other. 'If I'm there she's going to know it's related to the McQuarrie investigation,' Challis said.

'Then let me question her. I'll say someone found a photo of themselves on the net and we're investigating.'

Challis sighed. 'Okay.'

28

'I didn't expect the big guns,' Tessa Kane said, puzzled to see Ellen Destry ushered into her office, late that Wednesday afternoon.

'Meaning what?' said Ellen curtly.

Hello, thought Tessa, the claws are out. She'd often wondered if the other woman had been jealous of her relationship with Hal Challis or troubled for professional reasons. Plenty of cops disliked and distrusted the media. It would be fun to let Destry stew a little, she thought, and said, 'Say hello to Hal for me, won't you.'

'It's possible we've got our wires crossed, Ms Kane,' Destry said coldly.

Keeping her manner blithe, Tessa gestured for the other woman to sit, then returned to her swivel chair and swivelled in it, smiling across her overcrowded desk. 'I assume you're here about my tyres?'

'Your tyres.'

'Someone slashed them this afternoon.'

Destry cocked her head alertly. Tessa, irritated to be on the receiving end of a CIU interrogation, with its evasions and games, snarled, 'Cut the crap, sergeant. What's this about?'

Ellen Destry leaned forward, looking pleased with herself. 'It could very well be about your slashed tyres.'

Tessa said nothing.

'Been up to something, have we?' the Destry woman continued. 'Stepping on toes?'

'You tell me.'

'I understand you've had hate mail, anonymous phone calls, a rock through your window, and now this. Maybe you offended one of your swingers.'

Tessa went very still, her mind racing, her skin tingling. Her article on the sex-party scene had been heavy on atmosphere, mood and human interest, without in any way describing people or place. No one reading it could possibly have identified himself—or herself. She waited. Destry would show her hand soon.

And she did, fanning half a dozen grainy photo enlargements across her desk. 'Do you recognise anything?'

Tessa looked. The quality was poor: dim lighting, amorphous shapes, no faces. 'No.'

'Look at the background,' Destry snapped. 'Furniture, light fittings, curtains, bedspreads, paintings on the walls.' She paused. 'Or maybe you recognise the odd hairy backside or sagging tit.'

Tessa knew where this was going. The photographs had been taken at a sex party. She'd recently written an article about a sex party. Ergo, there was a connection between the two.

'I have no idea where these were taken—certainly not at the party I attended. Are you saying I, or one of my photographers, took these photographs for the *Progress*?'

'We're not saying that at all.'

'Then what have they got to do with me?'

'How many parties did you attend?'

'One.'

'Where?'

'Rye. Miles from here.'

'Did you recognise anyone?'

'Like who?'

'Just answer the question, please, Tess.'

She hated being called Tess right then. 'I didn't recognise anyone. Are you saying someone recognised me, and that's why I'm being targeted? But what's this got to do with these photos?'

'We don't know that your tyres being slashed has anything to do with these photographs,' Ellen Destry said. 'But someone found a photo of himself on the net, part of a series of photos including these, and we're looking at a blackmail angle. You're our first obvious point of contact. We need names of those you talked to at the party, and the names of the people who organised it.'

'Sorry, no can do. Confidentiality issues,' said Tessa automatically, with a sweet, empty smile.

'We can get a warrant.'

'Good, you do that, sergeant.'

It was good to see Destry's frustration. Even so, she smelt a story. 'Maybe we can help each other.'

'How?'

'Tell me more, and I'll make contact with my sex-party people and see if they'll talk to you.'

'If you didn't attend this party,' said Destry, collecting the photographs and slipping them into her briefcase, 'then there's no reason to talk to them. As I understand it, there are many such parties in operation.'

Tessa waited until the other woman was going out the door. 'Tell me, sergeant, was Janine McQuarrie involved in the sex party scene?'

Destry said nothing, didn't even look back, but the set of her shoulders and spine said plenty.

Tessa Kane's investigative instincts began to kick in.

29

Challis waited at the door to the incident room, smiling tiredly, waiting for the jokes to subside, as Scobie and the others filed in one by one and spotted the enlargements of Janine McQuarrie's photographs, which he'd arranged on the display board. Ellen came in last, her movements tight and brisk.

'Sorry to keep you late,' he said, turning to the display board. 'This—' he pointed '—is Superintendent McQuarrie's son, Robert, husband of our murder victim.'

There were sardonic looks and murmurs, mostly jocular, and Scobie asked who had taken the photos, and where.

'Ellen and I found them stored on Janine McQuarrie's mobile phone. We don't know the location. Does anyone recognise the other men?'

They shook their heads. 'Presumably the super's son will know,' Scobie said. He paused. 'Are you going to tell him, boss?'

'Tell the son, yes,' said Challis. 'Tell the super? Not yet. I don't want to cause unnecessary harm or embarrassment, and please, I don't want copies of these photographs circulating, and I don't want anyone outside this room knowing that we have them.'

Ellen cut in, apparently still prickly with him: 'But we have shown select copies to Tessa Kane to see if she recognised the location. She says not. Needless to say, the inspector and I will be talking to Robert McQuarrie this evening.'

'So it's coincidental?' asked Scobie.

'That's still to be investigated,' Ellen said, with a glance at Challis.

'You think Janine McQuarrie was blackmailing people?' a Mornington detective asked. 'Blackmailed the wrong person?'

'It's possible,' said Challis. 'We know she could be censorious and vindictive.'

'Blackmailed her own husband?'

'Could be.'

'Maybe she was followed by one of her blackmail victims yesterday,' Scobie suggested. He had a scarf around his scrawny neck; he'd been about to go home when informed of the briefing.

'Yes.'

'Maybe she's been at it for a while,' Scobie went on, 'and her husband—or whoever—finally jacked up or discovered her identity.'

'It's also possible,' said Ellen heatedly, 'that she was getting more and more miserable in her marriage to a man who dragged her along to sex parties. Maybe he made her have sex with his mates and she didn't like it. Then she read Tessa Kane's article and decided to take advantage of the fact that everyone was talking about it.'

One of the Mornington detectives cast her a sardonic look, as though to say he'd expect a female detective to speculate about feelings like this. 'Or she got jealous of Robert for having sex with other women,' he said, and Ellen flushed.

'Maybe she was seen taking the photographs,' Scobie said.

'These are all candid shots,' Ellen replied. 'No one knows they're being photographed.'

Challis nodded. 'I shouldn't think that cameras are allowed at these parties. Janine McQuarrie took her mobile phone with her and either no one paid any attention to it, or it was well concealed—as you can see, some people are carrying towels and bits and pieces of clothing. It's as if Janine went there with the express intention of taking photographs of certain men in compromising positions. Did she want money? To ruin reputations? To break up relationships?'

They all continued to speculate, and Challis watched and listened, occasionally prodding, occasionally demurring. Night had closed in outside the windows, the black wet streets giving back ribbons of red and yellow from headlights and brakelights, and hissing as tyres passed back and forth in the hour leading to dinner and evening TV in warm rooms. He thought of his cold house and shivered.

'We need to find out who held this particular party,' he said finally, 'and where and how often, and whether or not they have guest lists. Above all, we need to identify these other three men and ask if anyone has attempted to blackmail them.'

'What do you mean, "anyone"?' said Scobie.

'Maybe Janine had an accomplice.'

They slumped at the thought, but continued to brood over the photographs and motives. 'Assuming someone was blackmailed,' Scobie said, 'he'll still be around. The killers he hired might not be, but he will.'

'That's assuming that he—or she—hired the killers,' said Challis. 'Even so, we need to show Georgia head shots of the three men other than her father to see if she recognises the driver or the shooter.' He cocked his head to stare at the photographs.

Ellen was watching Challis. 'But first we talk to Robert.'

Challis nodded gloomily. 'Tonight.'

'Sooner you than me,' Scobie said. The case was a potential career breaker and they all knew it.

Challis ignored him. 'With any luck, Robert knows who the other three are, and we'll hit them first thing tomorrow morning.'

Everyone was tired, a tiredness encouraged by the revelations, the sluggish heated air and the deepening darkness. Ellen yawned, setting off yawns in the others. After a while they stretched, stirred, tidied their folders and pulled on their coats. Challis thanked them and began to take down the photographs. 'Again, keep this to yourselves. These people might be pathetic and guilty of bad taste but they haven't broken any laws that I know of. We'll presume the sex was consensual and no one was under age. Janine McQuarrie's murder might have nothing to do with these people or the fact that she took their photographs. She might have been titillating herself, or herself and Robert. In other words, we don't want a situation where the rich and powerful suddenly find themselves on the internet or splashed all over the front page.'

'Boss,' they murmured, filing out good-naturedly.

30

At eight o'clock that Wednesday evening, almost thirty-six hours after Janine McQuarrie's murder, Challis and Ellen parked the unmarked Falcon in the street, said 'No comment' to a handful of reporters, and walked up the driveway of an Edwardian house set on a ridge above a rocky cove in Mount Eliza. The house was angled to allow million-dollar views down to Sorrento from one bank of windows and across the Bay to the irregular towers of the city from another, but right now the sea was black, the coastal towns a belt of twinkling lights, the distant city a yellow glow that swallowed the stars.

Meg answered, smiling tiredly in greeting and showing them through to a sitting room with drawn curtains and a heaped log fire burning briskly. 'Make yourselves comfortable,' she said. 'Robert's in his study. I'll let him know you're here.'

She was back a moment later. 'He won't be long.'

She chatted, Challis listening with half an ear, wondering why Robert McQuarrie was taking so long. Phoning his father to complain? Or was it a typical and unconscious exercise of power to make them wait? An insult, maybe? This room needs colours and clutter to soften it, he decided, glancing around. It was a vast, starkly white room with plenty of chrome, glass and polished wood everywhere in hard angles.

'You don't need to talk to Georgia, do you?' Meg asked anxiously. 'It took me ages to get her to sleep.'

Challis shook his head. 'No.'

Then Robert McQuarrie came in like a man burdened with fools, still wearing suit trousers, black shoes and a loosened tie over a pale blue cotton business shirt. Here was the busy tycoon who never rests, not even at home, not even when his wife has just been murdered. 'I hope you're here with good news,' he said.

Challis glanced at Meg, who got the message and hurried out wordlessly, casting them a shy, relieved smile. A moment later they heard a television in another room, the theme music to the American cop show where the main guy always muttered, 'Keep me posted'.

'Well?'

'Mr McQuarrie, this is a photograph of you having sex with a woman who is not your wife,' Challis said.

McQuarrie took the photograph, screwed his eyes shut and rocked on his feet. When his voice came it was hoarse and full of strain. 'This isn't what you think.'

'Oh?' Ellen demanded. 'And what do we think?'

'That I'm some kind of, you know…'

He couldn't finish and they waited for other reactions. Finally Challis fed him the photographs. 'The dozen or so photographs we've obtained seem to concentrate on four men. Here are the other three.'

'I have to sit down.'

'Would you like a drink?'

McQuarrie eyed a glass cabinet, dithered, and poured himself a scotch. 'Does my father have to know about this?'

Challis and Ellen said nothing.

McQuarrie perched stiffly on the edge of an armchair. 'Please. It would destroy him, destroy my mother.'

Challis shrugged and McQuarrie got encouragement from it. 'You got these from the Kane woman,' he said poisonously.

'Oh?' said Challis. 'Why do you say that?'

McQuarrie curled his upper lip. 'I'm not stupid. She published that article, and hey presto, these photos appear. Your relationship with her is common knowledge. You doing her dirty work, or is she doing yours?'

His demeanour seemed to say that Tessa was scum and so therefore was Challis, for consorting with her. Challis tensed, wanting to wipe the man's expression off his face.

McQuarrie saw something in him and paled a little, and swallowed heavily from his glass of scotch. It revived him. 'Tessa Kane's on the way out, you know. She's finished. She has no idea of community feeling and should never have been put in charge of a local newspaper.'

The bluster can mean two things, Challis thought: that Robert McQuarrie honestly thinks Tessa took the photos and they're unrelated to the murder of his wife, or he's a guilty man attempting to misdirect us.

'Can you tell me where the photos were taken?'

McQuarrie shifted uncomfortably. 'I don't think I should. It doesn't matter where. But I will be having words with them. Opening themselves to a journalist is one thing, allowing photographs to be taken is quite another.'

'Sir,' said Ellen with barely concealed contempt, 'the longer you hold out on us the more likely it is that these photos are passed around and find their way onto the net, to the media and to your parents. At present it's strictly need-to-know and involves only a handful of trusted officers. I can't promise it will stay like that.'

'You can't bully me,' McQuarrie said. He moistened his mouth.

Challis said evenly, 'I want you to tell us—immediately—who these other men are and where these photos were taken.'

'They have a right to privacy...consenting adults...gladly sue you *and* the Kane woman...' Robert McQuarrie muttered, jumping from thought to thought as his gaze jumped from object to object in the room.

'It's not illegal,' he went on. 'We weren't doing anything wrong.'

Ellen studied him. 'Doesn't it bother you to know that someone you trusted has been taking candid photographs of you having sex with strangers?'

'Trusted? Tessa Kane? That's a laugh.'

'Not Tessa Kane. We obtained these from someone rather closer to you than that.'

McQuarrie's face grew desolate for a moment as he looked down an empty, unpromising road. 'Who?'

'We think you know.'

'I don't, I swear I don't.'

'We think you do.'

'Shouldn't you be looking for whoever killed my wife instead of hassling me about my private life?'

'Mr McQuarrie,' Ellen said pitilessly, 'what do you *think* we're doing, showing you these photographs, asking these questions, if not investigating the murder of your wife?'

A pause while he took this in. 'A coincidence,' he said.

'Is it?'

'You can't honestly believe she was shot because she took part in some harmless...' He'd scattered the photographs across a coffee table but now grabbed and scrutinised them. 'These don't even *show* Janine.'

'Think about it, sir.'

'I don't know,' he wailed. 'Maybe someone's wife or girlfriend arranged to have her shot out of jealousy, but what's that got to do with these photos?'

'Or maybe her own husband got jealous and arranged to have her shot.'

'No! That didn't happen.'

'Then what did happen?' Challis said, putting plenty of whiplash into it; he was tired of Robert McQuarrie.

In a distant room the television continued to murmur and the wind blew around the house. 'Look, I don't know anything about these photos. I didn't see anyone with a camera, and Janine's not even in—' He froze, and Ellen saw the shock as he realised. 'Oh God,' he muttered.

'Exactly, Robert,' Challis said, the familiarity offending the superintendent's son, 'these photographs were found stored on your wife's mobile phone, the phone you were so anxious for me to return to you.'

McQuarrie looked stricken. 'I didn't know that! How could I have known that? Dad simply told me to make sure I got all of Janine's things back!'

'Did he?'

Ellen cut in. 'Did Janine enjoy the sex parties, Rob?'

McQuarrie gave her a look full of hate but said nothing.

'She didn't, did she?'

McQuarrie swallowed and looked about the room. 'She didn't really enjoy that side of our marriage.'

'So you thought you'd kickstart her erotic life?'

'You're demeaning her, you're demeaning me.'

'Or was it that you could have sex with as many women as you liked without feeling guilty, because it was all open and your wife was having sex with other men?'

'I don't expect you to understand. When you're highly sexed you—'

'Anyone less highly sexed than you I have yet to meet,' Ellen snarled. 'With these photographs, Janine had a hold over you. You'd be ruined if they were made public. A laughing-stock. A disappointment to your parents, especially your law-and-order father. Janine showed them to you, told you to be faithful or she'd ruin you, but misjudged you badly and she lost her life as a result.'

'I was in Sydney!'

'So who did you hire, Rob?' Ellen demanded.

Challis eyed her warily. She was tense with anger, disgust and disappointment. Their closeness of early in the day was quite gone. She wasn't a prude, but hated the dishonesty and sly tawdriness of the sex parties, the photographs and the actions of husbands like Robert McQuarrie. He wondered if she were thinking of deceit, illicit love and empty marriages.

Meanwhile McQuarrie was outraged. 'Do you think I know people like that, hired killers, hitmen, or whatever they're called?'

A fair question, Challis thought. He didn't answer it. Then McQuarrie followed it with another fair question. 'Besides, how do you arrange something like this in just a few hours?'

Ellen pounced. 'Meaning?'

McQuarrie saw the trap he was in and tried to backpedal. 'I mean, the killers obviously needed time to learn her movements, where she lived, where she worked, that kind of thing.'

'Robert, you said "a few hours". Janine showed you the photographs, didn't she? And you made a few phone calls and—'

'No!' He gave them a hunted look and shrank in his chair. 'She didn't show them to me. They arrived in the post.'

'The post?'

'In a plain envelope. I assumed Tessa Kane or someone at her office had sent them.'

'When was this?'

'Monday.'

'Was there anything in the envelope besides the photos?'

'No.'

'No blackmail demand?'

'No.'

'Did you keep the envelope and the photos?'

'Yes. I hid them. I wanted to hold onto them in case there *was* a blackmail attempt.'

'Wise man,' Challis said, his tone disbelieving.

'If I'd known Janine had taken the photos and sent them to me I would have tried to talk to her about it, I swear.'

They watched him.

'Have you talked to the other three men?' Ellen demanded.

'No.'

'But you know them?'

'Yes.'

And he gave them the names of a surgeon, an accountant and a funds manager.

'I don't want you alerting these characters,' Challis warned.

'Of course not,' Robert McQuarrie said, relieved now to think that Challis was letting him off the hook, if only for a while.

31

Tessa Kane worked late, stewing about the tone of her interview with Ellen Destry. Interview? Interrogation was more like it. Destry had been clearly hostile. Now it was after ten o'clock and she was locking up for the night, and had just returned the keys to her bag when a voice growled, 'Stay out of my private life.'

She jumped, convinced that her stalker had waited for her. He was escalating, making personal contact and not relying on hate mail and stones through windows any more. Swallowing, she forced herself to turn around. 'Mr Mead,' she said, oddly relieved.

It was short-lived.

'You called on my wife unannounced.'

He wore a heavy overcoat, his shoes gleamed, and drops of misty rain dotted his face, granting him a look of powerful emotions held barely in check. He took a step towards her, passing out of the range of the nearby streetlight. She glanced past him, seeking helpful passersby or escape routes, but the entrance to the *Progress* building was at the side, not the front, and screened by bushes. There was no comfort from the steady stream of traffic on the main road, and at that moment no pedestrians on the footpath.

'I'm not going to attack you, stupid cow,' Mead said. 'But I'm warning you to stay away from my wife.'

'I merely—'

'Well, don't, okay?'

There was a spasm of something in his face, not anger but doubt. Tessa felt her courage returning. 'Another perspective, that's all I want.'

'Ask me, if you're so keen to know.'

'I have asked you. I get nothing useful.'

Now Mead was his old self again. His lip curled. 'I don't do special favours. The information I give you is the same as the information I give the Melbourne and national media.'

'It's public relations bullshit, that's what it is. I write my own stories, not a rehash of some press release. You still haven't answered my specific allegations regarding falsified staffing levels and falsified reports being filed by your section heads. There are lots of irregularities that I intend to follow up on.'

'Go your hardest.'

'And what do you intend to do about the self-mutilations?'

Charlie Mead showed her his sharp teeth as he turned and walked away. 'My officers have all been offered trauma counselling.'

That was enough for Tessa. When she got home she fired up her laptop, a glass of red at her elbow, and began to trawl through the internet for what it could tell her about Charlie Mead.

Vyner had driven back to Melbourne after burying Gent and stowing the shovel and his outer clothing in builders' skips on the Nepean Highway. He showered, caught a movie, ate pasta at a sidewalk café on Southbank, and now was watching the late news on TV. Thank Christ there'd been no further developments, no more clues found or anonymous callers to cause him a headache. He switched off and peered out at the night through a gap in the curtains he kept permanently drawn. Tenth floor, but he didn't have one of the river and cityscape views, just views of wet streets and buildings reflecting light like panels of glass or ice. He shivered. No one was out there, but he could feel the world closing in a little. He got out his journal and wrote: *Sing out the names of the lost ages. Uncover the warrior codes of the universe.*

That was all the boost he needed. He was ready when his mobile phone received a new text message.

Sorted?

Vyner sent back confirmation. Yes, the anonymous caller was dead and buried.

Andy Asche knocked off a few beers in the main bar of the Fiddlers Creek pub after footy training and got home late evening to find Natalie Cobb pacing up and down in his sitting room, Jet blaring away on the CD player, pity the old pensioner who lived in the adjoining flat. She must have found his spare key—on top of the fuse box; he'd have to re-think that—and let herself in. She was still wearing a suggestion of her Waterloo Secondary College uniform and it was clear to Andy that she'd been choofing a weed or dosing herself with E or ice or speed since the burglary they'd pulled that afternoon, and was pretty hyper there in his sitting room.

And paranoid. 'I think this cop's wife is spying on me.'

'Who?'

'Sutton, a dee at Waterloo. Know him?'

Andy didn't know any of the detectives, or any of the uniforms except John Tankard, his footy coach. He went to the window and glanced out. Salmon Street was quiet, the bay dark and still beyond the mangrove flats. 'What about him?'

'His wife works for Community Health, looks in on me and my sister and my mum, but I know she's a spy. Fucking cow.'

Pacing up and down, beautiful and agitated and stoned out of her brain. 'Listen,' she went on, 'I need some dosh really badly.'

'Already? What happened to the cash I gave you earlier?'

As if he didn't know.

She doubled over then straightened, her fists tight against her breasts, beseeching him. 'Andy, please, can't we knock over another house?'

'Not tonight we can't,' he said firmly. 'People are watching TV, tucking the kids into bed. Besides, it's too soon.'

'*Please*, Andy. I'll pay ya back.'

In the end he scrounged up $100 and she slowed down enough to offer to do him with her mouth, her hands, even her feet if that's what he wanted. He smiled sadly. 'It's okay, Nat. You don't owe me anything. Listen, we'll pull another job tomorrow, okay?'

'Where have you been?' her husband demanded, the moment she set foot in the house.

Ellen removed her scarf and jacket unhurriedly and hung them on a hook beside the back door. She checked the time on her watch, still drawing out her movements: almost 9.30. The interrogation of Robert McQuarrie had taken an hour, the drive back to Waterloo—where she'd dropped Challis—and then home had taken twenty minutes. She was in a severely contestable mood anyway, without her husband setting her off. She'd badly wanted to punish Robert McQuarrie, and didn't trust her feelings around Challis, which made her mad. And now here was Alan, getting right in her face.

'Interviewing a subject,' she said, moving around him.

'I bet.'

'What's that supposed to mean?' she said, stalking by him into the kitchen.

'You gave you-know-who a lift home, right? What, did he ask you in for a drink? Whip you up something to eat? Or maybe you stopped off somewhere first.'

'Give it a rest.'

Her dinner, a congealed Thai curry from a can dolloped onto rice, sat mute and unloved on the table. The kitchen—table, benches, sink—was spotless. Ellen knew at once that she was expected to be full of praise and thanks. Instead, she wordlessly slid her plate into the microwave, set the timer and poured herself a glass of wine.

'So, were you?'

'Was I what?'

'Out with Challis,' said Alan tightly.

'Yes.'

'What did you do?'

'I told you, we interviewed a subject. In Mount Eliza, if you must know.'

There was a pause, and into it Alan said, 'Did you have to give him a lift home afterwards?'

She enjoyed being obtuse. 'Who? The subject?'

His jaw and fists went tight, and it occurred to her that he'd hit her if she pushed hard enough. She felt neutral about that right now, as though it were an unimportant hypothesis to be tested one day.

'Challis,' he said in his strangled voice.

She gave him a reprieve. 'He's got a loan car.'

Unfortunately, she wanted to add.

The microwave beeped and she fetched her plate, which hissed and steamed. Alan watched her eat. She wished he wouldn't.

'Like it?'

'Not bad.'

'I waited, but got hungry,' he said innocently, and she reckoned that she was supposed to see him, in her mind's eye, as boyish, vulnerable and uncomplicated again, the lad she married. She ate. She was ravenous.

'Saw the news. Still working the McQuarrie murder?'

'Yes.'

'Any contenders?'

'A few.'

'So no time off in the near future?'

'No.'

'I thought,' he said, 'that we could go up to town, spend a night in the Windsor, catch up with Larrayne.'

In and of itself, this sounded like a pretty nice idea to Ellen, but her instincts told her that Alan was proposing it because he wanted to keep her away from Challis and remind her that she had family responsibilities. *Wifely* responsibilities. And because he didn't know her, or know her any more, he thought a romantic gesture would deflect her.

'Impossible at the moment,' she said, draining her wine.

'You're owed time off for yesterday. I've got Friday off.'

'Alan, we're in the middle of a major inquiry.'

'You and Challis.'

'And the others, several others.'

He held up his hands placatingly. 'I just want you to look after yourself, that's all—not run yourself ragged.'

Yeah, right, Ellen thought.

'I mean, did you really have to rush off early this morning to pick up his highness? Why didn't he call for a taxi? Instead, you have to detour all that way and pick him up. Where does he live again?'

Ellen told him without thinking, then checked herself and eyed him closely. But her husband was a plausible man, a good actor, and was absentmindedly flicking through the cane basket of household accounts. God knew what fresh hell he'd find there. She poured herself wine that she didn't really want but which would occupy her hands and mouth for a while.

32

They formed three teams and early on Thursday morning hit the surgeon, the accountant and the funds manager. Six o'clock, no dawn light leaking into the sky yet, houses slumbering or only just stirring; an hour when heads are unclear and lips loose.

Challis and Ellen heard later from Scobie Sutton and the Mornington detectives that the surgeon and the funds manager had displayed plenty of genuine shock, dismay and outrage, so it was clear they hadn't been tipped off by Robert McQuarrie. After the outrage had come shame and fear. They asked to be understood; they asked that their wives be spared the truth. The surgeon had attended the sex parties with his sister-in-law, the funds manager with his secretary. Their alibis were solid, and they confirmed that yes, they'd received photos of themselves in the post on Monday: no accompanying note, but, like Robert McQuarrie, they'd assumed someone at the *Progress* had sent the photographs and were fearful of blackmail and media exposure.

The accountant was a different kettle of fish, nothing like Robert McQuarrie, the surgeon or the funds manager. His name was Hayden

Coulter and he lived alone in a rammed-earth loft house on a slope above Penzance Beach. The driveway was narrow and the turning circle awkward, so Challis did what he always did in unfamiliar places and unknown circumstances—parked the car so that it faced the road and allowed him and Ellen an unimpeded escape route.

Coulter greeted them at the door wearing a shirt and tie, trousers and carpet slippers. His face was clean and tight from the razor and there were comb tracks in his shower-wet hair. About forty, Challis guessed, and used to playing his cards close to his chest. He regarded them expressionlessly, invited them in out of the cold.

They followed him through to the kitchen, into the odours of fresh coffee and toast.

'Can I get you something?'

Ellen glanced at Challis and answered for both of them. 'Coffee, please.'

'Pull up a pew.'

Coulter poured the coffee and sat across the table from them, precise, contained, watchful, his grey eyes clear and untroubled. He said nothing and betrayed no curiosity or apprehension. He'll wait us out, Challis thought, sliding a photograph across the table.

'Is this you, Mr Coulter?'

'Yes.'

'What can you tell us about it?'

'I'm having sex with a woman, on a bed, being watched by other men and women.'

'Did you receive a copy of this photograph in the mail on Monday?'

'Yes.'

'What did you make of that?'

'I made nothing of it. I have nothing to hide. I cannot and will not be blackmailed.'

'You received a blackmail demand?'

'No.'

'Then how do you know it's blackmail?'

'I assume that I'm being softened up for blackmail,' Coulter said, blowing across the steaming surface of his coffee.

'You say you can't and won't be blackmailed,' Ellen said. 'Is that bravado?'

'I can't and won't be blackmailed because I simply don't care enough,' Coulter said. 'So what that I go to sex parties? I have no family who would be shamed if word got out, and my clients certainly wouldn't care. I represent interests in the horse-racing industry and my reputation with them rests solely on my ability to make and save them money—which I do very successfully.'

Challis disliked the man's coldness and vanity. 'Did you build this house yourself?' he asked, noting Coulter's work-hardened hands, incongruous against the soft, costly fabric of his shirt.

'I did.'

'Impressive.'

Coulter said nothing, aiming for a prohibitive silence.

Ellen drained her coffee. 'Have you any idea who sent you the photographs?'

'Janine McQuarrie. That's why you're here, isn't it? You think I killed her?'

'Did you?'

Coulter looked bored. 'Why? What would be the point?'

'She threatened your reputation.'

'Perhaps you weren't listening: I don't care about my reputation.'

'The photos—or Janine herself—were a threat in other ways.'

'I've never met the woman.'

'She was murdered not far from here,' Challis said. 'Was she coming to see you?'

'No. I wasn't here anyway, but in my office in Mornington and needless to say I can prove it. But perhaps she was on her way here with more photographs.'

It occurred to Challis then that if Janine was murdered because she'd attempted to blackmail someone, wouldn't that someone want to search her home and office for all copies of the photographs? Yet neither place had been broken into. On the other hand, Robert presumably had access to the keys.

As if reading his thoughts, Coulter said, 'Did she have copies with her when she was shot?'

Never let them ask the questions. 'How did you know that Janine McQuarrie took your photograph?'

'I saw her do it.'

'With what?'

'Her mobile phone. Look, I go to these sex parties to look at faces and responses. Everyone else watches the sex. I saw her, I saw what she was doing. It amused me—though I was surprised to get photos in the mail. I assumed she was taking photos to meet some kind of basic and boring erotic need.'

'Did anyone else see her?' Ellen asked. Challis could see tension in her jaw, meaning that she loathed Coulter.

'Possibly, but that's your job, isn't it? I can just see it: the police going in heavy-handed, knocking on forty or fifty doors, throwing a scare into people who until then thought their grubby secret lives were safe from scrutiny, and they're all going to deny knowing anything about Janine McQuarrie and her pathetic photographs.'

'You're the one who's pathetic,' Ellen said.

Coulter grinned to know that he'd goaded her and Challis saw at last, behind the cool façade, an empty man.

'Mr Coulter, you say your clients are in the horse-racing industry.'

'Yes, and I daresay some of them are dishonest, and a handful know the type of men who will shoot someone dead for a few thousand bucks.'

'Do you know such men?'

'If I do, they haven't announced themselves to me.'

'Do you hear whispers?'

'I've heard whispers all my life. Am I going to inform? No?'

'But you might know who to go to if you wanted someone shot dead?'

'I might, but I don't. I don't care enough about anything to want anyone dead. I can't raise the emotional heat. There's nothing I want to preserve, no gain I want to make. The woman could have published my photo on the net, for all I care. Now if that's all, I have an appointment at a stable in Mornington in thirty minutes.'

'Early,' Challis observed.

'Horse-racing people are early people,' Coulter said.

That's how it's going to be between us, Challis thought. No confession or clear signs of guilt. Just a hard slog through Coulter's past and present.

33

Robert McQuarrie and the other men had identified the settings of Janine McQuarrie's photographs as two bedrooms in a house in the old part of Mornington, where solid dwellings sat on leafy streets a short walk away from the park, the beaches and Main Street. Ellen drove, slowing at one point to indicate a low-slung modern building that had gone to seed: drifts of paper and cellophane caught in the fence, untended grass, peeling paint, playground equipment growing a patina of rust and mould. 'That was a heartbreaker,' she said.

She didn't need to explain. A childcare centre; allegations of sexual abuse against the husband and wife who ran the place; no charges laid after a fruitless investigation. But the case remained open.

'And a hundred metres further on we have the Wavells and their wholesome sex parties,' she continued.

Anton and Laura Wavell, aged in their early forties, and both at home at 8.45 on a Thursday morning. 'We work from home,' Anton explained, showing them into the sitting room. He was a thin, gingery, nondescript man with long pale fingers that fluttered from his belt to his mouth to his neck.

'We offer IT support,' Laura explained. 'System upgrades, data recovery, website design, virus eradication. So, if you ever have any problems...'

She's drumming up business, Challis thought, even as she suspects why we're here. He eyed the Wavells. He'd stopped being surprised by the resemblances that husbands and wives developed to each other: like her husband, Laura Wavell was gingery. She sported rampant freckles on a broad face, and coarse red hair tamed by large clips.

'Would you like to see?' she asked, indicating a closed door at the end of the room.

There was something desperate about the question, as though Challis and Ellen might think better of the Wavells if shown a room devoted to cutting-edge technology and evidence of plain, everyday hard work. In Challis's experience, guilt was never very far from the surface when it came to the sexual proclivities of ordinary people. Only hardened paedophiles never showed a conscience or remorse. The Wavells were probably close to protesting sulkily and fearfully that they were only helping others have a bit of fun. Challis had no moral opinion one way or the other about the sex parties: he didn't care what the participants did; he only cared when someone stopped playing the game.

'Another time,' he said, and sat in a pillowy sofa, obliging the others to sit. There was a plasma widescreen TV in one corner of the room, a small bar, a scatter of Ikea easychairs, bright rugs and cushions, track lighting on the walls and ceiling. With the wintry sun picking up dust motes and finger smears, the room held a less than tepid erotic charge. He distributed Janine McQuarrie's photographs over the surface of a coffee table that had been constructed from recycled floorboards in the form of a low, wide box with a pair of shallow push–pull drawers. 'These were taken in two of your bedrooms last Saturday night.'

For some time there was silence. Anton's hands were busy and he swallowed; Laura straightened her back, slanted her knees to one side, and folded her hands in her narrow lap.

'We did nothing wrong,' she said.

'We certainly didn't take these photos,' Anton said. 'Search the place if you like. No hidden cameras.'

'Cameras are strictly forbidden.'

'Against etiquette.'

'Oh, etiquette,' Ellen said, and Challis saw something dangerous in her face and voice. Ellen in full flight could be something to see. It even produced results from time to time.

'We have standards,' Anton said.

'Standards,' said Ellen flatly.

'Yes.'

'Do you know these men?'

'They come to our occasions.'

'Occasions. That's a good one,' Ellen said. 'I'll see if I can occasion my husband tonight, if he's not too tired.'

Anton flushed. 'I can read you like a book. You think there's something smutty about our parties because you yourself think sex is a smutty thing. It's not.'

'I love a bit of smut,' Ellen said. 'Hal?'

'Me too,' Challis said carefully, wondering if her fury came from disappointment with him. He'd wanted her yesterday, and the day before that, and she'd picked up on it. He hadn't acted: had she wanted him to?

He placed a photograph of Janine McQuarrie on the coffee table, the studio portrait taken for Bayside Counselling Services. 'Do you know this woman?'

They peered with dutiful frowns. 'She's been here.'

'Been to the sex parties?'

'Yes,' Anton said stiffly.

'One of the wives,' Laura said, as if to stress legitimacy.

Ellen leaned forward and with great sharpness and concentration said, 'She was murdered two days ago, almost to the hour.'

They knew. Janine's likeness had been plastered all over the TV news and daily press. 'I fail to see what that has to do with us,' Anton said.

'Don't you?'

'No.'

'She took these photos at one of your parties and now she's dead.'

A pause. '*She* took them? How?'

'Mobile phone.'

The Wavells shifted about as if kicking themselves for not anticipating that, for not policing it.

'But why?' Laura asked.

Ellen ignored her. 'Tell me more about these orgies of yours,' she said in her dangerous, reckless way.

'They're not orgies! Tell her, Anton.'

'They're not orgies.'

'Okay, group-sex gangbangs. Tell me more about them.'

'You're deliberately goading us, deliberately cheapening everything,' said Laura.

'We're not doing anything wrong, anything illegal,' said Anton. 'No drugs, no coercion, no underage girls, no sexually transmitted diseases, just healthy safe sex for consenting adults.'

'*Multiple* sex acts between *desperate* adults,' Ellen snarled.

'They're not desperate. Tell her, Anton.'

'*Couples*,' Anton said, 'who already have sexual partners and want to explore and extend the possibilities.'

'Sounds like desperation and fear to me,' Ellen said. 'You knew Janine McQuarrie was taking these photographs, didn't you?'

'No. Absolutely not.'

'You encouraged it.'

'No way.'

'You *commissioned* it,' Challis cut in. 'You're running a nice little blackmail racket and Janine was your partner. You sent these photographs to four of your potential victims to soften them up before making demands for money.'

'Don't be stupid. Why would we do that? Our parties, as you like to call them, would soon grind to a halt.'

'Power. Money. Revenge.'

'Not interested. We're decent people, not criminals.'

Into the silence that followed, Anton said meekly, 'Do we need a lawyer?'

Ellen pointed to a pale, grainy, globular backside. 'Here's one.'

He flushed angrily. 'Are you going to shut us down?'

'Shut you down?' said Ellen in amazement. 'Who do you think we are?'

34

That was the early hours of Thursday. A raw wind had risen by the time Challis and Ellen returned to CIU, and there was a message for Challis to telephone his elderly next-door neighbour. 'A huge gum tree's come down across your driveway, Hal. It's sticking out into the road. I tried to cut it up but can't start my chainsaw.'

'Try the shire,' Challis said, shrugging out of his coat.

'I did. There are trees and branches down everywhere and they can't promise they'll get around to it today.'

Challis cursed. Ten o'clock. He was obliged to attend the Navy inquest at eleven. 'I'll be there in fifteen minutes.'

He dragged on his coat again, grabbed his laptop and inquest notes, and stopped at Ellen's desk. 'I'll be out for two or three hours. I want you to call on Janine's sister. I doubt if Janine was the confiding type, but I'm pretty sure Meg intuited something about her recent activities.'

Ellen sat back in her chair, tapping a pen against her teeth. 'Everything in this case is a trace of a ghost of a faint chance of a possibility.'

He was relieved to see her smile. 'Eloquently put.'

Challis drove to his home along roads festooned with twigs, branches and long scraps of bark. By the time he'd cursed his chainsaw into life and sliced the tree up and rolled the segments of trunk out of the way, and showered and dressed again, he was late for the inquest.

The ruling was as expected: the Navy armourer had shot dead the Fiddlers Creek Hotel bouncer, and then committed suicide. He'd been drinking heavily in the main bar, but was also under the influence of a cocktail of drugs bought from a Navy cadet, and this, compounded by his sense of grievance at being ejected from the hotel, had disturbed the balance of his mind.

But the coroner went further. Reading from Challis's own report, he noted that the armourer had used a Browning automatic handgun from the armoury, and recommended that an investigation be held into how it had been removed despite electronic surveillance measures and bi-weekly spot checks on the inventory, and whether or not other weapons had been removed, and if so, who had them.

The proceedings continued briskly and by early afternoon Challis was stepping out into a ragged wind, fits of sunlight and obscuring cloud masses. He hurried to his car, checked his mobile, and saw that Superintendent McQuarrie had called him. Twice.

'Challis, sir.'

'Finally. Was your mobile switched off, Inspector?'

'Coroner's inquest, sir, that Navy shooting.'

'And?'

'Murder suicide.'

Into the pause that followed, the superintendent said tightly, 'I understand you went to see my son again.'

'Sir.'

'May I ask why?'

'Loose ends,' Challis said. Surely Robert hadn't told his father about last night's visit. The sister-in-law? No—most probably one of McQuarrie's spies, he decided.

'Such as?'

Challis debated with himself. Could he reasonably expect to keep the super from learning about the photographs? Either way, he was in a bind: damned if he told the super, damned if he didn't. 'It was partly a courtesy call, sir, and we went over old ground to see if he could remember anything further about his wife.'

'Old ground? What about new ground, Inspector?'

As if to suggest that Challis hadn't been thorough the first time around and liked to spend his days upsetting important and influential people.

'In the absence of leads we have to check phone records again,' said Challis, 'read correspondence, look for holes and inconsistencies in witness statements, as well as talk to new witnesses who might come forward.' *Jesus.*

McQuarrie was silent. Then he said, 'I thought we agreed this was a case of the wrong person in the wrong place at the wrong time.'

You agreed it, Challis thought. 'It's important to keep an open mind, sir.'

'Dig deeper into this witness protection woman.'

'Sir.'

There was another silence, and then McQuarrie seemed to tiptoe through his words: 'Is there anything about Janine that I should know, Hal? A secret lover? Was she skimming funds from the clinic? Blackmailing her clients?'

Is McQuarrie simply waiting to be told the worst? wondered Challis, or does he know something that we don't? 'Whatever it is, we'll find it,' Challis said. You had to say things like that to your boss and a fearful public. He meant it, but he was saying it to shut McQuarrie up. Anxious to get going, he finished the conversation and returned to his office in CIU and a backlog of paperwork that owed plenty to the superintendent's cost-cutting measures. The budget destroys resources, Challis thought, the paperwork destroys time, and the jargon destroys reason.

Fed up, he went in search of Ellen. 'Did Meg tell you anything?'

'Yes and no. They weren't close, but she did feel that Janine had seemed happier than usual in recent weeks.'

Challis drew his hands tiredly down his cheeks. 'An affair? Someone in the swingers scene?'

Ellen shrugged. 'There's nothing to indicate a lover in her e-mails, phone records or ordinary mail. She didn't confide in anyone. If there is a lover, she's covered her tracks well. Do you want me to keep looking?'

He shook his head absently, returned to his office and attacked his in-tray again. At one point he reached for his laptop. It wasn't there. It wasn't in his car. Then he remembered: he'd left it on his kitchen table. He'd gone home, changed into overalls, cut up the fallen tree, raced off to the inquest. Challis always paid attention to his instincts, and this one was a creeping sensation that told him not to waste a minute of time.

He ran downstairs to the carpark, climbed into the loan car and headed out of town. At the second roundabout he turned northwest, glancing briefly at Waterloo Mowers, where the lights were a dull yellow through a gauze of water droplets and a man in a japara was despondently assessing the ranks of lawn mowers parked on the grass outside. His tyres hissed and other cars tossed dirty scraps of water over his windscreen.

Soon he was driving between a dismal housing estate and a couple of waterlogged horse paddocks, and then was in undulating country, where costly lifestyle houses had scant views over Westernport Bay. Otherwise the houses here were older, faintly rundown fibro, weatherboard and brick-veneer farm dwellings amid rusty sheds, untidy pine trees, orchards and dams. It was turning out to be a wet winter, even this early in the season, and the dams were full, the clay backroads greasy, the roadside ditches running furiously, the floods washing drifts of grit and gravel from adjoining dirt roads across the sealed roads.

That's how Challis knew his own road, the dirty yellow-brown smear across the bitumen surface. He turned off, splashing through muddy potholes and hearing the heater fan cut out with a death rattle. He came to his driveway and turned in, passing the sawn logs and dead agapanthus stalks, and headed up towards the house, which looked damp, empty, almost forlorn, but familiar in all of its manifestations, and a true home, a haven through the years up until now.

And that's when he saw the marks in the lawn. Dark brown mud gouges stark against the green. His first thought was: *They got bogged.* His second and third were: *Who?* and *How did they get out?* His fourth, when he found the splintered back door, was: *Did they take the laptop?*

35

Challis made himself a coffee while he waited, careful how he touched things, even using his elbow to work the door of the fridge, and hooking out the milk container with the back of his thumb. As for the coffee pot, coffee jar and his 'old cops never die' mug, he'd yet to meet a burglar who paused to brew coffee. He didn't for a moment think the crime-scene techs would lift any prints other than his own—and some old ones of Tessa Kane's—but he knew the procedure, the irony being that, since he was a cop, his place would be given more than a cursory examination.

It was too cold to sit on his sundeck, and no sun anyway, only the grey light of a winter's afternoon, and so he set the central heating to high, sat at his kitchen table and made lists for his insurance company and CIU. Damage: jemmied back door, a broken fruit bowl (Italian, hand painted, a gift from Tessa), cracked CD covers. After a moment, he added the twin gouges in his lawn. Stolen: a jar of coins, approx. value $15; digital camera, $499; DVD player, $250; portable TV, $399;

answering machine, $70; cordless phone, $79; laptop, $2500; laptop case, $60. He walked through the house again, returned to the kitchen and added: Rockport walking shoes (new), $299; Swiss Army knife (ten years old, no longer have receipt); Walkman (broken); leather belt, $45. A third walk through yielded him the bedside clock, $25, and assorted jewellery (property of late wife), value approximately $2000.

Angela had wanted to take some of the rings and earrings into prison with her, but he told her they'd be the target of the other prisoners, and so, therefore, would she. 'They'll tear them off you,' he'd said, 'or they'll resent you. Everything will be here waiting for you when you get out.' And she'd said, 'But will *you* be waiting for me?' and he'd had no answer to that. As for the jewellery, he'd bought most of it—a watch, a white gold necklace, emerald earrings. The engagement ring had been his grandmother's, mercifully dead before she knew that Angela had tried to kill him.

He heard a car beyond his kitchen window and spotted Ellen arriving. The next stage would be routine: she'd assess the situation and then call for crime-scene technicians. He waited: there was a knock, and then she was standing in the kitchen doorway, concern on her face. 'You poor thing,' she said, making to cross the floor to where he stood by the window. He wanted her to, and wanted to cross to her, but things held them back.

She glanced about the kitchen, and then peered through the door into his sitting room. 'When you said damage, I was expecting to see a real mess,' she said.

He was puzzled. 'Minor damage,' he said, 'about what you'd expect in a burglary.'

'So it is a simple burglary?'

'Looks like it.'

'But you asked for me especially. I thought—'

'What?'

In a rush she said, 'I thought it might have been personal: you know, someone who had it in for you and wanted to cause major damage.'

He frowned, shook his head. 'Well, there's always someone, but no, this is a simple burglary, more or less.' He saw relief on her face then, as she shrugged out of her coat and swung it over the back of a chair. He said carefully, 'Did you think it was Alan?'

She flushed. 'Alan? No. Well, he can be jealous.'

Challis decided to let it go, but she seemed to fill the room and his senses, and oddly to make him feel less violated by the burglary. He pulled out a chair for himself and motioned for her to sit.

When she was settled she took out her notebook and headed an empty page with the date, time and location. But then, apparently in no hurry, she pushed the notebook aside. 'I'd really like one of your coffees.'

With relief he busied himself at the sink and cupboards. At times he passed quite close to her. Then he poured, set biscuits on a plate and sat with her again.

'So, Hal, burgled.'

'Uh-huh.'

He gave her a rundown on the damage and what had been stolen. 'Plaster casts of the tyre tracks on my lawn might help.'

'Will do,' she said.

He reached for her hand without thinking about it. 'There's a reason why I asked for you.'

She raised her eyebrows, but didn't withdraw her hand, which felt taut, bony but warm in his. Suddenly self-conscious, he jerked back. Was his neediness too apparent? Was he the subject of smirks and raised eyebrows among the female officers and civilians in the Waterloo police station? He saw himself as a clumsy man.

'This has to be low profile,' he said. 'I'm in trouble.'

He saw that he'd discomposed her. To cure it she reached for her notebook, all business now. 'In what way?'

He told her about his laptop.

'Oh dear.'

'I know.'

She stared at him through the steam from her mug. 'No password protection at all?'

He shook his head. 'I couldn't figure out how to set it up.'

'Dinosaur,' she said. 'Have you told anyone else?'

'My insurance company.'

'You didn't tell them what was on the laptop?'

'No.'

'You'll have to tell the super.'

Challis pushed his coffee away as if it were sour. 'How can I? He doesn't know about the photos.'

'But you've got case notes stored on it as well.'

'Yes.'

'He won't be pleased.'

'He's already pissed off with me. This will reinforce it.'

Ellen sighed. It was a sigh that said she commiserated with Challis, that she wasn't so different from him, that she'd stuffed up on occasion, too.

'Damage limitation. He'll want damage limitation.'

Challis nodded, and they were both silent for a time, picturing McQuarrie, the man's prim mouth, Rotary and golfing cronies, and air of satisfaction.

'Will you tell him, or will I?'

Challis was startled. 'I will, of course.'

'Into the breach.'

He nodded.

'How do I play it at the station?' she asked.

'Straightforward burglary, for now. Don't mention that the laptop contained sensitive material until I've squared it away with the super.'

'But if he wants it in my report, I'll have to—'

'Amend it. Don't worry, I'll cover your back.'

After a pause, Challis went on: 'Any other break-ins reported in the area today?'

She shook her head. 'There was one in Penzance Beach yesterday. An empty holiday house, but the next-door neighbour spotted a broken window.'

'One burglary among many.'

She glanced at him a little coldly. 'You'll get the full crime-scene treatment, Hal, don't worry.'

'Thanks.' He knew that simple burglaries generally didn't attract a concerted level of investigation. 'Have you any ideas? Does this fit a pattern?'

She shrugged. 'There are always break-ins, Hal, you know that. Town and rural.'

Challis nodded bleakly. 'I know.'

'Look at what was stolen. Small items, easily shifted and stored. We don't even know if it's the same gang or individual. A pattern only becomes apparent when specialist goods are taken and we can track where they end up.' She finished her coffee. 'Better make a start.'

They went from room to room, Challis indicating the location of each of the stolen possessions, Ellen taking notes for the crime-scene techs who would dust for prints.

Perhaps it was a combination of sensations, images and memories, and the conjunction of the homely with the erotic—a bedroom, the half light, a beautiful woman watching and listening, the particular arrangement of the bones and tendons at her throat and neck, his own months of deprivation—but Challis found himself reaching for Ellen. She reached for him. Out of their clumsy collision came a long kiss and then they parted sufficiently to look each other in the eye, slightly awed.

'I want you,' Ellen said simply.

'Me too.'

'You want yourself?'

It was the kind of dumb thing you said when the ground was slippery. Challis found the bare skin at her waist and spine, and they continued to stare at each other. 'Your hands are cold,' Ellen said, her skin seeming to crawl at his touch and absorb him at the same time. He leaned towards her again, and that's when a car growled over the gravel outside his window and Ellen said, 'Crime-scene techs.'

With a ragged sigh Challis said, 'You called them out before you came here?'

'Biggest mistake of my life.'

He planted a hungering, regretful kiss and looked at his watch. 'I'd better get it over and done with.'

'The super?'

'With any luck,' Challis said, 'I'll interrupt his golf.'

36

A bummer, Andy thought, getting bogged this morning.

And avoidable, too, if he'd twigged earlier that the day was going to turn out badly. First, Nat had been out of her skull. She'd turned up on time, thanks to a rare good-parenting impulse on the part of her mother, and was even dressed in her school uniform and carrying a packed lunch, but she'd turned up stoned.

Then, when timing and efficiency mattered, she'd been no use at all.

Andy had a special trailer for these Peninsula burglaries, towed each time by a ute or van stolen especially for the job. Andy's Mowing, like Jim's Mowing, that franchise operation you saw everywhere these days. High steel mesh sides, the handles of rakes, shovels, pruning shears and a lawnmower showing. A few padlocked aluminium lockers in the well of the trailer: anyone would think they contained secateurs, sprinkler nozzles, lengths of hose, weed poison, bags of blood-and-bone. They wouldn't think portable TVs, laptops, DVD players, leather coats, jewellery boxes, CD collections.

All that weight on board, he should have thought twice about letting Natalie drive, especially given the rain they'd been having lately. Before he could stop her she'd cut across the lawn on the way out, bogging the van. She'd then proceeded to cack herself laughing as she revved the motor and he pushed, getting himself sprayed with watery mud and grass in the process.

Then a tense moment when a guy delivering leaflets in a big four-wheel-drive had pulled up at the front gate, slipped a leaflet in the letterbox, and noticed their predicament. 'Need a hand getting out?'

'Yeah, thanks,' Andy had said, prattling on nervously about gardening work being slow in winter, and you had to be careful on these rural properties, three times he'd been bogged in the past month, and he'd have to come back tomorrow, do the right thing and patch the owner's lawn.

'Tell me about it,' the guy said, shoving a leaflet at him and hitching a towrope to the front of Andy's stolen Toyota van. Andy glanced at the leaflet as the guy pulled him out of the mud. 'Dave's Farm Drainage,' with a mobile number at the bottom.

'Thanks, Dave.'

'No problems,' Dave said, and was gone—Andy and Natalie forgotten, with any luck.

Andy took charge after that, grabbing the leaflet from the letterbox outside the gate, then removing copies from every letterbox along the road, and finally driving home to his place. With Natalie's 'help' he shifted the stolen goods to the back of the van and unhitched and stored the trailer. Finally he did what he always did with laptops: he transferred the contents of the hard drive to his PC with its 120 gig hard drive. He'd examine the files later. You got all kinds of stuff, porn, bank account details, sensitive documents. You never knew when it might come in useful.

And now it was mid afternoon and they were heading up to the pawnshops in the city. Nat was bored, restless, so he let her fiddle with the stolen laptop. She always got a kick out of scrolling through the intimate aspects of some stranger's life.

'Boring,' she said, her slender fingers flashing over the keys and rolling the cursor ball. 'Wait a minute.'

'What?'

'Wicked,' she said.

'What?'

Natalie was silent, her fingers busy. 'I think,' she said in a bright, wry, singsong voice, 'we hit a cop this morning.'

'Fuck!'

'Some case he's working on.'

Natalie continued to search the contents of the laptop. 'Hello. Dirty pictures.'

Andy thought a cop was as entitled as anyone to visit porn sites. 'So?'

'Not what you're thinking. These look like they might be evidence.'

'Evidence. Shit, Nat, I don't like it.'

Andy felt very tense suddenly. If they *had* hit a cop, and were in possession of evidence pertaining to a case, they were in deep shit. He wanted to put some distance in between the van and the Peninsula—quickly. They were on Stumpy Gully Road, approaching Eramosa Road, which would take them down to the highway. They could be out of the district and well on the way up to the city in less than thirty minutes. But should they hang onto the gear? He made the turn at Eramosa Road and headed down towards the Coolstores.

He slowed for a tractor hauling a trailer load of hay; he couldn't pass, too many cars coming the other way. 'Nat, I don't like it, let's dump the gear. It feels unlucky.'

She gazed at him, full of dope-head empathy, reached across and stroked him between the legs. 'Poor baby,' she said.

'There's a dumpster at the Coolstores.'

She shrugged. 'Whatever,' she said in her sunny voice, the dope still singing in her.

And so Andy steered into the Coolstores carpark, and a minute later there was a dinky little sports car pulling up next to them, a cop saying, 'Excuse me, sir.'

37

That Thursday afternoon it was Tank's turn to drive. As he steered the little Mazda through Somerville and headed on down Eramosa Road to the Coolstores, Pam Murphy gazed out at the roadside verges, noting how widespread pittosporum was on the Peninsula. She'd begun to see the place with new eyes, now that she belonged to the Bushrats. 'Did you know,' she said, 'that pittosporum is considered a weed?'

Tank seemed to shake himself awake. 'What?'

'Nothing.'

He glowered at the road ahead. 'That woman in the Passat. Do you know if she's reported us?'

So that was what he'd been brooding about. 'Lottie Mead? No. And I wouldn't worry about it if I were you.'

They neared the roundabout on the highway, stopping behind a build-up of traffic. Pam glanced at her watch: another two hours before they could knock off work. Then she happened to glance across at the Coolstores carpark, where a Toyota van with tinted windows was about to dart into an empty slot. It had the right of way but at the last minute stopped, the driver gesturing graciously to an elderly, panicked-looking woman driving an ancient Morris Minor. With a thankful wave and relieved smile, the old woman steered jerkily into the vacant spot. The van paused, idling, the driver casting about for another parking place.

'What do you reckon?' she asked Tankard. 'We haven't been exactly overwhelmed with courteous drivers this week. Give the guy a showbag?'

Tankard was rubbing his knee, releasing a powerful odour of athletes' liniment. He'd injured himself coaching football, and seemed obsessed with it. 'What? Didn't see it.'

The old Tankard, who'd liked to brush against her breasts and comment on the up-lift qualities of her bras, was almost better than this defeated slug. 'Wake up, Tank, you've got the rest of your life ahead of you,' Pam said, reaching across and gently tugging on the steering wheel.

'Don't get you knickers in a knot,' he said, flicking the turning indicator and steering into the carpark.

'Pull up beside that van,' Pam said, pointing to where the Toyota had parked outside the caravan owned by the community FM radio station. The other buildings housed a showbiz museum, craft shops, a restaurant and a café. The driver was opening his door when Pam's passenger door slid into view beside him. A young guy, clean cut, wearing sunglasses, and barely out of school, Pam thought, quickly sizing him up, and she reflected that it was almost comical the way everyone's first reaction to meeting the police was apprehension, tinged with panic and resignation, as if they'd all broken the law and the police had caught up with them at last.

'Excuse me, sir,' she said, winding down her window.

And the young guy slammed his door, gunned the engine and reversed with a raw squeal of tyres, shooting out of the carpark onto Eramosa Road. 'Jesus!' Tankard said, and then as Pam glanced inquiringly at him, he looked at his hands, which were beginning to tremble. She knew it: the slightest pressure and he would crumble. She didn't trust him in a high-speed pursuit, and screamed 'Swap places!' at him as she leapt from the car and hurried around to the driver's door and practically dragged him out from behind the wheel. She was already reversing as he hopped and skipped to get into the passenger seat.

The Toyota van had not entered the highway, where it could be tracked easily by helicopter, chased by pursuit cars or stopped by roadblocks, but had headed back towards farmland. Pam followed, now almost twenty seconds behind. A moment later, the van turned right onto a narrow sealed road that ran between flat, sodden paddocks and was lined by trees and bracken. She followed for three kilometres, the van reaching speeds of 120 kmh and snaking a little, the smaller sports car skittish and volatile on the uneven surface.

Tankard slammed his meaty hand on the dashboard. 'You'll never catch the prick if you drive like a girl.'

What a time for the old Tankard to show himself. Pam steered grimly, telling herself to ignore him and do this by the book. She ordered him to call it in: make, colour and registration number of the van, current position, direction, road conditions and other factors.

The radio dispatcher's voice was calm and unhurried. 'That vehicle was reported stolen yesterday. Description of the driver?'

Tankard looked to Pam, who muttered, 'Young male, late teens or early twenties, short dark hair, sunglasses, jeans and black football jumper.'

Tankard relayed the information. He glanced inquiringly at Pam again when the dispatcher asked, 'Passengers?'

She shrugged.

'Unconfirmed at this stage,' Tankard said.

'I'm sending pursuit cars to take over the chase,' the dispatcher said. 'Maintain visual contact of the suspect vehicle but don't spook him. You know the drill.'

'Easier said than done,' Pam muttered. She wanted to catch the driver of the van, but didn't want to be the target of an internal witch hunt, senior police displeased by another *High Speed Police Pursuit Ends in Fatality* story on the six o'clock news.

The Toyota shot through the intersection in the little settlement of Moorooduc, barely missing an LPG tanker, and Tankard radioed in that the van was driving riskily, at high speed. 'Request intercept cars from Waterloo and Mornington,' he said.

'Maintain position and report,' the dispatcher replied, as if ignoring him. 'Do not chase.'

The van was winding up to at least 130 kmh as it left the primary school and fire station behind. Pam followed, passing between open paddocks and a market garden. Around a bend, into a fold in the landscape, past vineyards, cattle standing in muddy grass, a conference retreat behind a stand of poplars. Kilometre after kilometre, with no sign of a helicopter, let alone other police vehicles. 'We're alone, Tank.'

He grunted, 'Why don't we just head the prick off?'

The Toyota seemed to be taking them in a wide skirting path, gradually heading southwest around Waterloo, which was several kilometres to their left. The grey rain was lifting; a weak, lowering sun lit the world of the empty backroads and slanted into Pam's eyes.

'What's that on the road?' Tankard said, pointing ahead.

She steered deftly around a deep pothole and a tangle of blackened pipes beyond it. 'He's torn off his exhaust system.'

Tankard shook his head. 'What the fuck's keeping the others? They should have headed him off by now. Go on, put your foot down.'

Pam bit her lip. The driver of the van had eased back on the accelerator, she was managing to keep him in sight, and that was all that was required of her officially. But she badly wanted to catch the guy. She'd driven pursuit cars at her last station; she had the training and the experience to chase the van rather than simply shadow it. But there were other police vehicles in the area: she could hear them trying to find the van from other directions. 'The post office says I live in Bittern,' one pursuit driver was saying, 'the shire says I live in Balnarring, the Electoral Commission says it's Merricks North, and they expect me to know where I am?'

'Strict radio procedure, please,' the dispatcher said.

'Stolen van,' Tankard muttered. 'That's why the guy ran.'

'Did you get a good look at him?'

'Didn't see him at all,' Tankard said, and in a fit of rage thumped the back of his fist against the removable hardtop of the Mazda. 'Can't see a fucking thing out of this sardine can.' Then: 'Oh, Jesus,' he said, his voice choking.

Pam saw it, too. A woman on horseback, the speeding van, the narrowness of the tree-lined road. The woman pulled back on the reins, trying to coax her horse onto a grassy gap between the trees, but the horse was spooked by the eruption of speed and noisy exhaust behind it. The Toyota clipped horse and rider and fishtailed, brake lights flaring too late, and shot between trees and through a wire fence. It could not sustain the high speed, the terrain or the shift in direction, and a hundred metres in from the fence it began to roll, then flipped onto its roof. Pam stopped, but whether for the horse, the rider or to give chase to the driver, now climbing from the overturned van, she couldn't say.

Still feeling a tug in the pit of her belly, Ellen watched Challis drive away. She wished she could accompany him, help him face the super, but knew that was impossible. She shook herself and went to greet the crime-scene technicians.

For the next hour she supervised their search for prints, and then directed them to the tyre marks in Challis's front lawn, watching them spray a fixing solution onto the muddy impressions first, before pouring the plaster.

'I need to know if these match tracks found at other local burglaries,' she said.

'We're on it, Sarge.'

She'd only just got back to the incident room when her mobile rang.

'Sarge? It's Pam Murphy.'

'Hi. What's up?'

Something about a crashed Toyota van, full of expensive gear, the driver legging it into a belt of trees. 'I remembered that you and Scobie Sutton had been working on a series of burglaries.'

Did you indeed, Ellen thought. In anyone else the explanation would have seemed fawning, but Pam Murphy had a good memory and the habit of making connections. She'd make a good detective.

'Are you sure the gear is stolen?'

'Well, the driver did a runner, and there's too much stuff: TV, DVD, digital cameras, jewellery, laptop.'

Ellen tingled. 'You're searching for the driver?'

'Yes, Sarge.'

'Stay there, I'm on my way.'

She collected Scobie Sutton and an unmarked car and set out for a corner of the map she'd never visited before. The Peninsula was endlessly variable, and here was the Devilbend Reservoir and remote houses set back from a winding dirt road.

'It's not as if she's new,' said Scobie Sutton as she drove.

Ellen guessed that he was talking about his goddamn daughter again. She'd heard about every cut, bruise, bowel movement, bad dream and spelling-test result. Roslyn Sutton was endlessly fascinating to her father. For Ellen, Challis and anyone else who worked with the man, the daughter had long become background noise. Ellen tried to pay attention. Today it was the child's dancing classes. Irish traditional? Ellen tried to remember. Riverdance stuff? Scottish jigs and reels? Something like that.

'She's as good as any of the other kids, but year after year the medals and honour certificates go to those girls whose mothers help out with the costumes and makeup. It's not fair, and she knows it's not. She tries to be grown-up about it, but it hurts her, you can tell. She'd like some acknowledgment, just once.'

'It's important,' Ellen said, thinking of her own daughter, nineteen now, sharing a house with other university students.

'I mean, Beth and I are too busy to help out with costumes and stuff. Why should Ros be penalised for that?'

'Exactly.'

A sudden roar and a helicopter flashed above them, low and straight.

'Just follow the chopper,' Scobie muttered.

Five minutes later they were at a scene of carnage. Ellen swallowed, feeling sick at heart. Blood, litres of it, had pooled dark as spilt oil across the road. A vet was administering a lethal injection to an injured horse, and a dead woman in full horse-riding jodhpurs, helmet and boots was being loaded into an ambulance. A wire fence had been torn open and deep tyre gouges scored the muddy surface of a paddock of grass and scattered apple trees, the remnants of an old orchard. Several police cars were parked on the verge, roof lights flashing. And there was the helicopter, hovering above an overgrown stand of trees at the far end of the paddock; closer to, one hundred metres inside the ruined fence, was an overturned van.

And there was her husband, questioning John Tankard, who was agitated and shaking his head. Pam Murphy stood watching them, biting her bottom lip.

Leaving Scobie to catch up on the details with Alan and Tankard, Ellen pulled on rubber boots and approached Pam, touching the younger woman's forearm reassuringly. 'Don't worry about my husband. The accident squad has to get involved. But it was a clean chase, right?'

'Yes, Sarge.'

'Good, then there's nothing to worry about. Has he talked to you yet?'

'No.'

'You'll be fine. Now, show me.'

They waded through wet bracken, Ellen glancing across the paddock, which sloped gently up to the stand of trees. Dead gums predominated, dry skeletal arms reaching above shorter, denser pittosporums and wattles. 'What's that place?' she said, pointing.

'Myers Reserve, Sarge.'

The air was damp, laden with the odours of nature disturbed in the process of decaying. They walked on.

'Sarge, mind your feet.'

They leapt over a small creek, murky water glinting beneath reeds, and came to the overturned Toyota. The rear doors had fallen open and Ellen peered inside. There, just as Pam had listed them, were several items that, on first impressions, matched items listed as stolen from Challis this morning and the Penzance Beach property yesterday. She went around to the front of the van and crouched at the broken windscreen. Laptop. She drew on latex gloves, reached in, and hooked it out.

'Sarge?'

Challis's Toshiba, complete with his initials scratched on the lid.

'Bingo.'

'Sarge?'

This was delicate. She needed to secure the laptop and return it to Challis; she didn't need every cop on the Peninsula to know that his laptop, containing sensitive information, had been stolen. At the same time, she didn't want to lie to Pam Murphy, or get her into trouble.

'Pam, I'm giving you a receipt for this, okay? If there are any questions, refer them to me.'

'Sarge, CIU's in charge now anyway, you can do what you like.'

Ellen nodded. 'This laptop was stolen this morning. It contains sensitive material.' She hoped Pam hadn't seen the initials, or twigged that they belonged to Challis.

'Sure, Sarge, whatever you say.'

'Good. Meanwhile we need the crime-scene people to dust the van for prints and make casts of the tyre tracks.'

'Sarge.'

Just then a couple of brightly festooned highway patrol cars came screaming in, one of them skidding as it braked. 'Only about thirty minutes behind everyone else,' Pam muttered.

'I'll need details,' Ellen said, as they returned to the road.

Pam described the incident at the Coolstores, the chase itself—'Strictly by the book, Sarge'—and then the Toyota clipping the horse and veering out of control through the fence.

'Rolled and landed on its roof. Nothing we could do. Tank stopped to help the woman on the horse, I tried running after the driver, but he disappeared into the reserve.'

'How long ago?'

'Almost an hour. It took a while for everyone to get here.'

Ellen looked up. 'So that chopper is probably wasting its time.'

She drew away, saying, 'I need to make a call, be with you in a couple of minutes, okay?'

'Sarge.'

Ellen flipped open her mobile and speed-dialled Challis.

Challis was at regional HQ in Frankston, tight and jittery in McQuarrie's top floor corner office, when the call came. He fumbled for his mobile, murmuring, 'Sorry, sir, I'd better take this.'

McQuarrie didn't glance up but continued to employ an age-old boss's tactic of frowning over documents with a pen and ignoring him.

'Hello.'

'It's me. Can you talk?'

He felt a surge of spirits, not only from hearing Ellen's voice but also from realising that its altered timbre—low and throaty—reflected what had happened that afternoon. 'Not exactly.'

'You're with the super? Blink your eyes once for yes, twice for no.'

He grinned, despite knowing that his career was about to be sunk. It probably gave Ellen a curious thrill to rag him like this, knowing he was with McQuarrie. 'Sergeant Destry,' he said, 'if you're really sure that you want to transfer to the traffic division then I'd be happy to write a reference.'

She snorted. The super glanced up, frowned, and returned to his stack of papers. 'Good news,' she said, and told him something about a crashed van loaded with stolen goods, including his laptop. 'It's definitely yours.'

His relief was palpable. 'You're a wizard.'

'Have you told the super?'

'Not yet.'

'Don't, Hal. There's no need to, not now.'

'Okay.'

'Catch you later.'

Challis felt buoyant, no longer afraid, no longer depressed by the atmosphere on the top floor, where policing was a rarefied thing, soundproofed and distant from the streets and the law courts. Policing here walked on carpets, wore suits and had university qualifications after its name.

He stretched his legs and gazed around him. There were leather-bound reports on the shelves, photographs of the super shaking important hands, a rubber plant as glossy and vigorous as a plastic fake, and a cluster of tiny silver picture frames in one corner of the huge desk, featuring Mrs Super, Robert and Georgia. Georgia's image had been scissored from a larger photograph. She'd been sitting on a woman's lap. Janine's?

He grew aware that the super had put down his pen and was regarding him with faint irritation and disdain, the face of a busy man on important tasks. 'You told my secretary this was urgent?'

Challis said, 'I'm afraid there's been a development, sir. It's delicate.'

McQuarrie's face shut down and he didn't say anything, but swallowed, as if steeling himself. Thank God I don't have to tell him about the laptop, Challis thought. I can show him the photos and retain the advantage.

'Go on, Inspector.'

'Sir, we found the missing mobile phone.'

'And? Get on with it.'

'Certain photographs were stored on it,' Challis said, taking them from his briefcase and fanning them across McQuarrie's desk.

For a long time, McQuarrie was motionless, inclined a little to examine the photographs but not touching them. Finally he looked up and said, his voice catching, 'When?'

'They were probably taken the Saturday before last. Of course, it's possible that—'

McQuarrie gestured irritably. 'I don't mean that—when did you find them?'

'Late yesterday afternoon.'

'You didn't think to tell me sooner?'

'We didn't want to cause any unnecessary distress.'

McQuarrie watched him in apparent disbelief, but then switched tack. 'I heard all about your raids this morning.'

His spies. 'The men in the photographs,' Challis said.

'You didn't raid Robert?'

'We interviewed him last night.'

'And?'

'Each man received a copy of his photograph in Monday's mail.'

'Janine was blackmailing them? One of them killed her? I take it she took the photos?'

'We can't be sure.'

'I can,' said McQuarrie emphatically.

'Sir,' said Challis, 'did you suspect something was going on?'

McQuarrie's façade slipped. He looked bewildered, pushing his fingers back through his hair and looking about wildly as if for deliverance. 'There was always something about her that wasn't quite right. Something missing. The wife and I did our best to make her welcome, make her one of the family, but Janine seemed to resent us, despise us. She was quite critical. I don't know what it was: jealousy, perhaps? She had quite a sharp tongue, often reducing my wife to tears. She had nothing good to say about anybody.'

His glance settled on Challis helplessly. 'My wife's not to hear about any of this. You can't show these photos to anybody. How many have seen them so far?'

'Only the members of my team.'

'Do you vouch for each and every one of them?'

'Yes.'

McQuarrie turned self-protectively nasty. 'If our friends in the media learn about these photographs, I'll know where to look.'

Challis knew how to play at this game. 'Sir,' he said, tapping Robert McQuarrie's photograph, 'apparently this has been going on for some time.'

McQuarrie flushed angrily. 'I'm sure she drove him to it. She was a cold little bitch. I bet it was all her idea.'

'Neither she nor your son gave you any indication that this was a part of their private lives?'

'Of course not.'

But you had niggling doubts about Janine, thought Challis, and when she was murdered they hardened into suspicions. You feared the reasons why she was murdered would reflect badly on you and your son, and this accounts for your apparent obstructiveness and lack of sympathy.

'We don't know why she took the photos or who else might have been involved,' he said.

'Are you saying my son's involved? He was in Sydney when she was shot. *He's in the damn photos*, for God's sake. Are you suggesting he and Janine were in this together and his photo's a smokescreen? Are you saying he's next?'

'No,' Challis said, remembering Robert's reactions the night before.

Meanwhile McQuarrie was gaining momentum. 'Are you saying I had prior knowledge of all this? That *I* killed Janine to save our reputations?'

'Did you, sir?' said Challis mildly.

'Don't be absurd,' said McQuarrie, pitching about in his chair. 'I resent the implication. Do you honestly think I wanted to bring all this down on myself?'

Challis didn't. In fact, if the shooting was related to the photographs, then why hadn't the killer searched Janine's house and office for further copies? 'Sir, I have to ask, but did Janine ever approach you, or your wife, with overt or veiled threats or attempts to blackmail you?'

'Absolutely not. She'd know I'd never have paid up and I'd have had her in handcuffs quick smart.'

McQuarrie had possibly never carried or used handcuffs. 'And there's no indication that she blackmailed these men,' Challis said, pointing to the photographs. 'We don't know why she chose them, took their photos or sent copies to them.'

McQuarrie said softly, 'But it's a hell of a motive for murder, Hal.'

'It is indeed.'

'She could have been at it for months, years.'

Challis had thought of that. 'Yes.'

'Was she in it alone? Maybe there's a lover we don't know about.'

'We're keeping it in mind, sir.'

McQuarrie seemed to want to tear at his sparse hair again. 'Who else knows? How are we going to keep a lid on it? I'm relying on you, Hal.'

39

Meanwhile, Andy Asche was back in Waterloo.

When the Toyota had finally stopped rolling, he'd found himself upside down and half strangled in his seatbelt. He'd released himself, remembering Natalie, but couldn't find her anywhere. She must have climbed out and scarpered.

So he'd run like hell through grass, bracken and cow shit, dodging around old apple trees, and vaulted a fence, darting into a dense wooded area. Damp in there, leeches probably, mosquitoes in summertime, rotten logs mossy green everywhere, gaunt dead trees, thriving pittosporum. Then out the other side, coming upon a road—Penzance Beach Road, he realised—carrying a fair bit of traffic at this time of the day. He'd ducked back into the trees and considered his options.

Hitchhike?

Hell no. It could take him an hour to get a ride, and the cops would be all over him before then. He remained in the shadows, beneath dripping trees, and finally saw a kid aged about fifteen come riding down a muddy driveway opposite. Saw the kid park his bike in the hedge at the entrance to the property—a winery, according to a wooden sign—and wait at the side of the road with a gym bag. One minute later, this woman in a Mitsubishi people-mover picks him up, the kid high-fiving it with other kids in the back.

Off to footy training. Maybe I'll be tackling that same kid at footy next Saturday morning, Andy thought, ducking across when the road was clear, jumping onto the bike, cramming the helmet on his head and pedalling away as fast as he could.

Cool bike, too. Lightweight, snappy gears.

Pity about the van and contents, he thought. Maybe I should get out of housebreaking, get into nicking bikes.

He pedalled hard for thirty minutes, down to Penzance Beach, where he met the bike path that meandered across to Waterloo. Here there were always cyclists, so he'd not attract attention. Twenty minutes later, he was home, thinking that he could give the bike to Natalie's brothers, see the looks on their faces. As for Natalie, she must have hitched out, left him behind, the bitch. He had to admire that. It's what he would have done.

But none of this would have happened if she hadn't insisted they pull another job. She was fast becoming a liability. If the pressure hadn't been on, he might have spotted that they were robbing a cop's house. Photos, commendations, an old uniform hanging in the wardrobe.

Thinking he'd better delete the files he'd swiped from the guy's laptop, Andy switched on his PC.

Back at the accident scene, Pam Murphy was standing at the broken fence, watching the crime-scene technicians dust the van for prints and take casts of the tyre tracks. The sarge was a few metres away, pocketing her phone after talking to Challis. Alan Destry called out from the other side of the road. 'Oi, Constable Murphy, over here, please.'

Pam stiffened. She saw him cast a half gloating look at his wife, then jerk his head and say, 'Straight away, Constable. I haven't got all day.'

'Alan,' the sarge said warningly.

'It's okay, Sarge,' Pam said, not wanting to get in the middle of a marital row.

'Don't let him bully you,' Ellen murmured, 'okay?'

'Okay, Sarge.'

Pam crossed the road to where Alan Destry stood with his rump against a police car. He opened his notebook. 'And how's my wife's little pal today?'

Pam eyed him warily, wondering about the undercurrents. And was she Ellen Destry's pal? Hardly. The sarge was fifteen years older, senior in rank, a detective, and married with children. Mentor might be a better word.

Did he expect a response? Did she address him as 'sir'?—after all, he was only a senior constable.

He folded his arms across his chest. 'Do you know what my job is?'

'Accident Investigation Squad.'

'Correct. I was in Traffic for years, drove pursuit cars, manned booze buses, taught defensive driving techniques, and coordinated high-speed chases as a pursuit controller. There's nothing I don't know about driving a motorcar. Nothing you can put over on me.'

So, a challenge. Pam frowned as if puzzled by his choice of words. 'I don't understand.'

'Oh, yes you do. Do you realise there'll be an inquest? The state coroner will be involved, possibly the Ethical Standards Department?'

'The Ethicals? Why them?'

'That depends on you, how you answer my questions, how your partner answers my questions, and on what I learn about your conduct during the pursuit.'

Pam stood very still, watched, and waited. She wanted to swallow. Maybe Lottie Mead *had* reported the stone incident after all.

'Everything suggests high speed,' Alan Destry said.

'The Toyota, not the police,' Pam flashed back.

Destry cocked his head disbelievingly, a solid, arrogant-looking man with cropped hair. 'If the Toyota was driving at high speeds—up to 130 kilometres an hour, according to John Tankard—then how come you witnessed the accident?'

'We were not pursuing,' Pam said, 'we were following.'

'Following at high speeds,' said Ellen Destry's husband, 'and spooking the other driver.'

'It wasn't like that.'

'Write it up and submit it before the end of the day. I've got tomorrow off, so expect a formal debriefing next Monday.'

'Formal debriefing.'

'Yes. What did you expect?'

Andy Asche was in a hurry. He had to get to the post office before five. Wearing latex gloves to screen his fingerprints, he loaded his printer with paper fresh from a new packet, clicked on the photo array that he'd transferred from the stolen laptop to his computer, clicked on the four thumbnails that clearly showed the faces of four men, and clicked 'print', making multiple copies.

The photos rolled out of the printer and he collated them into five bundles, which he slipped into five express-post envelopes. Before sealing the envelopes he typed up a letter, big font, plenty of bold, and printed out a copy to add to four of the envelopes. He typed a different letter for the fifth envelope. Finally he tore up the highway to Frankston, where no one knew him, and lodged the envelopes at the main post office.

With darkness settling over the mangrove flats beside her house, and feeling cocooned by her fleecy tracksuit and the warmth of her slow combustion fire, Tessa Kane continued to search the net, a glass of wine at hand. Last evening's Google search had been useful for consolidating the readily accessible information on Charlie Mead and ANZCOR—the bland public face—but now she was refining her search parameters, concentrating on the period before Mead and his wife came to Australia. She'd also made dozens of local and international phone calls since yesterday, speaking to men and women who'd once studied with, taught, worked alongside or served under either of the Meads.

At first, the results seemed promising. The deeper she dug, the more Charlie Mead's profile blurred at the edges. She found several Charlie Meads, or variations of the one. There had been a time in the 1970s and '80s—after he'd served with the security forces in Zimbabwe and later worked as a security consultant in South Africa—when Mead frequently changed addresses, but she could not discover why. To avoid creditors? There was also a question mark over his service record: certainly he'd served in the South African military, but had he ever been a highly trained commando with SAS connections, as he'd claimed? Later still he'd worked for a security company in the UK that specialised in surveillance, firearms training, bodyguards for travelling businessmen, and negotiating in hostage and kidnap situations. He was sacked in 1986 after South African authorities had interrogated him regarding an attempt to provide arms and mercenaries to insurgents in the Seychelles. In the early 1990s he'd joined ANZCOR and risen through the ranks.

Apart from references to a position held in the South African public service, she'd found almost nothing on Lottie Mead.

Tessa felt frustrated. The facts were sparse, and although they'd required a little digging, were on public record, and didn't point to anything obviously criminal or corrupt. What was the point in publishing an exposé if there was nothing to expose? Sure, Mead had probably cut corners all his life and his values were non-existent or deplorable, but in the current political climate, which admired cowboys, Mead was bound to have powerful supporters and be seen as a man who got things done.

There was one last strategy she could try. Reaching for the phone, she began to hire private detectives in South Africa, England and the US.

Ellen arrived home that evening to find Alan watching a DVD: a war movie, no surprise there. She almost went straight out again. 'Have you eaten?'

He gestured with the remote control, his gaze on the screen. 'Yep.'

So she heated leftovers and ate at the kitchen table. Usually Sunday night was movie night, but Alan had a day off tomorrow. Ellen had treasured Sundays when Larrayne had still lived at home. They'd eat pizza, fish and chips, or cheese on toast, plates on their laps, in front of the box, watching a good movie, like *Emma*, *Sense and Sensibility* or *Love, Actually*. Sometimes Alan watched with them, but it had to be an action movie for him to last the distance, and the only ones that Ellen and Larrayne could stand to watch were old James Bond and Indiana Jones movies, or action movies with a bit of class, like *Heat*. Or *Titanic*, which he'd endured more for Kate Winslet's tits and the ship turning arse up than the characters and storyline.

Now, with Larrayne living in the city, Ellen felt a sense of loss. Larrayne seemed to lurk in the corners of the house, the corners of Ellen's gaze. Ellen's widowed mother had suffered the same thing: 'I keep catching glimpses of your dad,' she'd say. 'Not his ghost, I don't mean that. The particular way he held the newspaper or walked through a door or put the dishes away.' Well, Ellen kept glimpsing Larrayne here and there, and even missed those quirks of Larrayne's that had driven her nuts at the time, like the way she would never stay put when cleaning her teeth but wander out of the bathroom and up and down the hall and in and out of rooms, electric toothbrush buzzing in the corner of her mouth.

Ellen picked at her food, seeing the dead horse and rider, the overturned van. Was Larrayne very vulnerable now?—away from home for the first time; drugs everywhere; evening lectures and a long walk home across a shadowy campus and down dark streets; getting attached to an axe murderer disguised as Mr Right; or even getting her heart broken, which was bound to happen sooner or later.

And so she phoned, several times. No answer. Larrayne, and her housemates, were out.

For the evening? The whole night?

Where?

Doing what?

With whom?

The old who, what, where, when and why of police work.

And all the while she was trying to tell herself that she would leave her husband on her own terms and not because Challis existed.

40

Challis spent most of Friday morning in CIU. It was proving to be difficult to get fast or accurate information from Witsec or the New South Wales prison service. Meanwhile, according to the findings of the DCs on loan from Mornington, Hayden Coulter was guilty of no more than massaging the books of his clients. Nothing solid tied him—or any of the other men in the photographs—to Janine McQuarrie's murder. Several people, including a racehorse owner, a trainer and a groom, alibied Coulter; various secretaries, receptionists and work colleagues alibied the other men. Finally, the investigation had not turned up a secret lover for Janine, and Challis could only suppose that she'd seemed happy to Meg because she'd thought of a way to stick it to her husband. The anonymous caller hadn't called back.

He checked with Scobie Sutton, who was manipulating the images stored on Janine's mobile phone into simple head-and-shoulders shots of Coulter, the surgeon and the funds manager, and which Challis would later show to Georgia McQuarrie. Scobie was hunched in front of his monitor, his whole body revealing distaste for the task, as though he feared he'd be soiled. Not for the first time, Challis wondered if the man was too sensitive and moralistic for the job. He said nothing and returned to his cubicle, wondering how Ellen was doing. She was out, following up on forensic evidence found at the murder and accident scenes, and talking to anyone who might have met or seen Christina Traynor.

Challis poured another mug of coffee and turned on his radio for the 10 a.m. news. First up was another young Australian arrested for attempting to smuggle heroin out of Indonesia, followed by an account of yesterday's inquest, in which a Navy public relations officer, responding to a question regarding cadets and drug abuse, said that the Navy's position was one of 'zero tolerance'. Challis's mind drifted. What would his parents make of the story? He often found himself measuring the world against them. He was the late-in-life child of a father who'd been a World War II RAAF navigator and a mother who'd been an Army nurse. Not much drug use back then, he didn't suppose, apart from alcohol and tobacco—and a bit of cocaine and heroin amongst inner-city bohemians. The two world wars had also established a simple set of values: Australians were defined as brave, practical, resourceful, egalitarian, clean-living and loyal to their mates. Conservative governments and the popular press continued to hold that view, but Challis thought that things *had* changed. Bravery, loyalty, egalitarianism, patriotism and a fine young mind in a fine young body were media images trotted out to suit sixty-five-year-old politicians, sports commentators and shock-jock talkback radio hosts who kept one eye on their ratings and another on their sponsors' kickbacks. Outmoded, irrelevant concepts that bore little relation to the real world. Drugs belonged now; the old Australia didn't. Drugs had made crime more prevalent, vicious and unpredictable, too, making Challis's job harder, but no one wanted to know about that.

When the walls seemed to close in on him he returned to the open space of the incident room with the McQuarrie file and sat and stared at a wall map of the area. The killers could have driven to Mrs

Humphreys's house from anywhere on the Peninsula—or further afield.

Feeling Georgia's sombre gaze on him then, he took out her sketches and arranged them side by side, trying to think his way into her skin: her vantage point, what she'd seen, what she couldn't have seen, what she might have invented. Her representations of the crime-scene seemed to be truthful if rudimentary. She'd not shown the shooter as a monster but a man with dark glasses, a coat, and a thin face. The driver had a round face and a shaven head, and she'd shown his arm hanging lazily out of the driver's side window.

Challis stared at that arm. Georgia's sense of perspective was skewed but her pen strokes were generally clean and precise, which didn't explain the lumpy appearance of the hand. He picked up the phone.

By late morning he was knocking on Robert McQuarrie's door in Mount Eliza. McQuarrie himself answered, demanding, with a red face, 'What do you want?'

Challis had assumed the man would be at work. 'I need a quick word with Georgia. I cleared it with Meg.'

'Well, she should have cleared it with me. My daughter's grieving, you know.'

'I must talk to her, Robert.'

Again the guy flinched at the use of his first name, and glared at Challis. 'You think I did it, don't you.'

It was a statement, not a question. 'Did you?'

'Absolutely not.'

Challis regarded him. 'Then you have nothing to worry about.'

With a kind of sob, Robert McQuarrie said, 'You showed my father the photos, you bastard.'

'It couldn't be avoided.'

'You're a shit, you know that? Am I going to see myself in the

Progress? Have you been flashing copies around?'

'Dad?'

It was Georgia, peering around at Challis from behind her father's legs. She wore a pink tracksuit and her hair had been freshly washed. Challis put his hands on his knees. 'Hi there.'

'Have you come to see me?'

'I have indeed.'

'I'm in the kitchen.'

McQuarrie, his face suffused with anger, stood back to let Challis enter. Challis followed Georgia to the kitchen, where she promptly sat at the table, a hot milk drink and half a honey pikelet on a plate at her elbow. Meg stood beside her, glancing nervously past Challis to the hallway. Challis turned his head: Robert McQuarrie stood there, and the moment extended, full of tension. Then McQuarrie turned irritably and stalked away down the hall.

Challis swung his gaze back to Meg and grinned. She returned it meekly and began to fill the kettle at the sink.

Georgia, munching the rest of her pikelet, said, 'I think I might go back to school next week. Do you think that's a good idea?'

Challis glanced at Meg helplessly, then smiled at Georgia. 'I think that sounds like a very good idea. Do you miss your friends?'

'Uh-huh,' Georgia said.

'Are you up to answering a few more questions for me?'

'Uh-huh. What do you want to know?'

Challis spread the photographs of Coulter and the other men across the table. Scobie had done a good job: there was nothing to indicate that the men had been photographed naked. 'Do you recognise any of these men?'

She glanced from one to the other. 'No.'

'The man who shot your mother? The man driving the old car?'

She shook her head emphatically. 'No.'

He collected the photographs and substituted her drawings. 'Remember these?'

Georgia eyed him brightly, seriously. 'That's my name in the corner, see?'

'Yes.'

'That's my mum on the ground.'

Challis nodded. 'I'm mainly interested in the driver of the car the bad men came in.'

'I've got other pictures,' she said.

'Have you?'

She left the room, Challis and the aunt exchanging polite, sad smiles. Meg passed him a cup of instant coffee. The central heating cut in and Challis felt warm air gust over him from a wall vent. He sipped his coffee: it was terrible coffee, weak, stale, and nothing would ever put it right: sugar, milk, or an extra spoonful of granules.

Georgia returned with three drawings. The situation was potentially morbid and unhealthy, a small child reliving her mother's murder through drawings and conversation, but Challis was reassured by the warmth and peacefulness of the kitchen, the fact that Meg wasn't chiding Georgia or hovering anxiously, and Georgia's own air of wisdom and maturity. 'These are good drawings too,' he said.

Two were essentially the same drawing, but the third showed the killer's car in profile. Cream body, yellow driver's door, just as she'd described it on the day of the murder.

Challis returned to the drawings that showed the driver, his arm hanging out of the window. It was a typical young tough's driving pose. And there was that same lumpy hand on one of the new drawings, the outline smudged.

Challis was wary of asking leading questions, so he pointed and said, 'I always had trouble drawing hands when I was a kid.'

Georgia frowned. Was Challis criticising her drawing skills, or merely admitting to his own? 'First I did a proper hand, then remembered and rubbed out one of the fingers.'

'Rubbed out?'

'Does it hurt,' Georgia said, 'if you get a finger chopped off?'

Challis went very still. 'I expect it does,' he said carefully. 'Do you remember which finger?'

She held up her right hand and gazed at it critically. 'This one,' she said finally, pointing to her ring finger.

It was lunchtime when he got back to the office. Ellen and Scobie were there, their hard, tense, hopeful smiles telling him there'd been a development.

41

Raymond Lowry's wife was a small, discouraged-looking woman with drawn features. 'It was more verbal than physical,' she said. She paused. 'Ray had anger-management issues.'

She used the term awkwardly. 'Is that the expression Janine McQuarrie used?' asked Challis.

Deborah Lowry shifted about in consent. They were in a CIU interview room overlooking the carpark. Ellen leaned forward and touched the woman's wrist. 'You say he was more verbal than physical, meaning he did sometimes hit you?'

'Yes.'

'So you sought counselling.'

'I wish I hadn't!'

'Why?'

'I didn't know what she was like!'

'Janine McQuarrie?'

'She went right off, said men like Ray needed to pay, a simple rap over the knuckles in court isn't enough, they have to be confronted.'

'And she confronted your husband.'

'She could have got me killed doing that! He came storming home afterwards, slapped me around, said he'd kill me, kill her.'

Challis sat back in the plastic chair and folded his arms. 'Is he capable of killing someone? Do you think he did it?'

Deborah Lowry shrugged, looked sulky, as if her choice of husband reflected badly on her character.

'You were concerned enough to come here today and make a statement,' said Ellen encouragingly.

'Ray's got a terrible temper. Who knows what he's capable of? Ever since he left the Navy he's been kind of drifting. His mobile phone business is struggling. He...' she finished, gesturing helplessly.

When she was gone, Challis called Dominic O'Brien at Bayside Counselling, who refused to hand over Janine McQuarrie's file on Deborah Lowry. 'Mrs Lowry is now my client, Inspector.'

'Ah.'

O'Brien pressed home his advantage with a tone of portly satisfaction. 'And I do not intend to reveal my own assessment of her.'

Challis sighed irritably. The irritation apparently communicated itself to O'Brien, who went on to say, 'However it is my judgment that Mrs Lowry is not a threat to herself, or anyone or anything else. Look elsewhere for your murderer, Inspector.'

At two o'clock that afternoon, Raymond Lowry was brought in for questioning. Ellen led by saying, 'You used to be in the Navy, Mr Lowry.'

Lowry examined his nails, a picture of boredom. 'So?'

'You travelled widely, ending up at the base near Waterloo. You liked the area, and when you left the Navy you decided to settle here with your wife.'

'So?' repeated Lowry, glancing at Challis as if to say that he knew where Ellen was getting her information from.

'A good place to raise a family and start a business.'

Lowry stared at her.

'But your wife doesn't live with you any more, does she?'

Challis, seated to one side of the interview room as if merely an observer while Ellen Destry asked the questions, saw Lowry's jaw tighten. He took in the man's powerful build, large teeth bared in a mocking smile, and small ears tight to the head. Ex-Navy, now a shopkeeper who sold mobile phones: what disappointments drove him?

Challis slid his gaze sideways to meet Ellen's and gave her a tiny nod. The tape machine was running. Lowry hadn't requested a lawyer yet.

'You and your wife had marriage difficulties, Mr Lowry?' Ellen asked.

Full of fake concern, and Lowry wasn't buying it. 'Nothing unusual about that.'

'Of course not. But not everyone seeks counselling from a psychologist.'

It was stuffy in the little room and Lowry had hung his polar fleece jacket on the back of his chair. He wore jeans and a V-necked cotton sweater over a white T-shirt. Under it all he was bulky from steroids or the gym. He frowned. 'What are you on about?'

'Your wife saw a psychologist, Mr Lowry. Didn't you know that?'

He shrugged. 'The Navy sent me to three bases in two years. That was disruptive. Plus she was scared I'd be sent to the Gulf and come back in a body bag.' Another shrug. 'Nothing to be ashamed about. That's why the Navy has a counselling service.'

'I'm not talking about the past, I'm talking about now, this past year. And I'm not talking about the Navy's psychologists. I'm talking about Janine McQuarrie.'

Challis watched Lowry scowl. 'I suppose my wife told you all about it.'

'It doesn't matter how we know. What matters is your response. You said, and I quote, "I could kill the bitch." Do you remember saying that, Mr Lowry?'

'Yep.'

'Well, did you carry it out?'

'Nope.'

He was abrupt, unruffled, contemptuous. Challis leaned forward. 'You were angry. We can understand that.'

'If I was to murder anyone it would be my wife.'

'Shoot her in the head like you shot Janine McQuarrie,' Challis said. 'We're searching your house and business, Ray. Are we going to find the gun you used?'

'You were questioning me on Tuesday morning. How can I be in two places at once?'

'So, who did you hire?'

'Look, am I under arrest?'

'No.'

'Do I need a lawyer?'

'I don't know—do you think you need one?'

Lowry continued to sit impassively. Eventually he said, 'I'll humour you for the time being.'

Ellen leaned forward and said, 'Janine McQuarrie tried to empower your wife, didn't she? And you didn't like it.'

'Doesn't mean I killed her.'

'But it was more than that, wasn't it, Ray?' said Challis, toying with his pen. 'Janine McQuarrie made contact with you. She confronted you.'

Raymond Lowry shrugged indifferently. Challis slammed the flat of his hand on the table. 'She *confronted* you, Ray.'

Lowry was unruffled. 'So?'

'Didn't that upset you?'

'Sure. But I didn't kill her and you can't prove I did.'

Challis sat back and folded his arms. 'We're the first to admit that she wasn't very well liked,' he said reasonably. 'In fact, many loathed her. She liked to confront people, particularly men. We can understand why you'd want to punish her, get even with her. Tell us, Ray: you'll feel better.'

Lowry sighed, as though they were slow and needed the obvious pointed out to them. 'You're describing someone losing it, flipping out, acting in the heat of the moment. Yeah, I admit, I've got a temper. But as I understand it, the bitch was shot dead by contract killers, which doesn't sound like heat of the moment to me.'

He gave them his arid smile.

'Maybe you got very calm and hired those killers, Mr Lowry.'

'How would I go about doing that?'

'You own a mobile phone shop,' Challis said. 'Is that how you kept in contact? You used cloned, throwaway phones to cover your tracks?'

'You thought you'd got away with it, too,' Ellen said, 'but we received an anonymous call from someone who knew quite a bit about the murder.'

Challis watched Lowry with interest. Lowry merely shrugged.

'Was that anonymous caller you, Mr Lowry?'

Lowry glanced at his watch indifferently. 'If I'd shot her, why would I call you?'

'Perhaps you only wanted to scare her, and things got out of hand.'

'I wasn't bothered by her, okay?'

'Are you protecting someone?'

'Like who?'

'You hired a mate. He let you down, but you're unwilling or afraid to tell the police about it.'

'Will that be all?' Lowry was saying. 'Or should I ask for one of the duty solicitors? Perhaps *he* will make you see sense.'

'*He?*' Ellen asked, amused. 'What if it's a woman? Oh, I forgot, you have trouble relating to women, don't you, chuckles?'

'Believe that, if it makes you happy.'

'Especially clever, articulate, fearless women like Janine McQuarrie.'

'Why waste a good bullet?' Lowry asked.

42

Challis had no choice but to release Lowry without charge. Later that Friday afternoon, the car repairer called to say that his Triumph was ready, so he swapped the loan car for it and returned to the station, where he called the last briefing before the weekend.

Outlining the results of the Lowry interview, he said, 'We need more: warrants for his home and office phones—including any second-hand phones he may have in stock, and phones brought in for repair—and warrants to search his house, shop and car. We need a weapon, ammunition, or anything that will tie him to the murder. Meanwhile, the funeral's on Saturday. Scobie, I want you to attend, photograph the mourners.'

'Boss.'

Challis rubbed his palms together. 'Getting back to Lowry. Ellen? Is he our man?'

Ellen shrugged. 'Janine McQuarrie liked to confront people— mainly men—who she thought were abusive in some way. She liked to rub their faces in it. She went too far, confronted the wrong man. But was it Lowry? She pissed him off, but as he said, Hal, he was being interviewed by you on Tuesday morning, just before Janine was shot.'

Challis nodded. 'But that doesn't let him off the hook. He could have hired someone to do the job.'

They brooded. Scobie Sutton said, 'Ellen's right about the pattern to Janine's behaviour. We know she confronted Lowry, and my wife has told me about similar incidents. By sending those photos to her husband and the others, Janine was being true to form.'

'So who else did she confront,' said one of the Mornington DCs, 'and why, and in what way?'

Challis cleared his throat. 'And were the photographs the first step, or was she following up an earlier, face-to-face confrontation?'

'All four men seemed shocked and puzzled though, Hal,' said Ellen.

'True,' said Challis, glancing at the uncurtained window. The day was closing in. They'd all be driving home in darkness. He said slowly, 'Did she confront the super? Maybe Robert refused to be cowed by her, so she went to his father.' They shifted uncomfortably at the thought of interviewing the super.

Later Challis was to refer to it as speak-of-the-devil. At that moment, McQuarrie appeared in the doorway of the incident room. Nostrils flared, he directed a hard bright smile at them one by one and said, 'Inspector, sit down.'

'Sir?'

'I said sit,' McQuarrie snarled.

Challis shrugged and complied. McQuarrie stood at the head of the long table and said, 'Now, which one of you devious shits sent this to my son?'

He tossed an envelope onto the table. After a moment, Challis picked it up gingerly by the bottom corner and shook out the contents. McQuarrie said irritably, 'You may put your dirty mitts on them, Inspector. They're copies—or copies of copies. The lab has the material sent to my son.'

Even so, Challis sorted the contents with a pen: the familiar photograph of Robert McQuarrie, naked, his face in a rictus of pain or ecstasy, and a sheet of A4 paper with a ransom demand printed on it. He went cold; his mind raced.

'My son stayed home today,' McQuarrie said, 'to be with his daughter, like any decent father, and found this, this *garbage* in the mail this afternoon. He came to me in tears—*in tears*—and showed it to me.'

The super glared and waited. No one spoke. 'It might interest you to know,' he went on, 'that Robert and I have already talked through the admittedly unfortunate matter of his participation in the sex party scene, and the fact that Janine had been taking candid photographs and sending them anonymously to him and to other men. Talked it through yesterday. But now *another* photograph has been sent to my son, *with* a ransom demand, *after* Janine's murder, so I can only conclude that someone in this room thought he—or she—could make a few dollars out of my son's misery.'

He paused. 'No one cares to comment? Your little ruse has backfired, backfired badly. Robert has admitted everything. He's hidden nothing. Yes, he's ashamed; yes, he knows his conduct was tawdry; but these so-called swinger parties were for consenting adults. We all make mistakes, and my son is man enough to face up to his. He swears that's the end of it, and I believe him. Meanwhile he's just lost his wife in the most appalling way—he loved her, despite the fact that she was taking these photographs—and he has a daughter who loves and depends on him. For Christ's sake, the funeral's tomorrow.'

McQuarrie had worked himself into a fine, livid rage. His spittle flecked the table. 'We were given assurances that nothing would be leaked to the media or to other police, so someone in this room, or a friend of someone in this room, must have sent the latest letter. But if you or your friends think you're going to get a cent out of us, you're sadly mistaken.'

They were silent.

'Well?'

Eventually Ellen stirred. 'Sir, perhaps it was sent by Janine and got delayed in the post.'

'Good try, Sergeant. It was sent by express post, guaranteeing next-day delivery, and lodged in Frankston yesterday afternoon.'

Challis read the blackmail demand again. Fourteen point bold: *$10,000 or I place this on the Net. Expect a call.*

'Sir, I can vouch for everyone in this room.'

'Bull*shit*, mister. The force is riddled with corrupt officers; don't you read the papers? I intend to make a formal complaint to Ethical Standards against each and every one of you unless I get a confession right this minute.'

Challis looked around at them all, their affronted faces. He couldn't see any of them being responsible for this. So it had to have stemmed from the theft of his laptop. He had to do the right thing by them.

And they would hate his guts as a result.

'Sir, I think I know what happened.'

McQuarrie curled his lip. 'I'm all ears.'

'My house was burgled.'

McQuarrie pounced. 'You took sensitive material home with you? From an active investigation?'

'In a manner of speaking,' Challis said, and he laid it out for them, glancing at them one by one, apologising but not asking to be absolved.

'Your laptop?'

'Yes, sir.'

'You should have reported it immediately.'

Ellen cut in. 'He did report it, sir. To me. Constable Sutton and I have been investigating a series of burglaries, and this seemed to fit the pattern.'

'But neither you nor Inspector Challis saw fit to report the theft to me.'

'Sir, with respect, we recovered the stolen goods a couple of hours later. That incident yesterday, the stolen Toyota van that struck the woman on her horse...'

'I'm aware of it.' Some of McQuarrie's fire abated. 'Presumably the burglars copied the files from your laptop, Inspector.'

'Sir.'

McQuarrie stared at him for a long time. 'I'd replace you in an eyeblink if you weren't so far advanced on the murder. I don't want a massive task force digging around, but I'll form one if you're not up to the job.'

Taken off the case, Challis thought. Another cliché. 'We're making good progress, sir,' he said, his face and voice unreadable.

'But afterwards, Inspector, afterwards...'

'Sir.'

'Find these burglars,' McQuarrie said, and left.

Challis, heartsick, tried to apologise. They waved it off:

'Forget it, boss.'

'Wouldn't be the first time someone took stuff home with them.'

Relieved, Challis said, 'It's late. Go on home.'

43

Scobie Sutton was getting ready to drive home when his phone chirped. 'Front desk, Scobe. A woman to see you.'

'Name?'

'Heather Cobb.'

'Okay, tell her I'll be right down.'

When he got there, Heather was wringing her hands. She wore a bulky stained parka over a windcheater and stiff new jeans. 'It's Natalie, Mr Sutton. I haven't seen her since she left for school yesterday morning.'

He took her to an interview room, gave her a cup of tea, and got the details. No, she hadn't fought or argued with Natalie. She assumed that Nat had gone to school: she was supposed to, she'd put on her uniform, but who knew with kids these days? Had she rung the school? No—would you do that, please, Mr Sutton? They don't like me down there. Friends? Well, Nat didn't really have many. In fact, the kids at her school were a bit jealous of her. Had she ever run away before, stayed overnight with a relative or friend? Well, sometimes, but she didn't make a habit of it. Boyfriend? You mean Andy? Heather hadn't thought to call him. It's not as if Nat had ever stayed over at his house.

'I'll ask around,' Scobie said. 'Don't worry, she won't be far away. Ring me if and when she shows up at home, okay?'

When Heather was gone, he rang his wife. 'Sweetheart, can you ask around about Natalie Cobb? She's gone missing. The kids at the youth centre or on the estate might know where she is.'

Next he contacted the collators. Andy Asche? They knew the name; he did odd jobs for the shire, but no record and no known criminal associates.

Scobie sighed and glanced at the clock. It was almost 6 p.m. and he was dying to go home, but Natalie Cobb had been missing for almost thirty-six hours now. He picked up the phone again, and dialled the missing persons unit.

Ellen gave Pam Murphy a lift to Penzance Beach, trying to get her to open up about Alan's attitude yesterday, but the younger woman was very circumspect, so she didn't push it.

She arrived home to find bales of insulation batts on the front verandah, glowing pink in the evening gloom, and a ladder in the hallway, the manhole open. Alan's day off, and clearly he'd been busy. His muffled voice reached her from inside the ceiling: 'That you, El?'

She shouted, 'Yes,' and walked through to the kitchen. There was paperwork on the table: three quotes to install ducted heating. She felt herself grow very still, very wary. Not triumphant, not grateful, not elated—not until she understood his motives. And where would the money come from?

It was 6.15 and she didn't say anything. She showered, changed into the tracksuit she liked to unwind in, and poured herself a glass of wine. Meanwhile her husband bustled between the crawl space in the ceiling and the insulation batts heaped on the verandah. She tracked his movements overhead, beams creaking, faint dust and plaster sprinkles marking his progress.

At 7 p.m. she put the dinner on and retired to the sitting room while it cooked. She watched the ABC news, idly aware of Alan taking the ladder back to the shed, sweeping the hallway, dumping his dusty clothes in the laundry, and having a shower.

She'd said nothing beyond their initial greeting, and he'd said nothing.

Alan joined her halfway through 'The 7.30 Report'. He sat beside her on the sofa and took her unresponsive hand. 'Dinner ready soon? I'm starving.'

At once she felt hostile and tried to remove her hand. Hurt, he shifted away from her. 'What's got into you?'

'What's got into *you*?'

He shrugged. 'I thought about what you said, that's all.'

'You said we couldn't afford it.'

'We'll do it in stages. Plus I've saved an incredible amount of money by insulating the ceiling myself.'

Fishing for compliments. Ellen said nothing. She shrugged in a way that was almost a thank you.

He said casually, 'How's young Murphy?'

There it was: according to canteen gossip, he'd been unnecessarily harsh on Pam Murphy at the accident site yesterday, and now felt bad about it. Ellen wanted to tell him to atone to Pam, not her. And an insulated ceiling didn't begin to heal a rift that was growing and probably permanent.

'First rate,' Ellen said.

In the *Progress* office in Waterloo, Tessa Kane was glancing at her watch. Rattled by the incident with Charlie Mead, and finding smashed lights on her car yesterday, she'd been taking a taxi to and from work. Tonight's cab was five minutes late. Well, it was Friday.

She looked again at the photographs that had arrived in the post that morning. The anonymous sender wanted $5000 in exchange for names, addresses and other key information. He—or she—was confident that Tessa would be interested, given her recent article on sex parties.

She recognised the setting from the photos that Ellen Destry had shown her. Was someone on Challis's team bent? Should she alert him? No—not before she got a good story out of it. Not before she got a statement from Robert McQuarrie.

Meanwhile, she could also smell a story in Raymond Lowry. According to one of her contacts, he'd been brought in for questioning, and later released. When she'd gone to his house and asked for an interview this afternoon, he'd slammed the door in her face.

Just when she was about to call the taxi firm again, Joseph Ovens stepped into the foyer, wearing neat dark trousers and a jacket. Aged in his sixties, he'd been retrenched by a bank and used his termination payout to purchase a taxi licence. She liked Joe, and generally asked for him. If work took her interstate, she'd always see if Joe was available to drive her to the airport. She'd give him the details of her return flight, and he'd always be there to collect her. She wasn't stupid enough to take a cab from the airport rank, not after her first couple of experiences, the drivers nervous about leaving the city limits for open countryside, having never driven without traffic lights before, or on dirt roads, or on unlit roads at night, or experienced so many trees or so many *absences* of familiar things. Their speed would drop, and drop, and drop, they'd drive with white knuckles, hunched low in their seats, they'd sweat, look hunted and afraid. She'd even had to draw maps so they could get back to the city.

So Joe was her regular driver whenever she needed a cab. But he'd been away fishing since Tuesday, so she'd had other drivers yesterday and this morning. She watched him for a moment, unobserved: a good-looking older guy, grey, a bit of a paunch, always genial, and knowledgeable and interested in the world around him. He began to wander idly around the foyer, examining the clippings from past editions that she'd had framed and fastened to the walls out there, between the rubber plants and the visitors' chairs. 'Come on through,' she called. 'I won't be long.'

He strolled in, glancing at the layout tables as she gathered her bag and coat and switched off her computer. Suddenly he went into a kind of shock, stepping back, his hand over his heart, his jaw dropping, white as a sheet. 'Joe,' she said, rushing to him. 'What's wrong?'

He pointed: the mock-up of next Tuesday's front page. Eventually he managed to say, 'I was there.'

44

The weekend arrived, and winter seemed to deepen suddenly, promising short, still, silent grey days, with little wind or rain, but dank and cold.

Challis held an informal briefing with Ellen and Scobie first thing on Saturday morning, mainly to tell them about the taxi driver. Scobie Sutton responded first, his expression mournful, a skinny man slumped in his chair like an arrangement of twigs. He was dressed for Janine McQuarrie's funeral in a dark suit, white shirt and black tie. 'How come we didn't find this guy earlier?'

A fair question. After all, they'd found everyone else who'd had cause to drive past Mrs Humphreys's house on the morning of the murder: neighbours, the guy who delivered the *Age* and the *Herald Sun*, a woman distributing leaflets for her yoga and massage clinic, a farrier, United Energy and Telstra linesmen, various tradesmen, delivery drivers, a vanload of Cambodian people—wearing conical straw hats—who'd been hired to prune the vines at a nearby winery. Even other taxi drivers.

But not Joseph Ovens.

'He took someone to the airport last Tuesday,' Challis said, 'and just kept heading north, fishing gear in the boot of his car. Didn't listen to the news all week, didn't read the papers. Came back yesterday, learnt about the murder, and realised what he'd seen.'

He explained about Joe Ovens's visit to the *Progress*. 'And the editor contacted me,' he added.

The editor, he said, to emphasise that his relationship with Tessa Kane was formal now, and had been for some time. Nevertheless, Ellen was gazing at him with an unreadable but complicated expression, and he felt himself colour a little. She looked tired, edgy, faintly crumpled in her slim-line jacket and trousers, her hair a little untamed. He searched for another reassurance, but she cut in, some of her old sharpness returning. 'How does this help us if his memories are hazy?'

'We use a hypnotist,' Challis said.

They all gave him pie-in-the-sky looks. 'You're joking, right?'

'No.'

'For when?'

'Monday morning was the earliest it could be arranged.'

Ellen cocked her head. 'That will blow the budget. How did you get the super to agree to it?'

Challis gave her a wintry smile. 'I haven't told him yet.'

Ellen watched him. 'Let me guess: Tessa Kane—or rather, her newspaper—is paying.'

'Correct,' said Challis a little heatedly, 'but before you all start scoffing, I want to point out that we've found a hypnotist who has worked successfully with the police before, and Ms Kane has agreed not to publish any details that might compromise the investigation. But she does get exclusive rights to a story in Tuesday's edition about a witness coming forward and undergoing hypnosis.'

Ellen gave him a mutinous scowl. Meanwhile Scobie Sutton was shifting in his seat, as if trying to find room for his long, restless legs, but Challis read the discomfort as psychological. He felt fed up with both of them.

'Boss,' Scobie said, 'what if that puts the taxi driver's life in danger?'

'Ms Kane won't name him, or what he does for a living.'

'No offence, but I think we have to think twice about what we reveal to the press from now on,' Scobie said, folding his arms with an air of finality. 'That's what I think.'

'Ellen?' Challis said.

Ellen had been watching them with a cold smile. 'Is Ms Kane going to be sitting in?'

They don't trust her, Challis thought. They think she'll publish everything that Joe Ovens reveals under hypnosis and the police can go jump in the lake.

They think I'm still involved with her.

He said tensely, 'Ms Kane has a right to sit in. She's paying for it, and has given me assurances.'

Ellen shrugged. 'Suit yourself. See you on Monday.'

Challis clenched, wanting to have it out with the pair of them, but told himself to count to ten, and barely acknowledged them as they made their way out of the incident room.

The funeral was at eleven. Scobie Sutton took fifty photographs with CIU's digital camera, then returned to the station and logged them in. Finally, tired of working on the McQuarrie murder, he went in search of Natalie Cobb.

'Andrew Asche?' he said, outside a flat in Salmon Street.

'Er, yep.' said, the kid in the doorway.

'You don't sound too sure.'

'I'm Andy Asche,' the kid said.

Scobie did what he always did, tried to read the body language, tried to pick up early-warning signals that Andy Asche was lying or feeling guilty. Ellen had the gift, Challis had it, but somehow it had passed by Scobie. He got his results from doggedness and the rulebook. Still, he suspected that he could train himself if he kept trying.

All he got was a neatly-put-together young guy who was understandably nervous about finding a policeman on his doorstep. That could be said of ninety-nine point nine per cent of the population, guilty and innocent alike. It's when you met an individual who wasn't that you took a step back, got out your gun, and called for backup.

'Natalie Cobb,' Scobie said.

A flicker in the kid's eyes. 'What about her?'

'You're her boyfriend?'

A non-committal shrug. 'Not really. We used to hang out a bit. What's she done?'

'I don't know that she's done anything,' Scobie said. It was chilly out here on the porch. 'Can we go inside?'

Asche thought about it, then gave in. 'If you like.'

Scobie followed him through to a sitting room in which everything was mismatched and second hand. Photographs of flash cars on the wall.

'You like cars.'

Andy shrugged. 'Yeah.'

'And a computer buff, I see.'

The kid really looked nervous now. He's been looking at porn, Scobie decided. There were sheets of screwed up printer paper in a cane wastepaper basket under a table against one wall, an impressive-looking computer on top of the table. A different sort of copper would tighten the screws about now, just for the hell of it—search what was on the computer, go through drawers and the waste paper.

Andy Asche said, 'Has Nat been hurt or something?'

'I don't know. Has she?'

'I'm asking you,' Asche said, getting some of his nerve back.

And fair enough, too, Scobie thought. I'm no good at rattling cages. 'Her mother hasn't see her since Thursday.'

'Thursday,' the kid said flatly.

'Correct. Have you seen her since then?'

'We're not that close.'

'But have you seen her?'

'No.'

'You're sure?'

'Yes.'

'When did you see her last?'

Scobie watched Asche carefully. He was a good-looking kid; fit, neat, an earring, that's all. Was he going to lie?

'Haven't seen her for a couple of weeks.'

Yes, he was going to lie.

'So that wasn't you who picked Natalie up outside the Frankston Magistrates' Court on Tuesday?'

Slowly dawning comprehension. 'Oh, yeah, that's right, I forgot.'

'Where did you take her that day?'

'Back to school.'

'And have you seen her since then?'

Andy Asche was adamant that he hadn't seen Natalie Cobb since that day. 'She's been kind of moody,' he offered. 'All that crap about her mother getting arrested, stuff at school, you know.'

Scobie tried again to get the measure of Asche. 'If she contacts you, ask her to call home, and ask her to call me, can you do that, please?'

'Sure, no problem.'

Sunday was another still, grey day. It should have been a day of rest for Pam Murphy—'rest', in her case, meaning an opportunity to train for the triathlon—but she'd received official notification that she was to present herself for a formal interrogation on Monday, and spent the day going over her notes and trying to contact Tank, who wasn't at home or answering his phone.

She couldn't call the sarge. She couldn't call anyone. It was a miserable Sunday.

It turned miserable for Vyner, too.

When the text message came, he'd been writing in his journal, *Let there be one constant in all of your fine dreams—you own your own destiny.* Not original—it had been spouted at an own-your-own-life seminar he'd attended when he got out of the Navy—but what you did was adapt to or move on from what has already occurred. Then the message came, *Got another job 4 U*, and he was suddenly well and truly obliged to own his own destiny.

Vyner shot a message back. *OK.*

And back came the details.

30 thou, Vyner replied, upping his price, *half up front*.

45

Monday morning.

Tessa Kane, Joe Ovens and the hypnotist had been shown to a room called the victim suite, so-called because it was recognised that rape victims, lost or recently orphaned children and distressed adults needed a non-threatening room for their waiting and grieving. Soft lighting, comfortable armchairs, a box of cuddly toys in the corner. Coke, Fanta and mineral water in the fridge, spirits in a locked wall cupboard. A table and padded chairs, TV/VCR set with tapes of 'The Simpsons', 'The Wiggles' and *Notting Hill*.

Joseph Ovens was old school and promptly stood when Ellen entered the room ahead of Challis and Sutton, a smile on his broad, pleasant face. He gestured with a walking stick as Challis introduced him to the others. 'The leg's a bit gammy today.'

'Must be the fog, or hanging around rivers with a fishing rod,' Challis said with a grin. He knew Joe: Tessa Kane had recommended him. Joe often drove Challis to conferences, the airport and police headquarters in the city.

Challis turned inquiringly to the hypnotist, a short, plump woman with severely permed grey hair, who cast quick, assessing looks at each of the CIU detectives and immediately took control.

'My name is Fran Lynch,' she said. 'I'll state from the outset that I know very little about the case, or the witness, or the results of the police investigation. I prefer not to know. I don't want to bias my approach through foreknowledge, making assumptions, offering leading suggestions or asking leading questions, for the very good reason that I don't want any potential evidence thrown out of court. Fair enough?'

Challis shrugged. 'Sure.'

'I have no idea what Mr Ovens will say in response to my questions, I don't know if what he says will help you or not, and I don't even know if he'll make a good subject for deep hypnosis—no offence, Mr Ovens.'

'None taken.'

Ovens exchanged a grin with Challis. He was getting a kick out of this.

'As for my credentials,' Lynch continued, 'I trained as a psychologist and therapist, developing an interest in forensic psychology and hypnosis. I lived in New York City for many years, where I trained alongside an expert who was used regularly by the police and the district attorney's office. Here in Australia my hypnosis has covered everything from helping kids stop chewing their nails to getting descriptions that have put rapists and murderers behind bars.'

Challis nodded. There was a challenge in her voice, and he simply wanted to get the session over and done with.

Then the curtains were closed, the dimmer switch set to low, and Challis, Tessa, Ellen and Scobie sat in the shadows and watched. Ovens was shown into a deep, enveloping armchair, with Fran Lynch sitting opposite in a stiff-backed chair. She began in a low, gentle voice:

'Close your eyes and relax, you are letting go, feeling comfortable, no tension, no pain...

'Now I'm going to count to three, and on the count of three your arms and hands will feel pleasantly loose and heavy.

'You will continue to relax, drifting, drifting, deeper, deeper, all of your tensions draining away, no cares or worries, no fears or anxieties, just deeper and deeper.'

The lead-up took twelve minutes, at the end of which Lynch counted to three again and said, 'And now you feel totally relaxed, wonderfully peaceful in mind and body, and it's time to go back to a particular morning, you're heading along Lofty Ridge Road, a familiar route, and something you see lodges in your mind. There is a house that you've passed many times before, a steep driveway and an unfamiliar vehicle. Perhaps you could describe it to me.'

His posture limp, his voice slurred, Ovens said:

'I was driving along the road there where it runs higher than the level of the houses on either side, and there's this house and driveway I always watch out for because the old lady who lives there hires me to drive her to the shops or her doctor once or twice a month, in fact I drove her to hospital for a hip operation, so I don't expect to see a strange car in her driveway. *Two* cars.'

'Could you describe these two cars?'

'There was a newish silver Volvo station wagon near the house, and an older car coming up the driveway towards me.'

'Describe that car for me.'

'It was a Holden Commodore, mid 1980s vintage.'

'Can you be sure?'

'My son had one, his first car.'

'What else can you tell me about the Holden?'

'I noticed the number plate because it was sort of partly my initials and my phone number...'

At this point, Ovens's finger began writing, tracing numbers and letters on the soft leather arm of his chair. Lynch gently slipped a pad of notepaper under his hand and wrapped his fingers around a pen. Ovens wrote, then stopped.

'What else did you see?'

'The driver had to brake suddenly or he would have collected me. He was youngish, shaved head, puffy kind of face.'

'Any other distinguishing features?'

There was a long pause, and Challis wondered if Ovens had gone to sleep. Then, in a slow, even voice, 'Not that I can recall.'

Challis scrawled a hurried note and passed it to Lynch: *Ask if he noticed the driver's right hand.*

Lynch scowled, pondered, and said, 'Did the driver have both hands on the steering wheel?'

Joe paused and said slowly, 'Yes.'

'Did you notice anything about them?'

'I don't follow you.'

Challis could see that Lynch was struggling not to lead Joe. She lost the struggle and said simply, 'Was he wearing gloves, a watch, a ring?'

Joe, in a fog, said slowly, 'No.'

Challis sighed, disappointed.

'And the other man?' Lynch went on. 'Where was he sitting?'

'The passenger seat.'

'Describe him for me, please.'

'His face was obscured by his arm. I think he was putting on or taking off his cap, a black beanie. But he bothered me,' the taxi driver said. 'They both bothered me.'

'And the car, Mr Ovens. Can you be more specific about the car?'

This was the crucial question, and Challis leaned forward intently. He hadn't wanted to disturb the rhythm of the session, or offer Lynch leading material, but he did need to know if Ovens's description reinforced Georgia McQuarrie's.

Joe Ovens grunted, as if finding himself on familiar ground, and recited, 'Holden Commodore, early to mid 1980s, mag wheels, a dirty white colour, tinted windows—an amateurish job because you could see the bubbles under the film—and rust on the sill of the rear door but not the driver's door. That was a kind of pale yellow, like they'd got it from a wrecker's yard.'

Challis exchanged a smile and nod with Ellen and Scobie, their differences temporarily forgotten.

'You saw the car clearly, Mr Ovens?'

In his dull voice, Joseph Ovens said, 'I know all about cars. Plus I saw the driver's side of the car, then the front number plate, as I passed it.'

Ten minutes later, it was clear that Lynch would get nothing more out of Ovens. Challis gathered the tape, which would be transcribed immediately, and the notepaper on which Ovens had jotted those letters and numbers he could remember seeing on the Commodore: *OT?*, he'd written, *?59.*

46

Ellen was impressed by the session, despite herself, but Tessa Kane had been cool towards her, and afterwards, as they were all filing out of the victim suite, she'd overheard Challis ask Kane out to dinner, to say thank you. Yeah, right.

She hadn't heard Kane's reply, but the image of the pair of them seated in a restaurant burned inside her. So now, back in the incident room, she was sharp with Challis. 'Did this Joe character remember correct letters and numbers? Are they in the correct sequence? What if the O was a Q, or the T was a J or an I? What if the plates were stolen from another vehicle, or are from another state?'

Challis was defensive. 'What you say is true,' he said, 'and so we try all combinations. We also check the stolen car register and ask them to cross-reference to reports of stolen plates.'

'You'd think they'd have dumped or torched the car afterwards, but there have been no reports.'

'But earlier in the week we didn't know what make and model of car we were looking for,' said Challis impatiently, 'and we only checked locally for abandoned or torched vehicles.'

'They could still be driving around in it.'

'Then issue a general be-on-the-lookout to all stations,' he said heatedly.

'Keep your shirt on. The description of the driver might get us somewhere.'

They glanced across to the corner of the big room, where Scobie Sutton was seated with Joe Ovens before a laptop screen. Earlier in the year, Scobie had attended a training course aimed at helping the police generate computer likenesses based on witness descriptions. This was his first opportunity to use it.

'Georgia's certain about the missing finger?'

Challis nodded firmly. 'Absolutely certain.'

'She's just a kid, Hal,' Ellen said, still stroppy, but also aware of the irony: playing devil's advocate was often what she did when they were working together, and working well.

Challis eyed her warily. 'She shows the missing finger in several of the drawings. She was adamant, and I didn't have to prompt or lead her.'

There was an awkward pause. 'What are you doing now?' she asked.

Challis began to head towards his office, saying over his shoulder, 'Transcribing the hypnosis tape onto my laptop. Then when Scobie and Joe have agreed on a likeness, I'll install that, too.'

'And not let the laptop out of your sight?'

'And not let it out of my sight,' he said.

Ellen returned to her desk and began to search the databases. Plenty of crims with missing fingers but none who matched the other search parameters, none associated with the Peninsula, organised hits or getaway drivers. Even so, she thought, easing the kinks in her back, it was lucky that Joe Ovens had driven past Joy Humphreys's house at the moment the killers were leaving. Anyone else might have driven past and even glanced down the driveway, but the old taxi driver knew the elderly woman who lived there, and that she was in hospital. We lay personal maps over standard maps, Ellen thought. A taxi driver mentally maps the terrain with details about clients and traffic hazards, a police officer with the locations of unforgettable arrests, criminals, victims and crimes, and burglars with getaway routes, sensor alarms and guard dogs.

It took Scobie an hour to create a face that satisfied Joseph Ovens, after which he'd fed the details into the data base, and now he was scrolling through photographs of convicted crims whose features matched the computer-generated likeness, Ovens saying, 'They all look the same after a while.'

Scobie knew what Ovens meant. There *was* a certain sameness in the endless cascade of faces. Objectively speaking, these burglars, con-men, rapists, junkies, armed robbers and murderers possessed an endless variety of noses, chins, scars, eyes, lips and hairlines, but they all had something in common: a deadness, a soullessness, behind the eyes.

Half an hour later, Challis took Joseph Ovens's description of the Commodore and his photofit of the driver to the media liaison officer, who would release both to all of the newspapers and TV and radio stations. Then he attended to his in-tray for a while: minutes of meetings he could barely remember; agendas for meetings he intended to avoid; amendments to standing orders; organisational flow charts—the term 'information cascades' catching his eye; risk assessment papers; Ministry feedback on service performance indicators—whatever that meant; strategy papers on paedophilia and cyber porn; a report into the rise of secretive right-wing organisations with names like Australia First and The Borderers...

Then his door opened and McQuarrie barked, 'Inspector? A word.'

The man looked apoplectic. Challis followed, not hurrying, murmuring to Ellen as he passed her desk, 'I bet his spies have told him about the hypnosis session.'

She gave him a rueful smile and whispered, 'Good luck.'

He found McQuarrie opening the door to a conference room and barking 'Out,' at a clutch of probationers, who were cramming for a test.

Challis followed him in and closed the door. McQuarrie went to the window, and swung around, hands behind his erect back, lifting a little onto his toes and down again.

'Sir?'

'Correct me if I'm wrong, but Senior Sergeant Kellock informs me that you had someone hypnotised this morning? And your girlfriend attended?'

Challis counted to ten. 'That's correct.'

'Why a hypnotist?'

'To help the witness remember what he'd seen.'

'I warned you,' McQuarrie said tightly, 'to keep a lid on the more delicate aspects of the investigation. I don't want my son's photo plastered all over the media. I don't want his involvement in these blasted sex parties made public. And you go and hire a hypnotist with the connivance of Tessa Kane?'

It occurred to Challis that McQuarrie was blustering because he was afraid. Too much was happening, too quickly, and he couldn't control the fallout. 'You're well informed, sir.'

McQuarrie stepped abruptly away from the window, knocking a plastic cup of coffee or tea to the floor. Industrial grade carpet, a tufted, nightmarish brown-grey, and unlikely to register a stain. 'What's the trade-off?'

'Trade-off, sir?'

'Your girlfriend gets to publish all the details ahead of the metropolitan press? A scoop, in other words?'

'Ms Kane is not my girlfriend. And the witness approached her first. She has promised not to compromise the investigation in any way. She's agreed to describe the hypnosis session as a mood piece only. Meanwhile I've released a photofit image of the driver, and a description of the car, to all of the media outlets.'

'Which will drive the killers deeper underground. Look what happened after that anonymous tip-off story: a reverberating silence.'

'This time we have more concrete information, which should stir memories.'

'Do you trust Ms Kane? Trust the press in general? Don't be naïve, son.'

McQuarrie was suddenly Challis's kindly uncle. Challis went very still.

'Anyway,' McQuarrie said, drawing out a chair and indicating for Challis to follow suit, 'what do hypnotists, psychologists and clairvoyants have to do with proper police work?'

'They have their place.'

There was silence. McQuarrie brushed lint from his sleeve. 'What transpired?'

'We have the make and model of the car, a partial numberplate, and a description of the driver.'

'Does it tally with what my granddaughter told you?'

'Yes.'

'I suppose that's something.'

Challis waited.

'You're treating this information seriously?'

'I'm treating it as having potential, sir,' said Challis carefully. 'I'll submit it to standard investigative procedures, as I would any information.'

That last sentence sounded clumsy in his mouth, as if he'd swallowed one of McQuarrie's memos.

'Good. Anything else makes us look inept, as if we're clutching at straws.' McQuarrie paused. 'But getting back to this rag of yours.'

'Rag?'

'The *Progress*. There have been rumblings.'

When McQuarrie failed to elaborate, Challis said, 'What rumblings, sir, and what do they have to do with me?'

McQuarrie sat back in his chair and touched his fingertips together. Everything about the man is staged, a cliché, Challis thought, as McQuarrie said, 'It's felt, in certain quarters, that Ms Kane has been overstepping the mark.'

McQuarrie paused, but this time Challis didn't fill the silence. He gazed at the superintendent, forcing the man to elaborate.

'The material she chooses to publish is divisive, and potentially libellous.'

McQuarrie stopped. Challis said, 'Since when is that a police matter, sir? Has there been a formal complaint of actual wrongdoing?'

'It's a police matter,' McQuarrie snarled, 'when a senior officer has an affair with the editor and passes sensitive information to her.'

Challis felt a pulse of anger, quick and hot, and it must have shown in his eyes, for McQuarrie swallowed and braced himself in his chair.

'Don't do anything you'll later regret, Hal.'

Challis's voice, when he found it, was a low, dangerous rasp. 'My private life is no one's concern but my own. As for police matters, I would never jeopardise an investigation. Never.'

'But she's your girlfriend. You pass things on to her.'

'No,' said Challis. 'Sir, what's this about?'

'The *Progress* hasn't always been a friend of the police,' McQuarrie said, 'but we'll leave that aside.' He seemed to search for the words. 'I was wondering if you could have a quiet word with Ms Kane.'

Something about McQuarrie's wet mouth and eyes then said *nudge nudge, wink wink*, as if he were offering Challis a blokey endorsement for having sex with Tessa, for what might be said in bed before, during and after love play.

Challis stood. 'With respect, sir, you're not listening to me, and I have better things to do.'

His head was pounding when he reached the foyer of the police station. He felt enraged, fretful, impotent, and didn't trust himself to remain in the building. He hadn't eaten and his blood sugar was low. He threaded blindly through the people waiting for service at the front desk, intending to make his way to Café Laconic and its coffee and focaccias, when he heard footsteps and felt a tug on his sleeve.

'Hal,' beseeched the super, 'I need your help.'

47

That same Monday afternoon, Pam Murphy sat across an interview room table from Alan Destry and an Ethical Standards sergeant, and imagined herself running a marathon, gaining on the leaders. It's a murderous run, not for the faint-hearted. One by one the runners withdraw, exhausted. She comes upon Destry. He's gasping, thirsty, crippled by cramp, severe asphalt scrapes on his knees and palms. 'Help me,' he wheezes.

She smiles without any warmth at all and runs on by.

'Constable Murphy?' he said. 'You with us?'

Pam blinked. She sat erect and waited.

Suddenly he opened a folder and dealt a dozen photographs across the table.

'The scene of the accident,' he said. 'The fatality.'

Twin fatalities, Pam thought, if you include the horse. She leaned forward and glanced at the photographs one by one. As well as the horse, the rider, the ruined fence and the overturned Toyota van, there were several shots of the road itself and the grassy verge between it and the ruined fence. Plenty of skid marks, paint scrapes and gouges in the grass.

There was a digital recorder and playback machine at Destry's elbow. His finger hovered over a button. 'I have here a recording from D24, the police radio control and communications centre,' he said. 'I have listened to it.'

He seemed to be waiting for her to panic, begin justifying the high speeds reached, or her tactics in the little Mazda sports car. She stared at him neutrally. The Ethical Standards guy, she noticed, was fidgeting, frowning.

'Well?'

Pam shrugged. 'I have nothing to fear. I did everything by the book.'

Don't let him bully you, Ellen had said.

'Why don't you tell me in your own words what happened.'

'I did that on Thursday.'

'Since then,' he snarled, 'you and Constable Tankard have had time to get your stories straight, time to whitewash what happened.'

'Not true,' said Pam calmly. She wiped her damp palms on her thighs. The Ethicals guy was cocking his head at Alan Destry.

Encouraged, Pam said, 'Play the tape. I reported speed and traffic conditions, and—'

'Your pursuit controller ordered you to abandon the pursuit, is that correct?'

'Yes.'

'And did you?'

'Yes.'

'Yet you were on the scene in seconds. In fact, you saw it happen. I quote from the tape: "He's come to grief. We're with the vehicle, near where Penzance Beach Road passes Myers Reserve." Do you recall saying that?'

'Yes.'

'You went on to say: "Get an ambo...It doesn't look good." Correct?'

'Yes.'

'Doesn't look good,' Alan Destry repeated, staring at her. 'What do you mean by that? That you stuffed up?'

'No. It means that we'd witnessed a possible fatality.'

'You called for an ambulance and the helicopter?'

'Yes.'

'But not immediately.'

'I chased the driver of the Toyota across the paddock.'

'Answer the question put to you, not the question you'd like to be asked.'

'I didn't immediately call the ambulance, no.'

'Did you examine the horse and rider before, or after, giving chase to the driver of the van?'

Pam swallowed. 'After.'

'How soon after? One minute? Ten?'

Pam didn't want to shift the blame or get John Tankard into unnecessary trouble, but he had been there. 'Constable Tankard attended to the woman riding the horse while I tried to chase the driver on foot. I gave up after one minute. The driver had a head start and had disappeared into the nature reserve.'

'The rider died at the scene?'

'Yes.'

'Were you trying to intercept the Toyota?'

Pam blinked at the change in direction. 'No. We held back.'

'Yet the Toyota struck horse and rider, suggesting the driver was speeding and panicking.'

'We held back at all times.'

The Ethical Standards officer leaned forward, suddenly lean and hungry. 'You know what the lawyer hired by the dead woman's family is going to argue at the inquest, and afterwards when they sue the police, don't you? That you and Constable Tankard were negligent, if not reckless, in continuing to follow the van.'

Pam swallowed. She didn't have a friend in the guy after all. 'The chase had been formally abandoned, sir. We were merely shadowing the van, monitoring its movements, as ordered.'

'The dead woman's family is already making noises to the effect that the Office of Public Prosecutions should consider laying charges against you and Constable Tankard—on top of their talk of suing the force.'

'What charges, may I ask?'

'Culpable driving or reckless conduct endangering life.'

'The pursuit controller abandoned the chase, sir. Our presence was necessary in case the suspect vehicle doubled back.'

Alan Destry looked at her with a faint curl of his lip. 'Was that discussed over the air with the controller?'

'No.'

'No. You took it upon yourselves?'

'I thought the police service valued initiative?'

'Don't get smart, constable.'

'No, sir.'

The look he gave her then was personal, and spoke volumes about his grievances and paranoia. At one level, he was doing his job, but mainly he was scoring points—against me? she wondered. Against his wife?

'What did you know about the Toyota and its occupants?' demanded the Ethicals guy.

'The vehicle had been reported stolen. A young man was driving, but we don't know who else, if anyone, was with him.'

'A young man driving. Young men tend to take risks with their driving. Did you factor that in before giving chase?'

'A short-duration chase, sir. After that we merely followed at a distance.'

'Have you had training in high-speed pursuits?' the Ethicals guy asked.

'Yes, sir, when I was based in the city.'

'This wasn't your first high-speed chase?'

'No, sir.'

'Did any of the other pursuits you've been involved in come to grief?'

'No, sir.'

'Are you a risk taker?'

Pam thought long and hard. 'I do what's necessary to catch the bad guys, sir,' she said, and wondered if she'd lifted the line from a bad movie.

Then the unimaginable, after the atmosphere that had been cooked up in the past few minutes: the Ethicals guy nodded, gave her a brief smile, and closed his file. 'I too have heard the D24 recording. I think we need not detain Constable—'

'You were *pursuing* the Toyota,' Alan Destry cut in, red in the face.

He was like one of her father's old vinyl records, stuck in a groove. 'Yes,' she said, 'until the pursuit was formally abandoned, when I dropped speed and merely continued along in the same direction as the Toyota. The tape will show that. Blame the driver of the Toyota, not me.'

'We would if we could find him,' the Ethicals guy said.

'Prints, sir?'

'Plenty, but they're not on file anywhere.'

Why couldn't Alan Destry have told her that? She pondered the matter, almost forgetting that she was a witness rather than an investigator. 'Unfortunately I didn't see his face clearly,' she told the man from Ethical Standards. 'However, Sergeant Ellen Destry and DC Scobie Sutton have been working on a series of break-ins on the Peninsula, and—'

'Fine, thank you, that will be all,' Alan Destry said.

A few things were coming together in Scobie Sutton's head: Andy Asche's cutting edge computer gear, his job with the shire council,

Natalie Cobb's poise, and finally, her disappearance—*after* the accident. Telling Ellen that he was following up on the burglaries, in particular the theft of Challis's laptop, he drove around to Andy Asche's flat late that afternoon and pounded on the door. No answer. He went through Asche's rubbish bin and bagged a couple of bottles and cans and a strip of cellophane wrapping.

Meanwhile, Vyner was writing in his notebook: *I have been reborn in white light and perfect joy. I am prepared for the Great Catastrophe.*

Having followed the taxi that had collected Tessa Kane from her home that morning, he was now parked where he could watch the editorial offices of the Waterloo *Progress*. What a one-horse town. Yeah, there were cars, buildings and streetlights, but he could feel the open paddocks at his back. Much more of this and he'd suffer a bad case of urban withdrawal.

He shifted to get comfortable. This time he was in a stolen Camry station wagon. The Camry was just right for the environs, the carpark of the Pizza Hut. No one was going to question his right to be there, no one was even going to notice.

He tucked the notebook into his jacket pocket, wishing the Kane woman would hurry up and finish work for the day. He'd watched her set out on foot with an older guy this morning, shadowed her to the cop shop, of all places, and then back again, alone this time. Normally he'd want to follow her for a few days, get an idea of her movements, but the order was quite clear: hit her immediately.

48

At 8 p.m. Ellen sat alone in CIU, unwilling to go home. She'd finished adding some recent findings to the case narrative, noting that Janine McQuarrie's finances showed no debts or unusual amounts in or out over the past twelve months. In fact, Janine had died a relatively wealthy woman, with savings, shares and insurance bonds worth $300,000. But Robert was also wealthy, so murder for gain was out. Also, there had been nothing on her computers or in her e-mails and ordinary post to indicate a lover or anyone or anything shady or hidden—apart from the photographs she'd taken with her mobile phone, of course.

Finally, with the assistance of the murdered woman's husband, sister and business partners, and the super's wife, Ellen had identified everyone who'd attended the Janine's funeral as being a work colleague, friend or relative—which meant only that no strangers had been present, not that the murderer hadn't been. She'd also shown photographs of Raymond Lowry to Georgia McQuarrie, who'd shaken her head and said, 'I haven't seen him before.'

So, Ellen had put in a good day's work, but still she didn't want to go home yet. There were two reasons for that, one unfortunately related to the other but greatly outweighing it—at least in her mind.

First, earlier that day she'd encountered her husband on the ground floor, accompanied by a guy from Ethical Standards. They'd completed questioning Pam Murphy and John Tankard, and Alan had been looking pretty pleased with himself. She'd had to let him peck her on the cheek, and then he'd invited her for canteen coffee. By then she'd collected herself, and declined, to which Alan had said, 'Hal baby's got you on the run, has he?'—suspicion and frustration not far under the surface of his grin.

So she couldn't face him just now.

Second, Hal Challis was taking Tessa Kane out to dinner tonight.

Ostensibly it was to say thank you on behalf of the police, for bringing them Joe Ovens, but Ellen was reading more than that into it. Challis and Kane had been lovers once—no reason why they couldn't or wouldn't be again, even if only once more, tonight, for old time's sake, or simple lust's sake. They were unencumbered, weren't they?—unlike me, Ellen thought, gazing at the little array of family snaps on her desk, Larrayne as a toddler and later a teenager, Alan when he was young and worth loving.

And so she was keyed up this evening, her imagination on fire. It was like being eighteen or nineteen years old again, burning to know what her boyfriend was up to. Her feelings were juvenile, but they were powerful.

So powerful that they drove her to stow the photograph of Alan into her bottom drawer and then begin to prowl the dark streets in her car.

'What's wrong?' said Tessa Kane, buttering her dinner roll. 'I thought you wanted to thank me for bringing you Joe Ovens. Instead, you're as thankful as a wet week.'

Challis *had* wanted to thank Tessa with this dinner, had wanted to set the universe right a little. But that was before his talk with McQuarrie this afternoon. He toyed with his food, wondering how to begin. They were in a Mornington bistro, one of the few open on a chilly Monday evening in winter. A scattering of other diners, a vaguely Mediterranean décor and menu. Tessa looked fatigued: the pressure of getting copy ready for tomorrow's edition. To Challis, all of the kitchen sounds were jarring, the soft lighting too sombre, the room offering no refuge from McQuarrie's news or even the sleety wind and the blackness beyond the windows.

'You're holding out on something,' he said.

She went very still. 'I am?'

'According to McQuarrie,' Challis said, 'you're in possession of certain photographs.'

'Robert told you?'

'His father.'

'Ah. And he sent you to warn me off.'

'This is not about him, it's about your professional relationship with me in particular and my hard-working officers in general.'

She looked at him with her head on one side. 'Hal, listen to yourself.' Then she narrowed her eyes. 'Robert was sent copies, too, wasn't he? A blackmail demand?'

Challis wasn't about to confirm or deny. 'I need to see the copies you were sent. We need to check them, and the envelope, for prints. Was there also a letter?'

'Yes. But whoever sent it wouldn't have left prints.'

'Even so,' Challis said.

'You think it was the killer? I thought it might be a cop.'

'No.'

Tessa sighed. 'I'll make copies for you.'

'What did the letter say?'

'It referred to the article on sex parties, and said that for a fee of $5000 I'd learn who the men in the photos were and the circumstances in which the photos were found. The others received blackmail demands, right? The guy's trying to make as much money from the photos as possible.'

'Normally I don't care what you print,' Challis said, 'but if you publish those photos, or even allude to them, you'll jeopardise the investigation.'

Tessa toyed with the food on her plate. 'Was Janine McQuarrie into the sex party scene?'

'You know I can't tell you that.'

'The family's not going to like what I've written about her in tomorrow's edition.'

'Like what?'

'Janine was a poor therapist, she rubbed people up the wrong way, she enjoyed challenging men and accusing them of being abusive, and she kept inadequate records. In other words, she might have had enemies.'

Challis gave her a rueful shrug. 'That about covers it.'

'I need a big story,' she said, 'before I finish.'

'What about Mead and the detention centre?'

She shook her head and twirled her fork in a tangle of tagliatelle. 'That fizzled out.' She paused. 'He warned me off, you know, because I went to see his wife.'

Challis gave her a crooked smile. 'I met Lottie at a function once. She didn't strike me as the communicative type.'

'Correct.'

'Look, Tess, will you publish the photos, or mention them?'

She scowled. 'I might, when it's all over.'

Challis wanted to help her. But he couldn't point her in the direction of anyone yet, not even Anton and Laura Wavell, not while they, and their party guests, were potentially implicated in Janine McQuarrie's murder. If Tessa talked to them now, they'd very likely clam up to her and the police, speak only through a lawyer, and feel betrayed. And so he murmured something that meant nothing and within thirty minutes he was driving her back to Waterloo, the heater of the Triumph not working and the windscreen fogging up, obliging him to turn on the air-conditioning to clear it, obliging Tessa to burrow herself into her coat and her scarf and her gloves and scarcely trust herself to speak to him. 'What is it with the heaters in old British cars,' she said when they reached the kerb outside her house.

Said lightly, to mask her pain and let him off the hook, he supposed. He decided to take the question literally. 'They need time to warm up.'

'Some never do,' she said pointedly, getting out.

He watched her cross the footpath and approach her front door, bulky in her overcoat, her hair trapped in black folds by the turned-up collar. He knew that on the other side of the door she'd shed the coat and transform herself into someone slender and purposeful, but right now she looked cold, tired and burdened. He didn't watch her go in but sped off, the exhaust of his car booming down the street.

No shooting, this time, according to orders. This one had to look like an accident. So Vyner was going for a drowning in the mangrove swamp at the rear of the target's house. A pity: a shooting is quick and relatively clean. By the same token, if he shot her he'd have to get himself another pistol, and his Navy source was no good to him any more.

He had his third and last Browning with him, though, just in case.

8.45. 9.00. At 9.20 Tessa Kane appeared under the light outside the entrance to the restaurant, coat on, collar up, shoulders hunched, waiting for the boyfriend. Hello, trouble in paradise? The body language was spelling out tension. Vyner watched them walk to the boyfriend's junky car, and five minutes later he was following them back to Waterloo.

Yep, trouble in paradise. Instead of spending the night, the boyfriend dropped her off outside her house and drove away. The target let herself into her house, and Vyner was right there behind her.

Behind her neat behind.

49

The darkness was fully settled, an evening full of mist and hazy shapes, the crisp air laden with the stew of odours from the mangroves. Tessa, unlocking her front door, was thinking only about Hal Challis and why she should accede to his request not to pursue Robert McQuarrie and the sex party angle. She removed the key, stepped into her front hallway, and something punched her hard in the back, propelling her onto her knees. She heard the door slam. Someone straddled her; he smelt of the chilly blackness outside and of sweaty agitation. His fingers were twisted cruelly in her hair, jerking her head back. Then the tip of something long and metallic, creepily warm from his body, was grinding under the hinge of her jaw.

A gun, she realised, fitted with a silencer.

'Not a sound, bitch, okay?'

She choked her assent.

He kept pulling on her hair, stepping back, pulling her upright, the object on the end of the gun barrel travelling down her spine now, probing between her buttocks. 'You want this? I'll give it to you, you give me any grief, okay, bitch?'

The words were banal, but the heat behind them, and the man's turmoil and disorder, the rankness of his body, made her limp.

'Stand up.'

She tried to straighten her back, strengthen her knees. She said what she assumed everyone said: 'Please don't hurt me.'

'*Shut up.*'

'What do you want?'

He probed deeper with the gun. '*What did I just say? Shut up.*'

She complied.

His free hand snaked around to her stomach and indifferently explored her breasts and groin. It was a gloved hand. It parodied foreplay and she felt herself floating free, observing things from a great distance. She turned her head, glimpsing a dark coat, a dark woollen cap and narrow features, but his thick black leather fingers pinched a tuft of her pubic hair and pulled hard. '*Eyes front.*'

She averted her gaze, looked down her cold, unlit hallway.

'*Move.*'

'Where?'

'*Shut up. Back door.*'

He followed hard on her heels, one hand clasping the hair at the back of her head, the other pressing the gun against her coccyx, propelling her through to the back door.

'*Open it.*'

She tried to sort and assess her impressions of him. Wiry build, thin face, dark clothing, about her height, a harsh voice full of strain. She'd never identify him outside of this particular conjunction of time, place and circumstances.

Then they were through the back door and crossing her sodden lawn to the gate at the rear of the garden. Her mind raced. He was going to kill her out on the mudflats and dump her in a drainage channel. There were stagnant pools out there, covered in scum. She'd never be found and the fish and birds would strip her to the bone.

'Which one hired you? Lowry or Robert McQuarrie?'

'*Shut up.*'

He shoved and she stumbled. He jerked back hard, her hair coming out in his hand. Grass and bracken trailed wetly over her shoes and pants. Behind her he cursed softly.

'Who are you?'

'*Shut up.*'

She turned her head slightly. Up and down the fence line were the back walls of her neighbours, lights here and there: laundries, kitchens, porches, loos. She could hear 'Extreme Makeover' at full volume.

'Is it something I published?'

This time he slammed the gun against her temple and the pain was blinding. She began to cry. He'd destroyed her nerve and she had to cry.

'*Stop snivelling.*'

Now they'd met the serpentine path through the wetland: the raised gravel bed, the little treated pine bridges, the boardwalk itself. Tessa knew that Challis liked to walk here; she'd never seen the appeal of it. Then, curiously, someone was calling her name. Not Challis, but someone close to him.

50

Ellen parked two blocks away and cut through a side street that she recognised from a burglary she'd attended a month earlier. She stopped in the next street, her stomach fluttering with nerves, fluttering so badly that she thought she'd need to squat behind a bush and relieve herself. The air was still and very dark. She couldn't see Challis's car anywhere: maybe they hadn't returned yet, or maybe they'd gone to his house. She burned with jealousy and shame.

She crossed to Tessa Kane's house and heard voices, but there were no lights on inside, and so she went down the side of the house, feeling a little shabby about her motives now, ready to creep away again if she found proof that Challis and Kane had rekindled their affair.

There was a rainwater tank at the rear of her house and she barked her shins on the tap. She hobbled around in circles, silently screaming, and knew from the dampness that she'd broken the skin and blood had formed. She rounded the corner, limping and distracted, in time to hear the rattle of Kane's gate and then see her, a bulky shape in the light spilling across the back gardens of the neighbouring houses. For some reason, Kane was hurrying towards the mangroves.

Something was wrong. Kane's shadow split into two figures, then reformed, and Ellen read urgency in it. Then she heard a squawk, abruptly abbreviated.

Was the other figure Challis? Surely they weren't headed into the mangroves to have sex?

The figures were hurrying now, full of noise and panic, and so Ellen was able to track them. 'Hal? Tessa?' she called. 'Is that you?'

The figures paused, there was a flash and she heard a faint spitting sound. Something tugged at her coat sleeve. She'd been shot at. The coat was a burden suddenly. She shrugged it off, took out her gun, and stepped onto the spongy path edge, among the reeds and mangroves that would silence her footsteps and swallow her shape in the night. For good measure the gunman fired twice more and Ellen uttered a brief 'Oh' of pain. Her neck. A couple of centimetres to the left and she'd be choking on her own blood now. She fumbled for her handkerchief. Her hands shook. She tried to find her mobile and scarcely knew if she'd lost or forgotten it or if shock was closing her down.

Then Tessa Kane cried 'Help me!' and the man with her cursed, as if she'd torn free of his grasp.

Ellen cried *'Run!'*—but had she cried it? There was another muted shot and she ducked, her movements very slow now. She tried to straighten and go after the gunman but collapsed slowly onto the muddy ground where the shallow tidal water rose and spread in a primeval stink around her. She began to pat it like a child in a bath, looking for her gun and her phone.

There was the killer coming for her. Ellen tipped her head back to fix the man's shape but the night was full of hazy shapes. She lifted her hand to say stop or to beg for help and discovered that her .38 was still there. It bucked once, numbing her fingers.

51

Challis had barely reached home when he got the call. Shocked and numb, he returned to Waterloo, examined the body on the boardwalk, barely choking back his feelings, then acted hard and fast. By midnight he and Scobie Sutton had Raymond Lowry and Robert McQuarrie in separate interview rooms. They were sleepy, bewildered, affronted, and hadn't thought yet to ask for their lawyers, but that would change.

Lowry first.

'Where were you between the hours of nine and ten this evening?'

Lowry yawned and blinked. 'At home.'

'Can anyone vouch for that?'

Lowry gave another yawn, huge and jaw-creaking. 'Had a pizza delivered.'

'When?'

'Dunno. Some time.'

'Any phone calls in or out? Visitors? Trips to the bottle shop?'

Lowry, unshaven and smelling strongly of alcohol, shook his head. 'Must of fallen asleep watching TV.'

Scobie Sutton asked a Scobie Sutton question: 'You were drinking?'

'Yes.'

'Heavily?'

'I reckon. Look, what's this about? I feel buggered, I need to get to bed.'

'Tessa Kane questioned you after we released you on Friday,' said Challis tightly.

'That bitch. What's she saying about me now?'

Challis tensed in the depressing and claustrophobic conditions of an interview room in the dead of night. Images of Tessa's slack body and face, streaked with tidal scum and blood, surfaced in his mind, and he struggled to keep his voice even. 'You've been threatening her for some time now.'

Lowry's glance flickered. 'Don't know what you mean.'

'I think you do. Phone calls, hate mail, rocks through her windows, slashed tyres.'

'Not me, no way.'

Scobie leaned across the table and its scratched initials, gouges and coffee rings, its calligraphy of despair. 'You've had a grudge against Ms Kane for some time now.'

'Everyone hates that bitch.'

'Don't call her a bitch,' Challis said in a dangerous voice. He felt close to losing it.

Scobie shot him a warning look and opened a file. 'Late last year Ms Kane ran a couple of articles about an outfit called Fathers First. Are you a member, Mr Lowry?'

'So what if I am? I'm allowed.'

Challis chimed in heatedly. 'Your wife sees a family therapist about the state of your marriage—the violent state of it, to be precise—and soon leaves you, taking the children with her. She gains sole custody of them. You join Fathers First, a motley crew of wife-beaters, given to threatening Family Court judges. Tessa Kane runs an article about

274

you, implying that you're pathetic. Later she hears that you've made threats against Janine McQuarrie, and asks you about that.'

He leaned back, arms wide as if to display the obvious. 'Two strong women challenge you, and both wind up murdered.'

Lowry froze, his eyes darting, and he managed to swallow and squeak, 'Both murdered? The newspaper bitch, too?'

'Don't call her that,' snarled Challis. 'She was shot dead this evening and we need to know how you're involved.'

He still felt numb. Tessa hadn't deserved to die like that, hadn't deserved to die at all, and most of all hadn't deserved to die when things were unfinished and strained between them. He felt that he'd let her down—just as he'd let his wife down. He'd failed to look after them and they'd died.

'I was home all evening,' spluttered Lowry. 'Plus, I might have hated her but I didn't want her dead. I mean, Christ.'

'And one of my detectives was wounded, Ray,' Challis said. 'You know how we protect our own. We can get vengeful.'

Lowry shoved out his hands. 'Test me for gunshot residue or whatever it is you do, if you don't believe me.'

'The thing is, you were at home, but what about your mates?'

'I want a lawyer,' Lowry said.

Their run at Robert McQuarrie barely got started.

'I put Georgia to bed at eight, read to her for a while, then went to my study, which is where I was when your heavy-footed colleagues arrested me.'

'You're not under arrest, Robert.'

'Yeah, yeah,' said McQuarrie harshly, 'just helping with enquiries.'

'Can anyone vouch for your presence this evening?'

'My sister-in-law.'

'Who is very protective of you and your daughter.'

'I'm free to leave, yes? I'm not under arrest?'

'Well,' drawled Challis.

'That's what I thought. I decline to answer any more questions until my lawyer is present.'

'Tessa Kane had obtained photographs of you at a sex party—copies of photographs taken by your wife, in fact. You feared that she would publish them and so had her shot dead this evening.'

Robert McQuarrie was sitting well back from the table, as if to avoid dirt and germs, but now he leaned forward with a flicker of interest, almost of hope and relief. But was Tessa Kane's murder news to him, or had he ordered the hit and here was the confirmation he needed? 'Shot? Tessa Kane?'

'Was it the same team, Robert?'

'What same team?'

'As shot your wife.'

McQuarrie folded his arms. He wore suit trousers, a white business shirt, a waistcoat and an overcoat. He looked crisp enough to begin a full day's work, unlike Challis and Sutton, who were ending one, and showed it in their stubbled chins, bleary eyes and rumpled clothing.

'My lawyer, Inspector. You know the drill.'

And so Challis didn't get to see Ellen Destry until mid-morning on Tuesday, by which time he felt ragged from grief and lack of sleep. Reporters had laid siege to the entrance to the little hospital in Waterloo, baying because one of their own had been shot dead in a mangrove swamp just one week after the shooting death of another prominent local identity. Challis elbowed through the pack, ignoring their shouted questions and speculations, growling 'No comment.'

He encountered Mrs Humphreys in the hot air of the corridor. She'd come in for physiotherapy, she told him. 'If you like, I'll boot that rabble out of the way when it's time for you to leave.'

'Sounds like a plan to me,' Challis said, trying to return her grin. 'Any news from your god-daughter?'

'Not a word.'

Challis went on. He found Ellen in bed, her back against heaped pillows, entertaining her husband and daughter. Or not entertaining, it seemed to Challis, for they seemed to have run out of things to say to each other. He shook Alan Destry's hand after an awkward moment, then nodded hello to Larrayne, whom he hadn't seen for eighteen months. She'd outgrown her adolescent surliness and plumpness, and although she'd never be a beauty like Ellen—she had her father's bulky jaw and solid upper body—was nevertheless pretty and poised, and right now watchful and protective. She held a plastic water bottle in one hand and had a memory stick hanging from a strap around her neck, as though she'd come straight from her computer desk. She wore jeans and a heavy jacket over a brief top, her belly button winking at him as she uncoiled warily from the chair beside her mother's bed, so that Challis was obliged to go around the bed to peck Ellen on the cheek, the husband and the daughter watching him closely.

'Ow,' Ellen said, wincing, yet also smiling up at him, one hand going to her neck, which wore a heavy plaster. She looked haggard, embarrassed about looking haggard, and concerned for him.

'I don't want to tire you, Ells,' he said. 'Just seeing how you are.'

'I'm fine. Have you caught him yet?'

'Fraid not.'

He saw in her face then that she was struggling to convey many difficult messages. 'Hal, I'm so sorry.'

Alan Destry intervened. 'Come on, pal, give her a break. She's not up to being interrogated.'

Challis nodded slowly, knowing when he was beaten. 'Take care, Ellen. Take a few days off.'

Ellen stirred, fury animating her weakly. 'I'm fine,' she insisted, looking from her husband to her daughter and back again. 'I need a couple of minutes with Hal, CIU business, okay? Go and get yourselves a cup of tea or something.'

'Mu-um,' said Larrayne.

'No way,' said Alan.

Challis waited, guessing that Ellen would win. When they were alone, he said gently, 'Can you tell me why you were there last night?'

She glanced away and said, 'I was following up on a recent burglary in the next street, looking for links to *your* burglary, and happened to be passing.'

Challis knew that she was lying. He let it pass, for he wasn't innocent either. They were drawn to each other and it was illicit and still playing itself out, even if it led nowhere. 'Lucky thing that you were,' he said.

Her eyes filled with tears. 'Why? I didn't save her. All I did was get myself shot as well.'

'It could have been worse.'

She touched the graze on her neck as if to say that it was nothing. 'I couldn't see a thing. I had to feel my way in the dark. I shot at him, but presumably I missed.'

'We didn't find anything.'

'Apart from Tessa.'

'Apart from Tessa,' Challis repeated.

There was a pause. Ellen said gently, 'Hal, don't blame yourself.'

'Who says I am?' he demanded, more forcefully than he'd intended.

Ellen looked away, then back at him. 'What about Lowry and McQuarrie?'

'Lawyered up. Alibis.'

She sank back. 'I couldn't see anything, but I don't think it was one of them.'

'Get some rest.'

'Alan brought me today's *Progress*,' Ellen said. 'Tessa's take on Janine was pretty accurate.'

Challis nodded. He'd read it over breakfast, and heard Tessa's voice in his head, her special qualities of fierceness and irony coming through clearly. He blinked his eyes.

Ellen affected not to notice. 'Is there a link between the two murders?'

'Get some rest.'

'I'm coming in tomorrow.'

'Don't be silly.'

'I'm coming in,' Ellen said, 'and stop pitying yourself.'

Challis almost snapped at her, but went out to the carpark, avoiding the cameras and microphones. Behind the wheel of his car, he told himself to breathe deeply, evenly. There was no avoiding it: he *was* self-pitying. Then he remembered something that Tessa had once said about him, that he tended to feel guilt where it wasn't warranted or necessary, that guilt in many circumstances was a wasted, a crippling, emotion. That was the truth. She'd given him gifts of wisdom and he'd been too self-involved to see it.

52

At four o'clock that Tuesday afternoon, Vyner wrote, *Men are continents, men are islands, but I am a rocky shoal beneath the surface.*

He'd just collected $500 from a woman in Glen Iris, the mother of an Army signaller who'd stepped on a mine on the Iraqi side of the border with Kuwait. Yep, a hero, great guy, single-handedly saved Vyner's life on one occasion, but too modest to claim the credit. The mother's eyes glistened, Vyner's glistened. It was very moving, and while it lasted, Vyner believed every word of it.

It was getting hard to remember who he was, though. The personal, private, *real* Vyner was the Navy guy who'd refused the anthrax injection and been discharged for that and a few other minor matters, and later spent a couple of years in prison here and there. The pretend Vyner was the Army mate of some poor prick who'd died on foreign soil. The emerging Vyner was a hitman for hire—and a part-time conman.

That's when another text message came in on his mobile phone. No congratulations for a job well done in wasting Tessa Kane last night, only an angry query, wanting to know why descriptions of Nathan

Gent and the car had been released to the media. *Xplain or no fee*, the SMS concluded.

Christ. Vyner hadn't read the paper closely this morning, but now he did. The front page was full of last night's shooting, so he flicked through, and there it was on page 5, an accurate description of the car and a pretty accurate photofit image of Nathan Gent. His mouth dry, he sent back an SMS: *Gent ded car torchd*.

Who saw us? he wondered. There's no description of me, so does that mean I wasn't seen clearly, or do the cops have a description and this is some kind of trick?

He did a line of coke to chill out. He'd have to get himself another gun. He was fresh out of Browning pistols after last night.

That same afternoon, Scobie Sutton received a call from the lab. There were several usable prints on the bottles, cans and cellophane he'd collected from Andy Asche's rubbish bin, and they matched one print not on the Toyota van itself but on the stolen goods recovered from it. That was good enough for Scobie.

'You ever have a kid called Andy Asche in your home?' he asked Challis.

'No,' said Challis, looking sad and distracted.

'Then he's definitely one of our burglars. He also owns cutting edge computer gear.'

Challis rubbed his face. 'You think he copied my files and printed out the photos? Get a warrant for his computer and bring him in for questioning.'

Scobie shifted uncomfortably. 'I think he's done a runner.'

'Look for him then,' said Challis curtly.

'Boss,' Scobie said.

In his experience, you didn't often catch crooks through detection and investigation but through chance or luck. Cops aren't necessarily smart, he believed, but the bad guys are often dumb. You catch them red-handed, or they give themselves up, remain at the scene, punch a loved one who informs on them, find themselves arrested for a different crime, or draw attention to themselves by breaking the speed limit with a body in the boot, for example.

But now and then you got to detect, and Scobie went looking for Andy Asche on flight manifests. Assuming that Andy would not be flying under his real name, it was a process of elimination. First he rejected women's and unlikely names like Aziz, Hernandez and Nguyen. Then he rejected reservations made some time ago (Andy had left in a hurry, leaving his wheels behind), return reservations, credit card purchases, Frequent Flyer purchases, and special requests (Scobie doubted that Andy was a vegetarian, and in too much of a hurry to request a special meal even if he was). Scobie also couldn't see Andy trying to leave the country—unless he had a false passport, and that didn't seem likely—or flying to a small regional airport. Andy would seek out a big place, a place where he could lose himself. Finally, Scobie concentrated on tickets booked and used recently.

He could feel the panic in Andy Asche. Maybe I'm a good cop some of the time, he thought, or good in some ways. And maybe that's sufficient.

Andy was on the beach, working on his tan, blending in, another dropout or backpacker amongst thousands of them on the Gold Coast, where the sun never set. Except how many beach bums his age went on-line at the local library to read the Melbourne newspapers?

And how many had twelve thousand bucks in their pockets? Twelve grand, his total savings. He could maybe string that out for almost a year, but kiss goodbye to his dream of buying a BMW sports car.

The way everything had conspired against him. First, that cop, Scobie Sutton, asking if he was Natalie's boyfriend, telling him she was missing. Missing? Andy seriously doubted that—old Nat was off somewhere getting coked out of her brain—but it unnerved him to have the cops sniffing around. Then, a day after sending out the blackmail demands, he'd been reading an old copy of the *Progress* in the shire canteen and there, on the front page, had been a photograph of a guy in one of the photos he'd found on the laptop. Robert McQuarrie. A cop's son. A *senior* cop's son. And, according to the story, grieving husband of a woman who'd been shot dead.

So anyone sending this guy a blackmail demand is going to find himself a murder suspect, right?

Time for the lad to make himself scarce.

It had been a low-speed rather than a high-speed escape. Andy had gone straight to High Street and cleaned out his savings account, all twelve thousand. He'd debated going home, but what if they were watching his pad? He stood on the footpath, trying to do a casual scan of High Street. Trouble was, everyone had looked like an undercover cop on stakeout.

So he hadn't gone home. Instead, he went to the travel agent and bought a $99 Virgin Blue one-way flight to the Gold Coast. That was the high-speed part. Getting to the airport was strictly low-speed. He'd walked to the station, waited an hour for a Frankston train, got to Frankston, walked through the shops to the Nepean Highway, waited ninety minutes for the airport mini-bus, ridden the bus for another ninety minutes, then waited another two hours for his flight to leave. Wandered around the airport shops while he waited, almost bought a change of clothes, then told himself not to be stupid, nothing's cheap at the airport. He'd go to a jeans and T-shirt place on the Gold Coast and get kitted out there.

He'd stay a week on the Gold Coast, and then head to somewhere north of Cairns. He could keep drifting north. It didn't cost much to sleep on the beach.

53

Ellen appeared in the incident room just after lunch on Wednesday, a plaster on her neck, moving stiffly, all of her loose-limbed grace vanished, fatigue lines and pallor marking her face. But she was cheerful and itching to work—and itching to know how Challis was. She couldn't read him; he put her with Scobie Sutton, checking the public's responses to Joe Ovens's descriptions of the Commodore and the driver. Before very long she was sighing. It was soon clear that—as usually happened when photofits and vehicle descriptions were released by the media—the investigation had moved from a position of no help from the public to too much.

'Here's a good one,' she said, reading from a message slip. 'To quote: "Hypnosis takes the subject into another dimension, and so anything Mr Ovens saw relates to a different time and place."'

Scobie grunted. Like her, he'd divided the message slips that had come in since Monday evening into two piles: 'immediate attention' and 'maybe'. All would be checked, however: even the crazy and the greedy tell the truth sometimes. 'Half of these want to know if there's a reward,' he said.

'And the other half want to do the dirty on their husbands, brothers or ex-boyfriends,' Ellen said. She paused. 'Here's another, female caller, wouldn't give her name: "The man in the picture is a well-known al Qaeda operative. He is wearing white face paint to disguise his dark skin."' She caught Scobie's eye, hoping for a chortle, but Scobie merely looked sad, as if he wanted to help all the crazy, lonely people in the world. She wished she were doing this with Challis. With Challis you could have a giggle. She put the woman's message slip on the maybe pile, muttering, 'Your TV is talking to you again, love.'

She glanced across the room to Challis's partitioned office. The door was ajar; he was going through a list of numberplate combinations and matching them to 1980s Holdens. He looked drawn.

She kept sorting, then stopped. 'Ah,' she murmured.

Scobie looked up. 'Another sad creature?'

She ignored him, went straight to Challis, knocking and pulling the spare chair up to his desk. He was on the phone, saying, 'I deny that. She was good at her job,' and hanging up. 'The super,' he said.

Ellen understood. 'He read Tessa's profile of Janine.'

Challis nodded tiredly. 'What's up?'

'Something promising. A call early this morning from a mechanic in Safety Beach. Until about six months ago he used to service a 1983 Commodore, off-white in colour, one pale yellow door. In fact, he sourced the door for the owner from a wrecked car.'

'Owner's name?'

'Nora Gent, an address in Safety Beach,' Ellen said.

She watched Challis scan a list, and was relieved to see his mood lighten. 'Here it is, Nora Gent, registered owner of a 1983 Holden Commodore, QQP-359.' He paused. 'Registration has lapsed. It was due for renewal four months ago.'

'She sold it? Dumped it? It was stolen?'

'Who knows? But we have to talk to her.' He reached for the telephone directory and leafed through it, muttering, 'Gent, Gent, Gent. Not listed.'

'She moved away? Got married and changed her name?'

'Useless to speculate,' Challis said. 'I'll take Scobie and have a word with her.'

'No,' Ellen said.

'No?'

'Take me.'

'Your neck...'

'I'm fine.'

He shrugged. 'Grab your coat.'

Challis drove, headlights on, heading towards the other side of the Peninsula. It was mid afternoon on a day that would struggle to reach 13 degrees. Another sea fret, the fog mostly burnt away but hanging in dismal patches here and there over the highway and in the hollows of sodden paddocks. Ellen hunched deeper into her coat, wishing Challis would say something. The recent past seemed to fill the space between his seat and hers like an intrusive backseat passenger. It was made up of guilt, embarrassment and desire that she knew was reciprocated but could not—and should not—play itself out.

I have to grow up, she told herself. I'm married. I have responsibilities. And workplace romances are tawdry and clichéd.

No, this one wouldn't have been, she amended a moment later. This one would have been special. Wrong, but special.

Not feeling very much better about the situation, she coughed and said, 'Hal, I'm sorry about Tessa.'

He nodded. 'You did your best. I'm sorry you got shot.'

She wondered how to put it. 'You must feel bad.'

'Of course I do. No one deserves to die like that. She was leaving the job, you know.'

'I didn't know.'

'Ellen,' he said, 'to put it plainly, I was fond of her, I'll miss her, but there was no future for us.'

And none for us, Ellen told herself.

Twenty minutes later, they were in Safety Beach. Here the wind blew cruelly off the bay, and the mechanic took them into his office, wiping his hands with an oily rag. Greasy thumbprints everywhere, on invoice books, work sheets, the *Progress*, out-of-date calendars, spare-parts brochures. Ellen was careful not to sit, but she didn't mind the grime or the odours of oil, grease and petrol. There was something solid and dependable about the mechanic and his garage.

'I went back through the paperwork,' he told them. 'Nora Gent, lives right here in Safety Beach.'

'What can you tell us about her?'

'Cheerful, not that old—about thirty?—and always paid her bill on time.'

'You fitted a yellow door to her car?'

'That's right. Hers had rusted through, a cop magnet—no offence—so I found her another door from a wreck.'

'Which door?'

The mechanic stared at the ceiling and back through the months. 'Driver's door,' he said finally.

'What else can you tell us about her?'

'Like what? I can't see her shooting someone, if that's what you mean. Lovely girl.'

'Her job,' Challis said patiently, 'boyfriend, brother, husband.'

'She worked for a travel agent, I know that much, always trying to get me to book a holiday. "I'll get you a good deal," she'd say.'

'Family and friends?'

'Don't know, sorry.'

'You say she stopped coming to you about six months ago. Do you know why?'

'Wouldn't have a clue. I have short-term customers and long-term customers. They don't always tell me what their plans are. But if you want me to hazard a guess, she sold the car and moved away.'

'Or moved away and took the car with her?'

The mechanic shook his head emphatically. 'The car's still around, only she's no longer driving it.'

Ellen stiffened. 'Still around?'

'Yeah. I see it here and there, off and on.'

'Driving by? Stopping off for fuel?'

'Just here and there.'

'Who's driving it?'

'Some guy.'

'Name? Address?'

'Wouldn't have a clue, sorry.'

'Can you describe him?'

'Let me see now... Not that old, shaved head, a bit scruffy and overweight.'

'Is there anything else you can tell us?'

'That's about it, sorry.'

'You've been a great help,' Challis said.

And they drove around to Nora Gent's address, where a tall Ethiopian woman showed them a small white card on a hallstand inside the front door. On it, in a bold purple hand, was the name Nora Gent and an address in New Zealand.

54

Challis briefed them first thing on Thursday, wearing a dark suit and a black tie. Tessa Kane's funeral was at ten o'clock, and he was one of the pallbearers. He stood in his customary position at the head of the long table and felt a little disassociated from the room, his detectives, and the investigations. Mugs of tea and coffee steamed around the table; a basket of croissants sat within reaching distance. No sea fret today, just a brisk wind pushing billowy cloud masses across the face of a low, weak sun.

'Nora Gent,' he began, 'aged twenty-seven, now residing in New Zealand. She works for JetAbout Travel and they sent her to their Auckland office six months ago. She owned a 1983 Commodore, off-white with a pale yellow door, but sold it to her cousin before leaving the country. Nathan Gent, twenty-three, ex-Navy, served in the Persian Gulf in 2003, where he lost a finger in an accident. After that he became unstable, and left the Navy. Settled in Dromana, nothing further known about him. Apparently he didn't get around to registering the car in his name, and in fact let the registration lapse.'

'Like the super said,' Scobie muttered, 'we're not dealing with brain surgeons. Are we pulling him in?'

Challis nodded. 'We have warrants for his arrest and to search his house and the car.'

'Let's hope he was dumb enough to keep the car.'

Challis rested his hands on the back of his chair and said, 'The thing is, he may have done a runner. The New Zealand police weren't able to contact Nora Gent until this morning. I spoke to her by phone a couple of hours ago, got her cousin's address, and drove past to check it out. No car, curtains drawn, plenty of junk mail crammed in the letterbox.'

Ellen drained her coffee and reached for a croissant, but the movement strained her wound, and she winced and thought better of it. 'The car bothers me,' she said, easing back in her seat. 'It's not been spotted since the murder, not abandoned, not burnt, so has he driven off in it, made his way to far north Queensland?'

'If he's as dumb as we think he is, then yes,' Scobie said. 'Maybe he fled in it the same day, then dumped or torched it later on some back road the other side of Mount Isa.'

'I've put out a nationwide alert,' Challis said. 'But you're right, we may never find it.'

'Or he saw the description in the paper,' a Mornington DC said, 'and fitted stolen plates and a door that matched the colour of the car.'

'That's possible, too,' Challis said. 'But first we need to get inside his house, arrest him if he's hiding there, and search it and his life from top to bottom.' He paused. 'The Navy link needs further investigation.'

They gave him inquiring looks. 'First,' he said, 'both Gent and Lowry served at the Navy base, and may have known each other. Second, several handguns are missing from the Navy armoury. Lowry had motives to kill Janine McQuarrie and Tessa Kane. Did he hire Gent and the shooter? Is the shooter also ex-Navy? Did our shooter buy any of the missing guns? Did Lowry or Gent broker the deal? It's worth tracking their movements in the Navy, cross-referencing with the dead armourer and anyone who might have left the service under a cloud.'

'Robert McQuarrie also had motives to kill both women,' Ellen pointed out, 'but there's no Navy link.'

'He's still in the frame,' Challis said, 'but until new evidence comes to light on him, we dig deeply into Nathan Gent. The shooter hooked up with him somehow.' He paused. 'Unfortunately, he's been on a pension since leaving the Navy, meaning no workmates, and no one knows anything about his social life.'

Ellen was tapping the end of her pen against her teeth. 'All we seem to be doing is answering the how,' she said, 'when we need to answer the why. We still don't know why Janine was targeted, or even if she was the intended target, and we don't know if Tessa Kane was murdered by the same man or not.'

Challis nodded. 'Back to first principles: look long and hard at Janine. At the same time, dig around in Gent's Navy and civilian activities, and see if we can find a link to our dead armourer.'

55

And there both investigations stalled. A search of Nathan Gent's house uncovered evidence only of an arid life. No diary or personal letters, no computer, and neighbours who were indifferent and unobservant. Gent seemed to have been entirely jobless and friendless. Of the man himself there was no sign. If he had been the driver, and had gone on the run—as seemed probable, given the empty fridge and the hold on his mail—then he had a pretty unbeatable head start on the police.

There was one recent photograph, but it showed Gent with a full head of hair, and Georgia McQuarrie couldn't be certain that he was the man she'd seen behind the steering wheel of the Commodore. She was more confident about the likeness generated by Scobie Sutton and Joseph Ovens.

As a second, then a third week passed since the murder of Janine McQuarrie, the investigation concentrated on Gent's and Lowry's Navy records.

Nothing tied either man to the murder of Tessa Kane.

Meanwhile, there were no further blackmail demands and gradually Superintendent McQuarrie receded as a thorn in Challis's side. A warrant to examine Janine McQuarrie's files was finally granted, but Janine had kept minimal records and no warning bells sounded when Challis read through them. Dominic O'Brien, only barely helpful, said, 'Janine was a true professional. If any of her clients had failed the three-threats test—i.e., they were a threat to themselves, another person or the criminal code—she would have reported it immediately.' Challis nodded, ignoring him, jotting down names, dates and addresses.

Then came news that Blight had been knifed in the showers of Long Bay prison. Dead. But while there was still a faint chance that Blight had put out a contract on Christina Traynor, and it was still active, Challis thought it best that she remain overseas, and so he kept the news from Mrs Humphreys.

The only relief for Challis came when he spent two days in Shepparton with the Homicide Squad, short-staffed owing to a strain of Hong Kong flu. A market gardener had been shot dead, execution style. The man sold his produce to the Victoria Market, in Melbourne, and that pointed to organised crime. Either the man had belonged to the wrong side in a dispute, or he hadn't paid protection, or he owed money, or he'd been skimming off the top. The murder was unlikely to be solved, so Challis was released from the investigation.

Otherwise, he spent hours trawling through the written material that had accumulated since the murder: reports of attending officers; preliminary CIU and autopsy reports; investigation and crime-scene worksheets; witness lists and statements; canvass field notes; crime-scene sketches, photographs and videos; taped interviews; the ongoing investigative narrative, consisting of terse updates provided from time to time by himself, Ellen Destry, Scobie Sutton and other officers. There was also a folder of clippings from the metropolitan newspapers, and finally Georgia's drawings and Janine McQuarrie's phone records.

Nothing clarified for him, and he tried not to think of Tessa Kane or Ellen Destry. The *Progress* came out under a new editor and, as expected, it was utterly lacking in character. He saw his parents a couple of times. He managed to talk them out of investing, sight unseen, in a housing development on the coast of Queensland.

One night the phone rang. It was the man from the aircraft museum in San Diego. 'Mr Challis, sir,' he said, gravely courteous. 'We got your e-mail. I'm afraid we'll have to pass on your fine airplane at this time. But keep us in mind, sir, keep us in mind.'

Suddenly, Challis no longer wanted to sell. He felt obscurely that Tessa would have been disappointed in him if he had.

Ellen Destry used the hiatus to leave her husband, making a clean break of it. Why postpone the inevitable with marriage guidance and endless recriminations, breast-beatings and blame-laying? She told Alan that she was leaving, and simply left.

He was stunned. He was hurt, he was suspicious and he was nasty. 'Is it Challis?'

'No.'

'I don't believe you.'

'Believe what you like. The answer is no.'

Sure, Hal Challis had been a catalyst, but she wasn't leaving Alan to be with Hal, or make herself available to Hal. She was leaving to be with herself, for herself. She'd waited until she was damn sure of that.

Her new place was a house in Mornington, sharing with another woman, a recently divorced DS from the Community Policing squad. When she gave Challis the address and phone number, he gave her a searching look but then simply nodded. It was his way of saying that he understood how things would be.

Larrayne was furious, no sisterhood there. 'Are you having an affair or something?'

'No.'

'Dad's really upset.'

'I know.'

'You're a selfish bitch sometimes, Mum.'

Ellen's hand went to her neck, still faintly puckered from where the bullet had grazed her.

One day Scobie Sutton came home to find his daughter, Roslyn, mute and scared in front of 'The Simpsons' and his wife in the kitchen, in semi-darkness, still wearing her overcoat. She must have been sitting like that for over two hours. 'Sweetheart, what's wrong?'

She thrust a crumpled sheet of paper at him. It was a print copy of an e-mail, addressed to her at work. He scanned it rapidly, then looked at her in dismay. 'They *sacked* you?'

'By *e-mail*, Scobie,' Beth said furiously. 'Seven of us on the Peninsula. We're run by managers who are too scared, contemptuous or ignorant to tell us to our faces.'

In that moment, Scobie Sutton's politics shifted minutely to the left. The world is getting more callous, he thought. Goodwill doesn't work any more. The needs of business now outweigh ordinary human needs. The heroes of business are those who can cut costs rather than create jobs and add to happiness. Cutting costs means cutting staff, and it's an abstract exercise for those faceless people and their MBA degrees. Nothing messy and human like gently taking someone aside to apologise, explain and praise. Bad enough that it should infect the business world, but to bring that same heartlessness to bear against public servants, especially those—like Beth—who helped the disadvantaged, really sucked as far as he was concerned.

'One day it's going to rebound on the bastards,' he said.

'But what am I going to do?' wailed his wife.

He rocked her, thinking about it and not getting very far.

One day in late July, Senior Sergeant Kellock called Pam Murphy and John Tankard into his office and said, staring at each of them in turn, swinging his huge, bull-like head, 'You'll be pleased to know that the accident investigation boys have completed their inquiry and don't intend to take further action against you.'

Relief surged through Pam; her body felt looser suddenly, and she realised how tense she'd been for the past weeks. Even her daily jogging and training had been painful. Maybe now she'd enjoy the easy articulation of her joints and limbs again.

Tank asked, 'Sir, what will our records show?'

'Nothing,' Kellock assured them. 'No black marks, no long memories.'

'The civil suit, sir,' Pam said. 'The dead woman's family wants to sue us.'

'The Federation will support you, there's a fighting fund to cover legal expenses.'

That was good to know, but what Pam wanted was for the lawsuit to go away. 'No one else's put in a complaint about us?' she asked, thinking of Lottie Mead.

'No. Meanwhile,' Kellock said, smiling as if doing them a huge favour, 'there's a forty grand sports car sitting in the yard.'

'Sir, have you *driven* the thing?' Tankard protested. 'It's—'

Kellock went still and dark. 'Constable…'

'Sorry, sir.'

'Get on with it.'

'Sir,' they said, and took to the roads again, looking for polite drivers—a contradiction in terms, as they well knew.

Vyner waited and waited, then sent an SMS: *U O me 15 thou.*

He sent it again, and again.

Sometime later came the reply. Even rendered in SMS symbols and abbreviations, the tone was blistering. He'd fucked up. He'd shot Tessa Kane instead of staging an accident, and he'd shot a cop in the neck. 'You can whistle for your money' seemed to be the main thrust of the message.

56

The case began to break open on a Sunday in early August, almost four weeks after the murder of Janine McQuarrie. It started when Pam Murphy drove to Myers Reserve and parked beside the road. She was a little spooked to recognise it as the place where the Toyota van had killed the horsewoman, but it was a Bushrats working bee this morning, clearing the reserve of new pittosporum shoots. She locked her car and walked along the fenceline that divided the reserve from the remnants of orchard and untended farmland beside it. A blustery wind was blowing, cloud scraps scudding across a dismal sky, the ground spongy under her feet. Ten o'clock: the Bushrats would work until noon, and then retire to her house for a barbecue, for it was her turn to have them all for lunch.

She found it a curious experience, involving herself in the local community—even if with a faintly obsessive minority component of it. Most police members spent their leisure time out of the public eye or with other police, for the very good reason that they tended to unnerve the innocent and arouse the hatred of the guilty. But Pam felt welcomed by the Bushrats; it made no difference to them that she was a police officer. And it was a powerful antidote to the daily misery and pointlessness of crime to see ordinary people placing a value on openness, collaboration and benefiting the community without expectation of personal reward.

Last Friday she'd attended a public meeting held to discuss the fate of several stands and avenues of pine trees on the outskirts of Penzance Beach. Some of the pines were immense, casting permanent shadows over nearby houses. Others had died and looked ugly. All had inhibited the growth of grasses and native trees. Some residents had been in tears of fury and outrage that anyone should want to rid Penzance Beach of its pines, but Pam had sided with those who believed the pines should be chopped down and replaced with indigenous plants. A divided community, sure, but one in which the factions were talking and listening.

Reaching a wooden gate, she perched on the top rail and waited for the other Bushrats to arrive. The rail was damp and mossy under her thighs but she wore old jeans and didn't care. She sat staring out over the orchard where the stolen Toyota had come to rest, and then glanced around at the reserve. The driver of the Toyota had fled towards it, but then she'd lost sight of him and he could easily have doubled back amongst the clumps of old apple trees. Andy Asche was his name, according to Scobie Sutton. Where had he been headed with the stolen gear?

'Hello, there!'

A voice, torn into ribbons of sound by the wind. Pam turned her head. A fellow Bushrat, slogging across the paddock towards her. He must have parked further down the road; probably feared getting bogged, she thought. He was in his sixties and made heavy work of it. Partly his weight, partly the sodden terrain, for the old orchard was full of corrugations and drainage channels. He waved. She waved back.

Suddenly he stopped dead. Even from a distance of fifty metres, she saw his jaw go slack, his face white. He stared down at his feet, sunk in dead grass and tussocks.

His voice failed him on the first attempt. He tried again. 'There's a body in the drain.'

57

Ellen Destry stared gloomily at the body, which lay face down in a reedy drainage channel. Female, judging by the skirt, tights, smallish trainers, hair-tie and ankle bracelet. She guessed that the face, which lay in water, would be too decomposed to allow immediate identification, but she recognised the Waterloo Secondary College uniform, and the hair was blonde, so this was probably Scobie Sutton's missing teenager, Natalie Cobb. Scobie Sutton had tied her boyfriend, Andy Asche, to the stolen gear found in the Toyota, so it was reasonable to suppose that she'd been along for the ride. If so, she must have been thrown out when the Toyota overturned, then dragged herself or stumbled for some distance before collapsing into the drainage channel, which was partly obscured by long grass and nearby apple trees.

Ellen swallowed, feeling a stab of pity and guilt. Would Natalie have been found if she'd ordered a grid-pattern search? Was she dead already, or had she lain in the grass for a while, before falling into the channel? Ellen looked across at Pam, who was securing the scene with tape. I accepted her word that there had been only one occupant. Always check, she admonished herself. Always check.

Then she was running: the Bushrats were entering the reserve. 'Sorry,' she gasped, 'you'll have to cut down pittosporum elsewhere this morning.'

There were eight of them, wearing old clothes and kindly smiles. 'We won't get in your way,' they said politely.

'I'm afraid you will,' Ellen said. 'I'm securing the reserve as a secondary crime-scene.'

She saw understanding dawn on their faces, and then they were moving off obediently, one woman touching her arm and murmuring, 'You poor thing, I hope you keep dry and warm.'

Ellen returned to the body. Pam joined her, and together they waited for the crime-scene techs, Scobie Sutton, and the ambulance that would take the body away. No need to call Challis, not unless Dr Berg ruled it a suspicious death. But, suspicious or accidental, what if the girl's death was unrelated to the crashed Toyota? What if she'd been murdered and dumped here at a later date? Or had come here to party and died of an overdose or something? Ellen turned to Pam and said, 'Let's have a scout around for empty bottles and cans, joints, any kind of drug paraphernalia,' she said.

'Sarge,' said Pam, moving off, and then stopping. 'Do you think she was in the van?'

'Did you see a passenger?'

'No. Tinted windows.'

They searched for several minutes, then returned to the body. 'Maybe she wasn't wearing her seatbelt,' Ellen said. She swallowed, thinking of Heather Cobb's grief and feeling suddenly vulnerable and helpless. The last time she'd seen her own daughter there had been a blazing row, Larrayne furious with her for leaving Alan. She badly wanted to fish out her mobile and call Larrayne, to see if she was safely tucked up in bed on this Sunday morning, but knew she wouldn't get any thanks for it if she did.

'Sarge,' Pam said, breaking into her misery, 'look at her hands.'

The right hand was outstretched and touching the bank of the drain. Two fingers were missing. The left lay in the water, the skin partly detached, like a glove. Ellen grimaced: she knew that the 'glove' could be removed by the pathologist, distended and then fingerprinted, but she was hoping that the dead girl's teeth would provide all the identification they needed.

'You don't have to stay here, you know,' she told Pam.

The wind blew, laced with misty rain. They both shivered. 'I'd like to stay,' Pam said. 'Keep you company and watch and learn.'

'Appreciated,' Ellen murmured. She cleared her throat. 'By the way, I'm glad the inquiry cleared you.'

An awkward moment. She knew exactly what a prick her husband had been. 'By attacking you,' she wanted to say, 'Alan was attacking me. By taking broader swipes—at Challis, CIU, and the conduct of plainclothed police—he was attacking me.'

But she didn't say any of this and they talked desultorily of other things. Thirty minutes later, several vehicles arrived: Scobie Sutton, a crime-scene photographer, a video operator, an exhibits officer, the pathologist and several uniformed police. Ellen stationed a couple of the uniforms on the road to wave on the gawkers, and directed another half dozen to search the orchard and along the fence line, then rejoined Scobie and Pam, who were watching the pathologist and her assistant work on the body, which had been pulled from the water and now lay on its back in the grassy verge. The face was pulpy; Ellen looked away.

'Doc,' she managed to say, 'I don't want to influence you, but this could be related to an incident that happened here about three weeks ago.'

Freya Berg glanced up at her quizzically.

Ellen pointed. 'A van crashed through the fence and rolled, coming to rest just over there.'

'About three weeks ago? I'll bear it in mind.'

They moved away while the pathologist worked. 'I should have searched the area more thoroughly, Scobe,' Ellen said.

'I should have done a lot of things in my time,' he said gloomily.

She was pretty sure he'd come from church: he'd thrown an old gardening jacket on over a good shirt and trousers. Even more morose than usual, it was clear that he was taking the sacking of his wife pretty hard. 'I think it's Natalie Cobb,' she said.

'I'd say so,' he said.

'And you found her boyfriend's prints on the stolen gear?'

Scobie nodded gloomily. 'He's done a runner, but I tracked him as far as Queensland.'

'A big state.'

'Yep.'

'Do you think he knew she was dead?'

Scobie shrugged. 'It's possible. When I questioned him, he didn't seem to know she was missing, but he might have put two and two together and come looking for her.'

Ellen glanced around at the deceptive folds in the land, the grass, weeds and clumps of old, unpruned apple trees. 'An awful place to die.'

Scobie nodded in his mournful way.

Dr Berg glanced up at them. 'Preliminary findings?'

'Sure,' Ellen said.

'I found a student ID card in the name of Natalie Cobb, Waterloo Secondary College. Now, immersion in water does terrible things to the skin over time, but her clothing did protect her to some extent, and there are marks on her abdomen suggestive of seatbelt bruising. I also found the usual signs of exposure and putrefaction on the exposed areas, her face and hands. Her right hand appears to have been gnawed by animals. All in all, I'd say that she's been in the water for at least two weeks. A body immersed in water decomposes at half the rate of a body left in the open—depending on temperatures, insect and animal activity and dampness, of course. But I'll know more after the autopsy.'

'But can you say for certain that her death was related to the accident?'

Dr Berg shrugged her expressive shoulders, humour in her dark eyes. 'Sorry, Ellen. Her presence here, and manner of death, might be quite unrelated to it.'

'More complications,' Scobie muttered.

'I'll know more in the lab,' the pathologist continued. 'There appears to be some head trauma, and I might find internal injuries, and these might have killed her. Or she drowned.'

Ellen saw a twist of anguish in Scobie Sutton. All of his emotions were there on the surface. He felt things too keenly, too quickly. He imagined everyone's heartache. For a moment then, Ellen sympathised, seeing her own daughter sprawled dead in the muddy grass. 'Pam,' she said, 'you're wet through. Go on home. It's all under control here.'

The younger woman looked relieved. 'If you're sure, Sarge.'

'I'm sure.'

Ellen watched her walk away, then called after her: 'When you saw the driver legging it into the reserve, was he carrying anything?'

'Not that I could see,' Pam called back, slipping through the fence to her car.

Ellen brooded. She'd still have to search the reserve. The driver—this Andrew Asche—could easily have dropped something in the reserve when he fled, something that would tie him to the Toyota, to Natalie, to the burglaries.

And what if there had been two passengers, and another lay dead in the reserve?

Calling for Scobie and a couple of constables to accompany her, Ellen made for the railing fence and climbed through it into the reserve. An hour later, restless and frustrated, she found herself in a small clearing. She crossed it, bending occasionally to pull up pittosporum saplings in sympathy with Pam Murphy and the Bushrats. Her hands and back ached; a misty rain had blown across the reserve.

Pittosporum everywhere. Poor Bushrats. Ellen straightened the kinks in her back, then leaned over again to jerk a sapling from the rich soil. And some confluence of circumstances then—the light, the angle of her bent head, the sense that the surrounding soil and grass had been altered in some way, and, finally, knowledge and instinct—told her that she was looking at a shallow grave.

58

Challis found vehicles up and down the fenceline at Myers Reserve: photographer, video operator, exhibits officer, crime-scene technicians and the forensic pathologist. A couple of uniforms stood by the access track, one to sign in those authorised to attend, the other to keep onlookers away. Several uniformed police officers were searching the adjacent paddock in a grid pattern, supervised by Ellen Destry. Challis pulled on rubber boots and slogged through wet grass to join her.

'Over here,' she said.

She took him into the reserve, the ground soft under their feet. Bracken brushed their thighs and soon Challis's trousers were hopelessly sodden. 'What made you think it was a grave?'

Ellen grinned, oddly pleased with herself. 'The ground looked different. A regular shape, rectangular, a faint depression of the surface, and the grass and weeds were somehow more vigorous.'

Challis grunted. They came to a clearing and an inflatable forensic tent, under which Freya Berg was brushing leaf mould and damp soil away from a body. A crime-scene technician was sifting the nearby soil for objects that might have fallen from the body or whoever had buried it.

'So, Freya,' Challis said, 'two for the price of one.'

'Wait until you get my invoice,' Freya said. 'I was halfway back to the city, dreaming of a long hot shower, and your good sergeant calls me and says "Guess what?"'

'What have we got?' he asked in his 'CSI Miami' voice.

She grinned, speaking as she worked. 'Youngish male, fully clothed, hard to say how long he's been here.'

'Approximately?'

She sighed. 'There's no adipocere, so we're not talking months.'

Challis swallowed involuntarily. He knew all about adipocere, the crumbly, waxy substance that appears over large areas of the skin as body fats convert to long-chain fatty acids. He'd once touched the stuff: never again.

'There are complicating factors,' Freya went on. 'Contact with the soil, the type of soil, its moisture content—all these affect the rate of putrefaction.'

As Challis and Ellen watched, Freya and the forensic technician lifted the body onto a stretcher, and then the technician peered into the grave. 'There's a section of matted leaves here, not fully broken down yet.' He looked up, pointed silently at a stand of nearby poplars, on the paddock side of the railing fence. Skeletal now, but only weeks earlier they'd been losing their leaves.

Challis nodded. Now the technician was digging down to consolidated soil, ready to begin the process of sifting the loosened material. Challis touched Ellen's forearm. 'You've combed the area around the grave?'

'Of course.'

He needn't have asked. 'Thanks.'

Ellen nodded.

'The clothing hasn't rotted,' Freya said, 'no root growth through the rib cage or pelvis, nothing interesting in fact, just a young man interred in a shallow grave—sometime in the past month or six weeks, would be my guess.'

'You're not paid to guess, Doc,' Ellen said, attempting humour.

'Until I get him into the lab, I am,' said Freya said. She was peering at the body, a vaguely human shape covered in damp soil and leaf mould. 'I can't see any insect activity, so he was probably buried soon after he died. And no signs that the foxes had got to him. They would have, eventually.'

'How did he die?'

'It's possible he was shot in the chest,' Freya replied, glancing down at the body. 'There's a hole in his upper clothing and what appears to be blood. If so, there's no exit wound, but I can't at this stage confirm that it was a gunshot or that it killed him.'

She turned to Challis. 'Release the body. I'll do the autopsy tomorrow.' She glanced at Ellen. 'Who will attend for the police?'

'I will,' he said.

'And the dead girl?'

Scobie Sutton opened his mouth to speak, but Challis stopped him. 'No sense in tying two of us up, Scobie.'

Sutton nodded, relieved. 'I have to inform her mother anyway,' he said, trudging away from them to the collection of private and official vehicles parked at the side of the road.

'I haven't searched his pockets for ID,' Freya said, as she backed away, peeling off her gloves.

'I'll do that now,' Ellen said.

She crouched over the body, feeling the pockets, examining the hands and wrists for rings or a watch. 'Nothing,' she said eventually, but then stood, a strange excitement in her body. 'Except for one thing.'

'Except for the missing finger,' Freya wryly.

Challis tingled. He felt alive suddenly, and leaned over to look. The ring finger of the right hand. 'Foxes, Doc?'

Freya Berg shook her head. 'The finger was torn off some time ago. Years rather than weeks or months.'

59

On Monday Challis drove to the city, reaching the Institute by one o'clock. A chilly wind was blowing in off the bay, and he felt it accompany him into the Institute's viewing room, a small, glassed-in space that overlooked a huge laboratory. It was an eight-bay lab, and handled all types of reportable deaths: suicides, accidents, drug overdoses, and murders. Natural light flooded down from windows high above the dissecting tables, giving a false impression of warmth.

Freya and the Institute technicians worked in blue hospital pyjamas, green surgical gowns, and white rubber boots and disposable aprons. They worked cheerfully and efficiently. They were jokers, like cops and ambulance officers, but the humour was less black and self-protective—probably because they're around bodies every day, Challis thought, bodies in all kinds of extremes. Not even homicide cops were faced with that. He watched as the clothing was removed from the Myers Reserve corpse, vegetable matter sponged away from the body, the scalp peeled back to admit access to the bone saw, and the chest cavity cut open in a Y incision. Organs were removed and weighed; the clothing was searched; a molecular biologist took DNA samples;

a toxicologist endeavoured to find useable liver tissue, eye fluid, and bile, blood and urine samples. Finally a dental record was made as a potential aid to identifying the dead man, before the body cavity was packed and the various incisions deftly sealed with sturdy thread and a curved needle.

There were still forms to fill in, and Freya took Challis into her office, where she spoke as she ticked, scribbled and signed. He'd sat with her like this many times before. It's not that he thought her job macabre, her pleasant, cool professionalism jarring, but he was nevertheless always pleased to note the little vanities in her life, such as her dangly earrings and beautiful Mont Blanc fountain pen.

'You can still get ink for that?'

'Oh yes.'

Finally she capped the pen and sat back in her chair. 'So, there you have it. Until the tests come in I can't be positive about time of death. Our man had all of his teeth—apart from one that was probably knocked out, for there's some damage to the gum—indicating that he was young rather than middle aged. A cross-sectional analysis of his teeth should give us his age, plus or minus one year. Furthermore, his skull hadn't quite knitted fully, another indication that he's young—but not a teenager, more probably early twenties. I can't be accurate about his height, owing to cartilage contraction and some decay of the soles of his feet, but he was medium height, a little under six feet in the old imperial measurement. The absence of maggot cocoons indicates that he was buried soon after death. Finally, he'd been shot in the heart.'

'Leaving the best bit till last,' Challis said.

'Make 'em laugh, make 'em cry, make 'em wait,' Freya Berg said, and Challis watched her appreciatively. 'In the centre of the chest, here,' she went on, placing her hand between her breasts. 'I found the bullet and it's been sent to ballistics for analysis. At first glance they said it was a 9mm.'

Challis nodded. An intact bullet, with distinctive markings, could always be matched to the pistol that fired it. 'Nothing else?'

'No other cause of death that I can see. Toxicology might reveal he'd also been poisoned, but I'm pretty certain it was the shot that killed him.'

'Personal possessions?'

'This cash register receipt.'

Challis examined it. Nothing to indicate the shop or service; only the date—two days before Janine McQuarrie was murdered—and the amount, $2.95. A ham sandwich from a milk bar? A blank video from a bargain shop? It was a fruitless lead.

'That leaves us with his missing finger,' Challis said.

'Ring finger of his right hand, to be exact,' Freya said. 'As I suspected yesterday, it didn't happen recently, but some time after adolescence. And it was torn rather than cut off cleanly. Some kind of accident? Explosion? Caught in machinery? I can't be more certain than that.'

'It's something to go on,' Challis said. 'It ties in with a witness account in another crime. And the dead girl?'

Freya shook her head sadly. 'Drowned. She might have lived if someone had pulled her out of the water sooner.'

Drowned?

In far north Queensland a couple of days later, Andy Asche was reading the *Age* online. He concealed a sob and read the item again. Drowned. That's what it said.

He stumbled out into what passed for a winter's day in the tropics. Sure, Nat had probably been concealed by reeds and scummy water, but the cops couldn't have been looking very hard. He blinked his eyes. He shouldn't have run. He should have stayed behind and pulled her out onto the grass. But would he have been in time to save her life? He pictured it, her body cold, wet, floppy, heavy. He shouldn't have abandoned her.

Then he tried to tell himself that it wasn't his fault. Anyone would have assumed she'd escaped, run off in a different direction.

Drowned.

If he hadn't run he could have saved her.

Vyner had also read the papers, and seen the news on TV. 'Shallow grave,' they went on and on about a shallow grave. Yeah, well, he defied anyone to have dug a *deep* grave in that reserve. Sure, the soil had been soft, but it was also interlaced with roots.

Then came an SMS: if Vyner wanted his fifteen grand, he had to pull another job for free.

Vyner fumed. It was a no-brainer, but he fumed.

That same day Challis received confirmation from dental records that the buried man was Nathan Gent, and that evening he took Ellen with him to confront Robert McQuarrie. They didn't get further than the front doorstep.

'Did your wife ever treat a man named Nathan Gent?'

No flicker in McQuarrie's soft, sulky face. 'I have no idea.'

'Young, shaved head, missing a finger on his right hand.'

A look of distaste. 'She treated people from all walks of life, including riffraff.'

'Perhaps you befriended this man.'

'What are you implying? That I hired him to kill Janine?'

'Did you?'

'No, now leave. I'm not going to say it again, if you want to interrogate me, my lawyer has to be present. Can I get that through your thick skulls?'

Meanwhile Scobie Sutton was chatting quietly with his wife, Beth slicing onions and occasionally sniffing and blinking, her hands still then slicing rapidly again. She was often teary these days, but he didn't know if it was the onions this time or distress over her job. 'What did you do today?'

She had thrown herself into volunteer work for their church, and he was hoping that this would keep her from falling into depression or something.

'I went to see Heather Cobb,' she said, still slicing.

'Did you? I called on her this morning.'

Beth put down her knife and turned to him with the baffled smile she'd often worn when dealing with people from the local housing estates. 'Scobie, you wonder how their minds work sometimes. Heather knows we're married, but she didn't say a word about your visit. I mean, normal people in those circumstances would have mentioned it.'

This was a subject that Beth and Scobie could get passionate about. People's bad manners, careless manners, sheer indifference and ignorance and lack of social graces.

Just then Roslyn tiptoed in and placed a sheet of paper at Scobie's elbow. '*Please can I watch the Simpsons yes* ☐ *or no* ☐*?*' With a rush of love he kissed her and ticked the 'yes' box. Roslyn scurried away.

Beth turned around and saw his dopey love. 'What?'

'Nothing.'

The front door buzzer sounded. Scobie said, 'I'll get it,' and found two figures standing there, hunched miserably against the cold.

'He showed up at footy training,' John Tankard said.

Scobie nodded. 'Hello, Andy. How was Queensland?'

Andy Asche's jaw dropped. 'How did you know?'

'I'm a detective, remember?'

'I couldn't stand it, Mr Sutton, I had to come back. I thought my head was going to explode.'

'There's no rush,' Scobie said. 'Come in and get warm.'

60

On Thursday John Tankard said, 'This is a bullshit gig.'

'So you keep saying.'

Pam concentrated on the road ahead, trying to ignore Tank, who was heaving about in the passenger seat, fooling with the seat adjustments, trying to find room for his heavy legs.

'Piece of Japanese shit.'

Actually, it wasn't. Pam had come to appreciate the virtues of the little sports car. It was riding with John Tankard that spoilt the experience. But she was feeling pretty good now, training for the triathlon again, no disciplinary action hanging over her head.

Tank should count his blessings. He was off the hook too.

Coolart Road, a 90 kmh zone, several roundabouts, deceptive undulations here and there. She was sitting on 90, the rest of the traffic on 100 or more, and that was frustrating. Still, their job was to find courteous drivers, and they weren't armed with speed cameras.

She skirted Somerville, crossed Eramosa Road, for the T-junction at the Frankston end of Coolart Road. Beside her John Tankard sighed heavily and she said, 'Spit it out, Tank, what's the matter?'

'Andy Asche turned up last night,' he said. 'Poor guy.'

'Killed a woman riding her horse, killed the horse, left his girlfriend behind to die. Yeah, poor guy.'

Tank stirred and scowled. 'He's not a nasty piece of work, not like some we've dealt with over the years. Good footballer. A real waste of talent.'

'So you're saying he should be forgiven because he's a good footballer,' Pam said flatly.

Being sports mad herself, she hadn't come quickly or easily to the realisation that the system regularly allowed young footballers and cricketers to escape rape and sexual assault charges. When policemen, lawyers, judges and millionaire club presidents went dewy-eyed over sporting heroes, what chance did complainants stand?—especially when the wider community, men and women alike, shrugged the issue away with the words 'She was asking for it.' And heaven help you if you caused the accidental death of a sportsman. In the great outpouring of grief and rage that followed, you'd be hounded by the police and demonised by the media.

'Footballers can do no wrong, is that it, Tank?'

'I'm not saying that. I'm saying it's a real waste, that's all.' He paused. 'Sometimes his chick was there.'

'Watching him as he trained?'

'Yeah. Poor kid.'

The new, softer John Tankard. Pam braked gently for the car ahead, which in turn had braked for the red Mitsubishi ahead of it. All three came to a complete stop, allowing a huge semi loaded with pine vineyard posts to reverse into a narrow gateway. Clearly the driver had been waiting some time for an opportunity to complete the manoeuvre, but the traffic had been heavy, impatient, not prepared to give him a break. It was a rare good deed, and Pam followed the traffic right at the intersection and then left over the railway line. By now the Mitsubishi was directly ahead of them.

'Where are we going?'

Pam said impatiently, 'That car, Tank, didn't you see?'

'See what?'

'Stopped to let that truck reverse just now.'

'Oh.'

Tankard straightened, seemed to make an effort. 'Look at that guy.'

A man tying a banner to a picket fence: '*Devilbend Reservoir: Out*'.

'So?'

'Guerrilla tactics,' Tankard said, rubbing his meaty hands together. 'Come back after dark and rip it down.'

Pam thought he might, too. 'So much for free speech.'

Tankard scowled and muttered, an inarticulate man full of impatience and insupportable burdens. Pam thought he was probably representative of most people and there was no point in probing into his views. 'There,' she said, taking her hand from the steering wheel and pointing.

The township of Baxter was behind them. They were passing through farmland again, but halfway up a long slope ahead of them was a cyclone fence and a vast yard of wrecked cars. The red Mitsubishi slowed, indicator light blinking, and pulled into the parking area outside the main gates. Peninsula Wrecking, according to a faded sign.

Pam pulled in alongside the red car and introduced herself to the startled driver, a pleasant-looking man in his sixties. He was delighted to get the bag of rewards, but protested that he didn't deserve to.

'My wing mirror,' he said, pointing. 'Swiped it off getting petrol.'

Pam appreciated the irony: it was a roadworthy item. 'Even so, sir, you're a courteous driver, and I just know you're going to fit the replacement mirror before driving away from here.'

She grinned, he grinned.

She returned to the car, but Tank was standing at the fence, looking in at row after row of cars, some damaged, others mere shells. 'We couldn't stop for a few minutes, could we?'

'What for?'

'Busted window winder.'

Pam pictured the wallowing, barge-like station wagon in which he carted around young footballers and their gear on Saturday mornings. 'Sure, why not.'

While Tank asked for directions in the office, Pam wandered. The huge lot had been sectioned according to make and type of vehicle and was a scrounger's dream. Down one row she went, up another. She was struck by how few of the cars were damaged. Many were simply old or had no resale value except as a source of secondhand parts. The sun had taken its toll on the paintwork, the rain on exposed metal, and so at first she didn't register the significance of the dirty-white 1983 Commodore sitting on its axles in mud and grass in a row of similar sad old wrecks.

Challis spent Friday morning away from the incident room. The breaks were coming quickly now, and he felt impatient. He visited the car impound and watched for a while as the forensic techs printed the Commodore found by Pam Murphy and examined it for fibres, hair and traces of blood and other fluids. Then he spent a frustrating hour speaking to Nathan Gent's neighbours. When he returned to the Waterloo police station it was to a scene of chaos at the front desk. At least twenty people were lined up waiting for customer service.

He poked his head around Kellock's door. 'What's up?'

The senior sergeant shrugged his massive shoulders tiredly. 'Maybe this doesn't apply to you hotshots in CIU, but the Police Association has announced a go-slow.'

It was hard to determine where Kellock stood on the matter. 'Ah,' Challis said.

'The usual: better pay rates and working conditions. And so we have no unpaid overtime, no court attendances except by subpoena, bans on management duties, the assigning of custodial nurses rather than police members to medicate prisoners, and the issuing of discretionary warnings or summonses to appear in court, rather than penalty notices.'

As if Kellock were reading from a press release. Challis sympathised with the Federation, always had. He nodded briefly, then headed for the stairs, encountering Pam Murphy in the corridor. 'Sir,' she said, walking on.

'Wait.'

'Sir?'

'That was a good job you did, spotting the Commodore. Well done.'

She blushed. 'Thanks. Sir.'

Challis nodded and headed upstairs.

An hour later he called a briefing.

'Here's what we have: on Sunday, Ellen discovered a shallow grave in Myers Reserve. We're fairly certain the body recovered at the scene is that of Nathan Gent. The age is right, the clothing, the missing ring finger on the right hand. We expect dental confirmation soon. We know that Gent had bought—but not registered—his cousin's 1983 Holden Commodore. Two features of this car match the car seen leaving the scene of Janine McQuarrie's murder by the taxi driver, Joe Ovens: a mismatched driver's door and part of the registration. As you know, Georgia McQuarrie described the driver as missing a finger on his right hand, but didn't recognise a photo we found in Gent's house because it showed him when he was younger, with long hair. The neighbours describe him as overweight, with a shaved head. Since then his sister has sent us a more recent photograph, and both Georgia and Joseph Ovens are certain that he's the man driving the Commodore.'

He paused. One of the civilian clerks came in with a container of freshly brewed coffee. Challis thanked her, waited for her to leave, and went on:

'Meanwhile, we've had a ballistics report. Dr Berg recovered a 9mm slug from the body.'

He showed them photographs. Scobie Sutton sat up, alert. 'Doesn't match the slugs recovered from Janine McQuarrie or Tessa Kane, by any chance?'

'No.'

Scobie slumped. They all did.

'However,' Challis said, smiling at them, 'there is an anomaly common to all three sets of slugs: a faint but telling scrape mark. Our shooter used a suppressor. Either he didn't fit it properly each time, or there's a slight flaw in its design or manufacture.'

'He used different pistols but the same suppressor,' Ellen said.

'That's the theory,' Challis said.

'So all three shootings are related.'

'Yes.'

'Our shooter tops Janine,' a Mornington DC said, 'and later tops the guy who drove him—cleaning up loose ends?'

Challis caught Ellen's compassionate glance, and gave her a brief smile. If he hadn't let the media run with the anonymous caller story, Nathan Gent might still be alive. But right now he couldn't afford to think about that. 'Then later he shot Tessa Kane,' he said, 'probably acting alone this time. The motive's still unclear, except that the sex parties link both women and both murders.'

Challis let them brood on that, then told them more about Nathan Gent. 'After he lost his finger he was offered a desk job, but declined, electing to leave the Navy instead. According to one of the psychologists who assessed him at the time, he was deeply depressed. Maybe that grew into disaffection. He leaves the Navy and hooks up with other disaffected ex-Navy types—or at least one other, our shooter.'

He watched them absorb that, and went on: 'Then he's hired to be the driver on a hit, and makes a mistake, uses his own car. Realising his mistake, he sells it to a wrecking yard near Baxter. No plates, but the owner remembers Gent and gave a good description. As yet,' he said, glancing around the big table, 'there's no useful forensics. Plenty of prints—too many. That car was stripped of its seats, steering wheel, radio, seatbelts, rear view mirror, glovebox lid, virtually everything. But the lab's running the prints as we speak, so let's hope they find a match to someone who's in the system.'

'We're sure it's the car?'

'Yes. The plates were removed but we matched the VIN and engine numbers to the car owned by Nora Gent.'

'All we need is one print, boss.'

'True, but maybe our shooter's never been printed. Maybe he wore gloves the whole time. And we'd expect to find Nathan's prints.'

They absorbed that. They had half an ear to the phones in the room. It was like waiting for a watched pot to boil. In fact, they were standing to file out of the room when the call came. Challis motioned for them to sit, then replaced the receiver and grinned at them. 'We've got our one print,' he said. 'Apparently our man checked his appearance in the mirror attached to the sun visor.' He paused. 'Trevor Vyner, done time for assault and armed robbery. And,' he said, 'he's ex-Navy.'

They all seemed easier in their chairs now.

61

By late afternoon they had an address for Vyner, search warrants and an arrest warrant. Four Armed Response officers would go in first. Challis supposed they were necessary, but they made him nervous. The country had almost zero gun ownership, so what did they do from one day to the next but train and fantasise? Over-trained and under-experienced, they had nothing to model their behaviour on but American movies. He watched their swagger in the foyer of Vyner's building, young, trigger-happy men dressed in the latest street combat gear. They knew who Challis was: the cuckold whose wife set him up to be murdered by a fellow cop. They knew who Ellen was: the cop—the *female* cop—who'd let herself get shot. Well, that wasn't going to happen to *them*, their gum-chewing jaws seemed to be saying.

Challis was almost glad that Vyner's flat was empty. He'd asked for a watch on the place while the warrants were being sworn, and nobody had been spotted going in or out, but that hadn't meant Vyner wasn't there, prepared to shoot it out to the death. He stepped through the splintered doorframe—management had made a key available, but that wasn't the Armed Response team's style—and quickly prowled through the four spare, unloved Ikea rooms. He guessed that Vyner carried the habits of teenage detention, Navy life and prison with him, and had little room or need for possessions.

'You can go now,' he said, tired of edging around big men who were armed to the teeth.

'What if he comes back?'

'Post two officers in the corridor and two in the foyer,' Challis said.

They filed out, their uniforms and equipment creaking and clinking. Challis stood at the window and looked out over the acres of new apartment buildings that had reclaimed some of the old factory districts beside the river. He'd lost touch with the city. He'd walked along Southbank with Ellen just now and wondered who the people were, eating in the outdoor cafés, walking along the river path and watching the jugglers. He guessed there was a lot of disposable income around nowadays. You didn't see it in Waterloo.

'Hal,' said Ellen, coming up beside him. The setting sun was warm through the glass, bringing on a drowsy kind of desire in him, and he almost put his arm around her.

'Find something?'

'These,' Ellen said.

She showed him a couple of notebooks. Challis flipped through them, stopping at key phrases here and there. 'Some kind of anti-government, fundamentalist, Aryan survivalist nutcase?' he surmised.

Ellen grinned. 'Can you be more specific?'

'Doesn't make him any less dangerous.'

'No.'

'Here you are,' said a voice.

They turned. McQuarrie stood there, brisk, overcoated, slapping fine leather gloves against one palm. Off to a Rotary dinner, guessed Challis sourly.

'Sir.'

'I understand you've identified the man who shot Janine?'

'Yes, sir,' said Ellen, stepping forward as if to forestall criticisms the man might want to make. She began to lay it out for him, Vyner's past and the possible importance of the Navy connection, but he was soon nodding impatiently and finally cut her off. 'I expect this means my son is now in the clear.'

It was issued as a challenge, not a question. Ellen looked to Challis for guidance, but Challis felt a surge of anger, which went unrecognised by McQuarrie, who went on, 'You were way off beam there, Hal, admit it. Wasted man-hours, unnecessary—'

The anger built in Challis, the product of weeks of frustration and grief. It was hot and blinding. He had to blink. He said tightly, 'No one's in the clear, least of all your son. He was, and is, a logical suspect.'

'Logical? You dislike my son. There's no logic involved.'

Ellen coughed. 'I'll continue searching,' she said, and slipped out of the room. The men ignored her. They were facing off rigidly.

'What have you got against Robert? Is it that he's successful at what he does?'

Challis felt goaded. He fought it. 'Identify and eliminate,' he said. 'That's what we do. You know that.'

McQuarrie flushed. He curled his lip. 'The politics of envy, Hal. My son explained it to me. It's insidious, spread by people like Tessa Kane, but I have to say I didn't expect that *you* would ascribe to—'

Too late he realised that he'd gone too far. 'No offence,' he said, taking a step back.

Challis advanced on him, stabbed a forefinger against the man's softly padded breastbone. 'She was a better person than you or your son will ever be.'

'Take it easy.'

'I will not take it easy. You've interfered in this case every step of the way. I'm sick of it. Back off.'

'All right, all right, you've made your point.'

They'd gone well past admitting to a difference in rank, but they'd also talked out their fury. Their chests heaving, they stared at each other. They swallowed. Finally McQuarrie nodded curtly, left, and Challis stood for a while, willing himself to be fully calm again. Then Ellen was there, comfortingly close. 'Pissing contest over?' she said, nudging him.

He laughed, and it was a great release. 'Let's bring Lowry in again.'

It was late, dark and cold in Waterloo. 'They were ex-Navy, Ray, just like you,' Challis said, his voice clipped, in a little interview room along the corridor from Kellock's office.

Ellen took that as her cue to remove photographs from the file in front of her and slide them across the table. 'Nathan Gent and Trevor Vyner.'

'Never heard of them. Never met them,' Lowry said.

'At one stage, all three of you were serving at the Navy base in Townsville.'

'So? It's a huge base.'

'On duty, off duty, you had plenty of opportunities to meet them.'

Lowry's legal aid lawyer, who looked about eighteen, gained sufficient nerve to say, 'My client has answered your question, Sergeant Destry.'

Ellen ignored him. She tapped the photos. 'They murdered Janine McQuarrie. Gent was the driver, Vyner the shooter. Then Vyner shot Gent, fearing he was a loose cannon, and later still he shot Tessa Kane.' She looked up. 'You had a beef with both women, Ray.'

Lowry's lawyer said, 'Unless you have hard evidence that my client knew these men, or conspired with them to kill anyone, then I suggest you let him go.'

'Trevor Vyner,' Challis said. 'Ex-Navy, served two terms for fraud and burglary in New South Wales in 2003.'

'So?'

'Some Browning pistols went missing from the Navy armoury. The armourer was your mate. Did Vyner get those pistols direct from him or did you broker the deal?'

'My client doesn't know anything about missing guns or these murders,' the lawyer said. 'He left the Navy some time ago and is now a respected businessman.'

Challis said nothing but simply stared at Lowry. They had Vyner's print on the car and he'd sent a pair of Vyner's walking shoes to the lab, hoping the traces of vegetable matter in the treads would link Vyner to the shallow grave in Myers Reserve. But proving that Lowry had hired Vyner was not going to be so easy. There were no e-mails or phone records to link the three men to each other. Then again, Lowry had a shop full of mobile phones.

That's when a uniformed sergeant entered the little room and motioned Challis to join him in the corridor. 'Sorry, Hal, but we've got a woman at the front desk who claims her husband ordered the McQuarrie and Kane murders.'

62

'Is he still at the detention centre?' Challis asked.

Lottie Mead shook her head. 'Probably at home,' she said. 'Charlie's generally home by six.'

'Does he know you're here?'

'No! And you mustn't tell him, not until he's locked up!'

They were in the victim suite because the interview rooms were being used and they couldn't question a potential witness amid the files and wall displays of the incident room. Challis was leaning against the wall in his habitual pose, Ellen was perched on the edge of a straight-backed chair, and Lottie Mead sat jittery and scowling at one end of the room's ugly sofa.

Ellen reached out and touched the other woman's knee reassuringly. 'You're safe here, Mrs Mead.'

Lottie Mead, wearing jeans, boots and an expensive costly-looking jacket, stared glumly at her feet, then up. Challis studied her, recalling the civic function at which she'd given nothing away but allowed Charlie to do all the talking. She had narrow features, tightly compressed, as if she'd never revealed many emotions and was unused to it now. 'You don't know what he's like. You got shot because of him,' she said, and made as if to touch Ellen.

Challis watched and listened. Lottie's South African accent was strong: she's Afrikaner South African, he guessed, not English, poorly educated, unconfident around powerful people. She looked demoralised, and he wondered if Charlie Mead had kept her subjugated. Yet she must have found a spark of courage and will, enough to seek help from Janine McQuarrie—who typically had given her poor advice and false courage.

'Why didn't you contact us sooner? Another woman died.'

'I was scared.'

'Scared,' Challis said flatly.

'Hal,' Ellen said warningly.

'Really scared,' Lottie Mead said, looking at the floor again. 'I thought he'd find out and kill me.' Her cheeks were damp when she raised her head. 'But at the same time, he's so arrogant he believes I'm too scared to cross him.'

Challis's mind was racing, imagining this woman's life with Mead, a man who ruled her thoughts and actions. 'Tell us again about Janine McQuarrie. Your name's not on her client list.'

'I used my maiden name. Charlotte Strydom.'

Challis looked. The name was there. He found the case notes and leafed through them. 'You started seeing her only a few weeks ago.'

'Yes.'

The notes were typically cryptic and dashed off: abbreviations, simple words and phrases followed by question marks, virtually unreadable handwriting. 'What sort of counselling were you seeking from her?'

'My marriage was unhappy.'

As he often did with interview subjects, Challis let scoffing and doubt rule his features. He waited. Lottie Mead said, 'Charlie's being sent to manage a prison in Canada. I want to stay here.'

Challis continued to stare at her, wondering where this was going.

Lottie Mead shifted about on the sofa. 'I was scared.'

'Scared of how he'd react if you said you didn't want to go with him?'

Mead's wife looked astounded that Challis could be so naïve. 'Scared he'd kill me.'

'Kill you,' said Challis disbelievingly. It wouldn't be the first time that someone had used a major investigation to make false accusations against a spouse.

'You don't know what he's like! He has to get his own way. He hates to be crossed. It was bad enough that I was seeing Janine, but telling him I wouldn't be going to Canada with him, well, he's not the kind of man to take it lying down.' She paused. 'He'd make it look like an accident.'

Challis and Ellen exchanged doubtful glances. 'So you saw Janine McQuarrie for advice. Did you tell her of your specific fears concerning your husband?'

'Some.'

'Some. Did she tell you to leave him?'

'Yes.'

Challis watched Lottie Mead for a moment. The next question was obvious: 'Did Mrs McQuarrie then confront your husband?'

'Yes.'

'Did you ask her to?'

'God no! That would be a death wish.'

Challis nodded. Janine had acted true to form. But would a reasonable man respond by hiring a hitman to kill her? Would an *un*reasonable man, for that matter? So far, all that he and Ellen had was another situation similar to Raymond Lowry's, and there were bound to be still others.

'So you think he killed Janine because you'd gone to her and she'd confronted him?'

'Yes.'

'Did he say or do anything to you?'

'He hit me.'

'Is that all?'

'He told me to stop seeing Janine.'

'And did you?'

Lottie Mead sneered a little. She was an unappealing woman. 'You don't know my husband. Of course I did, and she was dead a few days later.'

'Did he tell you he was going to have her killed?'

'He didn't have to. He didn't care what I thought or knew. He knows I'm scared of him.'

'Yet you had the courage to see Janine, and now you've come to us.'

Lottie Mead shrugged. Ellen leaned into the gap between them. 'We need more, Mrs Mead. You're not making a strong case.' She paused. 'Forgive me for asking this, but have you and your husband been attending sex parties?'

Lottie Mead straightened in shock, which became outrage. 'How dare you. Certainly not.'

'Janine McQuarrie and Tessa Kane were murdered by the same man—you say under orders from your husband. The only thing we can find that links both women is the sex-party scene.'

'No, absolutely not,' said Lottie Mead, shaking her head violently. 'Charlie had them shot, but not because of *that*.'

'What, then?' said Challis. 'Spit it out, for God's sake.'

Lottie flushed. She examined her bony hands sulkily. 'They both knew things—' she muttered '—or Charlie thought they did.' She looked up. 'Don't you see? I went to Janine to talk about my feelings, Charlie thought I went to her to talk about *facts*. That's why he killed her. And Tessa Kane.'

'What facts?'

Lottie Mead was absorbed with her hands again. 'Doesn't matter.'

'I think it does,' said Ellen harshly. 'We will talk to your husband eventually—we'll *have* to—but we've also talked to other husbands just like him, who'd been challenged by Mrs McQuarrie. What makes your husband so special?'

Lottie Mead remained stubbornly uncommunicative, and Challis, watching her closely, realised that she was more calculating than bewildered or afraid, as though she had things to hide. The murder of Tessa Kane suddenly made sense. He remembered her file on the Meads—there had been many gaps and question marks. Had she uncovered information that she'd not yet recorded?

'Tessa Kane was writing a story on you and your husband,' he said. 'Is there something you're not telling us?'

Lottie Mead was glumly mute. They waited, watching her. The little bar fridge switched on and whirred softly. The room seemed cloying suddenly. 'It happened a long time ago, in South Africa.'

They gazed at her without expression. 'The apartheid era,' she said eventually.

'And?'

'Me and Charlie worked for the government.'

She explained haltingly. It was a story of the interrogation, torture and summary execution of black leaders, for which her husband had displayed a certain proficiency. He'd almost been outed during the hearings of the Truth and Reconciliation Commission, but friends had covered up for him. 'It was a long time ago, everyone's changed now, but he didn't want it made public.'

'What was your role back then?'

'I was in a different department,' said Lottie Mead, not meeting their gaze.

'Did you tell Janine McQuarrie about your husband's past?'

'I can't remember.'

Challis was tiring of her evasions. 'Did you tell Tessa Kane?'

'No, I wouldn't let her in the door.'

'Did Ms Kane challenge your husband?'

'She might have done. He doesn't tell me anything,' Lottie said. She paused. 'Are you going to arrest him?'

'We'll talk to him,' said Challis cautiously.

'He'll get away with it, he always does.'

'We know the identities of the killers. Do the names Trevor Vyner and Nathan Gent mean anything to you?'

'I've never heard of them, but Charlie was in charge of a prison before this. He would have met all types, including killers for hire.'

'We can check,' Challis said. He passed her photographs of Vyner and Gent. 'You might not know the names, but do you know the faces?'

She froze over Vyner's photograph. 'He was at the house this afternoon, looking for Charlie!' Her eyes danced, excited and alarmed. 'He looked angry.'

'What did you tell him?'

Lottie Mead put her hand to her mouth, appalled with herself. 'I told him to come back at six!'

63

Vyner had got there around 4 p.m., the appointed hour, a little curious, a little wary, but with a buzz on, too, looking forward to this next job, and getting his $15,000. Curious because Lottie was normally super cautious, avoiding face-to-face contact, and wary because she was mad and dangerous, and he didn't want to get on the wrong side of her.

A huge house with trees, deep hedges and a gravelled driveway, the tyres of his stolen Magna crunching down it with a sound that spelt status, seclusion and success. The Brisbane house, where she'd been living when he was pruning her roses, on day release from her husband's jail—rehabilitation through gardening—had been a lot humbler. She was ambitious, old Lottie. Charlie Mead might never have been promoted from deputy manager of the prison if the manager hadn't encountered an armed 'burglar' one night. Vyner had got five grand from Lottie for that one. Then no word from her for three years, and suddenly she'd needed him again.

He parked the Magna and knocked on the heavy front door, a door weighted with significance, like the fresh, clean, crisp gravel of the driveway. Lottie answered, he offered her an old-time's-sake grin, but she wasn't having it. 'You're late.'

'It's a long way down here. Plus the traffic.'

She peered past him at the Magna, opened her mouth, thought better of it and ushered him inside. 'It can't be traced to me,' he assured her.

'Trevor, it's bright yellow.'

He followed her through to a sitting room, where vast leather sofas faced off across a busy Turkish rug on polished boards. A fire crackled, faintly smoky. There were African masks, shields, spears and art on all of the walls. Vyner had lived most of his life confined, personal gear at a minimum, and hated the room at first sight. 'Who's the target this time?' he asked.

'My husband.'

He was shocked. 'Charlie?'

Uh oh, he'd set her off. Her face transformed itself in an eyeblink, from timid mouse to feral cat, and she began to pace and snarl, little fists tight. 'After all I've done for him.'

'I know,' said Vyner commiseratively, but without a clue.

She whirled on him. 'He'd be nothing without me, and how does he repay me? Says he's going to dump me for someone else.'

Things made sense now. 'Janine McQuarrie?' Vyner asked, double-checking.

'Who do you think?' said Lottie. 'And she wasn't even a good therapist.'

'Charlie needed therapy?' Vyner asked. The idea amazed him.

'Don't be stupid. I was checking her out.'

'Ah. So how did Charlie—'

'He met her at the detention centre a couple of months ago. She was relieving for another therapist who had the flu.'

Vyner nodded. Why a bunch of ragheads and sand niggers should need therapy, he didn't know.

'I've been with him twenty years, and he wants to leave me for someone he's known only a few weeks!' Lottie said. She paused. 'Five minutes with her and I knew she was incompetent, but love is blind, right, Trevor?'

'Right,' said Vyner stoutly. He looked around, locating all of the potential weapons in the room: poker, spears, vases, lamp, a wooden chair at a writing desk.

'He actually *grieved* for her, as if he didn't care I'd be hurt by that.'

Charlie had betrayed Lottie, Vyner understood that. 'Didn't he suspect you?'

'Never.'

And right in front of his eyes, she reverted again to the little brown wispy mouse. 'Right,' he said. Then, treading carefully, he went on, 'You could have divorced him, left him, got a good lawyer and screwed him for everything he's got.'

'But he would have her, and I couldn't allow that. I had to act fast.'

'Right.' He watched her while she paced again. 'How do you want to play this?' he asked eventually. 'Accident? Home invasion? What?'

She turned on him lashingly. 'Accident? Like you did with Tessa Kane?'

She subsided, muttering.

Vyner had to know. 'Kane asked me all these questions,' he began cautiously. 'Like, "Was it something I published?" and "Who are you working for?"'

'Nosy bitch.'

Vyner waited. He felt restless. A drink would be nice.

'She was getting too close,' Lottie said, coming right up to him and shouting in his face, spraying him.

'Right.'

'I get a phone call from Johannesburg,' yelled Lottie. 'Middle of the night.'

She turned inwards darkly, her face mottled and fists tight. 'Uh-huh,' said Vyner encouragingly.

Lottie blinked. 'Someone I used to work with. He's a private investigator now.'

Vyner nodded to keep her going.

'He wanted to warn me. Tessa Kane had hired him to dig around in my past, mine and Charlie's. I couldn't allow that.'

And a lot of dark stuff in your past, too, Vyner thought, gazing at Lottie. 'Getting back to Charlie: how about half of the fifteen grand you owe me up front?'

'I don't think so,' said Lottie, and somehow she had a little automatic pistol in her hand, no bigger than a .25, pretty quiet, unlikely to be heard next door, given the thickness of the walls and the intervening blanket of trees outside, and she shot him in the face with it.

Vyner reeled for a bit, clutching his blasted jaw and frothing. At one point she shot him again, a punching sensation between his shoulder blades. He went down gratefully, curling up on the rug, which had been Scotchguarded recently, unless his senses were deceiving him. She fired another shot into the wall.

Time passed and he bled and his heart and lungs laboured. He was dimly aware of someone—had to be Lottie—digging around in his parka and finding his new gun, which had cost him $650 in an alley behind a pub in Collingwood.

Then later, as he bled out, there were voices. Vyner recognised Charlie Mead's, in argument with Lottie, who sounded deranged. Who shot who, then? There was more than one shot. He dreamed. By the time he'd regained consciousness again, and was on his hands and knees, his gun was in his right hand. How had that happened? He swung his poor head and saw Charlie Mead on his back, one finger caught in the trigger-guard of Lottie's little pistol. There was no sign of her.

Vyner crawled out to his car, uttering frightful sounds from his ravaged mouth, thinking about gunshot residue.

64

They were not the first on the scene. The first were two uniformed constables from Rosebud, requested as back-up by Challis. He arrived with Ellen to find both officers crouching behind their patrol car, guns drawn. Challis soon saw why: at the end of the Meads' densely hedged driveway was a scene that seemed poised for grief: a yellow Magna stood on the gravelled turning circle, motor running, driver's door open, a figure sitting behind the wheel; the main door of the house was ajar; and bright security spots cast a harsh light over everything.

'Go around to the rear,' Challis told one of the officers, 'via the next-door garden. Check it out, report back by radio, but stay there. Arrest anyone who tries to run.'

'Sir.'

They waited. A couple of minutes later, the radio crackled. 'The door's locked. No lights on. I can't see or hear anyone.'

Challis thanked him. Just then the car outside the Mead's front door shook and the engine coughed, ran raggedly and died. 'Badly tuned, or run out of fuel,' said the Rosebud officer. The smell of poorly burnt exhaust drifted towards them.

'Have you called in the plate number?' Ellen asked.

'Stolen in Southbank this afternoon.'

'Vyner,' said Challis.

A minute passed. 'Sir, the guy's just sitting there.'

'He could be hurt,' said Challis, 'dead or waiting for us to show ourselves.'

The figure seemed to move then, his shadowy form slipping, and suddenly the horn blasted and wouldn't stop.

'Ellen, come with me. Constable, stay here. Don't let anyone in or out.'

'Sir.'

They ran at a crouch to the waiting car. The man in the driver's seat had slumped over the steering wheel. There was blood on the ground, the door, the seat, the man's back and neck. Challis was reluctant to interfere with a body at a crime-scene, but the horn was insistent and unnerving. Besides, the man might still be alive. He grabbed the collar and pulled. The racket blessedly ceased and a bloodied mobile phone fell to the floor pan of the car. There was a pistol on the passenger seat. He stared at the ruined face and guessed that he was looking at Vyner. 'Been shot twice. In the back and in the jaw.'

Ellen reached past and touched Vyner's neck. 'There's a pulse.'

'Call it in.'

Then they advanced on the house, keeping to either side of the open door, and entered together, making a swift, silent sweep of all the rooms, Challis feeling faintly ridiculous, as though he were watching himself in a training video. There was no one alive, only blood slicks in the hallway, leading all the way to the front door, a pool of blood on the sitting room rug, and a body, Charlie Mead, shot in the chest. But Mead had also got off a few shots: into Vyner, apparently, and into a wall of the sitting room. A small-calibre pistol lay beside his hand.

Their hearts hammering, Challis and Ellen stood for a while, willing stillness. They edged closer to each other. It was unconscious.

Eventually Ellen murmured, 'Why would Vyner want to shoot the man who'd hired him?'

The knuckles of Challis's gun hand brushed her thigh. He holstered the gun, unwilling to step away from her. 'Revenge, fear of discovery, money, the usual,' he said.

Outside, dying behind the wheel of the car he'd stolen in Southbank that afternoon, Vyner wanted the woman with the gentle voice, the woman who'd placed her cool fingers on his neck and found his pulse, to come back so that he could apologise for panicking that time on the boardwalk, for almost shooting her dead. He didn't feel like a rocky shoal, doom-maker, custodian of the codes or any other fine thing right now. He felt like a mere mortal, and a pretty dumb one at that.

But Lottie had always been several moves ahead of everyone else, he reminded himself, as he died.

Always several moves ahead.

He had a few moves of his own. Dying moves. He'd barely been able to operate the keys of his mobile phone, barely been able to spell it out for the cop with the gentle hands, given that his own hands were so slippery with the last of his blood.

But able enough.

Continue reading for a sneak preview of the next
Hal Challis investigation

Chain of Evidence

Down here in Victoria he was the Rising Stars Agency, but he'd been Catwalk Casting up in New South Wales, and Model Miss Promotions in Queensland before that. Pete Duyker figured that he had another three months on the Peninsula before the cops and the Supreme Court caught up with him again, obliging him to move on.

'Gorgeous,' he said, firing off a few shots with the Nikon that had no film in it but was bulky and professional-looking, and emitted all of the expected clicks and whirs. For his other work he was strictly digital.

The mother simpered. 'Yeth,' she said, reminding Pete of that old Carry On movie, the doctor with his stethoscope saying 'Big breaths' and the tarty teenager in his consulting room saying, 'Yeth, and I'm only thixteen.' He fired off a few more shots of the woman's five-year-old. The brat's lank hair scarcely shifted in the breeze on the top of Arthur's Seat, the waters of the bay and the curve of the Peninsula spreading dramatically behind her, the smog-hazed towers of Melbourne faintly visible to the northwest. 'Just gorgeous,' he reiterated, snapping away.

She wasn't gorgeous. That didn't matter. Plenty of them *were* gorgeous, and had factored in to his plans over the years. This one had skinny legs, knobbly knees, crooked teeth and a ghastly pink gingham outfit. It hadn't taken Pete very long to figure out that a mother's love is blind, her ambition for her youngster boundless.

'Golden,' Pete said now, fitting a wide-angle lens from one of his camera bags, the bag satisfyingly battered and worn, a working photographer's gear. 'That last shot was golden.'

The mother beamed, a bony anorexic in skin-tight jeans, brilliant white T-shirt, huge, smoky shades and high-heeled sandals, her nod to the springtime balminess here on the Peninsula. Hers was the ugly face of motherhood, the greed naked. She was seeing a portfolio of flattering shots of her kid and the television work that would flow from it, all for a once-only, up-front charge of $395 plus a $75 registration fee. In about a week's time she'd start to get antsy and call his mobile, but Pete had several mobile phones, all of them untraceable clones and throwaways.

He looked at his watch. He'd led her to believe that he had to rush back to Melbourne now, to update a client's portfolio, the kid who played little Bethany in that Channel 10 soap, 'A Twist in Time'.

'You'll hear from me by next Friday,' he lied.

'Thankth,' said the mother as the kid scratched her calf and Pete Duyker drove off in his white Tarago van, erasing them from his mind.

The time was 2.45, a Thursday afternoon in late September. The primary school in Waterloo got out at 3.15, so he was cutting it fine. There was always Friday, and the weekend, but the latter was risky, and besides, the impulse was on him now, fine and urgent, so it had to be today.

He drove on, heading across to the Westernport side of the Peninsula, winding through townships and farmland, many of the hillsides terraced with vineyards and orchards. Not entirely unspoilt, he thought, spotting an ugly great faux-Tuscan mansion, and here and there whole stands of gum trees looked dead. Pete racked his brains: 'dieback' it was called. Some kind of disease. But the thought didn't dent his equilibrium, not on such a clear, still day, the air perfumed and the Peninsula giddy with springtime growth all around him:

orchard blossom, weeds, tall grass going to seed beside the road, the bottlebrush flowering.

He reached the coastal plain and soon he was in Waterloo. Pete was a bit of a sociologist. He liked to get the feel of a place before he went active, and he already knew Waterloo to be a town of extremes: rich and poor, urban and rural, privileged and disadvantaged. You didn't see the wealthy very often. They lived in converted farmhouses or architectural nightmares a few kilometres outside town or on bluffs overlooking the bay. The poor lived in small brick and weatherboard houses behind the town's couple of shopping streets, and in newer but still depressing housing estates on the town's perimeter. You didn't see the poor buying ride-on mowers, reins and bridles, lucerne hay or $30 bottles of the local pinot noir: they ate at McDonald's, bought Christmas presents in the $2 shops, drove huge old inefficient V8s. They didn't cycle, jog or attend the gym but presented to the local surgeries with long-untreated illnesses brought on by bad diets, alcohol and drug abuse, or injuries from hard physical labour in the nearby refinery or on some rich guy's boutique vineyard. They were the extremes. There were a lot of people who ticked over nicely, thank you, because the state or local governments employed them, or because rich and poor alike depended on them.

Earlier in the week Pete had driven into town via the road that skirted the mangrove flats, but today he drove right through the centre of Waterloo, slowly down High Street, reflecting, spotting changes and tendencies, making connections. He wouldn't mind betting the new gourmet deli might flourish, but wasn't surprised to see For Sale signs in the camping and electronic shops, not with a new K-Mart in the next block. It made him mad, briefly. His instincts were to support the little man.

He drove on, passing a couple of pharmacies, a health food shop, bakery, ANZ bank, travel agency, Salvation Army op-shop, the library and shire offices, and finally High Street opened onto the foreshore reserve: extensively treed parkland, picnic tables, skateboard ramps, a belt of mangroves skirting the bay, and an area given over to the annual Waterloo Show, not busy today but all of the rides and sideshows would be in full swing on the weekend.

Pete passed the Show, making for the far end of the reserve, where he parked beside a toilet block that he'd scouted out earlier in the week: grimy brick, odiferous, no disguising what it was. He went in, checked that he was alone, and changed into a grey wig, grey paste-on moustache, white lab coat and black horn rims with clear lenses. Then he drove to Trevally Street and parked where the sunlight through the plane trees cast transfiguring patterns over himself and his van. He wasn't a smoker, but had been known to toss other men's cigarette butts at a scene, to throw off the cops.

Now Pete waited. He waited by the van's open door, a clipboard in his hand. Time passed. Maybe she had detention, or after-school care, or was dawdling on the playground. He walked to the corner and back. Surely she'd be along soon, dreamily pumping the pedals of her bike, helmet crooked on her gleaming curls, backpack bumping against her downy spine.

Of course, she might not come, but twice now he'd watched her take this detour after school. Rather than ride straight home she had made her way along Trevally and down to the waterfront reserve, to the magic of the Waterloo Show, with its dodgem cars, Ferris wheel, the Mad Mouse ride, the Ghost Train, fairy floss on a stick. The Show was a magnet to all kinds of kids, but Pete had chosen only one kid. He paced up and down, the van door partly open, listening to the bees in some nearby roses.

But then she appeared. Just as he'd imagined. He stood and waited as she approached.

Finally she was upon him and he stepped into her path, saying, 'Your mum was taken ill. She wants me to take you to her.'

She gave him a doubting frown, and quite rightly, too, but his lab coat spelt doctor, nurse or ambulance officer, and he was counting on her natural impulse to be at her mother's side. 'It's all right,' he said, glancing both ways along the street, 'hop in.' If necessary, he'd show her the fish-gutting knife.

She dismounted prettily from the bike and her slender fingers played at her arched throat, undoing the buckle of her helmet. Pete was overcome. When she got into a fluster with the helmet, her backpack and a small electronic toy she had hanging from a strap around her neck, he itched to help her get untangled.

'Would you like a drink?' he said, when she was buckled into the seatbelt and bike, bag and helmet were on board. They'd both forgotten the toy, which lay on the grassy verge alongside a crooked brick fence. 'Lemonade,' he explained, shaking an old sports drink bottle. 'Do you like lemonade?'

She took the bottle. He watched the motions of her throat. 'Thirsty girl,' he said approvingly.

He started the engine. He could see that she would start to fret before the Temazepam took effect. She'd want to know where her mother was and where he was taking her.

But, astoundingly, that didn't happen this time. 'Oh, what a cute puppy,' she gushed.

Puppy? What puppy? Pete followed her gaze, and sure enough, some mutt of a dog lay curled on the old sleeping bag he kept in the back, one drowsy eye on the girl. It beat its tail sleepily, gave a shuddering sigh.

Must have jumped in when my back was turned, Pete thought. He assessed things rapidly. If he ejected the dog now, he'd upset the girl. The dog would ease the girl's mind. Ergo...

'Where are you taking me?'

'To see your mum.'

Frown. 'But she went up to Melbourne,' the kid said, as if she'd only just remembered it. 'To the races. She'll be back late.'

'She had an accident on the freeway,' Pete said.

The girl didn't buy it. 'Let me out,' she mumbled, already feeling the Temazepam.

They were clear of the leafy grove by now and on the access road, with cars, kids wobbling home on their bikes and a knot of people yarning and eating ice creams at the bench seats outside the only corner shop in this part of Waterloo. Pete concentrated. The girl, fading rapidly, turned heavy eyes to her side window and mouthed 'Help me' at Mrs Elliott, the library aide at her school, who had stopped by for a litre of milk. Mrs Elliott gave her a cheery wave and disappeared, and soon Pete had, too.

That was Thursday.